Heman Merwin

Merwins Conn. River Business Directory for 1867 8

relating to the business interests of the cities, towns and villages, on the line of the

river from Saybrook, Conn., to Newport, Vermont - Vol. 1

Heman Merwin

Merwins Conn. River Business Directory for 1867 8
relating to the business interests of the cities, towns and villages, on the line of the river from Saybrook, Conn., to Newport, Vermont - Vol. 1

ISBN/EAN: 9783337302139

Printed in Europe, USA, Canada, Australia, Japan

Cover: Foto ©Andreas Hilbeck / pixelio.de

More available books at **www.hansebooks.com**

MERWIN'S

Conn. River

BUSINESS DIRECTORY

For 1867-8.

CONTAINING A CLASSIFIED LIST, ALPHABETICALLY ARRANGED,

OF BUSINESS FIRMS, MANUFACTURING ESTABLISHMENTS,

JOINT STOCK COMPANIES, ETC.,

WITH OTHER INTERESTING MATTER RELATING TO THE BUSINESS
INTERESTS OF THE CITIES, TOWNS AND VILLAGES, ON
THE LINE OF THE RIVER FROM SAYBROOK,
CONN., TO NEWPORT, VERMONT.

COMPRISING,

Saybrook, Lyme, Essex, Deep River, Chester, East Haddam, Haddam, Chatham, Middletown, Portland, Cromwell, Meriden, New Britain, Rocky Hill, Glastenbury, Wethersfield, Hartford, East Hartford, Windsor, Warehouse Point, Suffield, Thompsonville, in Connecticut; Long Meadow, Springfield, Chicopee, Holyoke, Hadley, East Hampton, Northampton, Hatfield, Whately, Sunderland, Deerfield, Montague, Greenfield, Northfield, Bernardston, in Massachusetts; Hinsdale, Walpole, Charlestown, Claremont, Lebanon, Hanover, Lyme, Oxford, Piermont, Haverhill, in New Hampshire; Guilford, Vernon, Brattleboro, Dummerston, Putney, Westminster, Rockingham, Springfield, Wethersfield, Windsor, Hartland, Hartford, Norwich, Thetford, Fairlee, Bradford, Newbury, Barnet, St. Johnsbury, Lyndon, Burke, Barton, Newport, in Vermont.

PRICE, $2.00.

H. MERWIN, Publisher,

HARTFORD, CONN.

CONTENTS.

PREFACE.

In presenting to the public the first edition of the CONNECTICUT RIVER BUSINESS DIRECTORY, the Publisher would express his hope and belief that the information which the work embodies, will meet their approval, and subserve their interests.

Extra efforts have been made in compiling the work to render it as complete and reliable as is compatible with the unavoidable defects accompanying such an undertaking, and of a character that will enhance the business interests of the localities to which it is confined, by pointing out their great models of industrial enterprise.

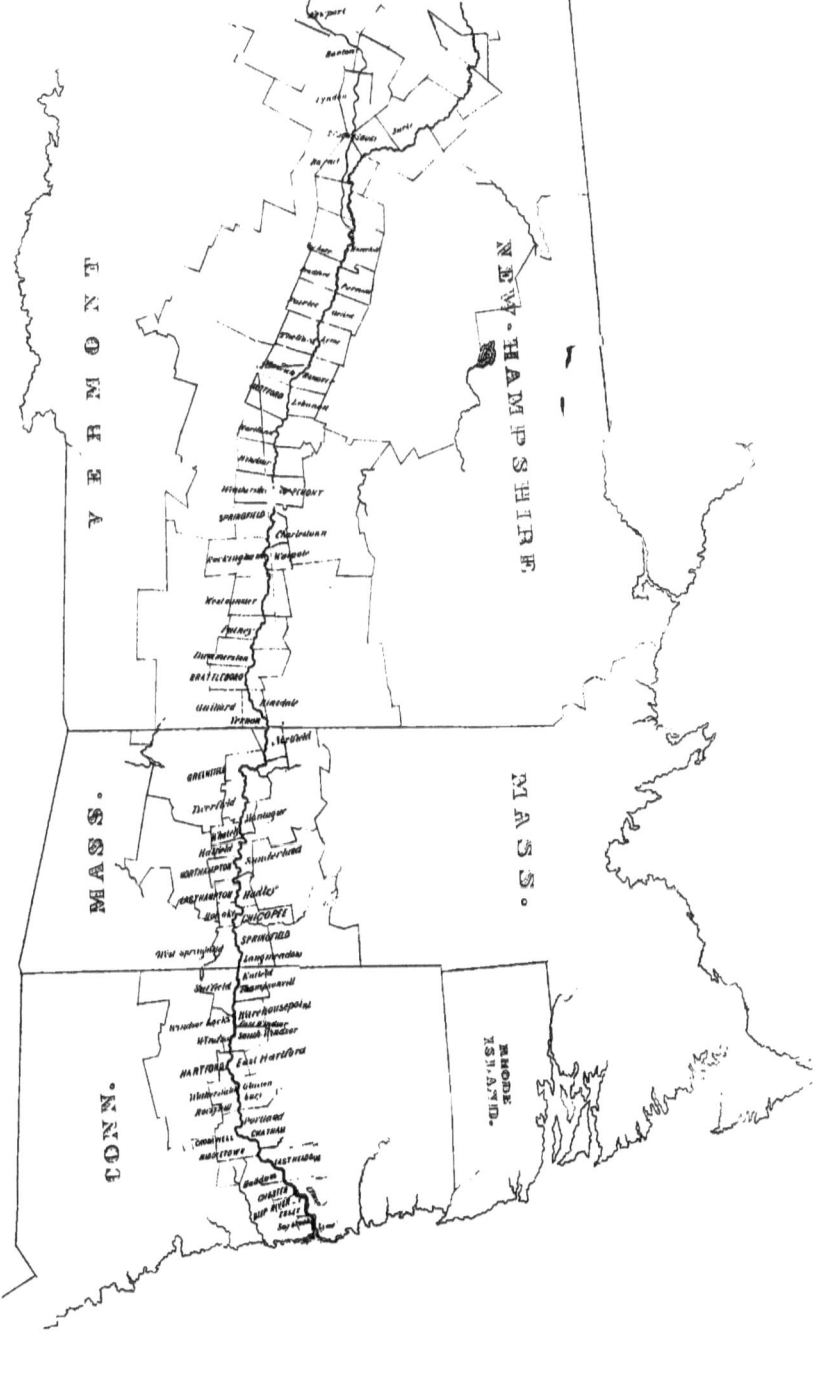

INTRODUCTION.
The Connecticut River Valley.

THE rank that New England occupies in the Union, the influence her institutions have, and are exerting upon the civilization of the present century, are duly appreciated by all intelligent men. Now if any one will scan the map of New England, and trace the course of the Connecticut from its source to its mouth, carefully considering its ramifications—the small tributaries that flow into it—the amount of water-power they furnish, and the business they thus sustain, he will see that the valley of the Connecticut, the main artery of New England trade and enterprise, occupies no very insignificant place in the scale of forces that help to make New England what it is. A brief history of the settlement and the progress of this valley, cannot fail to make an interesting and appropriate introduction to this volume. The Aborigines who inhabited this valley, hunted in the forests that skirted its banks, and caught fish out of its prolific waters, called it the Quonchtacut. It was not known to any civilized people until some years after the English and Dutch, the original settlers of the country, had established themselves at Plymouth and New Netherlands.

In 1631 Wahquimacut, a sachem whose people lived upon the river, made a journey to Plymouth and Boston, and earnestly solicited the Governors of each of the Colonies established there, to send men to make settlements upon the Connecticut river. He referred particularly to the exceeding fruitfulness of the country, and promised the English, if they would make a settlement there, that he "would supply them with corn annually, and give them eighty beaver skins." He suggested that two men might be sent in advance to view the country; and had this invitation been accepted it might have prevented the claim of the

Dutch from New Netherlands, who subsequently came up the river and built a fort at Hartford, at a place now called Dutch Point. Had this been done the controversy that afterward arose between the settlers of these separate colonies in consequence of the claim which the Dutch thus established, might perhaps have been avoided, and an extensive trade, we mean extensive for the time, might, no doubt, have been opened with the Indians in hemp, furs and deer-skins. But the Governor of Massachusetts paid no attention to the proposal, though he wisely treated the sachem courteously and generously. The Governor of Plymouth, however, Mr. Winslow, judged the subject to be worthy of more attention, and he accordingly, soon after, went to Connecticut "and discovered the river and the adjacent parts." The Commissioners of the United Colonies, in their declaration against the Dutch in 1653, said: "Mr. Winslow, one of the Commissioners for Plymouth, discovered the Fresh river when the Dutch had neither trading house nor any pretense to a foot of land there."[*] It soon after appeared that the earnestness with which the Indian sachem solicited the English to settle upon the river, originated in the distressed state of the river Indians, who were being overpowered by the Pequots. The Indian king imagined that if he could persuade the English to make settlements along the river, they would defend him against his too powerful enemies.[†] The next year (1632,) the people of Plymouth made new discoveries on the river, and founded a place at Windsor, which was subsequently settled, though the first settled town on the river was Wethersfield, four miles below Hartford, which was visited by an exploring party from Watertown, who erected a few huts in 1634–5.

The Dutch rested their claim to the discovery of the river and the ownership of its lands, on the fact that the seacoast adjacent to its mouth, with a portion of the river itself, were first explored by them; the counter claim of the English was based on a patent of Connecticut issued by Robert, Earl of Warwick, President of the Council of Plymouth, Lord Say and Seal, Lord Brooke, Sir Richard Saltonstall, and their associates, "embracing all that part of New England in America, extending in breadth 120 miles, as

---

[*] Records of the United Colonies.
[†] Winthrop's Journal.

the coast lieth, from the Narragansett River toward Virginia, and in longitude from the Western Ocean to the North Sea," meaning thereby from the Atlantic to the Pacific Ocean. The Dutch retained possession of their trading house at Dutch Point for some time after Hartford was settled, but finally sold out to the English and vacated. There are many facts of historical interest relative to these first settlements, but we cannot, of course, notice them in detail here, and besides, they are mostly familiar to those acquainted with the early history of New England.

The Connecticut has its source "in that grand ridge of mountains" which divides the waters of New England and Canada, and extends northeasterly to the Gulf of St. Lawrence. The source of its highest branch is in about forty-five degrees and a half of north latitude. Where it enters New England it is ten rods in breadth, and in running sixty miles further it becomes twenty-four rods wide. The country through which it passes is gradually descending from north to south, and its course corresponds therewith. Its wide and deep valley separates not only two mountain ridges, but two solid masses of highland. The level of its broad bed is broken by a series of terraces. In the first quarter of its course it has a rapid fall of twelve hundred feet, this being from its source to the mouth of the Passumpsic River, on the parallel of the White Mountains, where its surface is but four hundred feet above the sea, two hundred miles distant. From that point, in eighty miles, to the long and flat bottom between Windsor and Bellows Falls, in Vermont, it descends only one hundred feet; thence it sinks one hundred and sixty feet to the plains of Deerfield; and at Springfield, eighty miles above its mouth, it is but forty feet above the ocean. It runs with a gentle flow, as its course is, between three and four hundred miles. Its breadth through Connecticut, this portion only being navigable for large vessels, varies from one hundred rods to half a mile, and near its mouth, to a mile, and more. In the spring of the year high floods are common, reaching from twenty to twenty-five feet above low water mark, and a vast tract of country is often inundated, as the banks of the river are generally low. Much of the land flooded is meadow land, which by this process is irrigated by natural means, and is thus fertilized to a considerable extent. One feature about these floods, or "freshets," as the river people invariably term them, is a constant changing of the channel in many places. Between Hartford and Middletown, localities can be pointed out where the bed of the river formerly was, which are now pasture lots or marshes. The banks continually wash away, and the tendency of the floods, which are frequently aggravated by walls of ice, is to fill up certain spots in the channel where the current is swift, so that dredging machines are necessarily employed to remove the accumulations of sand or other deposits, so that navigation may not be obstructed.

We have said that the valley of the Connecticut separates not only two mountain ridges, but two solid masses of highland. To regard these highlands, which form so important a feature of New England geography, as simply two ranges of hills, would not be to conceive of them correctly. They are vast swells of land, of an average elevation of a thousand feet above the level of the sea, each with a width of forty or fifty miles, from which as from a base, mountains rise in chains or isolated groups, to an altitude of several thousand feet more. In structure the two belts are unlike. The western system, which bears the general name of the Green Mountains, is composed of two principal chains, more or less continuous, covered, like several shorter ones which run along them, with the forest and herbage to which they owe their name. Between these a longitudinal valley can be traced, though with some interruption, from Connecticut to Vermont. The space between these mountain ranges and the Connecticut, is mostly occupied by a rugged tableland, measuring in height from a thousand to fifteen hundred feet. In Massachusetts this is deeply furrowed by transverse valleys, through which torrents like the Westfield and Deerfield Rivers descend to the Connecticut. In Vermont both heights and streams assume a more gentle character. From a height of less than a thousand feet in Connecticut, the mountains rise to an average of twenty-five hundred feet in Massachusetts, and forty-four hundred feet in Vermont and New Hampshire. In Connecticut the bottom of the valley is from five hundred to seven hundred feet above the level of the sea; in southern Massachusetts it is eight hundred feet; it rises thence two hundred feet to Pittsfield, and one hundred more to the foot of Greylock Mountain, whence it declines to the bed of the Housatonic in one direction, and to an average height of a little more than five hundred feet in Vermont in the other.

The commerce of the river is confined to that portion lying between Hartford and its mouth, a distance of fifty miles. Small craft, flat-bottomed affairs, more useful than ornamental, go as far as Springfield, about thirty miles above Hartford, though few go above Windsor Locks, an intermediate point. They carry freight in small quantities. The navigation of the river for practical purposes, closes at Hartford, and to this place vessels drawing eight and nine feet of water can readily pass except in cases of unusual drought. A fine line of steamers connects the head of navigation with New York, the largest boat of the line being of twenty-two hundred tons burthen. A large proportion of the vessels engaged in river traffic, are employed in freighting stone from the extensive free-stone quarries at Portland, opposite Middletown, twenty miles below Hartford, and these vessels on their return trips from various commercial points on the river, do a good business in the conveyance of miscellaneous freight. At Essex, Deep River, East Haddam, Higganum, Middle Haddam, Middletown, Portland and Hartford, there are ship-yards, from which many vessels for the coasting trade are yearly launched.

This navigable portion of the river affords delightful scenery throughout its whole distance. It is not so bold nor so sharp in its outlines as the scenery of the Hudson, yet in variety and picturesqueness it is grandly superior to much that appears on that river, and the traveler cannot fail to enjoy the many natural charms that rise on every hand as he passes along the stream. At a point called the Straits, two miles below Middletown, a mountainous range is broken by the sweep of the river, and the banks on either side tower aloft for a distance of more than a mile, forming a beautiful stretch of bold river scenery; but the general features of the country through which the river passes, have none of the bold characteristics seen at this particular point. For the most part, a receding valley is formed, with fine distances opening up well-cleared farms, handsome slopes through diverging valleys, and mountain ranges in the extreme view; though all along the variety is so great that whatever there might be of monotony, is broken in the continual production of some new scene "fairer than the rest." Through this fifty miles of country,

2

watered by the Connecticut, one can see more of a general character of the topography of a considerable portion of the valley
in a short time than of any other portion, because he may pass
through it by daylight on a steamer, and obtain a view of the
whole landscape at every turn.

Above Hartford, to the sources of the Connecticut, there are
many attractions of an historical nature, which the local resident
can point out to the cosmopolitan. In colonial days, the Indians
kept close to the river, because it afforded good grounds for
hunting and fishing, and it was in the settlements established by
the English along its banks, where most of the horrible deeds of
atrocity were committed by the savage warriors. The Indian
wars in Massachusetts, the most terrible of any, left many traces
which are pointed to to-day, with great local interest, in all the
country along the valley where the early settlers suffered and
died in their efforts to resist the deadly hatred of the red men.
Though familiar to almost every school-boy, one story connected
with the localities we have alluded to, may serve to show the
character of some of the incidents which have been handed down
to the present time from the days of bloody massacres. We
quote from Stiles' History of the Judges—the Regicides—
Goffe and Whalley: "While Goffe was secreted in Hadley, in
1675, the Indians attacked the town while the inhabitants were
at public worship. The people were thrown into the utmost con-
fusion, till Goffe, entirely unknown to them, white with age, of a
venerable and commanding aspect, and in an unusual dress, sud-
denly presented himself among them, encouraging the affrighted
inhabitants, and put himself at their head, and by his military
skill, led them on to an immediate victory. After the dispersion
of the enemy he instantly disappeared. The wondering inhabitants, while ignorant whence he came and where he retired,
imagined him to be an angel sent for their deliverance." It was
into this section of country that Philip, sachem of the Wampa-
noags, and for a long time the terror of New England, fled from
Rhode Island, and excited hostilities against the whites. All of
our New England histories contain more or less graphic accounts
of the sanguinary struggle which followed.

The Connecticut itself, above its navigable head, waters a fertile section, through which prosperous towns are scattered, with

an abundant promise of future growth. At Holyoke there is an extensive water-power, owned chiefly by Connecticut capitalists, who made an early investment, and who have reaped already a considerable pecuniary harvest from it. At other points there are privileges on a smaller scale, but there is hardly any doubt that in the course of time, very much of the upper Connecticut will be utilized to the development of manufacturing interests. The natural scenery of this portion of the valley is in very many parts unsurpassed. In its rugged, mountainous features, it is grandly superior, and is attracting the attention of tourists more and more every year.

Of the population of this fertile valley it seems superfluous to say that it is composed of a people distinguished for their habits of industry and their moral culture. Some of the finest farms in New England lie along the Connecticut, and upon these toil many of New England's sons, whose frugality enables them to reap from their soil abundant harvests, that give to the New England farmer independence and competence. The sturdy self-reliance, and indefatigable energy, which are peculiar to New England character, are no more thoroughly marked and made a sterling part of the composition of communities, than through this flourishing valley. The people seem to draw to themselves the chief characteristics of the climate, being, as we may say, moderate, rather than excessive or hasty, standing midway between the torrid or impulsive, and the frigid or cold-blooded classes to be found in other portions of our continent.

It is, perhaps, not generally known, that within the past two or three years the tide of summer travel has been diverted from other sections, and has found its way, to a large extent, to New England, and particularly to the Connecticut valley. Thousands of delighted tourists no longer crave the salt breezes of the ocean strand, or seek recreation in tedious voyages across the Atlantic, but going up this valley, find the bracing air of New England more congenial to health, and the attractions of the country ample to supply the most feverish desire for "something new." Sojourning all over our territory we shall find these contented tourists—on quiet farms, in pleasant villages, by river and lake, stretching from Long Island Sound up to the highest point of "the Green Mountain State."

This region, to-day, is filled with the hum of industry; its population and wealth are rapidly increasing; its people are growing in intelligence and refinement; invention and art are daily adding to its stock of utilities, and to its refining and chastening influences; so that in a generation, or a century more, if the inhabitants are left undisturbed by those dissensions that often destroy and blight the prospects of the happiest people, this valley will be unsurpassed in everything that can contribute to the comfort of a great people, by any other locality of equal extent on the surface of the globe.

Special Business Directory.

For Business Cards see Alphabetical List immediately following this Directory.

Agricultural Implements.
Way, Geo. M. & Co., 344 Main St., Hartford, Conn.

Agricultural Tool Manufacturers.
Belcher & Taylor, Agricultural Tool Company, Chicopee Falls, Mass.
Whittemore, Belcher & Co., Chicopee Falls, Mass.

Architects.
Gardiner & Perkins, corner Main and Fruit Sts., Florence, Mass.
Pratt, Wm. F., 2 Union Block, Northampton, Mass.

Attorneys at Law.
Allen, J. Wm., 21 Merchants Row, Northampton, Mass.
Davis & DeWolf, Main St., Greenfield, Mass.
Hall, Alfred, Middletown, Conn.
Merrill, M. E., 248 Main St., Hartford, Conn.

Auctioneers.
Toohy, Wm., 506 Main St., Hartford Conn.

Bakeries.
Sykes, F. A., 7 Allyn House Block, Hartford, Conn.

Bell Manufacturers, (House.)
Gong Bell Manufacturing Company, East Hampton, Conn.

Basket Manufacturers.

Williams, T. A. & Co., Greenfield, Mass.

Bobbin and Thread Spool Manufacturer.

Bassett, Joel L., East Hampton, Mass.

Book Binders.

Claremont Manufacturing Company, Claremont, N. H.
Case, Lockwood & Co., corner Pearl and Trumbull Sts., Hartford, Conn.
Drake & Parsons, 150 Asylum St., Hartford, Conn.
Parsons, Charles, 338 Main St., Hartford, Conn.
Talcott, W. H., 13 Asylum St., Hartford, Conn.

Book Publishers.

Claremont Manufacturing Company, Claremont, N. H.
Case, Lockwood & Co., corner Pearl and Trumbull Sts, Hartford, Conn.
Bridgman & Childs, 19 and 20 Merchants' Row, Northampton, Mass.
Hartford Publishing Company, 155 Asylum St., Hartford, Conn.
Hale, A. S. & Co., 97 Asylum St., Hartford, Conn.

Books and Stationery.

Bridgeman & Childs, Northampton, Mass.
Hall, T. E., 161 Main St., Hartford, Conn.

Boot and Shoe Manufacturer.

Mooney, H. A., Railroad St., St. Johnsbury, Vt.

Bridge Builders, (Iron and Timber.)

Briggs, A. D. & Co., Fort Block, Springfield, Mass.
Harris, D. L. & Co., 1 Charles St., Springfield, Mass.

Carpet Warp Manufacturer.

Johnson, Emory, Moodus, Conn.

Carriage Manufacturers.

Austin Brothers, Suffield, Conn.
Clark, Edson, Chicopee, Mass.
Darling, John A., Lyndon, Vt.
Davis, R. B. & Co., South St., Northampton, Mass.
Kenney & Gay, 24 and 26 Sheldon St., Hartford, Conn.
Phelps, George S., Masonic St., Northampton, Mass.
Staples, George M., 34 Wells St., Hartford, Conn,
Smith, David & Co., 2 Park St., Springfield, Mass.
Quimby & Hudson, Springfield, Mass.

Carriage and Saddlery Hardware and Trimmings.

Lee & Baker, 78 Main St., Springfield, Mass.

Casket and Coffin Manufacturers.

Washburn & Chase, corner Sanford and Market Sts., Springfield, Mass.
Heyer, James H. St. Johnsbury, Vt.

Children's Carriages, Hardware Manufacturers.

Munson, J. M. & Co., Greenfield, Mass.

Clothing Manufacturers.

Day, A. F. & C. G. & Co., 54 and 56 Asylum St., Hartford, Conn.

Clothing, (Wholesale.)

Day, A. F. & C. G. & Co., 54 and 56 Asylum St., Hartford, Conn.

Clothing and Gent's Furnishing Goods.

Hitchcock & Hosley, Exchange St., Chicopee, Mass.

Coal Dealers, (Wholesale and Retail.)

Banks, J. H. & Son, 253 Main St., Springfield, Mass.

Cocoa Dipper Manufacturer.

Maltby, E. C., Northfield, Conn.

Confectionery Manufacturer.

Barret, Henry E., Claremont, N. H.

Copper and Brass Castings.

Emory, P. P. & Co., Hampden St., Springfield, Mass.

Copper Plate Printer.

Nevers, Roderick, corner Pearl and Trumbull Sts., Hartford, Conn.

Cottage Organ Manufacturers.

Estey, J. & Co., Flat St., Brattleboro, Vt.

Cotton and Cotton Waste, (Wholesale.)

Day Brothers, 208 State St., Hartford, Conn.

Cotton Seine Twine Manufacturers.

Johnson, Emory, Moodus, Conn.
Day Brothers, 208 State St., Hartford, Conn.

Cracker Manufacturers.

Barrett, Henry E., Claremont, N. H.
Carr, Smith, Northampton, Mass.

Crockery, China and Glass Ware.

Skilton, O. A., 8 Pleasant St., Northampton, Mass.

Cutlery Glasses Manufacturer.

Briggs, Wm. H., Claremont, N. H.

Curtain Fixture Manufacturer.

Belcher, B. B., Chicopee Falls, Mass.

Dentists.

Bullock, C. & Son, 346 Main St., Hartford, Conn.
Cody, John, 251 Main St., Hartford, Conn.
Crofoot & Powers, 251 Main St., Hartford, Conn.
Greenleaf, Jas. M., 2 State St., Hartford, Conn.

Dental Supplies, (Wholesale.)

White, Samuel S., 16 Tremont Row, Boston, Mass.

Dental Materials, (Wholesale.)

White, Samuel S., 16 Tremont Row, Boston, Mass.

Cement Drain Sewer Pipe and Masonry.

Bissell, H. & S., 17 Pearl St., Hartford, Conn.

Druggists.

Parsons, S. C., 28 Merchants' Row, Northampton, Mass.
Thompson, C. F., Main St., Brattleboro, Vt.
Williams, Geo. W. & Co., 204 State St., Hartford, Conn.
Vinal, L. C., 151 Main St., Middletown, Conn.

Dry Goods, Groceries, Crockery, Hardware, &c.

Gilman, W. C. & Son, Newport, Vt.
Prichard, Geo., (Agent,) Bradford, Vt.

Dyers.

Brattleboro Dye House, Thomas Kaye, Brattleboro, Vt.
Greenfield Dye House, Philip Burg. Greenfield, Mass.
New England Fancy Dye Works, 139 Trumbull St., Hartford, Conn.
Smith, Geo., 39 Wells, 9 Pearl St., Hartford, Conn.

Engine and Hand Lathe Manufacturers.

Flather & Co., 11 River St., Nashua, N. H.

Eave-Trough Manufacturers.

Bartlett, Child & Co., Taylor St., Springfield, Mass.

Express Companies.

Merchants Union Express Company, Springfield, Mass.

Extension Table Manufacturer.

Belcher, D. E., Liberty St., Springfield, Mass.

Electrotypers.

Lockwood & Mandeville, corner Pearl and Trumbull Sts., Hartford, Conn.

Fertilizers.

Kellogg, Rodney, 201 and 205 Commerce St., Hartford, Conn.

File Manufacturers.

Claremont File Works, Henry E. Austin, Agent, Claremont, N. H.
St. Johnsbury File Works, James Nutt, St. Johnsbury, Vt.

Fire Extinguisher.

American Fire Extinguisher Company, 46 Congress St., Boston, Mass.

Flour, Grain and Broom Corn.

Fletcher, J., St. Johnsbury, Vt.
Shattuck, S. L., Depot Store, Greenfield, Mass.
Thayer, Sargeant & Co., Main St., Northampton, Mass.

Furnaces, Ranges, Stoves, &c.

Chubbuck, Levi, 336 and 338 Washington St., Boston, Mass.

Fresco Painter.

Wiese, F., 13 and 15 Pynchon St., Springfield, Mass.

Furniture Manufacturers.

Kilburn, L. & Co., Orange, Mass.

Furniture.

Butler, Geo. L., Bradford, Vt.
Fisher, Buckhause & Knappe, 5½ Burt's Block, Springfield, Mass.
Robbins, Winship & Co., 209 Main St., Hartford, Conn.

Garden Engine and Force Pump Manufacturers.

Burnham, H. & E., Main St., Brattleboro, Vt.

3

Gas Cook and Heating Stove Manufacturers.

Child & Bull, 189 Main St., Hartford, Conn.

General Jobbers.

Eldredge & Hastings, 283 Main St., Springfield, Mass.

Gold and Silver Leaf Manufacturer.

Perry, F., 120 Fulton St., Brooklyn, N. Y.

Gold and Silver Refiners.

Austin & Carpenter, 38 Clifford St., Providence, R. I.

Gold Foil Manufacturers.

Ashmead, James H. & Sons, corner Pearl and Trumbull Sts., Hartford, Conn.
Ney, J. M. & Co., 59 Pearl St., Hartford, Conn.

Gold Foil, Gold and Silver Plate, Solders, &c., (Wholesale.)

White, Samuel S., 16 Tremont Row, Boston, Mass.

Gold Chain Manufacturer.

Shumway, Robert G , Springfield, Mass.

Gold Pen Manufacturer.

Packard, Charles N., Main St., Springfield, Mass.

Gong Bell Manufacturers.

Gong Bell Manufacturing Company, East Hampton, Conn.

Gunsmiths.

Gifford, J. H., 3 State St., Springfield, Mass.
Newton, P. S., 26 Kingsley St., Hartford, Conn.

Hair Restorative Manufacturer.

Queen, George H., Sanford St., Springfield, Mass.

Hardware Dealers.

Blodgett, R. F. & Co., 140 State St., Hartford, Conn.
Skilton, O. A., 8 Pleasant St., Northampton, Mass.
Way, George M. & Co., 344 Main St., Hartford, Conn.
Thompson, C. F., Main St., Brattleboro, Vt.

Hardware, Machinery and Tools, (Wholesale.)

Green, John C., 108 Center St., New York.

Hats, Caps, and Gent's Furnishing Goods.

Bailey, L. W., 10 Bank Row, Greenfield, Mass.
Bunce, J. W., 307 Main St., Hartford, Conn.

Hoop Skirt Manufacturer.

Chace, George H., 179 Main St., Springfield, Mass.

Horse Rake Manufacturer.

Kimball, George, (Kimball's Patent,) Springfield, Vt.

Hosiery and Gloves.

Kinsman, W. D., 214 Main St.., Springfield, Mass.

Hand Stamps, Seal Presses, &c.

Snow, Justin, Hartford, Conn.

Hotels.

American House, Hanover St., Boston, Mass.
American House, opposite Railroad Depot, Fitchburg, Mass.
Aldrich House, Providence, R. I.
Crystal Lake Hotel, Barton, Vt.
Atlantic House, Bridgeport, Conn.
Champion House, East Haddam, Conn.
City Hotel, 217 Main St., Hartford, Conn.
European Hotel, corner Wells and Mulberry Sts., Hartford, Conn.
Fitchburg Hotel, 162 Main St., Fitchburg, Mass.
Holyoke House, opposite Depot, Holyoke, Mass.
Hampden House, corner Main and Court Sts., Springfield, Mass.
New Haven Hotel, corner Chapel and College Sts., New Haven, Conn.
Round Hill Hotel, Round Hill, Northampton, Mass.
St. John's Hotel, 445 Main St., Hartford, Conn.
Strickland House, New Britain, Conn.
Samosett House, Holyoke, Mass.
Sullivan House, Claremont, N. H.
St. Johnsbury House, Main St., St. Johnsbury, Vt.
Massasoit House, Main St., Springfield, Mass.
Trumbull House, State St., Hartford, Conn.
Memphremagog House, Newport, Vt.
Union House, East Hampton, Mass.
Warner House, Main St., Northampton, Mass.
United States Hotel, State Street, Hartford, Conn.

Horse Power Machines, (Sawing, Threshing and Separating.)

Rollins, B. F., St. Johnsbury, Vt.

Ice Cream Saloons.

Sykes, F. A., 7 Allyn House Block, Hartford, Conn.
Briggs, H. S., 381 Main St., Hartford, Conn.
Gardener, Mrs. W. H., 387 Main St., Hartford, Conn.

Improved Upright Drill Manufacturers.

Bullard & Parsons, 23 and 25 Potter St. Hartford, Conn.

Insurance Companies.

Continental Life Insurance Company, 289 Main St., Hartford, Conn.
Connecticut General Life Insurance Company, 7 Central Row, Hartford, Conn.
Charter Oak Life Insurance Company, 240 Main St., Hartford, Conn.
Hartford County Mutual Fire Insurance Co., 321 Main St., Hartford, Conn.
People's Fire Insurance Company, Middletown, Conn.
Phœnix Mutual Life Insurance Company, 281 Main St. Hartford, Conn.
Putnam Fire Insurance Company, 240 Main St., Hartford, Conn.
Railway Passengers Assurance Company, 289 Main St., Hartford, Conn.
Travelers Insurance Company, 182 Asylum St., Hartford, Conn.

Insurance and Real Estate Agents.

Jewett, J. H. & Co., Northampton, Mass.
Kirkland, Harvey, Court House, Northampton, Mass.

Iron Foundries.

Buzzell, Luke, St. Johnsbury, Vt.
Clark & Chapman, Bellows Falls, Vt.
Green River Machine Shop and Foundry, Felt & Co., Greenfield, Mass.
Mitchell, James & Co., Springfield, Vt.
Hunt, Waite & Flint, Orange, Mass.
Phœnix Iron Works, Geo. S. Lincoln & Co., 54 and 60 Arch St. Hartford, Conn.
Union Manufacturing Company, New Britain, Conn.

Iron & Steel, (Wholesale.)

Blodgett, R. F. & Co., 140 State St., Hartford, Conn.
Fletcher, J., St. Johnsbury, Vt.
Prichard, George, (Agent,) Bradford, Vt.
Thompson, C. F., Main St., Brattleboro, Vt.

Knitting Machine Manufacturer.

Lamb Knitting Machine, Pynchon Bank Block, Main St., Springfield, Mass.

Lager Beer Saloon.

Siemer Ernest, 66 Trumbull St., Hartford, Conn.

Leather Belting Manufacturer.

Plympton, J. D., Chicopee, Mass.

Leather Manufacturers.

Ely, Homer, Ashleyville, Mass.
Ely, C., Ashleyville, Mass.

Lithographers.

Kellogg & Bulkeley, 245 Main St., Hartford, Conn.

Liquor Dealer, (Wholesale.)

Isham, A. B., corner Ferry and Commerce Sts., Hartford, Conn.

Livery Stables.

Alvord, E., Market St., Springfield, Mass.
Clark, C. S. & Co., opposite Depot, Northampton, Mass.
Richmond, F. & J. M., Sanford St., Springfield, Mass.
Strong, Ebenezer, rear Warner House, Northampton, Mass.

Loan Office.

Belden, Thos. H., 254 Main St., Hartford, Conn.

Lumber Dealers.

Bassett, Joel L., East Hampton.
Barrett, M. S., Pearl St., Springfield, Vt.

Lumber, Lime & Cement.

Pease, T. & Son, Thompsonville, Conn.

Machinery Broker.

Kimball, C. W., Springfield, Mass.

Machine Card Clothing Manufacturers.

Sargent Card Clothing Company, Junction Depot, Worcester, Mass.

Machinists.

Buzzell, Luke, St. Johnsbury, Vt.
Benham, Nathan, rear 262 Main St., Hartford, Conn.
Bullard & Parsons, 23 and 25 Potter St. Hartford, Conn.
Brown, W. H., 44 Exchange St., Worcester, Mass.
Clark & Chapman, Bellows Falls, Vt.
Cushman, Dwight, 21 Potter St., Hartford, Conn.
Flather & Co., 11 River St., Nashua, N. H.
Grant, Geo. M. & Son, Northampton, Mass.

Machinists—Continued.

Gerry, Geo. & Son, Athol Depot, Mass.
Green River Machine Shop and Foundry, Felt & Co., Greenfield, Mass.
Herrick, W., Northampton, Mass.
Holyoke Machine Company, Holyoke, Mass.
Humphrey, John, Keene, N. H.
Hunt, Waite & Flint, Orange, Mass.
Phœnix Iron Works, Geo. S. Lincoln & Co., 54 and 60 Arch St., Hartford, Conn.
Stacy, E. S. & Co:, Harrison Avenue, Springfield, Mass.
Stiles, N. C. & Co., West Meriden, Conn.
Turbine Water Wheel Mf'g. Co., J. D. Chase & Sons, Agents, Orange, Mass.
Wood, Light & Co., Junction Shop, Worcester, Mass.

Machinists' Tools Manufacturers.

Buzzell, Luke, St. Johnsbury, Vt.
Benham, Nathan, rear 262 Main St., Hartford, Conn.
Bullard & Parsons, 23 and 25 Potter St., Hartford, Conn.
Flather & Co., 11 River St., Nashua, N. H.
Grant, George M. & Son, Northampton, Mass.
Herrick, W., Northampton, Mass.
Holyoke Machine Company, Holyoke, Mass.
Humphrey, John, Keene, N. H.
Hunt, Waite & Flint, Orange, Mass.
Phœnix Iron Works, Geo. S. Lincoln & Co., 54 and 60 Arch St., Hartford, Conn.
Stiles, N. C. & Co., West Meriden, Conn.
Stacy, E. S. & Co., Harrison Avenue, Springfield, Mass.
Turbine Water Wheel Mf'g. Co., J. D. Chase & Sons, Agents, Orange, Mass.
Wood, Light & Co., Junction Shop, Worcester, Mass.

Marble Yards.

Andrews, George, Bellows Falls, Vt.
Batterson, James G., 650 Main St., Hartford, Conn.
Black & Ford, Main St., Northampton, Mass.
Cabtree & Short, 2 Bliss St., Springfield, Mass.

Manufacturers' Supplies, (Wholesale.)

Crompton & Dawson, 28 Front St., Worcester, Mass.

Meat and Fish Dealer.

Stevens, J. N. B., 34 and 38 Market St., Hartford, Conn.

Merchant Tailors.

Bailey, L. N., 10 Bank Row, Greenfield, Mass.
Ockington, B. F., corner Main and Pleasant Sts., Northampton, Mass.
Ray, Samuel C., 241 Main St., Springfield, Mass.

Metals and Paper Stock.

Hammond, S. T. & Co., Springfield, Mass.

Millinery & Fancy Goods, (Wholesale & Retail.)

Wallach & Schwab, 449 and 451 Main St., Hartford, Conn.

Millinery & Straw Goods, (Wholesale.)

Waters, Horace, Jr., 384 Main St , Hartford, Conn.

Mineral Water and Beer Manufacturer.

Brooks, F. A., 52 North Main St., Springfield, Mass.

Model and Pattern Maker.

Bliss, J. K., 18 Hampden St., Springfield, Mass.

Mop Holder Manufacturer, (Eureka Patent.)

Belcher, D. E., Liberty St., Springfield, Mass.

Mowing and Reaping Machine Manufacturers.

Warner, James M. & Son, St. Johnsbury, Vt.

Moulding Cutter Manufacturer.

Brown, Wm. H., 44 Exchange St., Worcester, Mass.

Music.

Maple Wood Music Seminary, East Haddam, Conn.
Grosvenor & Leonard's Quadrille Band, 45 Pearl St., Hartford, Conn.

Music Teacher.

Pellitier, O., Hungerford & Cone's Block, Hartford, Conn.

Newspapers.

Hartford Courant, (Daily and Weekly,) 14 Pratt St., Hartford, Conn.
Hartford Evening Press, (Daily,) 14 Pratt St., Hartford, Conn.
Hartford Morning Post, (Daily and Weekly,) 222 Main St., Hartford, Conn.
Meriden Weekly Visitor, Meriden, Conn.
New Britain Record, New Britain, Conn.
Northampton Free Press, (Semi-Weekly,) Springfield, Mass.
Springfield Union, (Daily & Weekly,) Springfield, Mass.
Vermont Record and Farmer, (Ed. P. Ackerman,) Brattleboro, Vt.
The Vermont Journal, Windsor, Vt.
The Vermont Chronicle, Windsor, Vt.

Nurserymen, Florists and Seedsmen.

Olm Brothers, 350 Main St., Springfield, Mass.
Whitmore's City Garden, 113 Wethersfield Avenue, Hartford, Conn.

Oakum Manufacturers.

Tibbals & Co., Cobalt, Conn.

Ornamental Carvers, (Wood.)

Prall & Drummond, 22 and 24 Mulberry St., Hartford, Conn.

Paper Box Manufacturers.

King, V. A., 66 State St., Hartford, Conn.
Tucker E. & Son, 139 Trumbull St., Hartford, Conn.

Paper Bags.

King, V. A., 66 State St., Hartford, Conn.
Tucker, E. & Son, 139 Trumbull St., Hartford, Conn.

Paper and Paper Stock Dealers.

Carroll, E. J. & Co., 243 State St., Hartford, Conn.
McCulloch & Burt, 117 Main St., Springfield, Mass.
Pitkin & Bartlett, 160 Commerce St., Hartford, Conn.

Pail and Bucket Manufacturers.

Fairbanks, M., Keene, N. H.
Whitney, Lord & Co., Orange, Mass.

Painters and Oil Dealers.

Smith & Jones, 3 Court St., Northampton, Mass.
Wilson, J. & Co., Main St., Greenfield, Mass.

Patent Agent.

Bliss, J. W., 240 Main St., Hartford, Conn.

Patent Medicine Manufacturers.

Harris, N. O., East Haddam, Conn.
Doty, C. C., Bradford, Vt.

Patent Right Agent.

Hauxhurst, G. W., 497 Main St., Hartford, Conn.

Piano Forte Manufacturers.

Hallet, Davis & Co., 272 Washington St., Boston, Mass.
New York Piano Forte Company, 88 Walker St., New York.

Piano & Melodeon Dealers.

Butler, George L., Bradford, Vt.
Clark, Kidder & Co., Union Block, Northampton, Mass.
Farris, John, 197 and 201 Main St., Hartford, Conn.

Picture Frame Manufacturers.

Dart, E. & Co., 219 Main St. Hartford, Conn.
Farris, John, 197 and 201 Main St., Hartford, Conn.
Witter, Albert G., 517 Main St., Hartford, Conn.

Pistol Manufacturers.

Stevens, J. & Co., Chicopee Falls, Mass.

Photographers.

Bliss, J. W., 240 Main St., Hartford, Conn.
Moore Brothers, Main, opposite Court Square, Springfield, Mass.
Oldershaw, J., 311 Main, and 3 Asylum St., Hartford, Conn.
Townsend, A. C. & Co., Main St., Springfield, Mass.

Physicians.

Norton, Daniel, 254 Main St., (Clairvoyant,) Hartford, Conn.
Lyon, J. L. Dr., No. 7 Postoffice Building, Hartford, Conn.

Plough Manufacturers.

Green River Machine Shop and Foundry, Felt & Co., Greenfield, Mass.
Mitchell, James & Co., Springfield, Vt.

Plumbers' Materials Manufacturers.

Whitfield, James M. & Son, 262 Water St., New York.
Buck, Fred. F. E., 14 Pratt St., Hartford, Conn.

Printers, (Book and Job.)

Case, Lockwood & Co., corner Pearl and Trumbull Sts., Hartford, Conn.
Claremont Manufacturing Company, Claremont, N. H.
Clark & Booth, 321 Main St., Hartford, Conn.
Cobleigh, F. D., Brattleboro, Vt.
Hanmer, S., 66 State St., Hartford, Conn.
Wiley, Waterman & Eaton, 152 Asylum St., Hartford, Conn.

Publisher, (Magazine.)

The Dental Cosmos, Samuel S. White, 16 Tremont Row, Boston, Mass.

Pump Manufacturers.

Douglass, W. & B., Middletown, Conn.
Norwalk Iron Works, (Earle's Patent Steam Pump,) 108 Sudbury St., Boston,
Mass.

Quarriers.

North Middlesex Quarry, (Freestone,) Cromwell, Conn.

Red Aberdeen Granite Dealer.

Batterson, J. G., 650 Main St., Hartford, Conn.

4

Reed, Harnesses, Shuttle, Spindle, &c., Manufacturers.

Miller, Frederick, 29 Canal St., Providence, R. I.
Weston & Place, Fitchburg, Mass.

Reed, (Weaving) Manufacturer.

Whitaker, Edmund, Holyoke, Mass.

Restaurants.

Briggs, Henry S., 381 Main St., Hartford, Conn.
Gardner, W. H. Mrs., 387 Main St., Hartford, Conn.
George, F. A., Bellows Falls, Vt.

Rope and Twine Manufacturer.

Church, Abner, (Agent,) 46 Morgan St., Hartford, Conn.

Saddles, Harnesses and Collars.

Payne, Wm., 35 and 37 Dwight St., Springfield, Mass.
Payne, H. W., 12 Merchants' Row, Greenfield, Mass.

Sawed Shingle Manufacturer.

Barrett, M. S., Pearl St., Springfield, Vt.

Screw Eyes and Hook Manufacturer.

Perry, A. T., Chester, Conn.

Sewing Machine Manufacturers.

Elliptic Sewing Machine Company, 543 Broadway, New York.
Gold Medal Sewing Machine, A. T. Johnson & Co., 334 Washington St., Boston, Mass.
Howe, A. B., 437 Broadway, New York.
Florence Sewing Machine Company, Florence, Mass.
Weed Sewing Machine Company, 240 Main St., Hartford, Conn.

Sewing Machine Agents.

Bailey, L. M., 10 Bank Row, Greenfield, Mass.
Chace, George W., 179 Main St., Springfield, Mass.
Forbes & Foster, American House Block, Greenfield, Mass.
Shaffer, Calvin, 5 Allyn House Block, Hartford, Conn.
King, V. A., 66 State St., Hartford, Conn.

Silk Manufacturers.

Cheney Brothers, 34 Morgan St., Hartford, Conn.

Show Case Manufacturer.

Belcher, D. E., Liberty St., Springfield, Mass.

Shafting and Mill Work.

Benham, Nathan, rear 262 Main St., Hartford, Conn.
Bullard & Parsons, 23 and 25 Potter St., Hartford, Conn.
Buzzell, Luke, St. Johnsbury, Vt.
Gerry, George & Son, Athol Depot, Mass.
Grant, George M. & Son, Northampton, Mass.
Turbine Water Wheel Mf'g. Co., J. D. Chase, Agent, Orange, Mass.
Holyoke Machine Company, Holyoke, Mass.
Stacy, E. S. & Co., Harrison Avenue, Springfield, Mass.
Phœnix Iron Works, 54 and 60 Arch St., Hartford, Conn.

Silver Plated Ware Manufacturers.

Pitkin, W. L. & H. E., 17 Hicks St., Hartford, Conn.
Roberts, E. M. & Co., East Hartford, Conn.

Shears, (Pruning) Manufacturers.

Stevens, J. & Co., Chicopee Falls, Mass.

Shirt Manufacturer, (Cotton and Woolen.)

Dewey, H. S., 24 Barnes' Block, Springfield, Mass.

Spectacle Manufacturer.

Coomes, W. W., Longmeadow, Mass.

Spring Bed Manufacturers.

Gerard & Forbes, 19 Artisan St., New Haven, Conn.

Spool Cotton Manufacturers, (White and Colored.)

Hadley Company, J. S. Davis, Agent, Holyoke, Mass.

Soapstone Stove Manufacturers.

Francestown Soapstone Company, F. A. Barton, Agent, Nashua, N. H.

Stationers' Ivory Goods.

Kelsey, Edward, Centerbrook, Conn.

Steam Engine Manufacturer.

Humphrey, John, Keene, N. H.

Steam and Gas Pipes.

Briggs, H. J. & Co., Main St., Springfield, Mass.

Steam Boiler Manufacturers.

Springfield Steam Boiler Works, Liberty St., Springfield, Mass.

Stove Manufacturers.

Mitchell, James & Co., Springfield, Vt.

Stone Cutters.

Brabazon, A. & S., 77 Potter St., Hartford, Conn.

Stoves and Tinware.

Chase, George A., Main St., Greenfield, Mass.
Child & Bull, 189 Main St., Hartford, Conn.
Philips, Wm. J., 220 Main St., Hartford, Conn.

Suspender Manufacturers.

Hartford Suspender Manufactory, 147 Main St., Hartford, Conn.
Nashawannuck Manufacturing Company, East Hampton, Mass.

Tag Manufacturers.

Dennison & Co., 66 Milk St., Boston, Mass.

Tar, Pitch and Rosin Dealer.

Church, Abner, Agent, 46 Morgan St., Hartford, Conn.

Tea, Coffee and Spice Dealers.

Gillette, A. B. & Co., 43 and 45 Asylum St., Hartford, Conn.
Hebaid, Sturtevant & Co., 260 State St., Hartford, Conn.
Park, Fellows & Co., 203 State St., Hartford, Conn.

Tinware Manufacturers.

Merriam Manufacturing Company, Durham, Conn.

Thread Manufacturers, (White and Colored.)

Hadley Company, J. S. Davis, Agent, Holyoke, Mass.

Tobacco and Cigars, (Wholesale.)

Burnham, J. D. & Co., 77 and 79 Asylum St., Hartford, Conn.
Brown & Oatman, 212 State St., Hartford, Conn.
Gabb, Charles N., Main St., Northampton, Mass.

Trunk Manufacturers and Dealers.

Cornwell, R. B., 434 Main St., Hartford, Conn.
Bullard, J. D., 90 Asylum St., Hartford, Conn.

Watches and Jewelry.

Forbes & Foster, Mansion House Block, Greenfield, Mass.
Steele, Thomas & Son, 340 Main St., Hartford, Conn.
Stevens & Rogers, corner Main St. and Central Row, Hartford, Conn.
Walter, M. F., 447 Main St., Hartford, Conn.

Water Cure Establishment.

Round Hill Hotel and Water Cure, Northampton, Mass.

Water Wheel Manufacturers.

Buzzell, Luke, St. Johnsbury, Vt.
Clark & Chapman, Bellows Falls, Vt.
Cushman, Dwight, 21 Potter St., (Cushman's Patent Turbine,) Hartford, Conn.
Green River Machine Shop and Foundry, Felt & Co., Greenfield, Mass.
Hunt, Waite & Flint, Orange, Mass.
Humphrey, John, (Improved Fourneyrow Turbine,) Keene, N. H.
Witherell, James & Co., Springfield, Vt.
Turbine Water Wheel Mf'g. Co., J. D. Chase & Sons, Agents, (Chase's Improved Excelsior Jonval Turbine,) Orange, Mass.

Weaving Reed Manufacturers.

Tilley & Clark, Commercial Row, Springfield, Mass.
Miller, Frederick, 29 Canal St., Providence, R. I.

West India Goods, Building Materials, &c., (Wholesale.)

Fletcher, J., St. Johnsbury, Vt.

Windows, Doors, Blinds and Glass.

Wilson, J. & Co., Main St., Greenfield, Mass.

Window Shade Manufacturers.

Fisher, Buckhause & Knappe, 5½ Burt's Block, Springfield, Mass.
Wiese, F., 13 and 15 Pynchon St., Springfield, Mass.

Wire Manufacturers.

Prentiss, George W., Holyoke, Mass.
Lamb, Horace, Northampton, Mass.

Wood Carvers.

Prall & Drummond, 22 and 24 Mulberry St., Hartford, Conn.

Woolen Machinery, (Wholesale.)

Crompton & Dawson, 28 Front St., Worcester, Mass.

Woolen Machinery Manufacturers.

Gerry, George & Son, Athol Depot, Mass.
Hunt, Waite & Flint, Orange, Mass.

ALPHABETICAL INDEX TO ADVERTISERS.

CONN. RIVER BUSINESS DIRECTORY.

SAYBROOK, Town of Middlesex County, Connecticut, is situated on the west bank and at the mouth of the river, bordering on Long Island Sound. Distance from Hartford 45 miles, and from New London 17 miles.

The principal street runs nearly north and south, and upon it the dwellings and stores are mostly located. Its situation on the sound makes it an excellent summer resort. Shad fishing is probably carried on more extensively here than at any other place on the river.

Steamboats plying between New York and Hartford, stop here. The town is also accessible by the Shore Line Railroad.

BUSINESS DIRECTORY.

Boots and Shoes.

Galin Dowd & Son.

Dry Goods and Groceries.

Bushnell, Giles
Sheffield, Amos & Son,
Whittlesey, Robert

Groceries.

Dickinson, Edgar
Potter, Henry
Redfield, L.
Spencer, William
Treadway, James

Hotels.

Sea Shore House, Wm. Spencer, Proprietor.
Saybrook Hotel, Jas. Rankin, Proprietor.

Millinery.

Burt, Sarah Mrs.
Chalker, Susan Mrs.

Oil Manufacturers.

Marine Oil Co.

Omnibus Line.

Williams, David J.

Physician.

King, Asa B.

Postmaster.

Dowd, G.

Restaurant.

Williams, David J.

LYME, New London County, Connecticut, is situated on the east bank of the river, 45 miles from Hartford and near the mouth of the river. The Township comprises the villages of Hamburgh, Hadlyme and East Lyme. Woolen goods are manufactured here to some extent, but the principal business is agriculture. The town contains about 1,400 population.

BUSINESS DIRECTORY.

Attorneys at Law.

Griffin, A. Hamburgh.
Parker, M. S. Hamburgh.

Blacksmith.
Beebe, W. H. Hamburgh.

Ferryman.
Bramble, H. G. Hamburgh.

Gristmill.
Comstock, Henry T. Hadlyme.

Merchants.
DeWolf, Roger   Lyme,   Dry Goods, Groceries, &c.
DeWolf & Rowland, "   "   "   "
Eabel & Conklin,   "   "   "   "
Brockway, W. Hamburgh,   "   "   "
Comstock, Henry Hadlyme, "   "   "
Gates, E. W.   "   "   "   "
Ely, S. C.   Hamburgh,   "   "   "
Lord, S. H.   "   "   "   "
Nichols Brothers, Lyme,   "   "   "
Parker, M. S. Hamburgh,   "   "   "
Reynolds & Bigelow, "   "   "   "
Sessions, S. B.   "   "   "   "
Spencer, William Hadlyme, "   "   "

Physicians and Surgeons.
Griffin, Ely Hamburgh,
Warner, Hiram Hamburgh.

Postmasters.
Sisson, S. B. Hamburgh,
Gates, E. W. Hadlyme.

Shoemakers.
Babcock, John Hamburgh.

Woolen Manufacturers.
Rathbone, A. C. G. & Co., Hamburgh.

ESSEX, a Post Town, Middlesex County, Connecticut, on the west bank of the river, distant from Saybrook 5 miles. Considerable business is carried on here, there being several manufacturing establishments, one Bank and two Hotels.

Centreville, a Post Village, two miles west of Essex, contains three extensive Ivory goods manufactories.

Population about 2,200.

BUSINESS DIRECTORY.

Auger and Bit Manufacturers.

Lewis & Co.

Banks.

Essex Savings Bank.
Saybrook National Bank.
J. D. Redfield, Cashier, C. R. Doane, President.

Block and Spar Makers.

Conklin, Geo. & Brother.

Blacksmithing.

Pratt, Edmund & Son.
Wright, William

Boot and Shoe Makers.

King, L.
Minke, J.
Redfield, J. C.
Sizer, R. H.

Boat Builders.

Gladwin, Frederick
Hurlbert, Jas.
Hayden, Jas. M.
Tucker, Harmon
Tucker, Niles

Cabinet Maker.

Dickinson, G. K.

Carriage Makers.

Morley, S. M.
Salter, Edwin

Cigar Manufacturer.

Hayden, Luther P.

Clothing and Gents. Furnishing Goods.

Dickinson, F. N.

Dentist.

Stevens, Benjamin

Druggist.

Whittemore, Elmore

Dry Goods and Groceries.

Hayden, T. S.
Spencer, Fuller

Fish Dealer.

Beebe, H. G.

Flour and Grain.

Post, M. H.

Grist Mill.

Bushnell, S. & Co.,
Williams, P. P.

House Joiners.

Buckingham, Ralph
Munger, Sylvester

Newton, Charles
Rose, Asa H.
Spencer, Chauncey
Starkey, George
Starkey, Charles F.
Stillman, George K.

Hotels.

Essex Hotel, W. B. Lane, Proprietor.
Union House, Geo. Harrington, Proprietor.

Justice of the Peace.

Redfield, E. W.

Lumber Dealer.

Wooster, H. O.

Marine Railway.

Hayden, Nehemiah

Meat Markets.

Burnett, Jas. R.
Champion, Richard

Millinery and Dress Making.

Brewster, Mrs.
Buckingham, Mrs.
Tyler, E.

Groceries.

Andrews, David
Pratt, A.
Spencer, Wilson
Starkey, F. & Sons.
Starkey, G. & Sons.

Organ and Melodeon Keys.

COMSTOCK, CHENEY & CO., P. O. Centre Brook.

Painters, (House.)

Hayden, E.
Hayden, Cicero
Hayden, J. G.
Knowles, David B.
Royce, George
Royce, William
Williams, W.

Physicians.

Hubbard, Charles
Mather, E. S.

Piano Forte Ivory.

COMSTOCK, DICKINSON & CO., P. O. Address Centre Brook.

Postmaster.

Williams, Richard S.

Restaurants.

Dolph, S.
Pratt, Charles
Smith, John

Rope Manufacturers.

Smith & Robbins.

Sail Maker.

Crystal, Thomas

Sash, Doors and Blinds.

Pratt, H. L.

Ship Builders.

Mack, David
Starkey, Noah

Shoddy Manufacturers.

Dickinson, T. N. & Co.

Stationers' Ivory Goods.

COMSTOCK, DICKINSON & CO., P. O. Centre Brook.
KELSEY, EDWARD   See adv. index.   P. O. Address
Centre Brook.

Stoves and Tinware.

Post, M. H.

Saw Mills.

Bushnell, S. & Co.

Tailors.

Gorton, William
Graham, George W.

Wood and Bone Turning.

GLADWIN, GRISWOLD & CO., P. O. Centre Brook.

Wood Turning.

Kelsey, E.

DEEP RIVER, Middlesex County, Connecticut, a post Village
on the west bank of the river, distant 33 miles from Hartford,
30 miles from New Haven, 18 miles from Middletown—population about 1,500.
Contains several extensive Ivory Goods manufactories.

BUSINESS DIRECTORY.

Attorney at Law.
Wilcox, W. F.

Auger and Bit Manufacturer.
Jennings, Russell

Banks.
Deep River National Bank.
R. P. Spencer, President, G. Parker, Cashier.
Deep River Savings Bank.
S. Snow, Secretary and Treasurer.

Boot and Shoe Makers.
Banning, Arbe
Banning, A. H. & Son.
Schlick, John

Brush Manufacturer.
Rogers, C. B.

Cabinet Maker.
Smith, C. D.

Carpenters and Builders.
Dickinson & Young.

Dry Goods and Groceries.
Richards, D. T. & Co.
Snow, S. F.

7

Groceries.

Lane, J. S.
Roberts, F. A.

Hotels.

Central House, C. G. Post, Proprietor.
Deep River Hotel, J. S. Southington, Proprietor.
Wahginnicut House, W. D. Worthington, Proprietor.

Insurance and Pension Agent.

Marvin, J. W.

Ivory Turning.

Rogers, C. B. & Co.

Ivory Combs.

PRATT, READ & CO.
PRATT, SMITH & CO.

Ivory Buttons.

Rogers, C. B.

Ivory Goods.

Rogers, C. B.
Pratt, Smith & Co.
Pratt, Read & Co.

Lumber Dealers.

Deep River Lumber Co.

Milliners.

Loomis, C. Mrs.
Shailer, Mrs. W.

Paper Box Manufacturer.

Wilcox, J. S.

Physicians and Surgeons.

Bidwell, Edwin

Tyler, E. C.

Piano Forte Ivory.

PRATT, READ & CO.

PRATT, SMITH & CO.

Piano Key Boards.

PRATT, READ & CO.

Saddlery and Harnesses.

Dixon, Thomas P.

Ship Builder.

Dennison, Eli

Tin Ware Manufacturer.

Williams, S. A.

Wood Turning.

Pratt, N. B.

CHESTER, a Post Village and Township of Middlesex County, Connecticut, on the west bank of the river, 31 miles from Hartford and 32 miles from New Haven. Population about 1000.

Manufacturing is carried on here to some extent, although principally a farming town.

BUSINESS DIRECTORY.

Auger and Bit Manufacturers.

Griswold, Charles L.

Jennings, Russell

Boots and Shoes.
Barker & Shipman.

Brush Manufacturer.
Rogers, C. B.

Clothing Dealers.
Barker & Shipman.

Cotton Twine Manufacturers.
Clark, J. L.
Marvin & Co.

· Dry Goods and Groceries.
Colt, S. H.

Grist Mill.
Gibbs, S. & Son.

Groceries.
Brooks & Jones.
Webb & Abbey.

Hotel.
Chester Hotel, C. H. Redfield, Proprietor.

Inkstand Manufacturers.
Silliman, S. & Co.

Iron Foundry.
Lord, J. L.

Ivory Goods.
Post, J. H.

Livery Stable.
Morse, Luther

Physicians.

Pratt, Ambros
Turner, S. W.

Postmaster.

Wright, S. A.

Satinett Manufacturers.

Gledhill & Hiff.

Sorghum Manufacturer.

Gilbert, A. H.

Screw Eyes and Hook Manufacturers.

Brooks, M. S.
PERRY, A. T., see adv. index.

Wood Worker.

Bogart, W. H.

A. T. PERRY,

MANUFACTURER OF

BRIGHT IRON GOODS,

Screw Eyes, Screw Hooks, Cornice Hooks, Meat
Hooks, Gate and Shutter Hooks and various other
kinds made to order with or without Screws.

Chester, Connecticut.

EAST HADDAM, Middlesex County, Connecticut, on the
east side of the river, about 32 miles from Hartford, is a thriving
and enterprising place, containing several large manufacturing
establishments. Population about 7000. The natural scenery
at this place is beautiful, and there are but few towns through

---

the Connecticut River Valley, which present so many attractions to the summer tourist. The Hartford and New York and Long Island Steamboats plying on the river, here have a landing.

The Champion House, situated near the steamboat landing overlooking the river for several miles, is one of the finest Hotels in New England. The rooms are large, and every thing connected with the house neatly and conveniently arranged.

Maplewood Music Seminary, a flourishing institution under the direction of Dwight S. Babcock, is pleasantly situated here, commanding a fine view of the river.

Moodus, a Post Village about 4 miles east, is noted for its extensive cotton manufactories.

BUSINESS DIRECTORY.

The Post Office address is given when it differs from the name of the town.

Attorneys at Law.
Clark, J. T.
Phelps, L. L.

Banks.
Bank of New England,
W. H. Goodspeed, President, T. Gross jr., Cashier.

Barber.
Webster, T. H.

Billiards.
Cook, H. J.

Blacksmithing.
Potter & Chapman,   Moodus.
Shailer, Austin S.

Boot and Shoe Makers.
Bammann, F. H.
Goff, Alfred   Moodus.
Mitchell, Samuel   Moodus.
Richmond, N. C.   Moodus.

Broom Manufacturers.

United States Broom & Brush Co.

Carriage Manufacturers.

Goff & Cook, Moodus.

Clothing.

Atwood, J.

Coffin Trimings.

Ray, J. S.

Confectionery.

Cook, H. J.

Cotton Goods.

Moodus Manufacturing Co., (Prints,) Moodus.
Boies, H. (Warp,) Moodus.

Cotton Twine Manufacturers.

Brownell & Co., (seine,) Moodus.
Cone & Purple, Moodus.
JOHNSON, E. see adv. index, Moodus.
New York Net and Twine Co., (seine,) Moodus.
Nichols, W. E. Moodus.
Silliman & Purple, Leesville.

Cotton Duck Manufacturers.

Atlantic Duck Co., Moodus.
East Haddam Duck Co., Moodus.
Silliman, J. B. Moodus.
Williams Duck Co., Moodus.

Dentist.

Arnold, Russell Moodus.

Druggist.

Harris, N. O. Dr. see adv. index.

Dry Goods.

Pratt, R. S.

Dry Goods and Groceries.

Brainard, W. R. Moodus.
Goodspeed, W. H.
Gates & Barton, Moodus.
Purple, D. S. & A. E. Moodus.
Rogers, E. J. Leesville.
Root, F. J. Leesville.
Tyler, W. S.
Smith, William
Stevenson & Lord, Moodus.

Furniture Dealer.

Cook, S.

Groceries.

Bingham, W. B. Moodus.
Martin, Samuel
Niles, H. B.
Spencer, R. D.
Warner, D. B.

Hotels.

CHAMPION HOUSE, D. Watrous, Pro. see adv. index.
Gelston House.

Livery Stable.

Swan Brothers.

Marble Yards.

MARSTON, E. (Marble and Brown Stone).
Mullins, J. M.

Meat Market.

Swan, George H.

Medicine Manufacturer.

HARRIS, N. O., McEckrons or Wigwam Liniment, Old Homestead Bitters, &c. (see adv.. index.)

Milliners and Dress Makers.

Brainard, W. R. Mrs. Moodus.
Miller, C. Mrs. Moodus.
Newbury, C. C. Mrs. Moodus.
Peck, Sarah A.

Music.

MAPLEWOOD MUSIC SEMINARY, DWIGHT S. BABCOCK, Principal. See adv. index.

Paper Box Manufacturer.

Bingham, W. H.

Patent Medicine Manufacturer.

HARRIS, N. O. See adv. index.

Physicians.

Carrington, R. Moodus.
Edmonds, J. D. Moodus.
Harris, N. O.

Restaurant.

Newbury, C. C. Moodus.

Ship Builder.

Goodspeed, W. H.

Silver Plated Ware.

Boardman, L. & Sons.

Spoon and Fork Manufacturers.

Boardman, L. & Sons.

8

Stoves and Tinware.

Boies, H. Moodus.

Tailors.

Boylston, J. C.

Thompson, G. W.   .   .

MAPLEWOOD MUSIC SEMINARY.

DWIGHT S. BABCOCK,

Principal and Professor of Music.

MISS VIRGINIE SHAILER,

Teacher of Piano and Cultivation of Voice.

MISS E. S. BABCOCK,

Teacher of Wax Work.

EAST HADDAM, CONN.

EMORY JOHNSON,

Manufacturer and Dealer in

SUPERIOR

COTTON SEINE TWINE,

Cotton Cord, Carpet Warp, &c.,

OF ALL THE VARIOUS SIZES,

MOODUS, CONN.

Dr. N. O. HARRIS,

ELECTRO-MEDICAL CHEMIST AND PHARMACEUTIST,

EAST HADDAM, CONN.

MANUFACTURER OF THE

ELECTRICAL WINE BITTERS.

From pure Native Wine, and the best of materials HIGHLY ELECTRIFIED, imparting a very invigorating effect in restoring exhausted vitality in debilitated constitutions from whatever cause, especially those of long standing. Its effects are truly MAGICAL in giving tone to the Stomach, in inadequate assimilation of food, and impaired appetite, Paralysis, Numbness, Nervous Debility, Flatulence, Colic Pains, Costiveness, Liver Complaint, Languor and Faintness. Particularly adapted to FEMALE WEAKNESSES and Incipient Consumption. These Bitters are highly recommended by Physicians of the highest standing.

Also manufacturer of McEckron's celebrated Liniment. This Liniment far surpasses any other liniment in the market, as thousands can testify who have used it, the best external application known in all kinds of Inflammation, especially. Inflammation of the Chest and Bowels it is a sure relief.

Also the Old Homestead Bitters, Grover's Celebrated Indian Salve, Ricord's Specific Pills for Spermatorrhea, &c. All orders promptly filled by

NICHOLS & HARRIS, Druggists,   Wholesale Agents,
NEW LONDON, CONN.

CHAMPION HOUSE,

D. WATROUS,

Proprietor,

EAST HADDAM, CONN.

This House is pleasantly situated, within a few rods of the Steamboat Landing, and affords a beautiful view of the River and surrounding country, for several miles.

Pleasant rooms with board by the day or week,

Good Livery Stable Attached.

HADDAM, Middlesex County, Connecticut, is situated on the west bank of the river, 25 miles from Hartford. Population about 2,500.

The Township includes the Village of Higganum.

BUSINESS DIRECTORY.

Attorney at Law.

Clark, Smith

Axe Helve Manufacturer.

Arnold, Justin

Balmoral Skirt Manufacturer.

Crosley, ———

Blacksmithing.

Smith, William   Higganum.
Hutchings, A. '

Carpenter and Builder.

Spencer, Hubbard

Cotton Goods Manufacturers.

Russell Manufacturing Co.   Higganum.

Dry Goods and Groceries.

Dickinson, Erastus
Gladwin, G. S.   Higganum.
Merwin, C. D.   Higganum.
Russell, A. S.
Smith, Oliver
Ventres, Hubbard

Faucet Manufacturers.

Smith & Gillett.

Feldspar Manufacturers.

Cook & Brainard.   Higganum.

Grist Mill.

Thomas Skinner.   Higganum.

Hoe Manufacturers.

Scovill, D. & H.   Higganum.

Meat Market.

Burr, Leander   Higganum.

Physicians.

Bailey, Samuel   Higganum.
Hazen, Dr.

Quarries.

Samuel & Isaac Arnold.
Whitmore & Burr.

Saw Mill.

Cook & Brainard.

Wool Carding.

Reed, Roswell

CHATHAM, Middlesex County, Connecticut, is pleasantly situated on the east bank of the river, about 20 miles from Hartford and 30 from New Haven, and includes the villages of East Hampton, Cobalt and Middle Haddam.

East Hampton is situated about 4 miles north-east, is celebrated for its extensive manufactories of Bells. Population about 2000.

BUSINESS DIRECTORY.

Attorney at Law.

Parmelee, L. Middle Haddam.

Blacksmithing.

Wall, William   Middle Haddam.

Bell Manufacturers.

Barton, W. E.   East Hampton.
Berin Brothers,   East Hampton.
GONG BELL MANUFACTURING CO. East Hampton. See adv. index.
Parmelee, Niles & Co.   East Haddam.
Sexton, Veazey & Brown.   East Hampton.
Wells, Clark & Brothers.   Middle Haddam.
Veazey & White.   East Hampton.

Coffin Trimmings.

Bailey & Brainard.   Cobalt.
Niles, Parmelee & Co.   East Hampton.
Watrous, E. W. & Co.   East Hampton.

Commission Merchant.

Johnson, Horace.   Middle Haddam.

Dry Goods and Groceries.

Whitmore, Titus   Middle Haddam.

Flouring Mills.

Bailey & Brothers.   Cobalt.
Parker, A. F.   Middle Haddam.

Groceries.

Carrier & Hurd.   Middle Haddam.
Clark, R. D.   Cobalt.

Hotel.

Whitmore Hotel, G. Whitmore, Proprietor.   Middle Haddam.

Iron Foundry.

Keeghley & North.   Middle Haddam.
Parker & Judson.   Middle Haddam.

Oakum Manufacturers.

TIBBALS & CO.   Cobalt.   See adv. index.

Physician.

Worthington, A. B.   Middle Haddam.

GONG BELL MFG. CO.,

EAST HAMPTON, CONN.

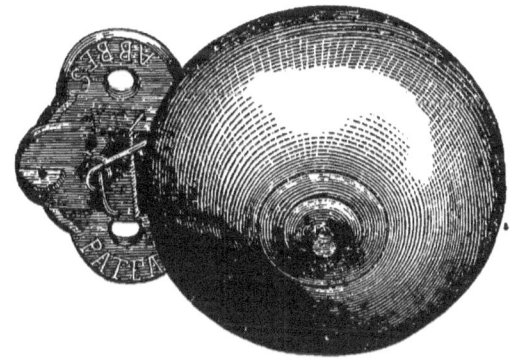

SOLE MANUFACTURERS OF

ABBES PATENT GONG BELLS

of all Sizes, from 3 to 24 inches in Diameter. Large Sizes fitted up in a very substantial manner, for Signal Bells for Hotels, Steamboats, Locomotives, Railroad Depots, Factories, &c. Also manufacturers of Cone's Patent Bronzed Steel Swing House Bells, with Bell Metal Shanks.

Agents wanted for hanging Bells in every State in the Union.

Please send for Circular.

TIBBALS & CO.,

MANUFACTURERS OF OAKUM,

AND DEALERS IN

PAPER STOCK, TRUNNEL WEDGES AND DECK PLUGS.

. J. N. TIBBALS.   R. E. TIBBALS.   R. D. TIBBALS.   D. S. TIBBALS.

COBALT, CONN.

MIDDLETOWN, Middlesex County, Connecticut, is situated on the west bank of the Connecticut River, 15 miles south of Hartford, 34 miles from Long Island Sound and 24 miles from New Haven A branch railroad connects this place with the New Haven, Hartford and Springfield Railroad.   The Hartford, New York and River Steamboats land here, there being spacious wharves and ample depth of water in the summer season.

The city is pleasantly situated on elevated ground, command-ing a fine view of the surrounding country, and contains many beautiful residences.   The principal public buildings are the Custom House and Court House, both constructed of Freestone. Middletown is a port of entry and shire town of Middlesex County, and contains about 12,000 inhabitants.   The extensive Pump manufactory of W. &. B Douglass, is located here.

Considerable business is done making Sewing Machines, Plated Goods, Machinery, &c.

Wesleyan University, a Methodist Institution, is located here, and occupies an elevated position overlooking the city and the valley of the Connecticut.

BUSINESS DIRECTORY.

Attorneys and Counsellors at Law.

Bacon, A. W.   124 1-2 Main St.
Brainard, N. L.   160 1-2 "
CALEF, A. B. (Attorney and Postmaster.)   Main St.   See adv. index.
Culver, M. 144 Main St.
Elmer, W. T. over Express and Telegraph office, Main St.
HALL, ALFRED (Attorney and Licensed Claim Agt.) Main St.
Robinson, S. A. Court House Building, Main St.
Roberts, J. L. S. over Express and Telegraph office, Main St.
Tyler, Charles C.   "   "   "   "   "
Vinal, Charles G. R. Court House Building,   "
Warner, S. L.   "   "   "   "

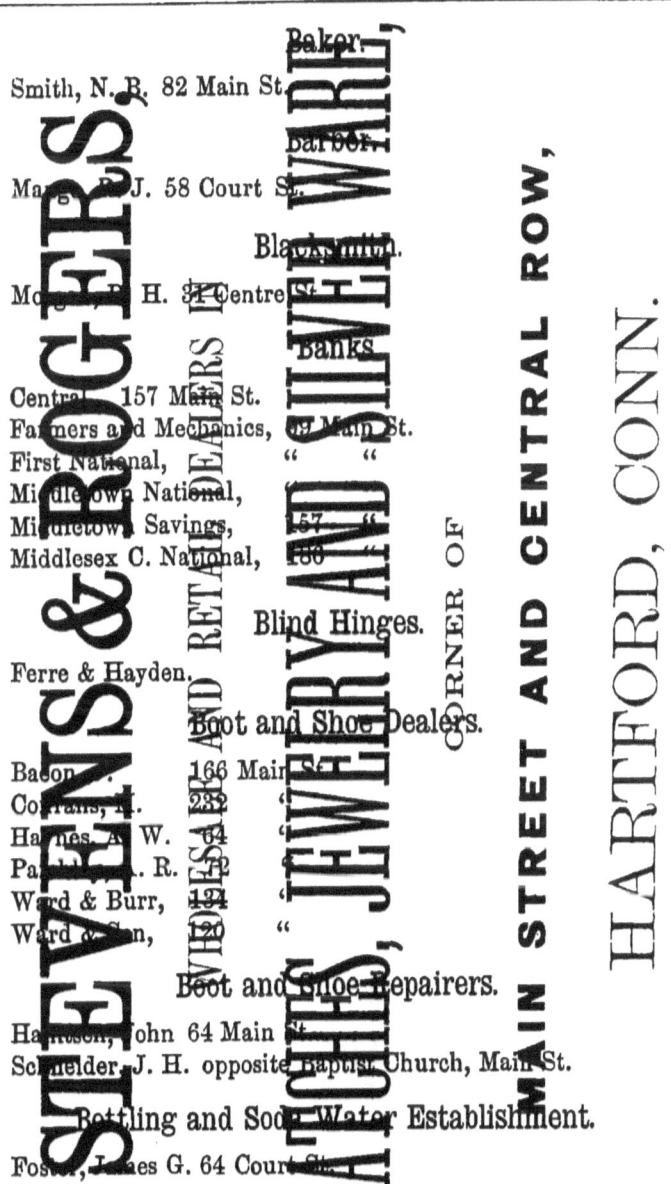

Smith, N. B. 82 Main St.

Baker.

Barber.

Ma... R. J. 58 Court St.

Blacksmith.

Mo... H. 8 Centre St.

Banks.

Central, 157 Main St.
Farmers and Mechanics, 87 Main St.
First National,   "   "
Middletown National,   "   "
Middletown Savings,   157   "
Middlesex C. National, 155   "

Blind Hinges.

Ferre & Hayden.

Boot and Shoe Dealers.

Bacon, 166 Main St.
Coffrans, H. 232   "
Haynes, A. W. 64   "
Pa... E. R. 72   "
Ward & Burr, 124   "
Ward & ..n, 120   "

Boot and Shoe Repairers.

Harrison, John 64 Main St.
Schneider, J. H. opposite Baptist Church, Main St.

Bottling and Soda Water Establishment.

Foster, James G. 64 Court St.

9

Books and Stationery.

Barnes, D.   144 Main St.
McLean & Wright, 118   "
Rockwell,   155   "

Carriage Manufactory.

Cornell & Warner, 51 Washington St.

Cartridge Manufacturer.

Sage, D. C.

Cigars and Tobacco.

Decker & Goetze, 99 Main St.
Decker, Lewis   62   "

Cigar Manufacturer.

Hodnett, P. H. 146 St. John St.

Clothing Dealers.

Jackson, R.   58 Main St.
Paragon, Branch, under McDonough House.
Roberts, Reuben   105 Main St.
Wolff, L. 88   "
Wolff, G. 41 East Court.

Cloak Making.

Lewes, J. E. Mrs. 160 1-2 Main St.

Coal and Wood.

White & Loveland, 81 Water St.

Coal Dealers.

Babcock & Carroll, corner Water and Court St.
Davis, Evan   2 College St.
Treadwell, R. B. 11   "

Confectioners.

Arnold, William R.   80 Main St.
Ferre, H. D. & F. E. 158   "
Finley G. R. 54 Parsonage St.
Hoffart, J. P. 222 Main St.

Coffin Warehouse.

Southmayd, George M.   262 Main St.

Cotton Goods Manufacturers.

Russel Manufacturing Co.

Crockery.

Hedge, W. A.   204 Main St.

Crockery and House Furnishing Goods.

Hale, C. & Co. 238 Main St.

Dentists.

Dibble, W. H.   80 Main St.
Graham, Chas. P. 151 1-2 Main St.
Pelton, 121   "

Deputy Sheriff.

Camp, John S.   134 Main St.

Druggists.

Collins & Pelton,   52 Main St.
Matheson & Bliss, 154   "
Woodward, Henry 124   "
VINAL, L. C.   151   "   See adv. index.

Dress and Mantle Making.

Shepard, Miss E. A. 225 Main St.

Dry Goods.

Ackley, E.   116 Main St.
Bunce, J. H.   162   "
Brewer, F.   150   "
Fagan, W. V.   160   "
Mitchell, Thos. F. 122 "

Dry Goods and Carpets.

Strauss & Schwarz, 106 Main St.

Express Companies.

Adams Express, 142 Main St.
Merchants Union Express, 62 Court St.

Fancy Goods.

Carroll & Co.   66 Main St.
Hackman, Isaac F.   220 Main St.
Dessauer, J.   306   "

File Cutters.

Hall, John W. & Co.

Fish Markets.

Brazos, A. 7 Parsonage St.
Leonard, H. 236 Main St.

Furniture.

Sheldon, E. F. 208 Main St.

Flour, Grain and Meal.

Union Mills, 1 Main St.
Barlow & Co., L. N. 202 Main St.

Galvanized Iron.

Wilcox & Hall.

Groceries.

Allison, S. S. 12 Sumner St.
Bidwell, A. M. 78   Main St.
Allyn & Meech, 204   "
Burr, G. E. 100   "
Bacon, J. P. & Son, 43   East Court St.
Burdeck Brothers, 14   Union St.
Clark, S. F. 21   "
Clark & Young, 1   Warwick St.
Chaffee & Camp, 138   Main St.
Chaffee, E & F. 136   "
Fuller, J. A. 290, 292   "
Hayden, J. O. 128   "
Hulse, O. 1 Parsonage St.
Hubbards & Roberts, So. Farms.
Pease, A. G. & R. A. 110 Main St.
Ryan, P. 234   "
Southmayd & Gardner, 68   "
Wilcox & Hall, So. Farms.
Young, H. R. 7 South Main St.

Gunsmith.

Radcliff, William 60 Main St.

Hats, Caps, Boots, Shoes, &c.

Stearns & Son, S. 146 Main St.
Hale, D. 298   "

Hardware and Crockery.

Atkins, H. 130 Main St.

Hardware Manufacturers.

Hubbard Hardware Co., Warwick St.

Hoop Skirt and Corset Manufacturer.

Gaines, E. C. 97 Main St.

Hotels.

Armory House, 56 Main St.   W. J. & J. R. Pitt, Proprietors.
Douglass House, 76 Main St.   D. B. Buck, Proprietor.
Farmers and Mechanics Hotel, 182 Main St.   J. L. Dickinson, Proprietor.
McDONOUGH HOUSE, corner Main and Court St.   Dickenson & Craig, Proprietors.

Insurance Companies.

Middlesex Mutual Assurance Co.   99 Main St.
PEOPLES FIRE INSURANCE CO., S. H. Butler, Secretary, Main St.   See adv. index.

Iron and Brass Foundry.

Sanseer Manufacturing Co.
Strond, William.

Livery Stables.

Hall, Walker   26 Court St.
Loveland, E.   42 Centre St.
Steel Brothers, 28   "
Wells & Wilcox, south McDonough House, Main St.

Lock Manufacturers.

Wilcox, William & Co.

Lumber Dealers.

Allen & Son, David,   59 Water St.
Hubbard Brothers, corner Centre and Water St.
Willard & Haskell,   85 River St.

Machinery Manufacturers.

Warwick Tool Co., Warwick St.

Meat Markets.

Coe, S. & O. & Co.   54 Main St.
Bacon, William   170   "
Hayes & Roberts, 172, 174   "
Southwick & Hall, 41 Court St.
Wright, G. W.   23 Main St.

Merchant Tailors.

Benham, D. R. opposite Court House.
Brewster & Co., F. D. 104 Main St.
Eaton, J. C. 160 1-2 "
Mooney & Wells, 70 "
Neale, P. J. 159 "

Millinery.

Dalton, M. A. 160 1-2 Main St.
Fitts, Miss H. E. 134 "
Greenfield, Miss L. 206 "
Luddington, Mrs. 96 "
Spalding, Miss H. M. 96 "
Tibbals, M. A. & E. F. 242 "

Middletown Gas Light Co., Main St.

Water Commissioners, 99 Main St.

Monuments, Grave Stones, &c.

Craig, J. 245 Main St.
Canfield, T. S. 263 "

Newspapers.

The Constitution, 129 Main St.
Our Own, 164 "

Paper Box Manufactory.

White, H. S. 202 Main St.

Paper Hangings, Paints, Varnish, Glass, &c.

Fountain, H. 166 Main St.

Picture Framing, Furniture Repairing, &c.

Tucker, N. D. 36 Washington St.

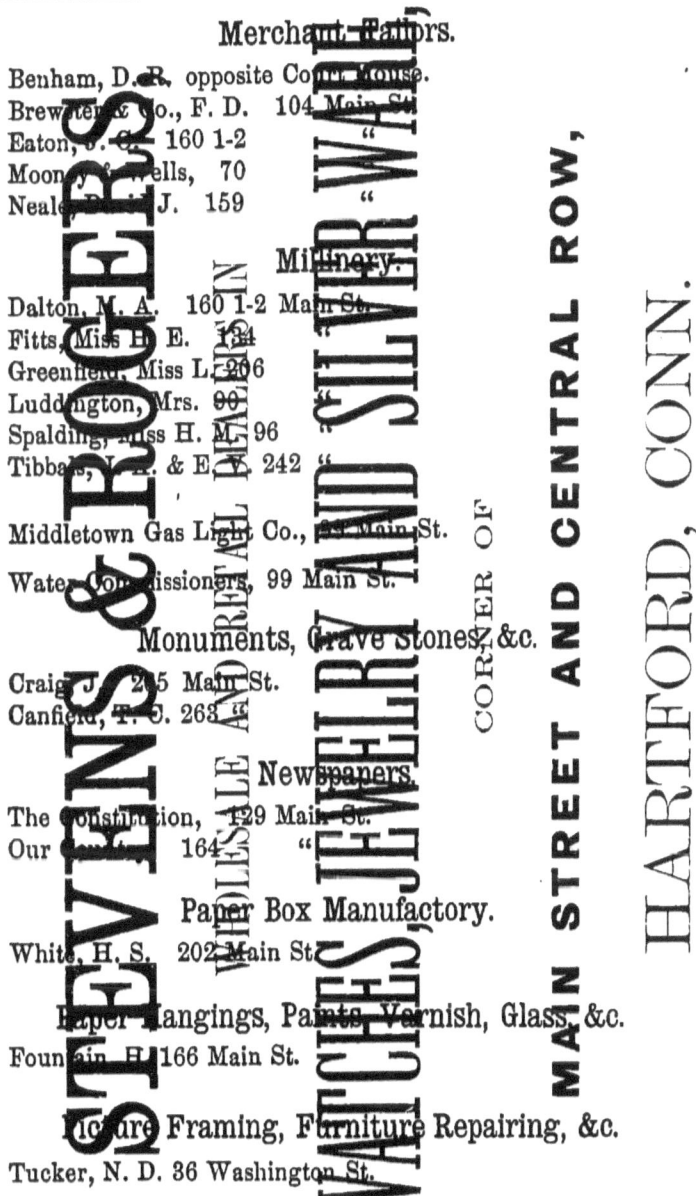

Plumbers and Gas Fitters.

Bacon, B. C. 92 and 94 Main St.
Ellis & Grigliette, 90   "

Photographers.

Bundy, Horace L. 136 Main St.
Hennigar, G. W. Main St., opposite McDonough House.

Pump Manufacturers.

DOUGLASS, W. & B., Williams St. See adv. index.

Saddle and Harness Manufacturers.

PRIOR, H. G. F. 176 Main St.
Southmayd, A. 46   "
Walsh, John T. 158   "

Seed and Plant Store.

Ryan, James 229 Main St.

Sewing Machine Manufacturers.

Alsop Arms Co. (Finkle & Lyons.)

Sewing Machine Needles.

Drake & Henshaw.

Silver Plated Goods.

Pelton, F. W. & O. Z.
Simons & Lawrence.

Soap and Candle Manufacturers.

Allison Brothers, 6 Sumner St.

Surgeons and Physicians.

Bailey, L. 254   Main St.
Baker, Rufus 165   "
Bell, W. C. 106   "
Burr, E. 85   "

Casey, Doct. 160 Main St.
Edgerton, F. D. 201 "
Maddox, Doct. 88 "
Nye, E. B. 39 Williams St.
Clark, Doct. 160 1-2 Main St.

Steel Yard Manufacturer.

Smith, Albert M.

Stoves, Tin Ware, &c.

Paddock, Edward   44 Court St.

Tin and Sheet Iron Manufacturer.

Bailey, J. S.   97 Main St.

Town Clerk and Real Estate Agent.

STARR, E. W. N. Main St.

Toy Tops.

Miner, S. A.

Watches and Jewelry.

Fairchild, J. S. ' 148 Main St.
Hall, Horace D. 152   "
Smith, J. L.   132   "

White Metal and Plated Goods.

Middletown Plate Co.

L. C. VINAL,

151 Main St.,

MIDDLETOWN, CONN.

10

W. & B. DOUGLASS,

MIDDLETOWN, CONN.,

BRANCH WAREHOUSE, 87 JOHN STREET, NEW YORK,

Manufacturers of the Celebrated Patent

REVOLVING STAND PREMIUM PUMPS,

PATENT ROTARY HAND & POWER PUMPS,

PATENT YARD PUMPS, DEEP WELL PUMPS,

Patent Double and Single Acting SUCTION and FORCE PUMPS, of various styles and capacity, both hand and power.

PATENT ROTARY BARREL PUMPS,

PATENT STEAM PUMPS,

PATENT PREMIUM HYDRAULIC RAMS,

Galvanized Pump Chain, Chain Wheels and Fixtures, Patent Cast Iron CURBS, Cast Iron SPOUTS for Wooden Curbs, Iron Well Wheels, Improved Premium.

GARDEN OR FIRE ENGINES,

Patent Ship Pumps, Barn Door Rollers and Hangers, Ornamental Iron Horse Posts, Grindstone Trimmings, Friction Rolls and Stands, Wrought Iron BUTS and HINGES, Washers, &c., &c.

Also the Patent AQUARIUS, a new and valuable HAND FORCE PUMP.

Incorporated by Special Charter, granted by the Legislature of Connecticut, in 1859.

BENJAMIN DOUGLASS, President.

WORKS FOUNDED IN 1832.

PORTLAND, Middlesex County, Connecticut, is situated on the east bank of the river, nearly opposite Middletown, with which it communicates by steam Ferry, 15 miles from Hartford and 34 miles from Long Island Sound.

In this town, upon the river bank, are the noted Portland Free-stone Quarries. The stone is transported long distances, and used principally for building purposes, being of superior quality, soft and easily worked, and is prized for its color and durability, which is improved by time. The town contains about 4000 in-habitants.

BUSINESS DIRECTORY.

Attorney at Law.

Hall, Alfred   Main St.

Banks.

First National Bank, Main St.   S. Gildersleeve, Pres., W. W. Coe, Cashier.

Free Stone Savings Bank, Main St.   S. Gildersleeve, Pres., W. W. Coe, Secretary and Treasurer.

Boot and Shoe Maker.

Henry, W. Main St.

Coffin Warehouse.

Spencer, W. C. Main St.

Dry Goods and Groceries.

Gildersleeve, S. & Sons.

Dry Goods.

Hall, Charles H. Main St.

Grocers.

Aheon, Morris Main St.
Crawford, Alex. "
Cooper, Geo. B. "
Goodrich, G. D. "
Laverty, Jas. "
Wall, M. "
Wilcox, S. W. "
Williams, David "

Hotel.

Union House, Edward Pease, Proprietor.

Livery Stable.

Laverty, Jas. Main St.

Meat Markets.

Hurlbut, Jas. Main St.
Strong and Mitchell.

Millinery.

Dunham, A. Miss Main St.

Physicians.

Buck, E. Main St.
Jarvis, Geo. O. Main St.
Sears, C. A. "

Seed Growers.

Strong, D. & Son, Main St.

Ship Builders.

Gildersleeve, S. & Sons.

Stoves and Tinware.

Buckland, O. C.   Main St.

Quarries.

Brainard & Co.   (Brown Stone.)
Middlesex Quarry Co.   "
Shaler & Hall Quarry Co.   (Freestone.)

CROMWELL, Middlesex County, Connecticut, situated on the west bank of the Conn. River, about 13 miles south of Hartford. The North Middlesex (Freestone) Quarry is situated in this town, from which large quantities of fine building stone are obtained, of a superior quality and beautiful color. The town numbers about 1800 inhabitants. The principal business of the town is agriculture.

BUSINESS DIRECTORY.

Dry Goods and Groceries.

Savage, R. B.

Eyelet Manufacturers.

Eyelet and Ferule Co.

Groceries.

Spencer, N.
Stocking, H.

Harness Manufacturers.

Allison, W. P. & Co.

Hotel.

C. Mather, Proprietor.

Iron Foundry.

Hubbard, Thos. S.

Physician.

Hutchingson, Ira

Skate Manufacturers.

Stevens, J. & E. & Co.

Toys and Hardware.

Stevens, J. & E. & Co.

Quarry.

NORTH MIDDLESEX QUARRY,
J. A. Bloomer, Agent. See adv. index.

ROCKY HILL, Hartford County, Connecticut, a small town on the west bank of the Connecticut River, 7 miles south of Hartford, and 42 miles from Long Island Sound. It contains about 1200 inhabitants.   Considerable is done in the manufacture of Hoes, Shears and Iron Castings.

New York and River Steamers have a landing here.

BUSINESS DIRECTORY.

Groceries.

Beaumont, L.
Parker, A. G.
Smith, Walter
Ward, William

Hotel.

Shipman's Hotel,
Shipman, Proprietor.

Iron Foundry.

Butler & Sugden.

Physicians.

Griswold, R.
Hodgkins, Dr.

Plantation Hoes

Wells & Wilcox.

Postmaster.

Parker, A G.

Restaurant.

White, George

Shear Manufacturers.

Butler & Sugden.

KELLOGG & BULKELEY, 245 Main St., Hartford, Lithographers. Checks, Drafts, Certificates of Stock, &c., Checks Stamped and Numbered, Lithographic work of every variety executed in the best style.

WETHERSFIELD, Hartford County, Connecticut, a small town on the west bank of the river, 3 miles south of Hartford, and is one of the oldest settled towns on the river. The location of the town is very level, the streets are broad and shaded with large and beautiful elms. It is connected with Hartford by Horse Railroad. Large quantities of seeds are grown here, and sent to all parts of the country. Here is located the Connecticut State Prison. The town contains about 1500 inhabitants.

BUSINESS DIRECTORY.

Attorney.

Adams, S. W.

Blacksmithing.

Talcott, Daniel E.

Druggist.

Cook, E. F.

Dry Goods and Groceries.

Lovell & Stillman.
Robbins, S. W.

Groceries.

Cowles Brothers.

Hammer Manufacturers.

Williams & Howe, Griswoldville.

Physicians.

Castle, Sr.
Fox, R.
Warner, A. S.

11

Produce Dealers.

Adams & Hanmer.
Warner & Adams.

Postmaster.

Smith, George

Seed Drill Manufacturer.

T. B. Rogers.

Seed Growers.

Comstock, Ferre & Co.
Griswold, Thos. & Co., Griswoldville.
Johnson, Robbins & Co.
Magget & Wolcott.

Restaurant.

Hill, E. A.

Short Horn and Alderney Cattle.

Robbins, S. W.

GLASTENBURY, a post town of Hartford County, 9 miles south of Hartford, on the east bank of the Connecticut River, contains the villages of South Glastenbury, East Glastenbury, Eastbury and Naubuc. Considerable is done manufacturing Woolens, Cottons, Leather, Anchors, &c.

The town contains about 3,500.

BUSINESS DIRECTORY.

Attorney at Law.

Goslee, William S.

Hotels.

GAINES HOUSE, W. H. Gaines, Proprietor.
Bates House, Charles Bates, Proprietor.

Merchants.

Gaines, C. F. Dry Goods and Groceries.
Taylor, William
West, O. C.
Bogue & Risley, Naubuc.
Bartholomew, C. H.

Millinery.

Grant, Mrs.

Physicians.

Bunce, H. C.
Kingsbury, Daniel
Hamnond, Dr.

Postmasters.

Andrews, E. H.
Bogue, A. A. Naubuc.

Spoon and Spectacle Manufacturers.

Conn. Arms and Manufacturing Co. Naubuc.

Soap Manufacturers.

Williams, J. B. & Co. Naubuc.

Tanners and Curriers.

Hubbard, D. L. & Co.
Hubbard & Broadhead.

Tailors.

Bunce & Seaver.
Reed, William

Woolen Manufacturers.

Eagle Mills, Eagleville.
Glastenbury Knitting Co., Eagleville.

MERIDEN, a city of New Haven County, on the New Haven, Hartford and Springfield Railroad, 17 miles from Hartford. Most of the manufacturing is done at West Meriden, where are located several large establishments for the manufacture of Britannia Ware, Cutlery, Hardware, Machinery, Balmoral Skirts, &c., &c.

The city is situated on a tract of level country, and contains about 10,000 inhabitants.

The State Reform School is situated here.

BUSINESS DIRECTORY.

Agricultural Implements.

Curtis, H. W.

Apothecary.

Block, J. B. Main St.

Attorneys at Law.

Fay, Geo. A. opposite P. O. West Meriden.
Platt, O. H. Colony St.
Smith, Geo. W. near P. O. West Meriden.

Bakers.

Emery, Ira West Meriden.
Williams, Thos. Main St.

Balmoral Skirt Manufacturers.

Wilcox, J. W. & Co. West Meriden.

Banks.

First National Bank.
Home National Bank.
Meriden National Bank, Joel Buckley, President, O. B. Arnold, Cashier.

Billiard Saloon.

Johnson, S. P. Colony St.

Blacksmiths.

Bicett, Joseph
. Burr & Hotchkiss, Main St.

Bonnet Bleaching.

Smith, F. S. & Co. State St.

Boot and Shoe Dealers.

Butler, J. & Co. Colony St.
Fales, C. H. State St.
Kenyon, S. R.
Southwick, D. F. Main St.
Sizer, A.

Boot and Shoe Manufacturers.

Fales, Charles H. State St.
Hunt, James Union Block, Main St.

Brass Founders.

Beadle, James West Meriden.
Foster, Merriam & Co. West Meriden.
Parker & Whipple, "

Britannia Ware Manufacturers.

Meriden Britannia Co.

Cabinet Ware Manufacturer.

Canfield, J. H. & Co. West Meriden.

Carpenters and Joiners.

Gay, George   West Meriden.
Rich, C. S.
Tyler, Richard.

Carpet Dealers.

Ives, John & Co.

Carriage, Coach and Sleigh Builders.

Perry, Northrup & Bryden, corner Court and Mill St.
Russell, J. W.

Cigar Dealers.

Clark, C. H. & Co. Railroad Av.
Curtiss, A. Rogers' Hotel Building.
Duis, J. Morgan's Block, Main St.
Hale, L. & Co. Colt's Building, Main St.
Phelps, C. A.   Main St.

Clothing Dealers.

Goldstein, S. corner Main and Colony St.
Keller, S. Morgan's Block, Main St.
Koerpel, L. Colony St. Byxbee House.
Levy, M. & Co.   Main St., Meriden House Building.
Stevens, J. H. Colony St.

Coal Dealer.

Fisk, W. H. State St.

Crockery, Glass and Earthern Ware.

Griswold & Searls.

Dentists.

Pember, C. P. Colony St.
Rust, T. L. Morgan's Block.

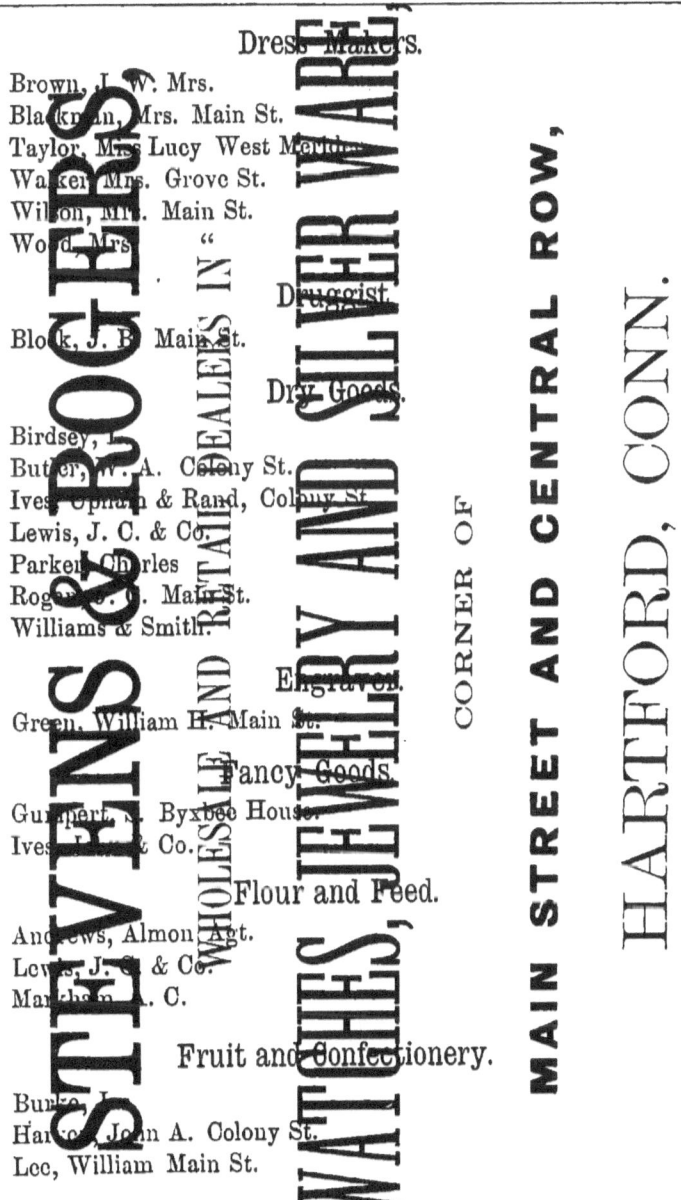

Dress Makers.

Brown, J. W. Mrs.
Blackman, Mrs. Main St.
Taylor, Miss Lucy West Meadow
Walker Mrs. Grove St.
Wilson, Mrs. Main St.
Wood Mrs. " "

Druggist.

Block, J. B. Main St.

Dry Goods.

Birdsey, L.
Butler, W. A. Colony St.
Ives, Upham & Rand, Colony St.
Lewis, J. C. & Co.
Parker, Charles
Rogers, C. C. Main St.
Williams & Smith.

Engraver.

Green, William H. Main St.

Fancy Goods.

Gumpert, S. Byxbee House.
Ives & Co.

Flour and Feed.

Andrews, Almon, Agt.
Lewis, J. C. & Co.
Markham, A. C.

Fruit and Confectionery.

Burke, L.
Harte, John A. Colony St.
Lee, William Main St.

Furniture Manufacturers.

Tooley & Gladwin, State St.

Furnishing Goods.

Golstein, L. corner Main and Colony Sts.
Williams, F. H. Colony St.

Furniture Fenders Manufacturers.

WILMOT BROTHERS, State St.

Gas Fitter.

Duncan, Alex.

Gas Company.

Meriden Gas Light Co. West Meriden.

German Silver Ware Manufacturers.

Meriden Britannia Ware Co. West Meriden.

Glass and Silver Ware Manufacturers.

The Parker & Casper Co., West Meriden.

Grocers.

Bassett, H. D.
Bradley, Hiram
Ernest & Pistorius, State St., West Meriden.
Hall, N. C. & Co., Colony "　　　"
Kirtland & Spencer, Loomis' Block, West Meriden.
Lewis, J. C. & Co., West Meriden.
Mechanics Trading Co., C. H. Coe, Agt., West Meriden.
Moran Brothers, Moran's Block, West Meriden.
Pomroy, N. W.　　　　　　"
Wilcox, H. T.　　　　　　"

Hair Dressers.

Bucse, Frederick D. Main St.
Fredens, W. Railroad.
Jeffrey, George L.
Jeffrey, R. A.

Hardware, Crockery and Glassware.

Curtis, H. W.

Harness Makers.

Backley, H. W.
Francis, G. W. Francis' Building, Main St.
Hall, P. E. Main St.

Harness Trimmings.

Warner, Chas. State St.

Hotels.

Meriden House, W. Lilley, Proprietor.
Byxbee House, Byxbee & Brothers, Proprietors.
Rogers' Hotel, H. Rogers, Proprietor.
Central Hotel, Samuel Brainard, Proprietor.

House and Sign Painter.

Graham, J. B. Middletown Turnpike.

Insurance and Real Estate Agent.

Morgan, S. B.

Iron Founders.

Park, Julius West Meriden.
Bradley & Hubbard.
Foster, Merriam & Co.

Ivory Comb Manufacturers.

PRATT, READ & CO.

Lamp Fixture Manufacturer.

Pierpoint, Chas. H. Colt's Building.

Livery Stables.

Merriman, Levi State St.
Parker, William Meriden House Stables.
Parker, G. A. opposite Wilcox's Tin Shop.
Williams, H. C. Main St.
Williams, Henry C. "

12

Lightning Rods.

Twiss, Ira L.

Lock Manufacturers.

Parker & Whipple, West Meriden.

Lumber and Coal.

Lyon & Billand, rear Wilcox Building, Main St.

Sawyers.

Fay, George A.
Platt, O. H. Colony St.
Smith, George W.

Machinists.

Canfield, J. H. & Co., West Meriden.
Meriden Tool Co., Nelson Camp, President.
STILES, N. C. & CO., see adv. index.
Wilder, Moses G. Main St.
UNION MANUFACTURING CO., J. Warren Tuck, Treasurer. See adv. index.

Manufacturing Companies.

Meriden Britannia Co.
Meriden Tool Co.
Wilcox, J. & Co.
UNION MANUFACTURING CO., J. Warren Tuck, Treasurer. See adv. index.

Match Manufactory.

Fenn, Nathan Main St.

Marble Yard.

Allyn, C. F. Main St., corner Grove.

Meat Markets.

Kelsey & Ives.
Coe & Austin, Main St.
Paddock, S. C. & Sons, Main St.

Milliners and Millinery Goods.

Beach, B. Mrs.
Dessauer, J.
Dudley, E. S. Miss Morgan's Block.
Dunham, V. Mrs.
Hall, Lottie Mrs.
Hall, J. S. Mrs·
Motley, Anna Mrs.
Parker, —— Mrs.
Parker, Charles 2nd.

Newspapers.

Meriden Recorder, Luther C. Riggs, Editor.
MERIDEN WEEKLY VISITOR, M. M. Eaton, Editor, State
St. See adv. index.

Newspapers and Periodicals.

Higgins, J. H. Main St.
Johnson, C. G.   "
Wright, L. A.   "

Oyster and Fish Markets.

Beach, John Rogers' Hotel Building.
Parker, J. I. State St.

Optician.

Pease, —— Wilcox's Building.

Paint Shops.

Carter Brothers, Main St.
Twiss, Ira L.   .

Paper Hanger.

Carter, B. State St.

Piano and Melodeon Key (Ivory) Manufacturers.

PRATT, READE & CO.

Photographers.

Wheeler, Frank Main St.
Everett, E. B. Morgan's Block, Main St.

Plated Goods Manufacturers.

Wilcox Silver Plate Co., West Meriden.

Physicians and Surgeons.

Averill, Jas. J. Main St.
Churchill, A. H. Main St.
Catlin, B. H.
Davis, T. F.
Davis, C. H. S.
Fitch, F. J. Colony St.
Hatch, Edward W.
Nickerson, N.
Tait, John
Wylie, James

Printers (Job).

Hinman, Frank A. Main St., West Meriden.
Jilson, Charles E. & Co., Colony St.

Real Estate Agent.

Morgan, Samuel B. Morgan St.

Roof Painter.

Twiss, Ira L.

Savings Bank.

Meriden Savings Bank.

Saloons.

Brainard, S. Main St.
Croway, Timothy Union Block.
Handells, C.
Hubbard, Wilber.
Keena, P. opposite Foster & Meriman.
Killiam, E. D. Main St.
Lakey, John State St.
Monahan & Kelleher.
Martin, Charles Lager Beer.
Remer, T. L. Main St.
Rich, C. West Meriden.
Welch, John State St.
Williams, A. J.

Sash, Doors and Blinds.

Piney & Clark, State St.

Silver Plated Ware.

Swan & Foote, State St.

Soap and Candle Manufacturer.

Megrath, A. P. Pratt St.

Stoves and Tinware.

Griswold & Searls.
Wheeler, F. J. Main St.

Tailor.

Benzard, E. C. Colony St.

Tin Ware Manufacturers.

Clark, S. L. Clark Building, Main St.
Ives, Rutty & Co.

Toy Manufacturers.

Tucker, T. O. & W. W. Main St.

Trunks and Valises, &c.

Hall, P. E. Main St.

Watches and Jewelry.

Dunham, Samuel Main St.
Pitel, John C.   "

Wood Engraver.

Green, William H. Wilcox's Building, Main St.

Undertaker.

Smith, William M. Main St.

Woolen Goods Manufacturers.

Wilcox, J. & Co.   (Balmorals.)

Young Men's Christian Association Reading Room.

Next to Byxbee House.

THE MERIDEN WEEKLY VISITOR.

THE HANDSOMEST WEEKLY PAPER

IN

CONNECTICUT.

Subscription Price, $2 per year.

Advertisements Inserted at moderate rates.

M. M. EATON, Editor and Proprietor.

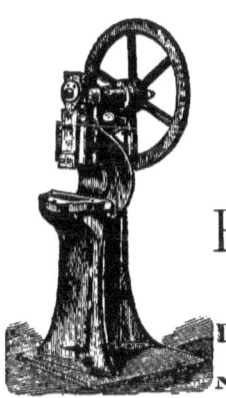

N. C. STILES & CO.,
MACHINISTS,
MANUFACTURERS OF
STILES'
PATENT POWER AND FOOT
PUNCHING PRESSES.
STILES' PATENT DROPS,
(With or without Patent Lifter,)
DIES, MACHINISTS' TOOLS, &c.
WEST MERIDEN, CONN.
N. C. STILES.   G. L. CLARK.

NEW BRITAIN, Hartford County, Connecticut, a flourishing town on the Hartford, Providence and Fishkill, and on a branch of the New Haven, Hartford and Springfield Railroads, 10 miles from Hartford, and 30 miles north of New Haven.

It is handsomely laid out, pleasantly situated and contains many fine residences which are surrounded with spacious and highly ornamented grounds. Here are located several extensive manufactories of Builder's Hardware, Saddlery Hardware, Jewelry, Rules, Levels, &c., &c.

It contains the State Normal School. Population of the town about 9000.

BUSINESS DIRECTORY.

Attorneys at Law.
Bronson, Merritt Main St.
Chambers, F.   "
Delavan, Marcus office in basement of Baptist Church.
Hart, Austin Main St.
Mitchell, C. M. "
Nash, H.   "

Barber Shops.

Agostino, Bertinis under Humphrey House.
Holston, John under Strickland House.
Jackson, Frederick G. Main St.
Minnis, T.   "

Bakeries.

Gridley, S. D. corner Arch and Walnut St.
Steele, William H. Myrtle St.

Banks.

New Britain National Bank, corner Main and West Main Sts.
Savings Bank of New Britian.
   Smith, W. H. President.
   Whitney, H. W. Vice President.
   Rockwell, S. Secretary.

Basket Manufacturers.

American Basket Co., Arch St.
   Comings, B. M. President.
   Lewis, C. M. Treasurer.

Bell Manufacturer.

Taylor, A. E.

Blacksmiths.

Burgess, C. A. Elm St.
Hayley, John F. Main St.
Martin, More   "

Builders and Hardware Dealers.

Bulkley, W. J. Main St.
Doen, Edward Kensington Av.

Boot and Shoe Manufacturer.

Fray, Charles Main St.

Boot and Shoe Stores.

Both, L. S. Main St.
Capron, D. P. "
Child, T. & Son, "
Murphy, John J. "
Seymour, Chas. "
Stanley, Samuel, "

Cabinet Warehouses.

Giddings, W. W. near Main St.
Thompson's Cabinet Warehouse, 2d store north of Green.

Cigar Store.

Long, Henry C. Main St.

Coal Yard.

Wilcox & Judd, Proprietors, rear Masonic Hall.

Clothing Dealer.

Norden, David, Main St.

Cooper.

Curtis, William, Lafayette St.

Dentist.

Dunham, Main St.

Dress Making.

Goodrich, Mrs. Arch St.
Harrison, Mrs. Main St.
Kenlock, E. Mrs. "
Medbury, Mrs. "
Peet, E. Mrs. "
Woodruff, L. Mrs. North Main St.

13

Dry Goods.

Andrews, G. C. Main St.
Miller, D. & N. G. "
Rogowski, B.
Whittlesey, F. & Co. Main St.

Dyer.

MINDER, JOHN D. Railroad Av.

Druggists.

Dickinson, C. &. J. Main St.
Rossetter & Goodrich, "

Dry Goods and Groceries.

Smith, J. B. South Main St.

Eating Houses.

Shoves, R. S. Main St.
Ward, John, "

Express Offices.

Adams Express Co., in Dickinson's Drug Store, Main St.
Merchants Union Express Co., in Thompson's Building.

Flour and Feed Store.

Williams, W. C. Main St.

Fruit and Confectionery.

Gould, Daniel, Main St.
Rhodes, A. A. "

Gent's Furnishing Goods.

Bailey, N. Main St.
Bennett & Marine, Main St.
Mahoney, William, "
Pratt, A. "
Talcott, C. M. "

Groceries, Retail.

Bassett, Chas. Main St.
Bigley & McInerney, Main St.
Bouge & Riseley,   "
Brown & Ellis,   "
Dowd, J. J.   "
Hawkins, B. & Co.,   "
Smith, Ira B. South Main St.
Thompson, James   "
Vessel & Brothers, Arch St.
Woodruff & Jones, Main St.

Hardware Manufacturers.

Union Manufacturing Co., Union St.
Butler, F. & Son, Stanley St.
Corbin of Stanley, Main St.
Corbin, P. & F.
Landers, Frary & Clark, Main St.
Russell & Erwin Manufacturing Co., Washington St.
North & Judd, East Main St.
Malleable Iron Works, West Main St.

Harness and Trunk Manufacturer.

Roberts, Horace, Main St.

Hotels.

Humphrey House, Samuel Beat, Proprietor.
STRICKLAND HOUSE, H. G. Arnold, Proprietor. See adv. index.

Insurance.

Fire, Life and Accident.
Northend, Charles, Agent, Main St.

Iron Founders.

Malleable Iron Works.
Swift, E. R. President.
Swift, E. R. Secretary.
Swift, M. C. Treasurer.

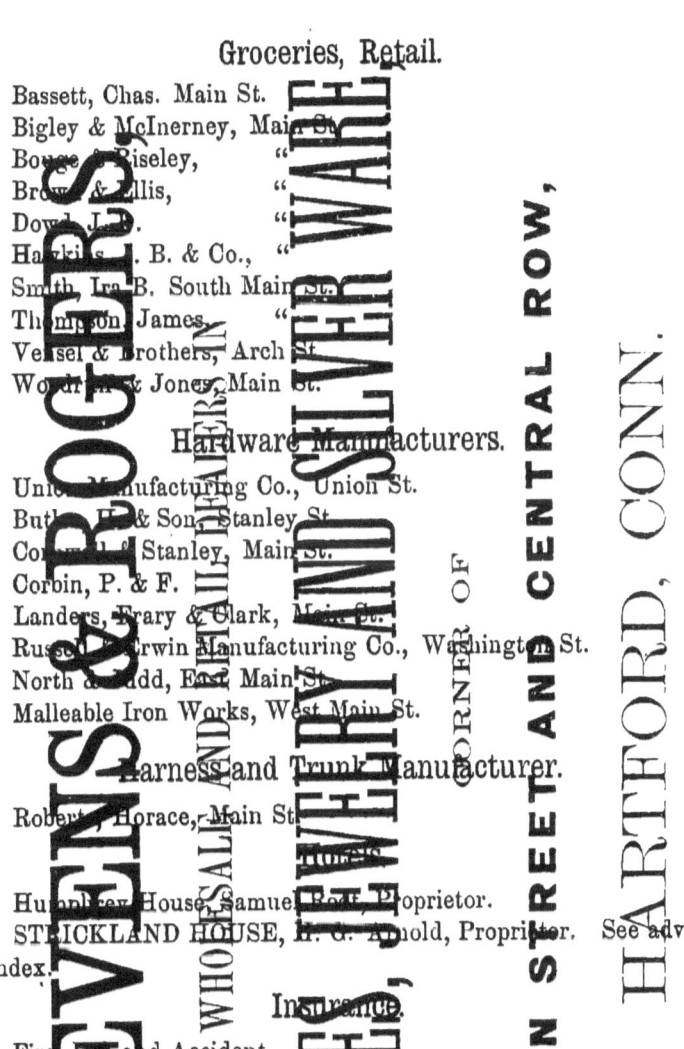

Jewelry Manufactory.

Churchill, Dana & Co., Main St.

Jewelry Stores.

Churchill, W. M. Main St.
Snauston, Robert,   "

Knitting Company.

New Britain Knitting Co., Elm St.
  North, F. H. President.
  Talcott, John B. Treasurer.

Livery Stables.

Bailey, H. Main St.
Merils, Robert, "
Root & Judd,   "
Spaulding, A. W.

Marble Yard.

Hanna, J. & W. Main St.

Machine Forging.

King, J. R. Main St.

Meat Markets.

Bassett, C. Main St.
Bogue & Risley, "
Hart, John G.   "
Moore, H. W. & S. A. Main St.
Stanley & Markeley,   "

Merchant Tailors.

Bailey, N. Main St.
Bennett & Maine, Main St.
Pratt, Alex. Main St.
Parker, Julius, Walnut St.
Pratt, A. Main St.

Job Printer.

OVIATT, J. N. Main St. See Adv. Index.

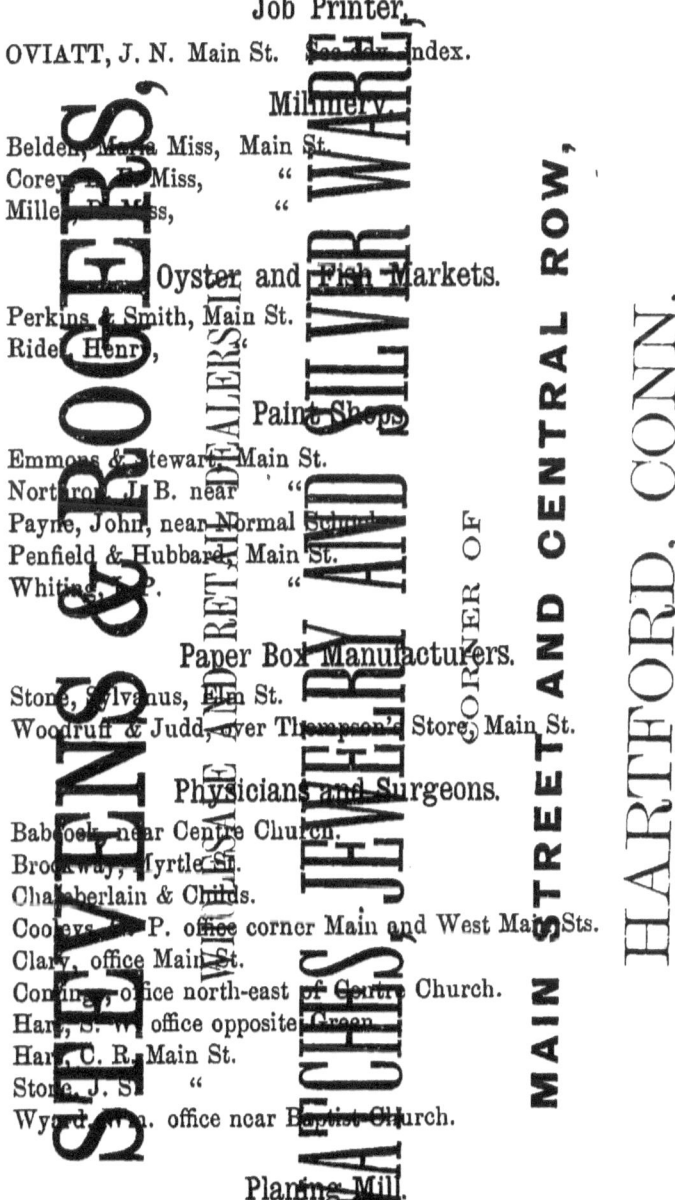

Millinery.

Belden, Maria Miss, Main St.
Corey, M. J. Miss, "
Miller, F. Miss, "

Oyster and Fish Markets.

Perkins & Smith, Main St.
Rider, Henry, "

Paint Shops.

Emmons & Stewart, Main St.
Northrop, J. B. near "
Payne, John, near Normal School
Penfield & Hubbard, Main St.
Whiting, P. "

Paper Box Manufacturers.

Stone, Sylvanus, Elm St.
Woodruff & Judd, over Thompson's Store, Main St.

Physicians and Surgeons.

Babcock, near Centre Church.
Brockway, Myrtle St.
Chamberlain & Childs.
Cooleys A. P. office corner Main and West Main Sts.
Clary, office Main St.
Comins, office north-east of Centre Church.
Hart, S. W. office opposite Green.
Hart, C. R. Main St.
Stone, J. S. "
Wyard, Wm. office near Baptist Church.

Planing Mill.

Woods, Chas. H. Elm St.

Printing Office.

OVIATT, J. N. Publisher of Record, Main St. See adv. index.

Photographers.

Fowlinson, Main St.
Judson, W. A. South part Main St.

Rule and Level Manufacturers.

Stanley Rule and Level Co., Elm St.

Real Estate Agents.

Bronson, Merrit
Cornish, Virgil, Main St.

Saloons.

Cawghlin, James T. Railroad Av.
Ruff, Mary,   "
Rich, William, Main St.
Martin, Frank A. "
Watts, J.   "

Saddler.

Capron, B. Main St.

Shirt Manufacturers.

Bingham, William, South Main St.
Lee, I. N. & Co., Main St.
Parker, Julius, Walnut St.

Stoves and Tinware.

Cloys & Co., Main St.
Payne, William G. Myrtle St.
Shepard, J. & Co., Stanley St.

Umbrella Stitching Manufactory.

NEW BRITAIN RECORD,

J. N. OVIATT, Publisher.

A FIRST CLASS FAMILY JOURNAL,

PERMANENTLY ESTABLISHED,

And with a rapidly increasing circulation, offering superior inducements to advertisers.

All kinds of Business printing neatly and promptly executed, upon reasonable terms. Orders for advertising or printing will receive immediate and careful attention.

HARTFORD, Hartford County, Connecticut, is situated on the west bank of the Connecticut River, 50 miles from its mouth, and distant from New York, 110 miles, New Haven 36 miles, Springfield, Mass., 26 miles, Boston 124 miles, Montreal, Canada, 336 miles, Providence, R. I., 90 miles, Albany 126, in Latitude 41 deg., 45 min., 59 sec., and Longitude 4 deg., 15 min., east from Washington. It may not be amiss in this book to give a brief historical sketch of the place. In 1633, on the point of land now known as "Dutch Point," at the junction of the Connecticut and Park rivers, the Dutch erected a Fort, which they named the "Home of Hope." Two years afterwards a settlement was begun by a company of settlers from Newtown, (now Cambridge,) Dorchester and Watertown, Mass.

Its Indian name was "Suckiaug." The white settlers first called it Newtown, but in 1636 formally named it Hartford, after Hartford, now called Hertford, in Hertfordshire, England, and during this year (1635) was held the first Town Meeting.

In 1654, by an act of the General Court of Connecticut, the Dutch were compelled to leave, and consequently the whole colony came entirely into the hands of the English. The first church was erected here in 1638, also a school was established the same year.

The first written Constitution ever formed in America, was here written and finished by five men, viz.: Ludlow, Haynes, Wolcott, Hopkins and Hooker, in the year 1639. In 1640 a House of Correction was established. The General Court, in the year 1644, ordered the establishment of an Inn, which in after years became historically associated with Col. Wadsworth and the famous "Charter," which he concealed in the hollow of an old oak. The tree was carefully preserved, and remained standing till within a few years.

The first Printing Office here was started in the year 1764, by Thomas Green, who commenced the publication of the Connecticut Courant. The act of incorporating the city was performed in the year 1784. Eight years afterwards the Hartford Bank and Hartford Charitable Society were organized.

The shipping interests of Hartford are quite large, there being 5 Steamboats, regularly plying between this point and New York, two river steamers, two lines of steam freight packets to Albany, Philadelphia and Baltimore, and regular lines of packets to foreign and domestic ports. Hartford is the leading Insurance city in the United States, there being no less than 22 companies in successful operation, consisting of Fire, Life, Accident, Live Stock, Steam Boiler, &c. Several more are chartered this season, which will soon be actively working. Among the large manufactories in the city may be mentioned Colt's Patent Fire Arms Manufacturing Co., with a capital of $1,000,000, and owning the largest and finest shop of the kind in the country; Sharps' Rifle Manufacturing Co., Cheney Brothers, Silk Manufacturers, Case, Lockwood & Co., Printers, Weed Sewing Machine Company, Woodruff & Beach Iron Works, Phœnix Iron Works, Bullard & Parsons, Machinists, with many others of lesser magnitude. There are 12 banks of issue in the city, with an aggregate capital of about $8,000,000, also 3 Savings Banks. The city has 25 churches, among which number are some of the finest church edifices in the country. The Park, bounded on the east, north and west by Park River, and containing 46 acres, is an ornament to the city. Colt's Dyke, one of the greatest improvements in the city, is 8,698 feet long, from 40 to 50 wide at the top, and cost about $80,000. This dyke encloses 123 acres of some of the most valuable land in the city.

The Hartford and Wethersfield Horse Railroad extends from Spring Grove Cemetery through Main, State and Asylum streets to Wethersfield, running cars past a given point every seven minutes. Hartford has a complete system of water works. Among the many public institutions in Hartford, may be mentioned the Hartford Hospital, built of Portland stone, which, exclusive of recent additions, cost about $50,000. Also the Connecticut Retreat for the Insane, situated on an elevation commanding a view of the city and meadow. The American Asylum for the Deaf and Dumb, was incorporated in the year 1816, and is the oldest institution of its kind in the country. The Wadsworth Atheneum is a granite building, 100 feet in length, 80 feet in depth. This building is occupied by the Young Men's Institute, Watkinson Library and Connecticut Historical Society. The growth of Hartford has been very rapid, as shown by census taken at different times. In the year 1800 the whole number of inhabitants was only about 5,000. At the present time the population is estimated at 45,000.

BUSINESS DIRECTORY.

Academies.

Bryant, Stratton & Remington, 395 Main St.
Hartford Female Seminary, 40 Pratt St.
Trinity College, Trinity St.
Theological Institute of Connecticut, 33 Prospect St.

Adjutant-General's Office.

Colin M. Ingersoll, Adjutant-General.

KELLOGG & BULKELEY, 245 Main St., Hartford, Lithographers. Checks, Drafts, Certificates of Stock, &c., Checks Stamped and Numbered, Lithographic work of every variety executed in the best style.

Agents.

Cook, C. W. Merchant's Dispatch, 2 Central Row.
Gates & Blakelee, American Improved Gas Light, 7 Central Row.

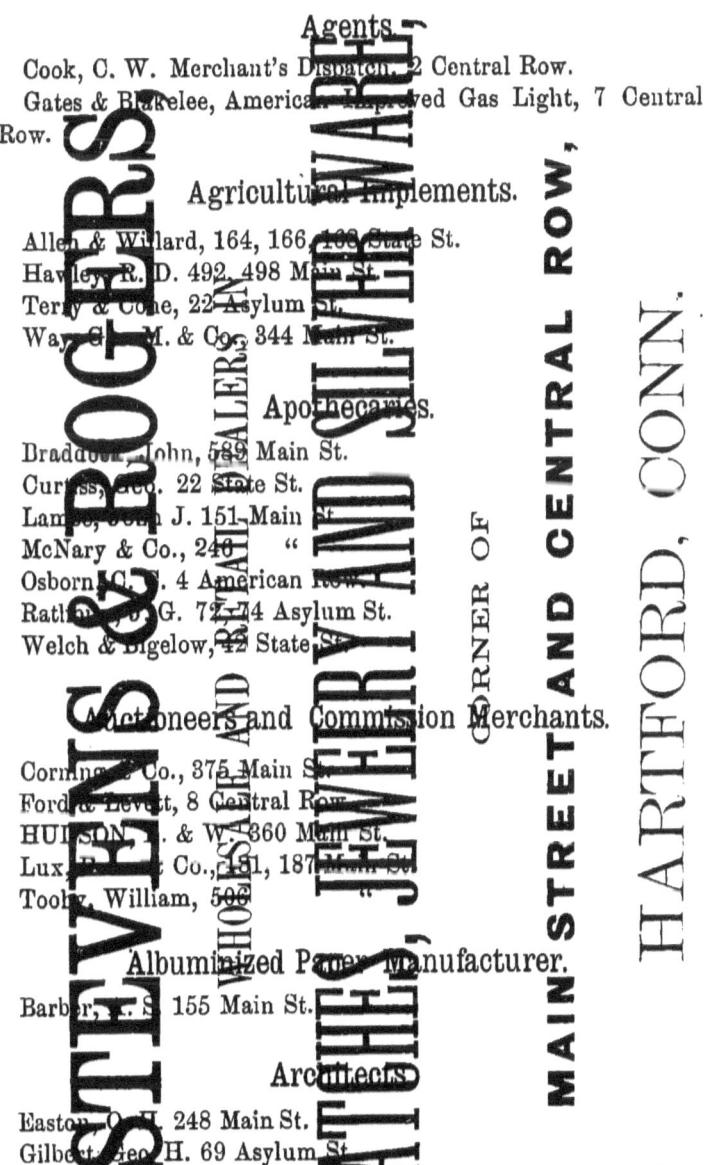

Agricultural Implements.

Allen & Willard, 164, 166, 168 State St.
Hawley, R. D. 492, 498 Main St.
Terry & Cone, 22 Asylum St.
Way, G. M. & Co., 344 Main St.

Apothecaries.

Draddock, John, 589 Main St.
Curtiss, Geo. 22 State St.
Lampe, John J. 151 Main St.
McNary & Co., 240 "
Osborn, C. J. 4 American Row
Rathbun, G. 72, 74 Asylum St.
Welch & Bigelow, 42 State St.

Auctioneers and Commission Merchants.

Corning & Co., 375 Main St.
Ford & Levett, 8 Central Row.
HUDSON, H. & W. 360 Main St.
Lux, R. & Co., 181, 187 Main St.
Tooly, William, 505 "

Albumized Paper Manufacturer.

Barber, J. S. 155 Main St.

Architects.

Easton, O. H. 248 Main St.
Gilbert, Geo. H. 69 Asylum St.

Attorneys at Law.

Adams, S. W. 274 Main St.
Bliss, J. W. 240   "   See adv. index.
Barbour, H. H. 321   "   Notary.
Briscoe, C. H. 311   "
Burton, H. E. 333   "
Buck, John R. 297   "
Case, S. N. 333   "
Chapman, C. & C. R. 8 State St.
Case, George, 279 Main St.
Chamberlin & Hall, 333 Main St.
Chambers, Francis, 274   "
Cole, Charles J. 297   "
Cornwall, H. 8 American Row.
Day, R. E. 2 Central Row.
Day & Stanton, 311 Main St.
Eaton, W. W. 240   "
Fellowes, F. 26 Pearl St.
Freeman, H. B. 274 Main St.
Goodman, Edward, 2 State St.
Goodman, Richard F. 2   "
Hamersley & Fellowes, 265 Main St.
Hooker, John, 333   "
Hubbard & McFarland, 245   "
Hurlbut, Wm. F. 248   "
Johnson & McManus, 289   "
Jones, S. F. 345   "   Notary Public.
Lyman, T. 333   "
Lounsbury, C. 241   "
MERRILL, M. E. 248   "   Judge of Police Court. See adv. index.
Owen, Chas. H. 297 Main St.
Parsons, John C. 353   "
Palmer, J. E. 2 Central Row.
Peters, John T. 289 Main St.

Perkins, J. G. 311 Main St.
Perkins, T. C. & C. E. 14 State St.
Robinson, W. C. 11 Central Row.
Smith, ?. ? American Row.
Spencer, ?. M. 333 Main St.
Shipman, ?. D. 345 "
Steele & Mathewson, 241 "
Sumner, Geo. E. 2 State S?
Terry, ?. 2?4 Main St.
Tucker, John D. 274 Main St.
Waldo & Hyde, 11 Central Row.
Welles, Roger, 34? Main St.
Welch & Shipman, ? Central Row.

Bakers.

Colson, James, 57 Ferry St.
Eaton, Geo. H. 23 Wells St.
Edwards, Ira, 57 Albany Av.
Ford, Wm. H. 185 Main St.
Lamb, Mrs. J. 132 Trumbull St.
Schneider, Charles, 160 Front St.
SYKES, E. A. 7 Allyn House Building. See adv. index.

Bailed Hay, Straw and Storage.

CHAPIN, HENRY, 130 Commerce St.

Ball Bats and Croquets Manufacturer.

Derby, Joseph, 30 Market St.

Barbers.

Bassett, W. T. corner Main and Asylum Sts.
Brunotte, William, 139 Front St.
Giese, Theodore, 141 Main St.
Hall, ?. ? City Hotel.

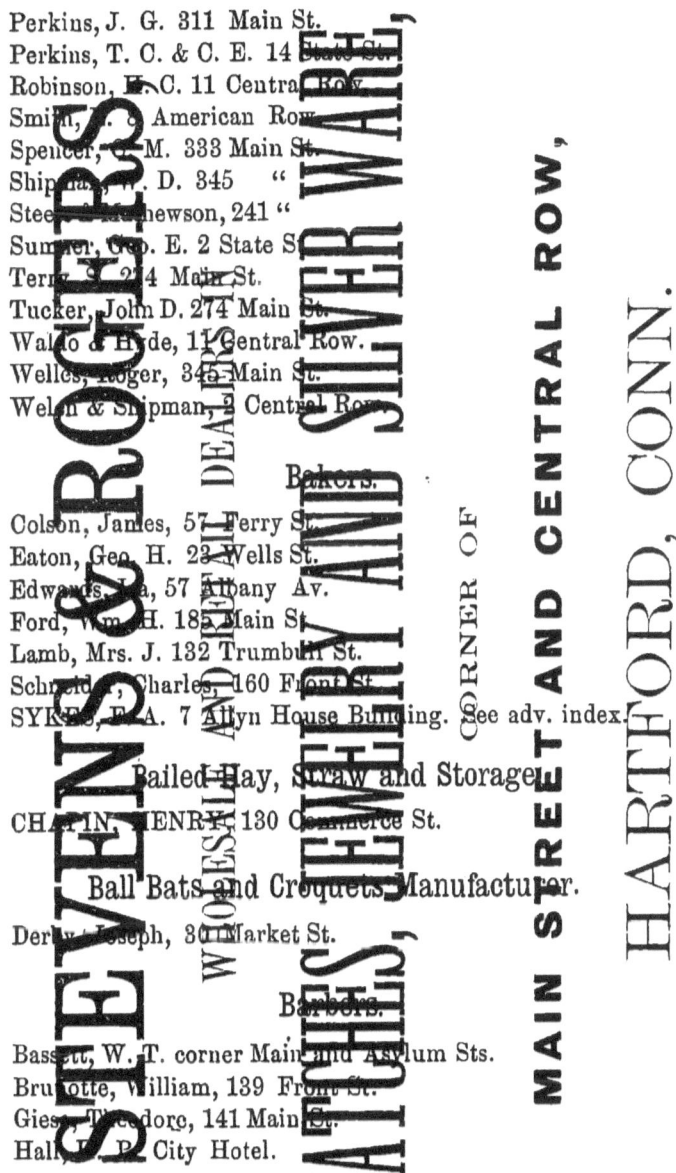

STEVENS & ROGERS, WHOLESALE AND RETAIL DEALERS IN WATCHES, JEWELRY AND SILVER WARE, CORNER OF MAIN STREET AND CENTRAL ROW, HARTFORD, CONN.

HILLS, WM. Allyn House, Hair Dressing and Bathing Saloon, 77, 79 Trumbull St.

Lathrop, Thos. S. 516 Main St.

Lathrop, S. B. 181   "

MILLER, CHARLES, 117 Front St. Bathing Rooms.

Ryan, Geo. M. 1 State St.

Stich, Martin, 295 Main St.

Seliger, Wendell, 14 Grove St.

Salvatore, Raineri, 24 State St.

Vandewater, James B. 129 Main St.

Whitmore, W. corner Main and Central Row.

Banks, (see Savings Banks).

Aetna National Bank, 224 Main St.

American National Bank, 258 Main St.

City National Bank, 348 Main St.

· Charter Oak National Bank, cor. Trumbull and Asylum Sts.

Connecticut River Banking Co., cor. Central Row and Prospect St.

First National Bank, 9 Central Row.

Farmers and Mechanics National Bank, cor. State and Market Sts.

Hartford National Bank, 60 State St.

Mercantile National Bank.

National Exchange Bank, 76 State St.

Phœnix National Bank, 303 Main St.

State National Bank, 299 Main St.

Bankers.

Bissell, Geo. P. & Co., 309 Main St.

Howe, Mather & Co., 346   "

Baths.

HILLS, WILLIAM, 77, 79 Trumbull St.

Bell Hanger.

Arthur, J. W. 131 Front St.

Belting Manufacturers.

Jewell, P. & Sons, 1 Trumbull St.
Palmer, N. & Co., 132 Asylum St.

Billiards.

Charter Oak Billiard Rooms, cor. Main and Pearl Sts.
Clinton House Billiard Rooms, Central Row.
Hewins, Matt., rear 262 Main St.

Blacksmiths.

Arthur, J. W. 131 Front St.
Cogan, D. 34 Mulberry St.
Hubbard, John. 6 Hicks St.
Sceery, M. 24 Wells St.
Morton, F. 5 Sheldon St.
Smith, Marcus, 46 Kilbourn St.

Block Letter Signs.

PRATT & DRUMMOND, 22, 24 Mulberry St. See adv. index.

Book Binders and Blank Book Manufacturers.

CASE, LOCKWOOD & CO., cor. Pearl and Trumbull Sts. See adv. index.
DRAKE & PARSONS, 150 Asylum St. See adv. index.
PARSONS, CHARLES, Blank Book Manufacturer, Paper Ruler, and Book Binder, 338 Main St.
TALCOTT, W. H. 13 Asylum St., over L. E. Hunt's Bookstore. See adv. index.

Book and Job Printers.

BUCK, FRED. F. E. 14 Pratt St. See adv. index.

CASE, LOCKWOOD & CO., cor. Pearl and Trumbull Sts. See adv. index.

CLARK & BOOTH, cor. Main and Asylum Sts. See adv. index.

Calhoun Printing Co., State St. (Job.)

HANMER, S. 66 State St., 2d floor. See adv. index.

Hartford Steam Printing Co., 18 State St.

Hutchings, W. C. 178 Asylum St.

WILEY, WATERMAN & EATON, 152 Asylum St. See adv. index.

Books and Stationery.

Brown & Gross, 313 Main St.

Corning & Co., 375 Main St.

Dowling, John, 10 Church St.

Fallon, B. K. 10 American Row.

Geer & Pond, 256 Main St.

HALL, T. E. 161 Main St.

T. E. HALL,
BOOKS AND STATIONERY,

News office, Circulating Library where books are loaned, Intelligence Directory. Also dealer in Magazines, Periodicals, Cheap Publications, bound books, toy books, games, Croquet and all kinds of Base Ball materials.

161 Main St., opposite St. John's Church.

Hamersley, Wm. Jas. 263 Main St.

HUNT, L. E. 13 Asylum St.

Rose, Abraham, 89 Asylum St.

Bonnet Bleachers.

Carter & Rezner, 22 Church St.

Greene, George C. 483, up stairs, Main St.

Warner, Luman, 390 Main St.

Book Publishers.

American Publishing Co., 148 Asylum St.
BRAINARD & SAMPSON, cor. Pearl and Trumbull Sts.
Belknap, Thos. 91 Asylum St.
Burr, J. B. & Co., 18 Asylum St.
CASE, LOCKWOOD & CO., cor. Pearl and Trumbull Sts. See adv. index.
Case, O. D. & Co., 41 Trumbull St.
HALE, A. S. & CO., 97 Asylum St. See adv. index.
HARTFORD PUBLISHING CO., 155 Asylum St. See adv. index.
Peters, S. A. & Co., 289 Main St.
Scranton, S. S. & Co., 126 Asylum St.
Stebbins, L. 248 Main St.

Boot and Shoe Dealers.

Aishberg, Henry, 447 Main St.
Chapman & Smith, 153 Main St.
Chapin & King, 495   "
Cohn, S. 483   "
Curry & Holladay, 145   "
Duffy, T. F. 99 1-2   "
Eldridge & Co., 278   "
Fairman & Holbrook, 370 "
Godard, Leonard, 519 Main St.
Goodwin, John H. & Co., 277 Main St.
Kenyon, S. C. & Co., 407, 443 Main St.
Kellogg & Maynard, 477 Main St.
Lynch, John, 171 Main St.
Lawrence, W. T. 183 Main St.
Richardson, Wm. H. & Co., 249 Main St.
Sawyer & Parsons, 267 Main St.
Selling & Rosenblatt, 404   "
Miller, W. H. 383   "
Wilcox & Son, 627   "

15

Winship, Thomas, 35 Main St.
Work, T. J. 122 State St.

Boot and Shoe Manufactures and Dealers.

Crittenden, L. S. 84 Asylum St.
Gleason, Eams & Co., 18 Ford St.
Hills & Goodman, 51 Asylum St.
Hunt, Holbrook & Barber, 130, 132 Asylum St.
Hills, I. & Sons, 202 State, cor. Front Sts.
Hutchinson & Avery, 76 Asylum St.
Marcey, F. A. 98 "
Wiley, Sylvester, 47 "

Boot and Shoe Makers and Repairers.

SEE ALSO DEALERS.

Burns, T. 89 Front St.
Crittenden, L. S. 84 Asylum St.
Eldridge & Co., 278 Main St.
Firth, H. H. & Co., 110 State St.
Goudolf, M. 46 State St.
Jordan, Horace, 345 Main St.
Kreuzer, C. 44 Asylum St.
Work, T. J. 122 State St.

Brokers, Money.

Abbe, B. R. 7 Central Row.
Bissell, Geo. P. & Co., 309 Main St.
Buel, Robert, 333 Main St.
Colt, E. D. Central Row.
Bissel, G. P. & Co., near cor. Main and Asylum Sts.
Russell, J. B. & Son, 62 State St.
Seymour, Harvey, 7 Central Row.
Robinson, A. S. Central Row.

Bottler.

Bacon, William A. & Son, 168 Main St.

Brewers.
Shannon & McCann, 18 Trumbull St.

Brass Foundry.
Blake, Thos. J. 30 Ferry St.
Cusick, Edward J. 18 Trumbull St.
Marshall, W. C. & Sons, 31 Wells St.

Building Stone Dealers.
Belden, Seth & Son, Commerce St.
BRABASON, A. & S. 77 Potter St.

Brush Manufacturer.
Whittemore, W. L. 48 Asylum St.

Broom Manufacturers.
Hubbard, Samuel & Co., 142 State St.

Bronzing and Gilding.
SEE BOOK BINDERS.

Pratt, W. F. & Co., 321 Main St.

Business Colleges.
Bryant, Stratton & Remington, 395 Main St.
Hannum, T. W. Hills' Block, Main St.

Cabinet Makers.
Avery & Colton, 169 Main St.
Lux, George, 181   "
ROBBINS, WINSHIP & CO., 209 Main St. See adv. index.

Candy Manufacturers.
BRIGGS, H. S. 381 Main St. See adv. index.
Thomson, E. C. 51 Albany Avenue.
Kibbe & Co., 7 American Row.

Carriage Manufacturers.
EVARTS, GEO. S. 39 Albany Avenue. See adv. index.
Hart, Lamby & Co., 12 Ford St.

KENNEY & GAY, 24, 26 Sheldon St. See adv. index.
King, Ralph, 177 Commerce St.
Keney & Joycox, 21 Charles St.
Mansuy, Louis, 17, 21 Elm St.
STAPLES, GEO. M. 34 Wells St. See adv. index.
SAFFORD, ADDISON, Manufacturer and repairer of Carriages, Buggies, Business Waggons, Sleighs, &c. 10 Ferry St.

Card Egraver.

Johnson, W. B. 333 Main St.

Carmen.

BALDWIN & DOWNING, 128 Commerce St.
Chamberlain, N. H. 31 Hudson St.
Ensworth & Co., 246 State St.
Hebard, C. & Co., 248 State St.
Webb Bros. 44½ Asylum St.

Carpet Manufacturers.

Hartford Carpet Company, cor. State and Market Sts.

Carpenters and Builders.

Case, Sam'l, 60 Pearl St. Builder.
Colton, H. 60 Pearl St. Builder.
Cornish, D. C. rear 30 Market St.
Green, Joel B. 30 Ferry St.
Kibbe, Geo. 56 Market St.
Bodge, Wm. C. 60 Pearl St. Builder.
Lay, John W. 60 Pearl St. Builder.
Phelps, Erastus, 27 Hicks St.
PARISH, L. F. 60 Pearl St. Builder.
Richardson, James, 60 " Builder.
Swan, Francis, 60 " Builder.

Cement Drain Tile Manufacturers.

BISSELL, H. & S. 17 Pearl St. See adv. index.

Children's Carriage Manufacturer.

Fuller, H. L. 153 State St.

Cigar Manufacturers.

Loomis, J. M. 488 Main St.
Montgomery, T. M. 553 "
Steinmeyer, Otto, 13 Albany Avenue.

Cigars and Tobacco Manufacturers and Dealers.

Bauman & Traute, 207½ Main St.
BROWN & OAKMAN, 212 State St. See adv. index.
Hebard, Sturtevant & Co., 260 State St. See adv. index.
Loomis, N. P. & W. G. 216   "
Long, Phil., 165 Main St.
Schott, James S. 159 "
Solomon & DeLeeuw, 6 Asylum St.

Civil Engineers.

Ellis, Theo. G. 2 Central Row.
Marsh, S. E. 2   "

Clergymen.

Burton, N. J. (Congregational.)
Clarke, Geo. H. (Episcopal.)
Crane, C. B. (Baptist.)
Fisher, C. R. (Episcopal.)
Gould, Geo. H. (Congregational.)
Herron, John M. (Presbyterian.)
Hodge, J. A. (Presbyterian.)
Hughes, James, (Roman Catholic.)
Leon, Louis, (Israelite.)
Lynch, John, (Roman Catholic.)
Mayer, I. (Israelite.)
Parker, Edwin P. (Congregational.)
Spaulding, Geo. B. (Congregational.)
Turnbull, Robert, (Baptist.)
Twitchell, J. H. (Congregational.)
Wildridge, H. A. (Methodist.)

Clothing.

Barnick, M. 707 Main St.
Beardslee, B. 81 Asylum St.
Brigham & Skinner, 19 "
Chapman, S. E. 94 Morgan St.
Clark, Franklin, 132 State St.
Clark, James, 29½ Asylum St.
Conklin, Skillman & Co., 264, 270 Main St.
Dow & Redfield, 11 Pearl St.
Ensign, Henry, 174 Main St.
Fisher & Co., 64 State St.
Freeman, S. 42 Asylum St.
Gemmill, J. & Son, 29 Asylum St.
Goodhart, J. (second hand) 198 State St.
Green, P. S. 10 Asylum St.
Hollander, A. Main St,
Hollander, A. 86 State St.
Kelsey & Hitchcock, 283 Main St.
Knoek, J. S. (second hand) 161 State St.
Koffman, Mitchell, 198 State St.
Legate & Fisher, 68　　　　"
Mayer, S. & Co., 8 Asylum St.
Selling, Henry, 188 State S.
SAUNDERS, T. P. 254 Main St.
Smith, James, 285　　　　"
Smith & Whittemore, 88 Asylum St.
Whittlesey, W. F. 20　　　　"

Dress and Cloak Making.

Benton, C. Mrs. 11 Ely's Block.
Brown, Mrs. L. M & Co., 781 Main St.
Callender, H. E. Mrs. 353　　"
Thompson, C. L. 353　　　　"

Clothing and Gent's Furnishing Goods.

SEE GENT'S FURNISHING GOODS.

Conklin, Skillman & Co., 264, 270 Main St.

Dow & Redfield, 11 Pearl St.
Kelsey & Hitchcock, 283 Main St.
Smith, James, 285   "
Williams, E. W. 297   "

Clothing Manufacturers, Wholesale.

DAY, A. F. & C. G. & Co., 54, 56 Asylum St. See adv. index.
Fenn, John T. 69 Asylum St.
Merriman, J. & Co., 51   "
Merriman, Griggs & Co., 14 Hick St.

Clothes Cleaning and Repairing.

Maureau, P. & Co., 153 State St.

Clothing, Wholesale.

MAMMOTH WARDROBE, 54 Asylum St. See adv. index.
DAY, A. F. & C. G. & CO., 54, 56 Asylum St. See adv. index.
Burpee, W. C. & Co., 56 Asylum St. See adv. index.

Coach Saddlery Hardware, Wholesale.

Corning Bros., 62 Asylum St.

Coal Hod Manufacturers.

CHILD & BULL, 189 Main St. See adv. index.

Coal Dealers.

Bronson, O. H. 103 Sheldon St.
Chapin, M. W. cor. Commerce and State Sts.
Carrier, W. B. 75 Front St.
Farnham, E. B. 253 State St.
Hatch & Tyler, 56 Commerce St.
Hartford Associated Coal Co., 13 Central Row.
Hatch & Tyler, 244 State St.
Kenyon, E. L. 171 Front St.
Lord, M. 111 State St.

Coffin Manufacturers.

Glafcke & Cook, 12 Pratt St.
WOOLLEY, G. W. & W. P. 175 Main St.

Coffin Trimmings.

WOOLLEY, G. W. & W. P. 175 Main St.

Coffee and Spice Manufacturers and Dealers.

Boardman, Wm. & Sons, 205 State St.
GILLETT, A. B. & CO., 43, 45 Asylum St. See adv. index.
HEBARD, STURTEVANT & CO., 260 State St. See adv. index.
PARK, FELLOWS & CO., 208 State St. See adv. index.

Commission Agent.

Kohn, M. 30 Market St.

Commission Merchants.

Buckland & Baker, 120 State St.
Boynton, J. W. (Machinery Agency,) 148 State St.
Bradford, Northam & Co., (Flour & Grain,) 129 State St.
Crosby, D. (Ship supplies,) 172 Commerce St.
CHAPIN & BURR, (Flour,) 75, 77 Ferry St.
Collins Bros. & Co., (Domestic Dry Goods,) 39, 41 Asylum St.
Cohen, Henry, 385 Main St.
Hunt, W. C. & Co., 141 State St.
Fox, Woodford & Co., (Grocers,) Central Row.
Fowler, Davis & Hoyt, 229 State St.
Slate & Simmons, 155 State St.
Wilcox, H. B. (Tobacco,) 169 Front St.
Whittlesey & Bliss, (Flour and Produce,) 33 Asylum St.

Commercial Schools.

Hannum, T. W. 19 Hills' Block, Main St.
Bryant, Stratton & Remington, 895 Main St.

Confectionery.

BRIGGS, Henry S. 381 Main St.   See adv. index.
Collum & Bryant, 143 Main St.
Kibbe & Co., 7 American Row.
Sykes, F. A. 86 Asylum St.
Thompson, E. C. 51 Albany Avenue.

Cordials, Bitters, &c.

ISHAM, A. B. 65 Ferry St.   See adv. index.

Contractors, Building.

Bissell, H. & S. 17 Pearl St.

Confectionery Manufactory.

Thompson, E. C. 51 Albany Av.

• Coopers.

Weeks, C. & H. Commerce St.

Cotton Dealers.

Dunham, A. & Co., 235, 237 State St.
Willard, W. F. 111 State St.

Cotton, Cotton Waste and Paper.

DAY BROTHERS, 208 State St.   See adv. index.

Copper Smiths and Brass Founders.

Blake, Thomas J. 30 Ferry St.
Cusick, E. J. 18 Trumbull St.

Cracker Manufacturers.

Edwards, Irad, 57 Albany Av.
EATON, GEORGE H. 22 Welles St.

Crockery, China, Glass and Earthenware.

Goodwin, Henry W. 272 Main St.
Fuller and Talcott, 389   "
Kendall, S. P. & Co., 231, 233 "
16

Newhall, John, 153 Commerce St.
Teft, Daniel R. 487 Main St.
Wells, J. G. & Co., 15 Asylum St.

Dancing Academy.

Reilly, P. H. 271 Main St.

Dentists.

Arnold, Edward, 94 Asylum St.
Blatchley, Wm. 14 State St.
BULLOCK, C. & SON, 346 Main St.   See adv. index.
Crane, S. L. G. 8 State St.
CROFOOT & POWERS, 251 Main St.   See adv. index.
CROFOOT, E. E. 251   "
CODY, JOHN, 251   "   See adv. index. .
GREENLEAF, J. M. 2 State St.   "   "
Hooker, C. M. 299 Main St.
Hitchcock, J. L. 356   "
McMANUS, JAMES, 251 Main St.
Munsell, R. A. 106 Trumbull St.
Newton, A. Talcott & Post's Building, Main S.
Parmelee, L. 25 Pratt St.
Porter, Wm. M. 390 Main St.
POWERS, C. A. 251   "
Riggs & Dwyer, 9 Asylum St.
Wille, E. C. 163 State St.

Designer and Engraver.

Curtis, H. C. 181 Main St.

Doors, Sash and Blinds.

Moody, L. B. & Co., 44 Market St.

Drain Tile Manufacturers.

BISSELL, H. & S. 17 Pearl St.   See adv. index.

Dress and Cloak Makers.

Adams, J. Q. Mrs. 19 Church St.
Crane, Mrs. 43   "
Chappell, F. M. Miss, 356 Main St.
Duley, James E. 311 Main St.
Frederick A Krabetz, 141 Main St.
Fenner, S. A. 499   "
French, E. M. 371   "
Kingsbury, Mrs. 108 Pearl St.
Martin, R. F. Mrs. 374 Main St.
Pollard, W. C. Mrs. 408   "
Ward, Miss 241   "

Druggists, Wholesale.

WILLIAMS, GEORGE W. & CO., cor. State and Front Sts.
See adv. index.

Drugs, Chemicals and Dye Stuffs, Wholesale.

Beach & Co., 209, 211 State St.
Riley, Hanmer & Co., 146 Main St.
WILLIAMS, GEORGE W. cor. State and Front Sts. See
adv. index.

Druggists, Retail.

Butler, J. V. B. 143 Trumbull St.
Bodwell, George, 139 Main St.
Braddock, John, 589   "
Bristol, J. H. 42 State St.
Curtis, Geo. 22   "
Goodwin, Henry A. 336 Main St.
Johnson, J. W. 555   "
Lambe, John J. 151   "
McNary & Co., 246   "   Seedsmen.
MOSES, S. G. & Co., 605, 587 Main St.
Osborn, C. C. 4 American Row.
Rathbun, J. G. 72, 74 Asylum St.
Sisson & Butler, 259 Main St.

Talcott Brothers, 354 Main St.
Sperry, I. J. 12 Grove St.
WILLIAMS, GEO. W. & CO., (Wholesale,) cor. State and
Front.   See adv. index.
White, Jas. 481 Main St.
Woodruff & Curtis, 94 Main St.

Dry Goods, Wholesale.

Bolles, Sexton & Co., 58, 60 Asylum St.
Griswold, Seymour & Co., 66, 68, 70 Asylum St.
Owen, Root & Childs, 73   "
Talcott & Post, 369 Main St.
Weatherby, Knous & Pelton, 335, 337 Main St.

Dry Goods, Retail.

Bliss, Benjamin & Co., 363 Main St.
Brown, Thomson & Co., 269   "
Bates, William, 97 1-2   "
Bloombargh, H. 466   "
Burkett & Ives, 386   "
CLAPP, C. W. 391   "
Clark & Latimer, 428   "
Corning & Co., 375   "
Duffy, T. 177   "
Denzig Brothers, 460   "
Gay & Hastings, 373   "
Frank & Frankenfield, 402   "
Goodman & Glazier, 474   "
Griswold, S. W. & Son, 414, 416, 418, 420 Main St.
Goodhue, J. M. 397 Main St.
Goldschmidt, H. & Co., 392 Main St.
Griffin, A. M. Mrs. 86   "
Hart, Merriam & Co., 325   "
Judd, W. M. 382   "
Langdon & Co., 359   "
LEWITH, HENRY, 235, 237   "
Martin, Geo. E. 532   "
Oppenheimer, Louis, 423   "
Pease & Foster, 364   "

Smith, C. H. & Co., 273 Main St.
TALCOTT & POST, 369 "
Weatherby, Knous & Pelton, 335, 337 Main St.

Dyers.

Davis, Rudolf, 30 Market St.
Degenhardt, H. John, 144 Front St.
Dumont, A. 30 Temple St.
Maureau, P. & Co., 141 State St.
NEW ENGLAND FANCY DYE WORKS, 139 Trumbull St.
See adv. index.
SMITH, GEO. 37 Wells and 9 Pearl St. See adv. index.

Eating Houses.

BRIGGS, HENRY S. 381 Main St. See adv. index.
BROWN, W. B. 33 Gold St. Cider at Wholesale.
The Continental, 9 American Row.
Dwyer, John, 172 Main St.
GARDNER, W. H. MRS. 387 Main St. Coffee House. See
adv. index.
Green, E. R. 35 Asylum St.
Gibbs, Geo. S. 598 Main St.
Indian Belle, C. W. Bradbury, 599 Main St.
Monitor House, 561 Main St. R. Sellew.
Taylor, Martin, 532 "
Union Dining Hall, Geo. W. Loomis, 134 Main St.

Edge Tool Manufacturers.

Collins Company, Axes and Knives, E. Colt, Sec., office 2
Central Row.

Electrotypers.

Hobbs, Richard H. 148 Asylum St.
LOCKWOOD & MANDEVILLE, cor. Pearl and Trumbull
Sts. See adv. index.

Engineers' Supplies.

Blair, H. P. 176 Asylum St.

Engraving.

Griswold, J. G. 25 Asylum St.

Envelope Manufacturers.

Plimpton, L. B. & Co., 178 Asylum St.

Express Companies and Agents.

Adams Express Co., 6 Central Row.
MERCHANTS' UNION EXPRESS CO., Wm. L. Matson,
Agent, 3 Central Row. See adv. index.

Fancy Goods.

Daniels, A. M. 422 Main St.
Fox, Gerson, 412   "
Kohners, M. 406   "
Mayer, Louis & Co., 368 Main St.
Miller & Haynes, 388   "
Rothschild, A. Mrs. 18 Church St.
Stern & Mandlebaum, 346 Main St.
Slesinger, S. 638   "
Thompson, F. C. 424   "

Fancy Saddlery.

Wilder, Lyman J. 147 Main St.

Fancy Dyers.

NEW ENGLAND FANCY DYE WORKS, 139 Trumbull St.
See adv. index.
SMITH, GEO. 37 Wells and 0 Pearl St.   See adv. index.

Farm Produce, Wholesale.

Fowler, Davis & Hoyt, 133 State St.
Whittlesey & Bliss, 33 Asylum St.

Fertilizers and Plastic Slate Roofing.

Clark, Merlen F. 12 Fairmount St.
Loomis, W. R. & Sons, 173 Commerce St.

Fire Arms Manufacturers.

Colt's Patent Fire Arms Manufacturing Co., Vandyke Av.
Sharps' Rifle Manufacturing Co., Rifle Av.

File Manufacturer.

Smith, Robert H. 129 Front St.

Fish Dealers.

Bryant & Hildreth, 76, 78 Ferry St.
Caswell & Bronson, 100 Main St.
Church, S. A. 29 Ferry St.   Fish Market.
Edgerton, E. A. 39, 41 "   "
Mason, E. 23 Albany Av.
Marsh, Jas. 118   "
Paine, T. H. 567 Main St.
STEVENS & BACKUS, 51, 53, 55 Kingsley St.

Flour, Grain and Feed.

Allen, E. L. 142 State St.
Deming & Moore, 619 Main St.
Ely & Co., 242 State St.
Giddings & Shaw, 542 Main St.
Hawes, W. 207 State St.
Holt, L. H. 581 Main St.
Rockwell, B. D. 187 State St.
Smith, Northam & Robinson, 129 State St.
Willard, W. B. 52, 54, 56 Ferry St.

Flouring and Grist Mills.

Daniels, L. 40 Elm St.
Willard, W. B. Ferry St.

Fruit and Confectionery.

Blackman, J. 132 1-2 Asylum St.
Brewer, F. A. & Co., 301 Main St.   Fruit Store.
Collum & Bryant, 143   "
Douthwaite, R. 207   "
Gregory, S. B. 178 State St.

Root, G. 145 Trumbull St.

Fruit Dealers, Wholesale and Retail.

Clapp, A. E. & Co., 127, 129, 131 Main St.
Buckland, L. H. & Co., 120 State St.
Gregory, S. W. 90, 92, 102 State St.
Maynard, Wilber, 14, 16 Asylum St.
Pendleton, A. & Son, 34, 36 Asylum St.
Pomeroy, J. 26 Asylum St.

Guano Dealer.

KELLOGG, RODNEY, 201, 205 Commerce St. See adv. index.

Gunsmith.

NEWTON, P. S. 26 Kingsley St. See adv. index.

Friction Pulley Manufacturers.

PHOENIX IRON WORKS, Geo. S. Lincoln & Co., 54, 60 Arch St. See adv. index.

Frames and Engravings.

Pelton & Webster, 241 Main St.

Foreign Exchange Office.

Jacobs, W. W. 13 Central Row.

Furniture Dealers.

Deming, E. M. 205 Main St.
Kellogg, Douglass & Seidler, 65, 67 Asylum St.
Read, Rawson, 385 Main St.
ROBBINS, WINSHIP & CO., 209 Main St. See adv. index.
Roberts & House, 393 Main St.

Gas Light Company.

Hartford City Gas Light Co., S. S. Ward, President and Treasurer, 99 Arch St.

Gas, Cook and Heating Stove Manufacturers.

CHILD & BULL, 189 Main St. See adv. index.

Gold Beaters.

Ashmead, Jas. H. & Sons, 41 Trumbull St. See adv. index.
Ney, J. M. & Co., 59 Pearl St. See adv. index.

Gold Foil Manufacturers.

ASHMEAD, JAS. H. & SONS, 41 Trumbull St. See adv. index.
NEY, J. M. &. CO., 59 Pearl St. See adv. index.

Gold Leaf Manufacturers.

ASHMEAD, JAS. H. & SONS, 41 Trumbull St. See adv. index.
NEY, J. M. & Co., 59 Pearl St. See adv. index.

Gold and Tin Foil Manufacturers.

ASHMEAD, JAS. H. & SONS, 41 Trumbull St. See adv. index.
NEY, J. M. & CO., 59 Pearl St. See adv. index.

Glass Cutting.

Houghton, Geo. 21 Potter St.

Grindstone Dealers.

Tuttle, S. & Sons, 488 Main St.

Gents. Furnishing Goods.

Bowers, C. A. 50 Asylum St.
Brigham & Skinner, 19 Asylum St.
Brockett, N. J. & Co., 10 State St.
BUNCE, J. W. 307 Main St. See adv. index.
Burpee, W. C. & Co., 56 Asylum St.

17

Conklin, Stillman & Co., 264, 270 Main St.
Clark, Franklin & Co., 132 State St.
DAY, A. F. & C. G. & CO., (Wholesale,) 54, 56 Asylum St.
See adv. index.
Dow & Redfield, 11 Pearl St.
Ensign, Henry, 174 State St.
Gemmill, J. & Son, 29 Asylum St.
Kelsey & Hitchcock, 283 Main St.
Legate & Fisher, 68 State St.
SAUNDERS, T. P. 254 Main St.
Smith, James, 285   "
Smith & Whittemore, 88 Asylum St.
Whittelsey, W. F. 20 Asylum St.

Grocers, Retail.

Adams, J. M. Agt., 646 Main St.
Barnes, L. W. & E. B. 634   "
Baker, J. W. 151 State St.
Bacharach, Henry, 80 Windsor St.
Bacon & Rowley; cor. Maple Av. and Retreat Av.
Blanchard, O. H. & Brothers, 199, 201, 203 State St.
Blumenthal, A. 40 Market St.
Bumstead, H. T..547 Main St.
Burdick, R. M. & Co., 541 "
Buckingham, Hiram, 243 "
Browne, J. 86 Front St.
Cadden, A. 60 Morgan St.
Case, O. P. & Co., 533 Main St.
Chalker & Wheeler, 433   "
Chamberlain, S. S. 179 State St.
Clapp, A. E. & Co., 127, 129, 131 Main St.
Crosby, D. & Co., 192 Commerce St.
Claffey, M. 21 Market St.
Cunningham, M. 97 Windsor St.
Delaney, Thomas, 170 1-2 Front St.
Donnelly, M. 75 Windsor St.
Donovan, John, 31 Albany Av.
Duffy, Bernard, 14 Elm St.
Fox, Woodford & Co., 17 Central Row.

Gaylord, H. 66 Morgan St.
Gilbert, E. S. 96 Main St.
Griswold, H. 157 Main St.
Glazier, J. M. 195 State St.
Gunn, Chas. 154 Front St.
Goff, Daniel, 97 Park St.
Harbison Brothers, 132 Main St.
Hendrick & Co., 84 Trumbull St.
Heublein F. 26 Market St.
Hilton, James, 564 Main St.
Holden, C. S. 63 Morgan St.
Katzenstein, W. 157 Front St.
Keane, H. P. 71 Potter St.
Kenny, W. M. 137 Front St.
Kenny, Wm. 85   "
Kellogg, Hawley, 149 Main St.
King, John, 47 Pearl St.
Kinne, H. F. 112 Albany Av.
Killen, James, 72 Morgan St.
Lee, Thos. 260 Front St.
Litchfield & Flower, 154 Asylum St.
Litchfield, T. J. 542 Main St.
Lorsch, S. & Brother, 44 Market St.
Lynch, Walter, 254 Front St.
. May, W. J. & C. 4 Ford St.
McColiff, Dennis, 81 Front St.
McGurk, Wm. 122 Albany Av.
MILLER, J. H. 711 Main St.
Mooney, James, 204 Front St.
Moses, L. M. 624 Main St.
Mullons, Matthew, 185 Front St.
Mulligan, Wm. 138   "
Otis, John D. 618 Main St.
Parish, Oliver, 145 State St.
Pease, H. K. 135 Asylum St.
Pease, J. W. 133   "
Pillion, Wm. 148 1-2 Front St.
Pomeroy, J. 26 Asylum St.
Post & Levally, 699 Main St.

Pond, C. J. 818 Main St.
Preston, Thos. 23 Trumbull St.
Ranney, J. H. & Co., 5 American Row.
Riley Brothers, 189 Front St.
Rice, N. 525 Main St.
Rhodes, H. B. 103 Main St.
Roche, Matthew, 39 Commerce St.
Rock, Bernard, 86 1-2 Pearl St.
Rosenblat, B. 149 Front St.
Roulston Brothers, 109 Park St.
Ryan Thomas, 288 Front St.
Sceery, Thomas, 48 Wells St.
Seyms & Co., 223 Main St.
Spayer, L. 197 Front St.
Spencer, A. 73, 75 Albany Av.
Strong, E. B. 144 Main St.
SWAN, HENRY, 40 Commerce St.
Tarbell, H. D. 128 Main St.
Whiting, H. L. 189 State St.
Wheeler, M. S. 799 No. Main St.
Willard, W. H. 84 Morgan St.
Williams & Goodwin, 439 Main St.

Grocers, Wholesale.

Chamberlain, S. S. 179 State St.
Danforth, J. W. & Co., 218 "
Farnham & Barnes, 238   "
Foster & Co., cor. Front and Grove Sts.
Glazier, C. & Son, 217 State St.
Keneys & Roberts, 700 Main St.
Litchfield & Flower, 154 Asylum St.
Redfield, A. B. & Co., 239 State St.
Smith, E. T. 232   "
Smith, C. G. & Co., 230   "

Gun Makers.

KELLOGG, E. C. C. 594 Main St. See adv. index.
NEWTON, P. S. 26 Kingsley St. See adv. index.

Hair Workers.

Lathrop, Thomas, 516 Main St.
Weildon, T. C. 342   "

Hay Dealers.

CHAPIN, HENRY, Commerce St.
Parish, O. 143 State St.

Hardware, Wholesale and Retail.

Bronson, W. S. & Co., 64 Asylum St.
Davis, Tracy & Co., 52   "
Francis & Co., 343   Main St.
Hawley, R. D. 492, 498 "
Terry & Cone, 22 Asylum St.
Thrall, Willis & Son, 10 Central Row.
WAY, GEO. M. & CO., 344 Main St., 22, 24 Kingsley St. See adv. index.
Whiting, G. S. 329 Main St.

Harness and Trunk Manufacturers.

BULLARD, J. D. 90 Asylum St.   See adv. index.
Brewer, Edgar, 5 Central Row.
Deming, Edwin, 86, 88 Morgan St.
Hawxhurst, Solomon, 25 Albany Av.
Hunter, N. W. 113 State St.
Lomax, R. 544 Main St.
Roberts, Wm. 147   "
Rooney, P. 567 1-2 "
Smith, Bourn & Co., 142, 144, 146 Asylum St.
Stiles, Leon, 228 State St.
Starbird & Pedlow, 595 Main St.
Wilder, J. L. (Fancy) 147   "

Hats, Caps and Furs.

BUNCE, J. W. 307 Main St.   See adv. index.
Boen, Samuel, 163   "
Daniels & Priest, 331   "
Daniels, James, 305   "

Dix, C. R. 4 Central Row.
Haff, Joel, 8 State St.
Hamilton, E. S. & Son, 349 Main St.
Stillman & Co., 347   "
Strong & Phelps, 351   "
Strong & Woodruff, 355   "
Watcrous, R. G. 319   "
Price, Louis, 165 Front St. ·

Hand Stamps, Seal Presses.and Conductor's Punches.

SNOW, JUSTIN, 289 Main St.   See adv. index.

Hide Dealers.

Martin, Thomas, 70 Morgan St.
Sage, E. E. 64, 66 Albany Av.

Hoop Skirt and Corset Manufacturers.

French, H. B. 410 Main St.
Hartford Skirt Co., 83 1-2 Asylum St.
Raffel, L. 468 Main St.

Horse Collar Manufacturers.

Baldwin, J. J. 129 Market St.
Deming, Edwin, 86 Morgan St.
Smith, Bourn & Co., 142—146 Asylum St.

Horse Railway Company.

Hartford and Wethersfield Horse Railway Co., 346 Main St. .

Hotels.

ALLYN HOUSE, R. J. Allyn, Proprietor, cor. Trumbull and
Asylum Sts.
Asylum Street House, T. Dooley, Proprietor, 157 Asylum St.
AMERICAN HOTEL, B. L. & S. P. Black, Proprietors, cor.
State St. and American Row.
CITY HOTEL, 217 Main St., Caleb Clapp, Proprietor.   See
adv. index.

CLINTON HOUSE, 22, 23, 24 Central Row, H. Keeney, Proprietor.

Eagle House, Ernst Helmrich, Proprietor, 114 State St.

EAGLE HOUSE, Joseph Rose, Proprietor, 4 Elm St.

EUROPEAN HOTEL, C. Brehm, Proprietor, cor. Mulberry and Wells St. See adv. index.

GERMANIA HOUSE, Colt's Dyke, Alex. Birkholz, Proprietor.

Hollister House, 193 State St. ·

Lafayette House, 8 Market St., Wm. Stratton, Proprietor.

Ryder's Hotel, 610 Main St., A. A. Bacon, Proprietor.

Sears' Hotel, 70 Ferry St., Calvin Sears, Proprietor.

ST. JOHN'S HOTEL, 445 Main St., L. Lane, Proprietor. See adv. index.

TRUMBULL HOUSE, J. M. Parker, Proprietor, 48 State St.

UNDERHILL HOUSE, 629 Main St., C. Gabrielle, Proprietor.

UNITED STATES HOTEL, D. A. Rood, Proprietor, 26 State Street.

WASHINGTON HOUSE, 64 Market St., Myer Stern, Proprietor.

Ice Cream Saloons.

BRIGGS, H. S. 381 Main St. See adv. index.

Collum & Bryant, 143 Main St.

GARDNER, MRS. W. H. 387 Main St. See adv. index.

SYKES, F. A. 86 Asylum St., 7 Allyn House Building. See adv. index.

Ice Dealers.

Hartford Ice Company, 15 Pearl St.

Insurance Agents.

Baker, W. E. 9 Hungerford & Cone's Block, Main St.

Conner, William & Co., 241 Main St.

Gillett, Ralph, 7 Central Row.

HYDEL, F. C. 15 Pearl St. (Fire, Life and Accident.)

Kimball, C. C. Hills' Block, 333 Main St.

Preston, C. 22 State St.

STEVENS, N. B. (Gen. Agt.) Charter Oak Life, 245 Main St.
Wallace, Wm. 333 Main St.

Insurance Companies.

Aetna Insurance Co., 226 Main St.
Aetna Life Insurance Co., 226 "
Aetna Live Stock Insurance Co., 258 Main St.
CHARTER OAK LIFE INSURANCE CO.,
    Jas. C. Walkley, Pres., S. H. White, Sec., Office 240 Main
    St. See adv. index.
CONNECTICUT GENERAL LIFE INSURANCE CO.,
    E. W. Parsons, Pres., Thomas W. Russell, Sec., Office 7
    Central Row. See adv. index.
Connecticut Mutual Life Insurance Co., 297 Main St.
Connecticut Fire Insurance Co., 12 State St.
CONTINENTAL LIFE INSURANCE CO.,
    John S. Rice, Pres., Samuel E. Elmore, Sec., Office 289
    Main St. See adv. index.
City Fire Insurance Co., Central Row.
Hartford Live Stock Insurance Co., 258 Main St.
HARTFORD STEAM BOILER INSPECTION AND INSUR-
ANCE CO.
    E. C. Roberts, Pres., H. H. Hayden, Sec., Office Hunger-
    ford & Cone's Block, Main St.
Hartford Fire Insurance Co., 295 Main St.
Hartford Life and Accident Insurance Co., 19 Pearl St.
HARTFORD COUNTY MUTUAL FIRE INSURANCE CO.,
Office 321 Main St. See adv. index.
    Merchants' Insurance Company, cor. Asylum and Trumbull Sts.
New England Fire Insurance Co., 258 Main St.
North American Fire Insurance Co., cor. Asylum and Trum-
bull Sts.
PHŒNIX MUTUAL LIFE INSURANCE CO.
    Edson Fessenden, Pres., Jas. F. Burns, Sec., Office 281
    Main St. See adv. index.
PHŒNIX INSURANCE CO.
    Henry Kellogg, Pres., W. B. Clark, Sec., Office 333 Main St.

PUTNAM FIRE INSURANCE CO.
Samuel Woodruff, Pres., Daniel Buck, Sec., Office 240 Main
St. See adv. index.
RAILWAY PASSENGER ASSURANCE CO.
Jas. G. Batterson, Pres., H. T. Sperry, Sec., Office 289
Main St., cor. Pearl. See adv. inside front cover.
TRAVELLERS INSURANCE CO.
Jas. G. Batterson, Pres., Rodney Dennis, Sec., Office 182
Asylum St. See adv. front cover.

Intelligence Offices.

Fallon, B. K. 10 American Row.
Hall, T. E. 161 Main St.
Rose, Abraham, 89 Asylum St.

Iron Castings.

Phœnix Iron Works, Geo. S. Lincoln & Co., 54—60 Arch St.
See adv. index.

Iron Founders.

Converse, C. A. & Co., 120 Grove St.
LINCOLN, GEO. S. & CO., 54, 60 Arch St. See adv. index.
Woodruff & Beach Iron Works, 73, 81, 60, 90 Commerce St.

Iron Railings, Fences, &c.

PHŒNIX IRON WORKS, Geo. S. Lincoln & Co., 54, 60
Arch St. See adv. index.

Iron and Steel, Wholesale and Retail.

Clark, Ezra & Co., 104 Front St.
BLODGETT, R. F. & CO., 140 State St.

18

Seymour, Charles & Co., 361 Main St.

Jewelry Dealers.

(See Watches and Jewelry.)

Junk and Paper Stock.

Callender, R. H. C. & Co., 64 Morgan St.
CARROLL, E. J. & CO., 243 State St. See adv. index.
Herlitschek, M. 68 Morgan St.

Knit Goods Manufacturers.

Glastenbury Knitting Company, 16 Ford St.
Henry R. Snath, Treasurer.

Lawyers.

(See Attorneys at Law.)

Lager Beer Brewers.

Frink, Angebrant, 110 Albany Av.
Koenig, David, 100 Commerce St.

Lager Beer Saloons.

Ahern, Matthew, 135 Main St.
Bauman, Chas. 64 Front St.
Bubser, Fidel, 17, 19 Mulberry St.
Ellenberger, F. W. 187 State St.
Fischer, John, 54 Temple St.
Harper, John, 25 Mulberry St.
Heublin, Andrew, 36   "
HEROLD, CHARLES, 60 Temple St.
Hayes, John, 26 Mulberry St.
Lutz, Jacob, 80 Front St.
Lippoldt, Augustus, 27 Mulberry St.
NEACY, MICHAEL, 70 Front St.
Kraus, B. 135   "
Link, Paul, 163   "
Merz, F. R. 26 Kingsley St.
Moehler, F. 159 Front St.

Meinerzhagan, Theodore, 66 Temple St.
Roske, Frederick, 41 Mulberry St.
Rosenbaum, Edward, 92 Front St.   Boarding House.
Roehrer, Charles, 174 Front St.
SIEMER, ERNEST, 66 Trumbull St.   See adv. index.
SIEMER, ERNEST, 52 Temple St.
Scoble, Wm. 15 Mulberry St.
Winter, C. 183 Front St.
Zelenka, Matheas, 118 Front St.

Leather Belting.
Jewell, P. & Sons, cor. Trumbull and Hicks Sts.
Palmer, N. & Co., 132 Asylum St.

Leather Manufacturers.
Jewell, P. & Sons, cor. Trumbull and Hicks Sts.

Leather Dealers.
Jewell, P. & Sons, cor. Trumbull and Hicks Sts.
Hunt, Holbrook & Barber, 130, 132 Asylum St.
Hills, I. & Son, cor. State and Front Sts.
Palmer, N. & Co., 132 Asylum St.
Wiley, Sylvester, 47   "

Leaf Tobacco.
BROWN & OATMAN, 212 State St.   See adv. index.
Pease, H. & Z. K. 222, 224   "

Lime and Cement.
Coburn, Charles, 171 State St.
KELLOGG, RODNEY, 201, 205 Commerce St.   See adv. index.
Sackett, E. 234 State St.

Line and Twine Manufacturer.
CHURCH, ABNER, 46 Morgan St.   See adv. index.

Lithographers.

Bingham & Dodd, 41 Trumbull St.
KELLOGG & BULKELEY, 245 Main St.   See adv. index.

Liquor Dealers, Wholesale.

SEE WINES AND LIQUORS.

Banman, Charles, 64 Front St.
CARSON, JAMES, Pearl St.
Fuller & Co., 220 State St.
ISHAM, A. B. cor. Commerce and Ferry Sts.   See adv. index.
Kane, Henry P. 71 Potter St.
Seymour, S. H. 216 State St.

Livery Stables.

Bailey, Harrison, 15 Kingsley St.
Burnham, Frank W. rear 185 Main St.
Cummings, F. B. rear 161 Main St.
Cosgrove, John, rear 575   "
CRITTENDEN, R. 104   "
Clapp, A. E. 13 Gold St.
Converse, L. 12 American Row.
Dean, Dow, rear 598 Main St.
DeWolf, H. P. 617   "
Fay, W. P. 48½ Asylum St.
Gaines, Albert, rear 171 State St.
Hills & Wheaton, rear Hills' Block, 339 Main St.
Ryder, S. N. rear 610 Main St.
Litchfield, M. 540   "
Sharpe, J. H. 629   "
Taft, Dan'l R. 485 Main St.
Spencer, Wm. 50 State St.

Loom Harness.

ELWELL, SHERMAN, 222 Main St.

Loan Office.

BELDEN, F. H. 254 Main St.   See adv. index.

Looking Glass and Picture Frame Manufacturers.

Deming, E. M. 205 Main St.
Glazier, Isaac, 276 "
WITTER, A. G. 517 " See adv. index.

Lumber Dealers.

Burgess & Co., Dutch Point.
Isham & Young, 20 Morgan St.
Chase & Co., Grove Works, Potter St.
MARSTON, C. T. & CO., 54 Morgan St.
Sanders & Bartholomew, Sheldon, cor. Commerce St.
Smyth, Isaac, F. 47 Sheldon St.
Taylor, E. cor. Sheldon and Commerce Sts.
White, W. S. rear 13 Albany Avenue.

Machinery Manufacturers.

Bynton, J. W. 148 State St. (Agency.)
Blair, H. P. 176 Asylum St. (Agency.)
BULLARD & PARSONS, 23, 25 Potter St. See adv. index.
Hoxie & Tolles, 11 Hicks St.
LINCOLN, GEO. S. 54, 60 Arch St. See adv. index.
Hunter & Sanford, 109 Commerce St.
WOODRUFF & BEACH, 98 "
BENHAM, NATHAN, rear 260 Main St. See adv. index.
Pratt, Whitney & Co., Foot Flower St.
PITKIN BROS. & CO., 152 State St.
CUSHMAN, DWIGHT, 21 Potter St. See adv. index.
CUSHMAN, A. F. 176, 178 Asylum St.

Machinists.

BENHAM, NATHAN, rear 262 Main St. See adv. index.
BULLARD & PARSONS, 23, 25 Potter St. See adv. index.
CUSHMAN, DWIGHT, 21 Potter St. See adv. index.
CUSHMAN, A. F. 178 Asylum St.
Hoxie & Tolles, 11 Hicks St.
PHŒNIX IRON WORKS, Geo. S. Lincoln & Co., 54, 60
Arch St. See adv. index.
Pratt, Whitney & Co., Foot Flower St.

Pitkin Bros. & Co., 152 State St.
Hunter & Sanford, 109 Commerce St.
WOODRUFF & BEACH, 98   "

Machinists' Tools.

BENHAM, NATHAN, rear 262 Main St. See adv. index.
BULLARD & PARSONS, 23, 25 Potter St. See adv. index.
Cushman, A. F. 176 Asylum St.
PHŒNIX IRON WORKS, Geo. S. Lincoln & Co. 54, 60
Arch St. See adv. index.
Pratt, Whitney & Co., Foot Flower St.
Hunter & Sanford, 109 Commerce St.
WOODRUFF & BEACH, 98   "

Machinery Agents.

Blair, H. P. 176 Asylum St.
Boynton, J. W. 148 State St.

Manufacturing Companies.

Cheney Bros. Silk Manufacturing Co., (silk) 34 Morgan St.
Coburn Soap & Washing Fluid Manufacturing Co., (Soap and
Washing Fluid.) See adv. index.
Colt's Patent Fire Arms Manufacturing Co., (Fire Arms,) Colts
Dyke.
Colt's Willow Ware Manufacturing Co., (Willow Ware) Wa-
warme Avenue.
American Silver Steel Co., office Hungerford & Cone's Block.
Collins Company, (Axes,) 2 Central Row.
Connecticut Peat Company, 15 Pearl St. (Peat.)
Glastenbury Knitting Co., 16 Ford St.
Hartford Eyelet Co., (Eyelets,) 148 State St.
Hartford Carpet Co., (Carpets,) 2 Market St.
Hartford Brick Manufacturing Co., (Brick,) 17 Pearl St.
Hartford Carver Pump Co., (Pumps,) 2 Central Row.
Hartford Sorghum & Machine Co., 148 State St.
Sharps' Rifle Manufacturing Co., ,(Fire Arms,) 11 Central Row.
New England Pump Co., 497 Main St.
MASON COUNTY MINING & MANUFACTURING CO., 2
Central Row.

Syracuse Coal & Salt Co., (Salt,) 347 Main St.
Union Manufacturing Co., (Cotton Goods,) 55 Asylum St.
WEED SEWING MACHINE CO., (Sewing Machines,) 240
Main St. See adv. index.
Willimantic Linen Co., (Thread,) 2 Central Row.
Woodruff & Beach Iron Works, (Steam Engines,) 98 Com-
merce St.

Marble Yards.

Adams, Thomas, cor. Temple and Market Sts.
Atkinson, John, 78 Albany Avenue.
BATTERSON, J. G. 650 Main St. See adv. index.
Batterson, S. S. & G. T. 796 North Main St.
Johnson, Fred A. 1 Talcott St.
McGowan, Wm. cor. Avon and Windsor Avenue.

Machinist and General Jobbing.

CUSHMAN, DWIGHT, 21 Potter St. See adv. index.

Machinists' and Tool Makers.

BULLARD & PARSONS, 23, 25 Potter St. See adv. index.
Hoxie & Tolles, 11 Hicks St.
LINCOLN, GEO. S. & CO., 54, 60 Arch St. See adv. index.
Pratt, Whitney & Co., Flower St.

Machinists' Tools.

BULLARD & PARSONS, 23, 25 Potter St. See adv. index.
LINCOLN, GEO. S. & CO., 54, 60 Arch St. See adv. index.

Meat Markets.

Altman, E. City Hall Market.
Bushnell & Kingsley, Arsenal Meat Market, 822 North Main
Street.
Barnett & Clark, 134 Asylum St.
Bacon, Henry, 569 Main St.
Brown, Geo. T. 287 Front St.
Cornish, George W. 53 Ferry St.
Caswell & Bronson, 100 Main St.
Dawson, J. 640   "

Downs, A. B. 18 Church St.
Filley, C. T. & A. D. 535 Main St.
FRANKLIN MARKET, H. W. & C. C. STETSON, Dealsrs
in Fresh and Salt Meats, Vegetables and Poultry, 142 Main St.
Gage & Williamson, 705 Main St.
Hall Bros., City Hall Market.
Kingsley, Frederick, 150 Main St.
Kelley, John, 146 Front St.
Olmsted, H. B. 102 Main St.
Peckham Bros., 125 Asylum St.
Spencer, A. 73, 75 Albany Avenue.
SEYMOUR & MILLARD, 142 Main St.
STEVENS, J. N. B. 34, 38 Market St.   See adv. index.
Smead, Geo. 514 Main St.
SISSON & ABBE, 134 "
Tennant, A. City Hall Market.
Waters, Horace, "   "
Wooster & Co., 133 Main St.

Merchant Tailors and Clothing Dealers.

Apgar & Wentworth, 85 Asylum St.
Anderson & Porter, 3 American Row.
Beardslee, B. 81 Asylum St.
Benning, F. 36 State St.
Bowers, C. A. 50 Asylum St.
Brown A. P. 613 Main St.
Chapman, Sam'l E. 94 Morgan St.
Conklin, Skillman & Co., 264, 270 Main St.
Darrow, Thomas 497 Main St.
Drake & Tuller, 64 State St.
Frasick, A. 2 American Row.
Freeman, S. 42 Asylum St.
Green, P. S. 10   "
Hollander, A. 430 Main St.
Legate & Fisher, 68 State St.
Larkum, G. B. 311 Main St.
Pettibone, H. C. & F. E. 384 Main St.
Pfeild & A. Schleicher, 12 Mulberry St.
SANDERS, P. H. B. 254½ Main St.

Schulze, H. 253 Main St.
Speil & Schleicher, 12 Mulberry St.
Smith & Whittemore, 88 Asylum St.
Stevens, Geo. L. 18 State St.
Torke, Wm. G. 166 Front St.
Vix, M. 384 Main St.
Whittlesey, W. F. & Co., 20 Asylum St.

Metal and Paper Dealers.

Carroll, E. J. & Co., 243 State St.
Callender, L. 173 Commerce St.
Herlitzschek, M. Morgan St.

Millinery, Wholesale.

Case & Prentice, 333 Main St.
Pratt & Todd, 395   "
WATERS, HORACE, Jr., 384 Main St. See adv. index.
WALLACH & SCHWAB, 449, 451 Main St. See adv. index.

Millinery and Straw Goods, Wholesale.

WATERS, HORACE, Jr. 384 Main St.

Millinery and Fancy Goods.

Bacharach, Wm. 469 Main St.
Ballerstein, Raphael, 398 Main St.
Crane, E. S. 475   "
Cornish & Kellogg, Misses, 594 Main St.
Daniels, A. M. Mrs. 422   "
Dibble, Carrie Miss, 154   "
Duffy, C. Miss, 163   "
Fuller, M. Mrs. cor. Trumbull and Chapel Sts.
Hunt, E. S. Miss, 408 Main St.
Hunter, M. J. Mrs. 271   "
Henchey, C. Mrs. 5 Pratt St.
Hinckley, N. G. 423 Main St.
Jennings, Ellen E. 9 Pratt St.
Livy, Bernard, 379 Main St.
MAYER, LOUIS, 427   "

19

McFarland & Co., 458 Main St.
Owen, G. Mrs. 377   "
Payne, Hattie E. 10 Church St.
Perkins, J. B. 372 Main St.
Phelps, Sarah S. Mrs. 473 Main St.
Pratt & Todd, 395 Main St.
Richardson, J. E. Mrs. 371 Main St.
Vinton, P. S. 368   "
WALLACH & SCHWAB, 449, 451 Main St. See adv. index.
West, P. Mrs. 173 Main St.
Wilson, J. J. 390   "
Woodmancy, Mrs. 374 "

Mining Company, Coal and Salt.

MASON COUNTY MINING & MANUFACTURING CO.,
SAM'L COIT, Prest., F. L. GLEASON, Treas., office 274 Main
Street.

Music.

GROSVENOR & LEONARD (QUADRILLE BAND,) 45 Pearl
and 11 Asylum Sts. See adv. index.

Musical Instruments.

Barker, L. & Co., 287 Main St.   Pianos, Organs and Music.
Babcock, W. J. 281   "   Pianos, Melodeons and Music.
FARRIS, JOHN, 197, 201 "   See adv. index.
Haven & Co., 11 Asylum St.

Money Brokers, See Brokers.

Buel, Rob't, 333 Main St.
Bissell, Geo. P.   "
BELDEN, THOS. H. 254 Main St. See adv. index.
Williams, J. D. 2 Central Row.

Monuments, Grave Stones, Fonts, Tablets, &c.

Batterson, Jas. G. 650 Main St. See adv. index.

Nails. See also Iron, Steel, and Hardware Dealers.

BLODGETT, R. F. & CO., 140 State St.   See adv. index.
Clark, Ezra & Co., 104 Front.
Way, Geo. M. & Co., 344 Main St.
Francis & Co., 343   "
Seymour, Chas. L. 361   "

Newspapers.

Christian Secretary, 338 Main St.
   E. Cushman, Editor and Publisher.   .
Connecticut Churchman, 97 Asylum St.
HARTFORD COURANT, (Daily and Weekly.)
HAWLEY, GOODRICH & CO., 14 Pratt St.   See adv. index.
HARTFORD EVENING PRESS, (Daily and Weekly.)
HAWLEY, GOODRICH & CO., 14 Pratt St.   See adv. index.
CONNECTICUT COURANT, (Weekly.)
   Hawley, Goodrich & Co., 14 Pratt St.   See adv. index.
HARTFORD MORNING POST, (Daily and Weekly,) 222
Main St.
   Geo. S. Hubbard, Publisher, Bernard Peters, Editor.   See
adv. index.   .
Hartford Times, (Daily and Weekly.)
   Burr Brothers, 254 Main St.
Religious Herald, 338   "
   D. B. Moseley, Publisher.

Newspapers and Periodicals.

Hall, T. E. 161 Main St.
Geer & Pond, 256   "
Rose, Abraham, 89 Asylum St.

Notaries Public.

SEE ATTORNEYS AT LAW.

Adams, S. W. 274 Main St.
HEMPSTED, CHARLES Y. 289 Main St,
Tucker, J. D. 274   "

Nurserymen, Seedsmen and Florists.

Affleck, George, 282 Asylum St.
CITY GARDEN, P. D. WHITMORE, Pro. 113 Wethersfield
Avenue, near H. & W. H. R. R. Depot. See adv. index.

Opticians.

Lazarus & Morris, 17 Hungerford & Cone's Block.
Burt, J. O. 321 Main St.

Oil Dealers.

WILLIAMS, GEO. W. & CO., cor. State and Front Sts. See
adv. index.
Sisson & Butler, 259 Main St.
Talcott Bros. 354 "

Oyster Dealers, Wholesale and Retail.

Goodsell, E. P. & Co., 119 State St.
Lewis, W. H. Asylum St.
Thomas, A. & Co., 30 State St.
Quintard, H. H. 152 Main St.

Packing Box Manufacturers.

Fitch & Hunt, Potter St.
Robertson, W. H. & L. H. Potter St.

Paints, Oils and Glass.

Burnham, George, 22 Central Row.
Sisson & Butler, 259 Main St.
Thompson & Hussey, 12 Central Row.
WILLIAMS, GEO. W. & CO., cor. State and Front Sts. See
adv. index.
Wright, Wm. L. & Son, 195 Main St.

Painters, House and Sign.

Cheney, C. H. 5 Sheldon St.
Enrigh, T. H. 274 Main St.
Hitchcock Brothers, 8 Pearl St.
Rice, F. F. 8 American Row.

Thompson & Hussey, 12 Central Row.
Wright, Wm. L. & Son, 195 Main St.

Paintings, Engravings and Chromos.

DART, E. & CO., 219 Main St. See adv. index.
Wheeler, W. R. 297   "   Portrait and Landscape.

Painters and Glaziers.

Bradley, William H. 522 Main St.
Martin, Chas. T. & Co., 638 "

Paper Box Manufacturers.

TUCKER, E. & SON, 139 Trumbull St. Sec adv. index.
KING, V. A. 66 State St. See adv. index.

Paper Bag Dealers.

TUCKER, E. & SON, 139 Trumbull St. See adv. index.
KING, V. A. 66 State St. See adv. index.

Paper Collars, Wholesale.

DAY, A. F. & C. G. & CO., 54, 56 Asylum St. See adv. index.
Griffin, C. A. & Co., 69, 71 Asylum St.

Paper Dealers.

CASE, LOCKWOOD & CO., cor. Pearl and Trumbull Sts. See adv. index.
Prescott, Plimpton & Co., 178 Asylum St.
CARROLL, E. J. 245 State St. See adv. index.
White, C. & Co., 134 1-2 Asylum St.

Paper and Paper Stock Dealers.

Callender, R. H. C. & Co., 64 Morgan St.
CARROLL, E. J. & CO., 243 State St. See adv. index.
McCrone, Wm. 90, 92 Morgan St.
PITKIN & BARTLETT, 160 Commerce St. See adv. index.
Herlitzschek, M. 68 Morgan St.
White, C. & Co., 134 1-2 Asylum St.

Patent Agent.

BLISS, JEREMY, W. (American and Foreign,) 240 Main St. See adv. index.

Patent Medicines.

(See Apothecaries.)

Braddock, John, 589 Main St.
Butler, J. V. B. 143 Trumbull St.
Lambe, J. J. 151 Main St.
MOSES, S. G. & CO., 587, 605 Main St.
McNary & Co., 246   "
Sisson & Butler,   "
Talcott Brothers,   "
Williams, Geo. W. & Co., cor. State and Front Sts.
Rathbun, J. G. 72, 74 Asylum St.

Patent Cement Roofing.

Holden, Burnham & Co., 8 Green St.

Patent Lamp and Gas Shades.

Emerson, C. W. rear 262 Main St.

Patent Right Dealer.

HAWXHURST, G. W. 497 Main St. (Patent Hoe and Bow Pin.) See adv. index.

Pattern Models.

PRATT & DRUMMOND, 22, 24 Mulberry St. See adv. index.

Peat.

Connecticut Peat Co., 248 Main St.

Piano Forte Dealers.

Babcock, W. J. 181 Main St.
Barker, L. & Co., 287 "
FARRIS, JOHN, 197, 201 Main St. See adv. index.
Wander, Wm. 313   "

Piano Forte Repairer.

Most, J. H. 130 Main St.

Photograph Album Manufacturers.

CASE, LOCKWOOD & CO., cor. Pearl and Trumbull Sts. See adv. index.

PARSONS, CHAS. 338 Main St.

Physicians and Surgeons.

Barrows, A. W.   Main St.
Beresford, S. B. 198 Asylum St.
Crabtre, A. D. 371 Main St.
Cottell, E. J. 554   "
Cutter, E. R. 266   "
Colley, C. E. 371   "
Ellsworth, P. W. 24 Pearl St.   ·
Fuller, H. 36 1-2 Church St.
Green, George S. 268 Main St.
Jarvis, G. C. 265   "
Hastings, P. M. 186   "
Lyon, J. L. 254   "
Lyon, Irving W. 78   "
Merrill, A. E. 607   "
NORTON, DANIEL, 254 "   See adv. index.
O'Flaherty, John, 147   "
Stearns, H. P. 196   "
Stephenson, A. L. W. 265 "
Storrs, M. 44 Church St.
Sperry, I. J. 12 Grove St.
Tremaine, W. H. 431 Main St.
Taft, C. A. 311   "
Wilcox, L. S. 552   "
Wayer, N. 268   "
Waite, Mrs. 140 Trumbull St.   Clairvoyant.

Picture Frame Manufacturers and Dealers.

Deming, E. M. 205 Main St.
DART, E. & CO., 219 "   See adv. index.

FARRIS, JOHN, 197, 201 Main St.　See adv. index.
Glazier, Isaac, 276　　　　"
PRATT & DRUMMOND, 22, 24 Mulberry St. See adv. index.
WITTER, A. G. 517 Main St.　See adv. index.

Photographers.

BLISS, J. W. 240 Main St.　See adv. index.
Camp, D. S. 69 Asylum St.
De Lamater, R. S. 258 Main St.
Kellogg, E. P. 279　　　"
OLDERSHAW, J. 311　　"　　See adv. index.
Prescott & White, 368　　"
Waite, S. H. 275　　　　"
Webster & Popkins, 297　"

Planing and Sawing.

BURGESS & CO., Dutch Point.
Chase & Co., Potter St.
Taylor, E. & Co., Sheldon St.
Moody, L. B. & Co., 42, 44, 46 Market St.

Plasterers.

Bissell, H. & S. 17 Pearl St.

Porcelain Pictures.

(See Photographers.)

Plate (Copper) Printers.

NEVERS, R. 41 Trumbull St.　See adv. index.
Willard, A. 150 Asylum St.

Post Office.

E. S. Cleveland, Postmaster, 254 Main St.

Plumbers and Gas Fitters.

Abbot, John C. 272 Main St.
Birch, Thomas & Co., 508 Main St.
Jones, Thos. S. 87 Asylum St.

Lawler, Edward, 151 1-2 Main St.
Robinson, Geo. 96 Asylum St.
Smith, Pratt & White, 16 Ford St.
Vail, J. R. & Son, 10 American Row.
Wilson, Nelson, 184 State St.

Pork Packers.

Moore & Johnson, 223 State St.

Poultry Dealers.

Bill & Bronson, 100 Main St.
Stetson, H. W. & C. C. 142 Main St.

Printers.

(See Book and Job Printers.)

Provision Dealers, Wholesale.

Chamberlain, S. S. 179 State St.
Fowler, Davis & Hoyt,   "
Moore & Johnson, 222   "

Pumping Engine Manufacturers.

Woodruff & Beach, 98 Commerce St.

Pump Manufacturers.

Carver Pump Co., T. Sheldon, Pres., H. H. Bartlett, Sec., 2 Central Row.
New England Pump Co., 497 Main St.

Publishers.

(See Book Publishers.)

Railway Supplies.

Howard, J. L. & Co., 176, 178 Asylum St.

Real Estate Agents.

Alden, William C. & Co., 271 Main St.
Brainard, J. H. 274   "
20

Buck, R. E. 18 Asylum St.
Clark, James W. 2 Central Row.
Dimock, J. W. 270 Main St.
Harris, N. 289   "
Hosmer, Luther & Sons, 241 Main St.
Lincoln, C. A. 265   "
Marven, Joseph, 2 State St.
Meek, J. S. 265 Main St.

Red Aberdeen Granite, Dealer and Worker.

BATTERSON, JAS. G. 650 Main St. See adv. index.

Restaurants.

Continental, 9 American Row.
Green, E. R. 35 Asylum St.
Phelps, O. 105 State St.
Pomeroy, J. 28 Asylum St.
POLLARD, CHAS. H. The Senate, 158 Main St.
LEONARD, HENRY O. 45 Pearl St.
Washburn, Geo. C. 255 State St.

Rifle Manufacturers.

Colt's Patent Fire Arms Manufacturing Co., Colt's Dyke.
Sharps' Rifle Co., 2 Central Row.

Rope and Twine Manufacturers.

CHURCH, ABNER, Agent 46 Morgan St. See adv. index.

Saddlery and Hardware, Wholesale.

Corning & Bros. 62 Asylum St.
Smith, Bourn & Co., 142, 144, 146 Asylum St.

Saloons.

SEE LAGER BEER SALOONS.

Salt Dealers, Wholesale.

Lyman, N. 260 State St.

Savings Banks.

Mechanics' Savings Bank, 13 Central Rowt
Society for Savings, 11 Pratt St.
State Savings Bank, 19 Pearl St.

Second Hand Clothing.

Getz, Jacob, 198 State St.
Solomon, A. 184   "
Kapper, Myer, 107 Front St.
Knoek, J. L. 161 State St.
Meikel, S. 187 .   "

Screw Machinery Manufacturers.

Pratt, Whitney & Co., Flower St.

Scroll, Sawing and Carving,

PRULL & DRUMMOND, 22, 24 Mulberry St.   See adv.
index.

Second Hand Furniture.

TOOHY, WM. 506 Main St. See adv. index.
Avery, E. 169 Main St.

Self Oiling Journal Boxes.

Bullard & Parsons, 23, 25 Potter St.

Sewing Machine Manufacturers.

Weed Sewing Machine Co., 240 Main St.   See adv. back
cover.

Sewing Machine Agents.

Griffin, C. A. & Co., 69, 71 Asylum St.
King, V. A. 66 State St.   See adv. index.
Miller & Haynes, 388 Main St.   Grover & Baker.
Perkins, J. B. 372 Main St.   Wilcox & Gibbs.
SHAFFER, C. (Singer's,) 82 Asylum St.   See adv. index.
Welch, H. L. 83 Asylum St., opposite Allyn House.

Screw Manufacturers.

National Screw Co., 59 Pearl St.

Scroll, Sawing and Turning.

PRALL & DRUMMOND, 22, 24 Mulberry St.   See adv. index.

Shirt and Collar Manufacturers.

Griffin, C. A. & Co., 69, 71 Asylum St.
Parker, E. A. 61 Asylum St.
Smith, A. M. & S. 7   "

Shipping and Commission Merchants.

CHAPIN & BURR, 75, 77 Ferry St.

Ship Builders.

Belden, S. & E. S. (Dutch Point.)

Ship Smith.

Leland, Henry, (Dutch Point.)

Sign, Card and Decorative Painters.

Enright, T. H. 2 Central Row.
Lincoln, W. D. 7   "
Rice, F. F. 8   "

Silver and Plated Ware Manufacturers and Dealers.

Ewins & Son, 221 Main St.
PITKIN, W. L. & H. E. 17 Hicks St.   See adv. index.
The Wm. Rogers Manufacturing Co., cor. Front and Grove
Streets.

Silk Manufacturers.

CHENEY BROS. 34 Morgan St.   See adv. index.

Soda Water Manufacturer and Bottler.

Etherington, James, 16, 18 Sheldon St.

Soap and Candle Manufacturers.

Benton, C. 82 Morgan St.
Coburn Soap and Washing Fluid Manufacturing Co., Colt's Dyke.
Gridley & Frisbie, 79 Talcott St.

Silk and Worsted Braid Manufacturers.

Kohn, T. 30, 36 Market St.

Spectacle Manufacturers.

Burt, John, 321 Main St.
Hibbard & Daniels, rear 262 Main St.

Stair Builder.

May, Chas. B. rear 30 Market.

Steam Engine Builders.

Benham, Nathan, rear 262 Main St.
Pitkin Brothers & Co., 132 State St.
Hunter & Sanford, Commerce St.
WOODRUFF & BEACH, 98 Commerce St.

Steam Heating Apparatus Manufacturer.

Blair, H. P. 176 Asylum St.

Steel Manufacturers.

AMERICAN SILVER STEEL CO., Office 274 Main St.
Sam'l Coit, Pres., F. L. Gleason, Treas.

Steam Saw Mills.

Burgess & Co., Dutch Point.
Taylor & Co., Sheldon St.

Stencil Plate Cutter.

Rice, F. F. 8 Central Row.

Stereotyper.

(See Electrotypers.)

Hobbs, R. H. 148 Asylum St.

Stone Cutters.

BRABAZON, A. & S. 77 Potter St.   See adv. index.

Stone Dealers.

Belden, Seth & Son, Commerce St.
Chaffee, J. H. cor. Charter Oak and Vandyke Avs.
BRABAZON, A. & S. 77 Potter St.   See adv. index.

Stoves and Tinware.

Allen & Willard, 164, 166 State St.
Brooks, David S. & Sons, 438 Main St.
Bronson, W. S. & Co., 64 Asylum St.
CHILD & BULL, 189 Main St.   See adv. index.
Kelsey, Henry P. 538   "
Kelsey, O. S. 524   "
Kenney, Francis, 6 Elm St.
Low, F. A. 106 Main St.
PHILLIPS, WM. J. 220 Main St.   See adv. index.
Roberts, Thomas, 9, 11 Kingsley St.

Stucco Ornamenting Cornices, &c.

BISSELL, H. & S. 17 Pearl St.   See adv. index.

Stove Manufacturers, Gas, Cook and Heating.

CHILD & BULL, 189 Main St.   See adv. index.

Stone Ware Manufactory.

Seymour Brothers, 50 Front St.

Straw and Millinery Goods, Wholesale.

Case & Prentice, 333 Main St.
WATERS, HORACE Jr. 384 Main St.   See adv. index.
Pratt & Todd, 395   "

Suspender Manufactory.

HARTFORD SUSPENDER MANUFACTORY, 144 Main St.
W. Johnson, Agent. See adv. index.

Tailors.

(See Merchant Tailors.)

Tailor's Trimmings.

DAY, A. F. & C. G. & CO., 54, 56 Asylum St.   See adv. index.

Tea Dealers.

Dugan & Quinn, American Tea Co., 19 Asylum St.
Fox, Woodford & Co., Central Row.
GILLETT, A. B. & CO., 43, 45 Asylum St.   See adv. index.
HEBARD, STURTEVANT & CO., 260 State St.   See adv. index.
PARK FELLOWS & CO., 203 State St.   See adv. index.

Thread Manufacturers.

Hartford Thread Co., Tomlinson & Holcomb, rear 262 Main St.

Telegraph Companies.

American Telegraph Co., 291 Main St.
Franklin Telegraph Office, 280 Main St.

Tin Plate and Metals.

Brainard, Charles H. 191 Main St.

Tobacconists.

Brown J. T. 6 American Row.
Block, Daniel, 208 Front St.
Goodrich, J. B. 479 Main St.
Haas Brothers, 282   "

Tobacco Dealers, Wholesale.

ADAMS, C. H. & CO., 137 State St.
BROWN & OATMAN, 212   "   See adv. index.

BURNHAM, J. D. & CO., 75, 77 Asylum St. See adv. index.
Gerry, Geo. E. & Co., 140 State St.
HEBARD, STURTEVANT & CO.   See adv. index.
King, Z. P. 92 Asylum St.
King, D. W. 154 State St.
Lee & Deane, 150   "
Seymour, D. M. 159, 161 Commerce St.
Woodruff, J. S. 233 State St.

Trunks, Valises and Bags.

CORNWELL, R. B. 434 Main St.   See adv. index.
Bullard, J. D. & Co.,   Asylum St.
Fuller, G. W. 57   "

Trunk Manufacturers.

Bullard, J. D. 90 Asylum St.
CORNWELL, R. B. 434 Main St.   See adv. index.

Toy Manufactory.

American Instructive Toy Company.
Goodhue, Douglass & Co., 42 Market St.

Twine, Wicks, Batts, &c.

DAY BROTHERS, 208 State St.   See adv. index.

Turbine Water Wheels.

CUSHMAN, DWIGHT, (Patent,) 21 Potter St.   See adv. index.

Undertakers.

Glafcke & Cooke, 12 Pratt St.
Hills & Knight, 2 Talcott St.   Upholsterers.
Ralph Foster & M. T. Russell, 602 Main St.
WOOLLEY, G. W. & W. P. 175   "

Variety Stores.

Burr, Edward, 465 Main St.
Cook, D. P, 128 State St.
Downie, A. 70   "

Peckham, Nathan, 16 State St.
Hart, Henry H. 491 Main St.
Humphrey, Philip, 563 "
Pond Brothers, 575 "
Wood, J. W. & Co., 88 "

Vegetable Dealer.

STEVENS, J. N. B. 34, 38 Market St.   See adv. index.

Veterinary Surgeons.

Bassett, A. rear 185 Main St.
Blumenthal, A. 40 Market St.

Vinegar Manufactory.

Herrman, J. 26 1-2 Sheldon St.

Watches and Jewelry, Manufacturers and Dealers.

Beeman, W. M. 6 State St.
Brace, Henry M. 10 Asylum St.
Buell, D. H. & Co., 323 Main St.
Cadden, A. 190 State St.
Deming & Gundlach, 20 State St.
Gerwich, H. 36   "
Griswold, J. G. 25 Asylum St.
Goodsell, Willis J. 293 Main St.
Hatfield, John, 219   "
Hubbard, C. K. 80 Asylum St.
King, Geo. W. 14 State St.
Mason, J. 8   "
Mahler, J. 84 Asylum St.
Mayer, David, 402 Main St.
Schall, Jacob, 207   "
Stevens & Rogers, 284 "
STEELE, THOMAS & SON, 340 Main St.   See adv. index.
WALTER, M. F. 447 Main St.   See adv. index.
Warner, Joseph, 8 State St.
Welles, L. T. & Co., 4 State St.
Woodford, E. A. 197 Main St.
21

Water.
Water Commissioners' Office, 10 Pearl St.

Water Wheel Manufacturer. '
CUSHMAN, DWIGHT, 21 Potter St.   See adv. index.

Wheelbarrow Manufacturer.
Butler, Samuel A. 12 Hicks St.

Wheel Stock Manufacturer.
EVARTS, Geo. S. 39 Albany Av.   See adv. index.

Willow Ware Manufacturers.
Colt's Willow Ware Manufacturing Co., Wawarme Av.

Wines and Liquors, Wholesale.
Baker, Wm. 130 Front St.
. CARSON, JAMES, 25 Pearl St.
ISHAM, A. B. cor. Ferry and Commerce Sts.
Kupper & O'Callaghan, 225, 227 State St.
Needham, M. C. 198 Front St.
SIEMER, ERNEST, 66 Trumbull St.
Silling, S. & Son, 194, 244 State St.
Wells, N. G. 59 Asylum St.

Wire Heddle Manufacturer.
ELWELL, S. 222 Main St.

Wood Engravers.
Clark, S. H. 221 Main St.
Curtis, H. C.   "

Wooden Ware.
Cobun, Chas. 171 State St.
Sackett, E. 62, 64, 66 Ferry St.

Woolen Goods, Wholesale.
Day, A. F. & C. G. & Co., 54, 56 Asylum St.

Wool Dealers.

Crosby, James B. 21 Arch St.
Ives, Blanchard & Co., 215 State St.
Judd, J. F. & Co., 231   "
Kellogg, E. N. & Co., 235, 237   "
Kingsbury, N. & Co., 148   "

Woolen Manufacturers.

CROSBY, E. & SON, 271 Main St.   Mills in Glastonbury.
Kingsbury, N. & Co., 148 State St.
Laprise, N. & Co., 271 Main St.

Wood Yards.

Crane, C. G. 75 Talcott St.
Gillette, G. F. 104 Sheldon St.
Steen, W. J. & A. 104 Pearl St.

Yankee Notions, Wholesale.

Clark, H. W. & Co., 48 Asylum St.
DAY, A. F. & C. G. 54, 56 Asylum St.   See adv. index.
Weatherby, Knous & Pelton, 335, 337 Main St.

JOHN FARRIS,

Dealer in

MUSIC AND PICTURES,

197 and 201 Main Street,

(Opposite the Athenaeum.)

HARTFORD, CONN.

PIANOS, MELODEONS AND CABINET ORGANS,

for sale and to rent on monthly and quarterly payments. Sheet Music and Music Books, Piano Stools and Covers, Violin and Guitar Strings, all kinds of Musical Instruments and Merchandise.

ALSO,

Paintings, Chromos, Engravings, Rustic Frames, Brackets, Easels, Artists' Materials, &c.

MIRRORS IN EVERY VARIETY OF STYLE.

Picture Frames made to order.

JAMES M. GREENLEAF,

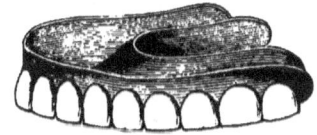

DENTIST,

No. 2 State St.,   Hartford, Conn.

A. & S. BRABAZON,

STONE-CUTTERS,

No. 77 Potter St.,

HARTFORD, CONNECTICUT.

Plain and Ornamental Stone-Cutting, of all kinds, promptly executed. Orders filled for all parts of the State.

CHENEY BROTHERS'

SILK MANUFACTURING COMPANY,

Mills at Hartford and South Manchester, Conn.

MANUFACTURERS OF ALL KINDS OF

Thrown Silks,
Skein Sewing Silk,
Spool Sewing Silk,
Machine Sewing Silk,
Machine Twist,
Tailor's Twist,
Saddler's Embroidering and Fringe Silk,

Trams and Organzines,
Fine Organzines for Silk Mixture Cassimeres,
Pongees, all widths and qualities,
Pongee Handkerchiefs, plain and printed,
Millinery Foulards, Florentines,
Tubular Neck Ties and Ribbons,
All Silk Belt Ribbons, C. B. Brand,
Silk Warp Poplins and Dress Goods,
And many other articles of Silk for special purposes to order.

AGENTS.

EDWARD H. ARNOLD & SON,	102 Franklin St., New York.
CHENEY & MILLIKEN,	4 Otis St., Boston.
LEONARD BAKER & CO.,	210 Chestnut St., Phila.
RICE, CHASE & CO.,	Baltimore.

PARK BOOK MANUFACTORY.

DRAKE & PARSONS,

BINDERS AND

𝕭𝖔𝖔𝖐 𝕸𝖆𝖓𝖚𝖋𝖆𝖈𝖙𝖚𝖗𝖊𝖗𝖘,

No. 150 Asylum Street, Hartford, Conn.

Books of every description bound by the edition, or Manufactured entire, including Electrotyping, Paper, Printing and Binding.

J. D. BURNHAM & CO.,

MANUFACTURERS AND JOBBERS

IN

TOBACCO, SNUFF AND CIGARS,

Nos. 77 and 79 Asylum Street,

HARTFORD, CONN.

J. D. BURNHAM. A. A. BURNHAM. E. D. WILLIAMS. J. H. BURNHAM.

EUROPEAN HOTEL,

BY

MRS. C. BREHM,

Corner Welles and Mulberry Sts.,

OVERLOOKING THE HARTFORD PARK,

AND

CENTRALLY LOCATED.

Also the only Hotel in the City kept on

THE EUROPEAN PLAN.

Business men will find this the most convenient and commodious House in the City.

PARK FELLOWS & CO.,

Wholesale Dealers in

CHOICE TEA, COFFEE AND SPICES,

203 STATE STREET,

HARTFORD, CONN.

Coffee Roasted and Ground daily.

PARK FELLOWS.   O. H. BLANCHARD.

COFFEE HOUSE,

(MELODEON BUILDING,)

387 MAIN STREET,

HARTFORD, CONN.

MEALS AT ALL HOURS.

Steaks, Tea, Coffee, Confectionery, &c.

Mrs. W. H. GARDNER.

A. B. ISHAM,

Successor to ASA FARWELL & SONS,

MANUFACTURER OF

Cherry Bounce, Cherry Rum,

CORDIALS, AND BITTERS.

DEALERS IN

FOREIGN AND DOMESTIC WINES & LIQUORS.

Stone Stores, cor. of Ferry and Commerce Sts.,

HARTFORD, CONN.

ABNER CHURCH, Agent,

MANUFACTURER AND DEALER IN

Hemp, Flax and Cotton Rope, Lines and Twines,

TAR, PITCH AND ROSIN, BLOCKS, &C.,

Manufactory and Office, No. 46 Morgan St.,

HARTFORD, CONN.

22

E. TUCKER & SON,

MANUFACTURERS OF

Paper Boxes of all Descriptions,

AND DEALERS IN

PAPER, STRAW BOARDS, AND PAPER BAGS.

139 Trumbull Street,

HARTFORD, CONN.

J. OLDERSHAW,

Nos. 3 Asylum, and 311 Main Streets,

Also cor. Main and Asylum Sts.

Photographs, Cartes De Visites, Ambrotypes,

AND

PORCELAIN PICTURES.

Particular attention paid to Copying Pictures, and Finished in Oil or Water Colors.

HARTFORD, CONN.

HORACE WATERS, JR.,

WHOLESALE DEALER IN

Ribbons, Silks, Millinery

AND

STRAW GOODS,

No. 384 Main Street,

HARTFORD, CONN.

HENRY S. BRIGGS,

381 Main Street, Hartford, Ct.

Ornamental Confectioner.

LADIES & GENTLEMENS ICE CREAM SALOON,

AND DINING ROOM.

WEDDING AND OTHER PARTIES,

SUPPLIED WITH EVERY REQUISITE.

THOMAS STEELE & SON,

DEALERS IN

Diamonds, Watches, Jewelry, Silver

AND PLATED WARE, CLOCKS, &c.

340 Main Street, Hartford.

THOMAS STEELE.   THOS. S. STEELE.

WM. J. PHILLIPS.

WHOLESALE AND RETAIL DEALER IN

Air-Tight Cooking Stoves, Parlor, Hall,

OFFICE & FACTORY STOVES, FURNACES, &C.

REPAIRING AND MANUFACTURING.

Tin, Copper, and Sheet-Iron Work done at short notice.

No. 220 Main St., First Store South New Ætna Building,

HARTFORD, CONN.

ROBBINS, WINSHIP & CO.,

Opposite the  Athenæum,

Manufacturers and   Dealers in

FURNI   TURE,

Offer to the   Public the most

Complete Assortment   of Furniture,

To be found in the   State, from the

Smallest Bracket to the Largest and most extensive Parlor or Chamber Sets.

150 DIFFERENT KINDS AND PATTERNS.

Of Bedsteads and Chamber Sets. Nearly 400 different kinds of Chairs, Looking Glasses, of every description. Side Boards, Library Tables, Hat Stands, Extension Tables, Office Desks, Center Tables, Mattresses, Feather Beds, Spring Beds of every description and price, Lounges, Camp Chairs, Cushions, &c., too numerous to mention.

209 Main St., Hartford, Conn.

GEO. W. WILLIAMS & CO.,
WHOLESALE DUGGISTS,
AND DEALERS IN

Paints, Window Glass, Brushes, Coal Oil, Burning Fluid, Neatsfoot, Lard and

MACHINERY OILS, &c.

Agents for Williams & Brothers Yankee Soap, Blucing, Blacking, &c.

Particular attention paid to supplying Country Physicians.

204 STATE STREET,
HARTFORD, CONN.

WILLIAMS'
CHOICE
Flavoring Extracts,
' GEO. W. WILLIAMS & CO.,

Hartford, Conn.

BROWN & OATMAN,
Successors to BROWN & ZWEYGARTT,

DEALERS IN

LEAF TOBACCO,
And Manufacturers of the
"Champion" and other Brands
OF
CHOICE CIGARS,
212 State Street, Hartford, Conn.
A. G. Brown. **L. Oatman.**

DAY BROTHERS,
COMMISSION MERCHANTS,
AND DEALERS IN

COTTON, COTTON WASTE & PAPER;
ALSO MANUFACTURERS OF

Twines, Wicks, Carpet Warp, Yarus and Batts,
OF EVERY DESCRIPTION.

Also Agents for C. F. HANKS' BABBIT METAL.

No. 208 State St., Hartford, Conn.
Samuel J. Day. **Asa W. Day.**

PHŒNIX MUTUAL LIFE INSURANCE COMPANY,

OF HARTFORD, CONN.

EDSON FESSENDEN, President. JAMES F. BURNS, Secretary.

Amount of Insurance, Nov. 1, 1866, ... $18,625,269.00
Assets, Nov. 1, 1866, ... $1,343,519.23
Income for 1866, nearly $1,000,000.00

DIVIDENDS DECLARED ANNUALLY, AND PAID TO ALL ITS MEMBERS WHO HAVE PAID FOUR PREMIUMS,

Dividends Paid in 1865, - - - - - - - - 50 per cent.
Dividends Paid in 1866, - - - - - - - 50 per cent.
Dividends being paid in 1867, - - - - - - 50 per cent.

In the settlement of all MUTUAL POLICIES a Dividend will be allowed for each year on which the Insured has received no Dividend.

THE

Connecticut General Life Insurance Company,

OF HARTFORD, CONN.

CAPITAL, - - - - - - - $500,000.

With a Surplus Securely Invested. CHARTER PERPETUAL.

EDWARD W. PARSONS, President. THOMAS W. RUSSELL, Secretary.
General E. W. WHITAKER, General Agent for Company.

ADVANTAGES PRESENTED BY THIS COMPANY.

SECURITY is the primary consideration in Life Insurance. This Company offers the security of a larger capital than ANY OTHER LIFE COMPANY IN THIS COUNTRY.
Its ratio of assets to liabilities (the real test of solvency,) is *larger than that* of any other Company in the United States. See Annual Report of Mass. Ins. Commissioner for January, 1867.
Its managers have had a long experience in all the departments of Life Insurance; and the Company is under the direction of men well known for their INTEGRITY AND PRUDENT MANAGEMENT.
The Company offers insurance upon the Stock Plan at the lowest rates consistent with security. This plan is increasingly popular.
If the mutual system is preferred, the Company offers the security of its large capital, and when the premium is $50, or upwards, will accept a note for 40 per cent. if desired.

Charter Oak Life Insurance Co.,

OF HARTFORD, CONN.

General Agents in New England.

N. B. Stevens for Conn. and West Mass., at Hartford, Conn.
I. M. Scofield for Mass. East of Conn. River, at Worcester, Mass.
Lou Weston for N. H. and Vt., at Concord, N. H.
S. H. McAlpine for Maine, at Portland, Maine.
A. A. White for R. I., at Providence, R. I.

Assets, - - - - - - - $3,500,000.
Income, - - - - - - - $2,500,000.

I. C. WALKLEY, Pres. N. S. PALMER, Vice Pres. S. H. WHITE, Sec.

CONTINENTAL LIFE INSURANCE CO.,

OF HARTFORD, CONN.

Assets, ...$550,000.00.

This Company is intended to combine all the advantages to be derived from the experience of Life Insurance Companies both in this country and Europe.

Being controlled by Directors pecuniarily interested in its welfare, with an abundant capital, and economy in its management, it is able to offer security to the insured surpassed by no other company.

If there is no Agent in your vicinity, send for a copy of its prospectus and examine its plans.

DIRECTORS.

John S. Rice, Roger Averill, Horace Cornwall, Ezra Hall, Allyn S. Stillman, Lucius J Hendee, Samuel E. Elmore, Wm. H. Post, H. K. W. Welch, Abner Church.

JOHN S. RICE, Pres. SAMUEL E. ELMORE, Sec. P. M. HASTINGS, Exam'g Physician.

Putnam Fire Insurance Company,

OF HARTFORD, CONN.

Cash Capital, $500,000—All Paid In.

DIRECTORS:

Samuel Woodruff, Milo Hunt, A. H. Welch, A. C. Dunham, Edward Kellogg, E. S. Cleveland, Chas. F. Howard, A. E. Ely, H. W. Conklin, Edwin H. Fenn, Frederick R. Foster, Geo. W. Quintard, N. Y. Henry O. Hubbard, Middletown. G. D. Talcott, Vernon.

SAMUEL WOODRUFF, Pres. DANIEL BUCK, Sec.

☞This Company is now prepared to issue Policies upon most classes of Hazard against loss or damage by fire, at reasonable rates of premium.

OFFICE--PUTNAM BUILDING,

240 MAIN ST., corner of Grove Street.

Hartford County Mutual Fire Insurance Co.,

OFFICE, 321 MAIN STREET,

HARTFORD, CONN.

Pledged Capital, ... $950,000.00
Cash Surplus, ... $61,450.26

CHAS. SHEPARD, Pres. D. D. ERVING, Sec. and Treas.

$5,000. To Loan, $5,000.

On Diamonds, Watches & Jewelry,

BY THOMAS H. BELDEN,

AT THE LOAN OFFICE,

No. 254 MAIN ST.,

(Over the Post Office,)

HARTFORD, CONN.

N. B. Business Confidential.

MONEY
MONEY
MONEY
MONEY

23

TRUMBULL HOUSE,

No. 48 State Street.

North of State House, Hartford, Ct.

JOHN M. PARKER, Proprietor.

This House has been established many years. Its reputation is believed to be

SECOND TO NONE IN THE CITY.

It is centrally located on the North side of State House Square, near the terminus of the city cars, which pass the House every ten minutes, and is particularly convenient for business men. Every effort will be made to maintain the former reputation of the House; and the subscriber hopes, by personal attention to his guests, to make it AN AGREEA-BLE AND PLEASANT HOME to all who may favor him with their patronage.

N. B.—This House is conducted on strictly Temperance principles.

JOHN M. PARKER.

DWIGHT CUSHMAN,
MANUFACTURER OF

Cushman's Patent Turbine Water Wheel,

From 6 inches to 60 inches in Diameter,
and using from 2 inches to 800 inches of Water.

ALSO,

SHAFTING, MILL GEARING, &c.,
AT SHORT NOTICE.

Send for Descriptive Circular.

GROVE WORKS,   **HARTFORD, CONN.**

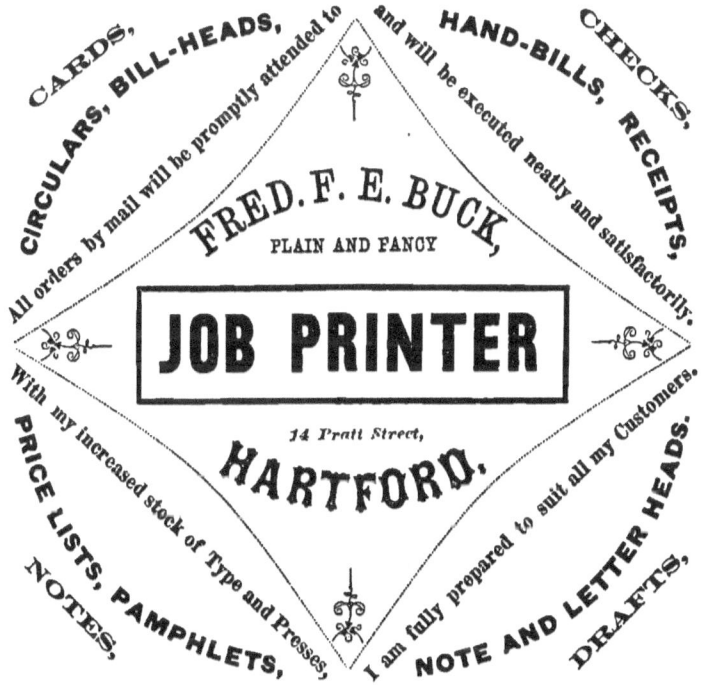

CARDS, BILL-HEADS, CIRCULARS, All orders by mail will be promptly attended to and will be executed neatly and satisfactorily. HAND-BILLS, CHECKS, RECEIPTS, With my increased stock of Type and Presses, I am fully prepared to suit all my Customers. PRICE LISTS, NOTES, PAMPHLETS, NOTE AND LETTER HEADS, DRAFTS,

FRED. F. E. BUCK,
PLAIN AND FANCY

JOB PRINTER

14 Pratt Street,

HARTFORD.

HARTFORD SUSPENDER MANUFACTORY,

147 Main St., Hartford, Conn.,

Suspenders, Shoulder Braces, Elastics,

AND ALL ARTICLES USUALLY FOUND IN THE TRADE.

ALL ORDERS WILL RECEIVE PROMPT ATTENTION.

THE

𝕳𝖆𝖗𝖙𝖋𝖔𝖗𝖉 𝕸𝖔𝖗𝖓𝖎𝖓𝖌 𝕻𝖔𝖘𝖙,

$3.00 PER ANNUM IN ADVANCE.

The Hartford Weekly Post,

$2.00 PER ANNUM IN ADVANCE.

OFFICE,   -   -   222 MAIN STREET,

Next door south of the Ætna Insurance Company's new building.

Published by GEO. S. HUBBARD.

BERNARD PETERS, Editor.

DURING the past year THE POST has passed under its present management. It has received the highest commendations from the public and the press, and, as the result, IT HAS MORE THAN DOUBLED ITS CIRCULATION. It has a larger country circulation than any other Hartford daily, and has made such important gains in the city, that it is now ONE OF THE BEST ADVERTISING MEDIUMS IN THE CITY.

In the management of the paper no pains are spared to make it acceptable to the family circle. The news of the day is carefully condensed and promptly given. Miscellaneous departments are kept up, in which a full variety of interesting items appear. Its editorial pages keep pace with the events of the day. Foreign and domestic matters are discussed with candor. Politically it does not follow the blind lead of any party, though advocating fearlessly the cause of the Union, it will always aim to cultivate amity and harmony on sound principles throughout the length and breadth of the land. If a truth is to be spoken, it will give it utterance boldly, not hesitating from motives of policy or expediency, till the truth itself becomes "flat, stale and unprofitable." It will seek to be in advance on all public questions, and will criticise men and measures independent of party considerations.

THE WEEKLY POST,

This a large sized four paged paper, issued every Thursday, and is crowded with every variety of interesting selected and original matter. It is the purpose of the proprietors to admit but a limited amount of advertising; this enables them to devote almost the entire space of the paper to reading matter. It contains more reading matter and is furnished to subscribers at a lower rate than any other paper in the State.

GAS COOK AND HEATING STOVES.
CRAIG'S PATENT.

Perfection Attained in Heating and Cooking by Gas.
CHILDS & BULL,
189 Main Street, Hartford, Conn.,

MANUFACTURE

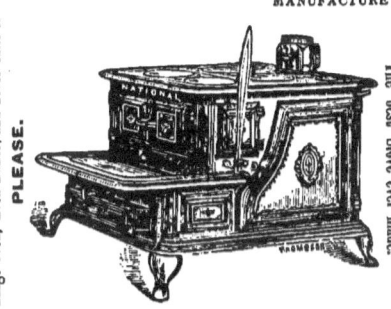

Large Oven, Even Baker, and never fails to PLEASE.

The best Stove ever made. THE NATIONAL.

Double Gas Cook Stoves.

Single " " "

Three Hole Gas " "

Four " " " "

and Coal Hods.

ALSO,

Wholesale & Retail

DEALERS IN

Cooking, Parlor, Gas & Kerosene Stoves, Ranges,

Furnaces, Cast Iron Sinks, Refrigerators, Tin Ware, &c.

G. W. HAWXHURST'S

ADJUSTABLE HOE,

Patented Feb. 13 and Oct. 23, 1866.

Premiums and Diplomas have been awarded at Fairs.

AND SELF-ACTING OX YOKE BOW PIN,

Patented April 4, 1865. Manufactured by G. W. Hawxhurst, sole proprietor.

N. B. At wholesale only to purchasers of TERRITORY, TOWN, COUNTY AND STATE RIGHTS, for sale throughout the United States, on reasonable terms, and the goods supplied.

OFFICE 497 MAIN STREET, **HARTFORD, CONN.**

For further particulars call on, or address as above. Send Stamp for circulars,

GEORGE M. STAPLES,
MANUFACTURER OF

Carriages, Business Waggons, Sleighs, &c.,

OF ALL DESCRIPTIONS.

HORSE SHOEING

AND

GENERAL JOBBING.

34 WELLS STREET, - - *HARTFORD, CONN.*

24

J. G. BATTERSON'S

Steam Marble Works,

650 Main, corner of Pleasant Street,

HARTFORD, CONN.

Monuments, Tombs, Grave Stones,
Mural Tablets, Fonts, Enclosures
for Cemetery Lots, &c.,

In great variety of design and material.

Particular attention paid to designing and executing

SOLDIER'S MONUMENTS.

Red Aberdeen Granite,

UNEQUALED FOR BEAUTY AND DURABILITY.

Mantels, Cabinet and Plumbers Tops,
Marble and encaustic tiling for floors,
Soapstone Sinks and Wash Trays,
Italian and American Marble,
and Soapstone, at wholesale.

H. & S. BISSELL,

No. 17 Pearl Street,

MANUFACTURERS OF

CEMENT, DRAIN AND SEWER PIPE,

BRICK MASONRY,

LATHING, PLASTERING,

AND

STUCCO, ORNAMENTING FOR CENTER PIECES, CORNICES, &c.

Also, Manufacturers and Dealers in

BRICK.

Also, Contractors for Buildings, &c. All work executed in the best and most tasty styles and durable manner, and to the satisfaction of customers.

E. DART & CO.,

MANUFACTURERS OF

PICTURE FRAMES,

AND DEALERS IN

PAINTINGS, ENGRAVINGS, CHROMOS,

CORD, TASSELS, STEREOSCOPES, &c.

219 MAIN STREET,

(Two doors North City Hotel,)

HARTFORD, CONN.

F. A. SYKES,

FANCY AND DOMESTIC BAKER,

NO. 7 ALLYN HOUSE, HARTFORD, CONNECTICUT.

ICE CREAM, JELLIES, CONFECTIONERY,

ORNAMENTAL WORK, &c.

Weddings and Parties furnished complete.

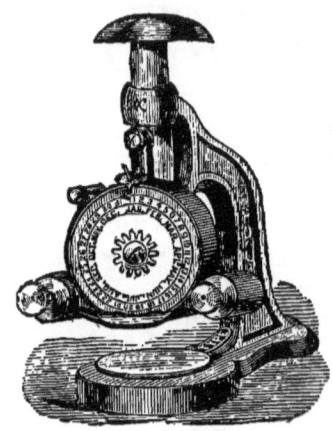

JUSTIN SNOW,

AGENT FOR

HAND STAMPS,

SEAL PRESSES,

AND CONDUCTOR'S PUNCHES.

289 Main Street,

HARTFORD, CONN.

EAST HARTFORD, a post town of Hartford County, situated on the east bank of the Connecticut River, nearly opposite Hartford, and 50 miles from Long Island Sound. The Township comprises the village of Burnside, where large quantities of Printing, Manilla and Bank note paper is manufactured. Agriculture is the principal business of the town, though something is done manufacturing Plated Silver Ware and Washing Machines. Population of town about 3000. A bridge spans the river between this place and Hartford.

BUSINESS DIRECTORY.

Carpenters and Builders.

West & Lapaugh.

Flour, Feed and Coal.

West, A. B.

Groceries.

Chandler, M. & Son. Burnside.
Darling, W.
Goodwin, S.
Olmsted, B. & A. G.
Roberts, M.
Sisson, B. & Co.

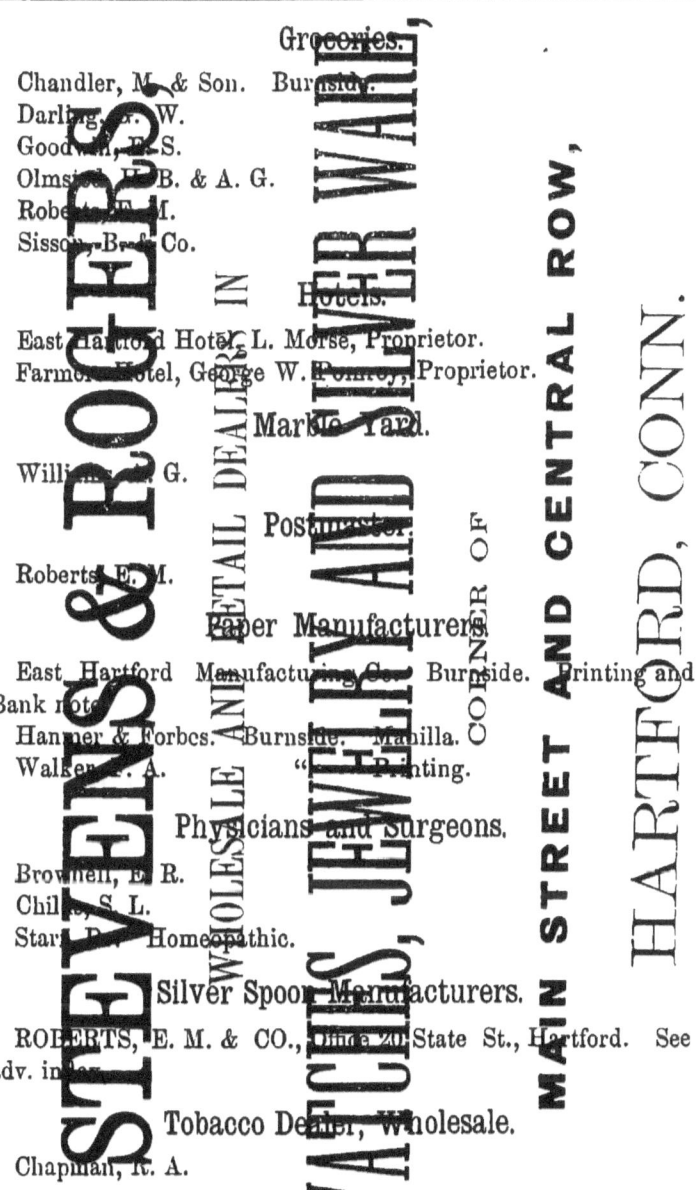

Hotels.

East Hartford Hotel, L. Morse, Proprietor.
Farmers' Hotel, George W. Pomeroy, Proprietor.

Marble Yard.

Williams, G.

Postmaster.

Roberts, E. M.

Paper Manufacturers.

East Hartford Manufacturing Co., Burnside. Printing and
Bank note.
Hanmer & Forbes. Burnside. Manilla.
Walker, A. " Printing.

Physicians and Surgeons.

Brownell, E. R.
Chilson, S. L.
Starr, Homeopathic.

Silver Spoon Manufacturers.

ROBERTS, E. M. & CO., 20 State St., Hartford. See
adv. in

Tobacco Dealer, Wholesale.

Chapman, A.

E. M. ROBERTS' MFG. CO.,

WINDSOR, a post town of Hartford County, Connecticut, 7 miles north of Hartford and 42 from New Haven, contains the villages of Poquonnock and Rainbow. Windsor is the oldest town in the State, having been settled in the year 1633, by a party of emigrants from Plymouth Colony, in Massachusetts. Windsor is one of the many rich agricultural towns through the valley, and large quantities of Conn. Seed Leaf Tobacco are raised.

Printing Paper, Cassimeres, Cotton Warps, Print Cloth and Yarns are manufactured here. Population of the town about 3,200.

BUSINESS DIRECTORY.

Blacksmiths.

Andrus, A. H.
Hoskin, H. B.
Loomis, S. O.

Brick Yards.

Barber, Martin
Filley, H. H. & Son.
Higinbothan, William W.
Loomis, S.
Loomis, S. B.
Loomis, E.
Loomis, W. W.
Mack, Geo. A.
Mack, William & Sons.
Moore, J. & O. B.
Thrall, H. & J.

Cabinet Maker.

Francis, E. B.

Cigar Manufacturers.

Phelps & Burns.

Cotton Manufacturers.

Dunham, Austin & Co.   Poquonnock.

Dentist.

Ellsworth, A. H.

Dry Goods and Groceries.

Ellsworth, Eli P. & Co.
Fenton, A.
Hatheway, C. W.   Poquonnock.
Leonard & Son.   Rainbow.

Groceries.

Rockwell, H. P.

Grist Mill and Saw Mill.

Simons, E.

Hotel.

Windsor House, Gillette, E. A. Proprietor.

Livery Stables.

Carpenter, H. Poquonnock.
Griswold, F. N.

Millinery.

Brown, K. L. Miss

Paper Manufacturers.

Brainard, L. & Co. Rainbow.
Hollingsworth & Whitney. Poquonnock.
Hodge & Merwin. Rainbow.
Springfield Paper Co. "

Physicians,

Morrison, A.
Wilson, S. A.

Postmasters.

Ellsworth, E. A.
Hatheway, C. W. Poquonnock.

Saloons.

Clark, Samuel
Hungerford, Joseph.

Wheelwrights.

Bedortha, L. L.
Griswold, Hudson N.

Woolen Manufacturers.

Laprise, N. & Co. Poquonnock.
Sequassen Woolen Company.

WINDSOR LOCKS, Hartford County, Connecticut, a manufacturing village situated on the west bank of the river, 13 miles
from Hartford, and has a station on the New Haven, Hartford

and Springfield Railroad. A canal was constructed here some years ago, around Enfield Falls, for shipping purposes, but since the construction of the Railroad the water is used for manufacturing purposes. Machinery, Steel, Thread, Paper and Woolen Goods are manufactured here quite extensively. The town numbers about 2000 population.

BUSINESS DIRECTORY.

Attorney.

Johnson, J. W.

Blacksmiths.

Chandler, L.
Whipple, Joseph

Boots and Shoes.

Schaeffer, L.

Clothing

Sisson, Charles S.

Carriage Makers.

Briscoe, Chas.
King, Ralph

Cigar Manufacturer.

Atherton, A. H.

Dentist.

Murless, M. T.

Dry Goods and Groceries.

Ashley, Wm.
Coogan, James

McCowan, R.
Mather, Wm.
Simms, E. B.

Fish Market.

Moran, John

Flour and Feed.

Swan & Easton.

Furniture and Undertakers.

Watrous, R. N. & C. W.

Hosiery, Shirt and Drawers Manufacturer.

MEDLICOTT, WM. G.

Hotel.

Charter Oak House, H. Cutler, Proprietor.

Insurance Agents.

Allen, B. R.
Watrous, R. N.

Iron Foundry.

Converse, H. A. & Co.

Lumber Dealer.

Benjamin, George
Somers, C. A., Agt.

Livery Stables.

Baldwin, N.
Stockwell, A. B.

Manilla Paper Manufacturers.

Dexter, C. H. & Co.

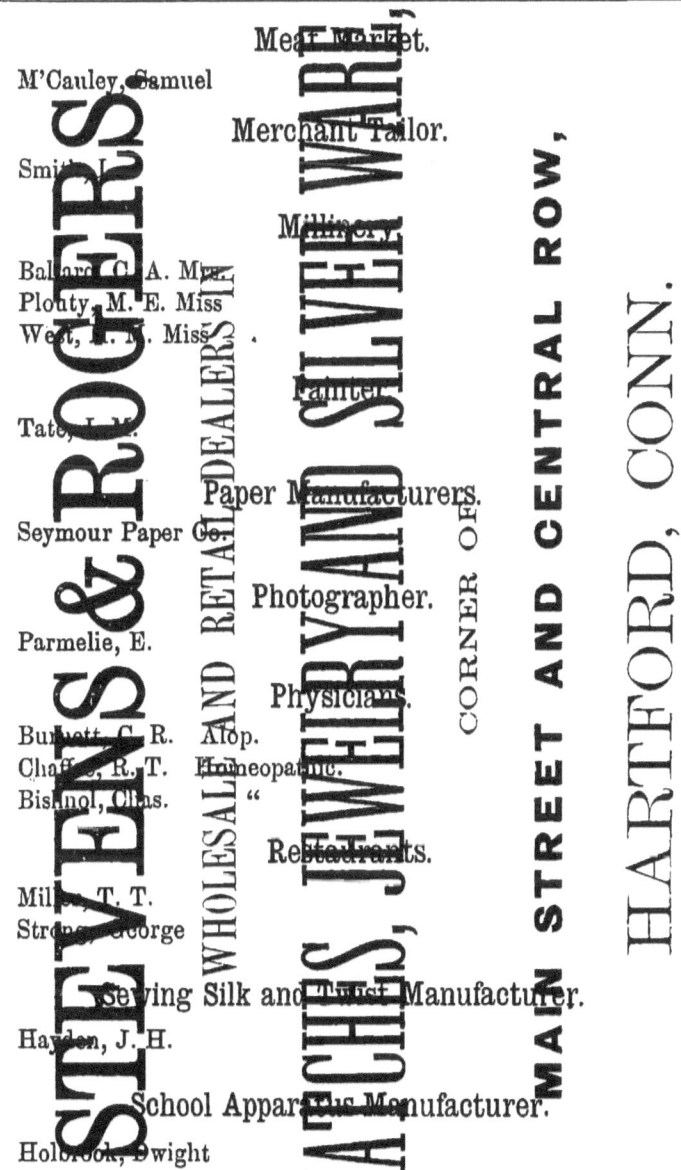

Meat Market.

M'Cauley, Samuel

Merchant Tailor.

Smith, L.

Millinery.

Ballard, C. A. Mrs.
Plouty, M. E. Miss
West, R. N. Miss

Painter.

Tate, J. W.

Paper Manufacturers.

Seymour Paper Co.

Photographer.

Parmelie, E.

Physicians.

Burnett, C. R. Alop.
Chaffee, R. T. Homeopathic.
Bishnol, Chas. "

Restaurants.

Miller, T. T.
Strong, George

Sewing Silk and Twist Manufacturer.

Hayden, J. H.

School Apparatus Manufacturer.

Holbrook, Dwight

Screw Chucks Manufacturers.

HORTON, E. & SON.

Stoves and Tinware.

Cornwall, Elias

Thread Manufacturers.

Conn. River Mills,
   L. M. Pinkham, Agt.

Wool Cleansing.

Coffin, H. R. & Co.

WAREHOUSE POINT, a post village in the town of East
Windsor, on the east bank of the Conn. River, 14 miles from
Hartford. The New Haven, Hartford and Springfield Railroad
has a station at this place. Woolen Goods are manufactured
quite extensively.

BUSINESS DIRECTORY.

Attorney.

Barnes, Wm.

Boot and Shoe Maker.

Moore, Thomas

Cigar Manufacturers.

Russ, A. J.
Woodruff & Barber.

Dry Goods and Grocery Dealers.

Barnes & Spooner.
Palmer, Joseph

Gin Distillery.

Barber, W. T. & H.

Grocer.

Baker, J. H.

Harness Manufactory.

Price, James

Hotel.

American Hotel, J. H. Baker, Proprietor.

Lumber Dealer.

Filer, A. P.

Physician.

Fisk, Dr.

Postmaster.

Woodward, Geo. G.

Restaurant.

Dean, Chester

Tailor.

Thiesse, F.

Tinware.

Abbe, George C.
McDonald, Daniel

Woolen Manufacturers.

EAST WINDSOR WOOLEN CO.
  B. Sexton, President.
26

SUFFIELD, HARTFORD COUNTY, CONNECTICUT, is situated on the right bank of the Connecticut River, 16 miles north of Hartford, and 50 miles from New Haven. Agriculture and the manufacture of Cigars, and Carriages, are the principal kinds of business carried on here. The town numbers about 3,500 inhabitants.

BUSINESS DIRECTORY.

Bank.

First National Bank.

Carriage Manufacturers.

AUSTIN BROTHERS.   See adv. index.
Case, J. W., West Suffield.

Cigar Manufacturers.

Austin, Albert
Austin & Newton.
Harrocks, McKinzie & Co.
Loomis, John W.
Wilson, Geo. M.
Wood, Benjamin

Dry Goods and Groceries.

Endress & Nichols.
Newton & Pomeroy.
Sheldon, Horace

Fine Cut Tobacco Manufactory.

Cowles, H. S.

Groceries.

Willeston, George

Paper Manufactory.

Eagle Mills Co.

Physicians.

Kellogg, O. W.
Mason, . K
Rising, A.

Postmaster.

Hale, David

Tobacco Dealers, Foreign and Domestic.

Kent, H. P.
Reed, S. N

Tobacconists.

Spencer, Alfred
Spencer, C. C.
Spencer, L. L.
Spencer, T. H.

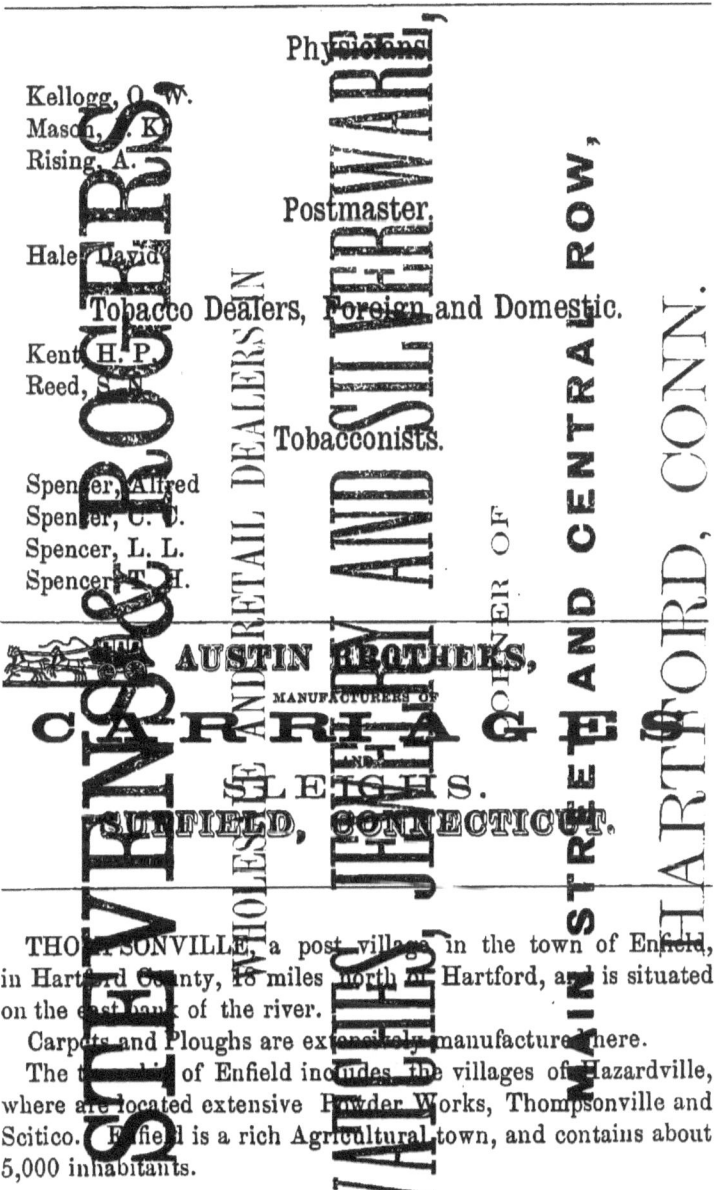

AUSTIN BROTHERS,
MANUFACTURERS OF
CARRIAGES
AND
SLEIGHS.
SUFFIELD, CONNECTICUT.

THOMPSONVILLE, a post village in the town of Enfield, in Hartford County, 18 miles north of Hartford, and is situated on the east bank of the river.

Carpets and Ploughs are extensively manufactured here.

The town of Enfield includes the villages of Hazardville, where are located extensive Powder Works, Thompsonville and Scitico. Enfield is a rich Agricultural town, and contains about 5,000 inhabitants.

BUSINESS DIRECTORY.

Agents.

Vanhorn, S. Adams Express Co., H. & N. H. R. R. Station Agent.

Ale Brewers.

Matherson & Gray.

Attorney.

Briscoe, C. H.

Barber.

Ebert, F.

Blacksmiths.

Bent, Joseph
Casey, Wm., Hazardville.
Lord, Geo., Enfield.

Boot Makers.

Bowman, D.
Wagner, Henry
McCarty, D.

Bonnet Manufacturers.

Hazardville Bonnet Co.

Brick Yard.

Alden, E.

Cabinet Makers.

King & Steel.

Carpet Manufacturers.

Hartford Carpet Co., Office, Hartford, Conn.

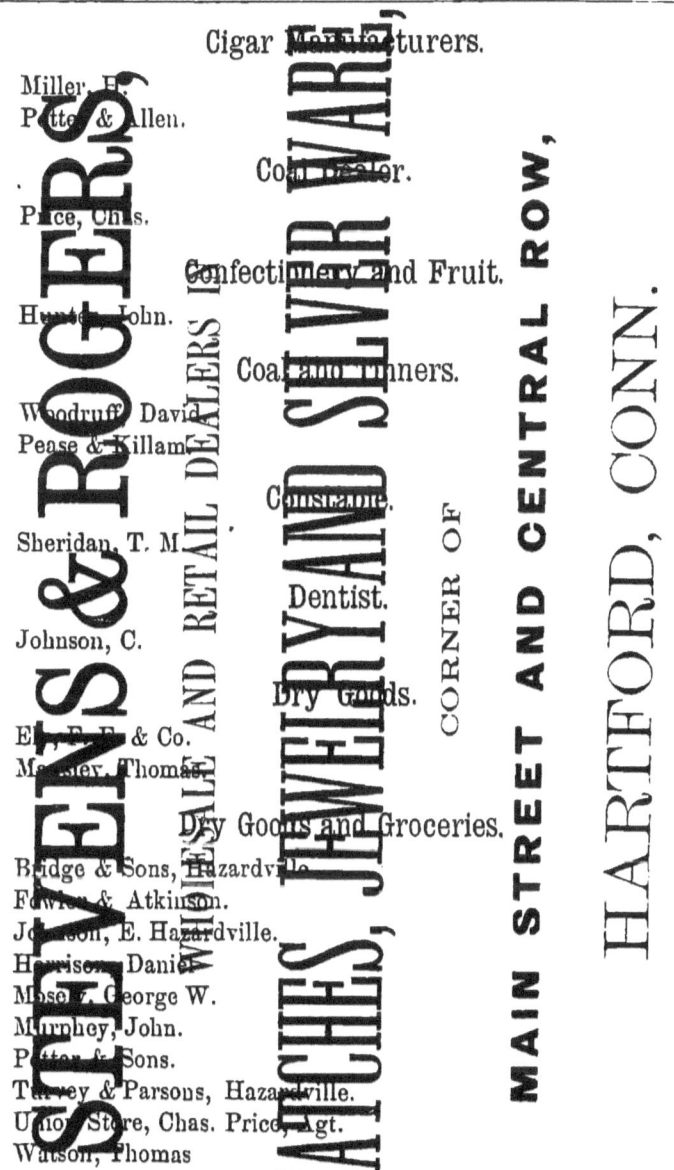

Cigar Manufacturers.

Miller, H.
Potter & Allen.

Coal Dealer.

Price, Chas.

Confectionery and Fruit.

Hunter, John.

Coal and Tinners.

Woodruff, David
Pease & Killam.

Constable.

Sheridan, T. M.

Dentist.

Johnson, C.

Dry Goods.

Ely, E. E. & Co.
Mansley, Thomas.

Dry Goods and Groceries.

Bridge & Sons, Hazardville.
Fowler & Atkinson.
Johnson, E. Hazardville.
Harrison, Daniel.
Mosely, George W.
Murphey, John.
Potter & Sons.
Turvey & Parsons, Hazardville.
Union Store, Chas. Price, Agt.
Watson, Thomas

Druggist.

Pease, L. H.

Fancy Dry Goods.

Ashley, F. E.

Fertilizers.

Ellis, H. R.

Fish Dealer.

Lavender, A.

File Manufactory.

Memnon & Kingsbury.

Gin Distillers.

Gowdy, Lorin,   Hazardville.
Gowdy & Stiles.

Grist Mills.

Watson, James
Spencer, Samuel,   Hazardville.

Grocers.

Burns Brothers.
Doyle, Michael
Morrison & Reynolds.
Warner, Henry

Harness Makers.

Lord, A. T.
Akin, Robert

House Builders

Bradley, F.
Pease, Warren,   Hazardville.
Woodward, H. & A.   Enfield.

House and Sign Painting.

Parsons, S.

Hotels.

Globe Hotel, H. A. Converse, Proprietor.
Hazardville Hotel, S. Charter, Proprietor.
John O'Neale, Hazardville.
Lyon Hotel, Wm. Abbe, Proprietor.
Philip Clarkin.
Thompsonville Hotel, B. F. Lord, Proprietor.

Ice Dealer.

Gray, Henry, Enfield.

Jeweler.

Lakin, J. A.

Lumber, Lime and Cement.

PEASE, THEODORE & SON. See adv. index.

Machine Needles.

Cooper, Charles

Meat Markets.

Davis, J. P.
Simpson, George, Hazardville.
Steele, James 2nd.

Melodeon Dealer.

Pease, L. T.

Millinery.

Smith, A. J. Mrs.
Wilson, H. & E. E.

News Office and Fancy Goods.

Hunter, James

Painter.

Parsons, S.

Photographers.

Sheriden, T. M.
Sweetser, C. A.

Physicians and Surgeons.

Adams, Dr.   Hazardville.
Converse, J. P.
Grant, H. A.
Miller, George H.   Homeopathic.
Parsons, Edward
Pease, L. S.
Strickland, Dr.

Plow Manufactory.

King & Clark.   Hazardville.

Plow and Waggon Manufactories.

King, Albert,   Enfield.
King & Clark.   Hazardville.
Potter & Parsons.

Postmaster.

Houston, John

Powder Company.

Hazardville Powder Co.

Restaurant and Bakers.

Abbe & Prickett.   Hazardville.

Saloons.

Barrett, Thomas,   Hazardville.
Harrison, John
Jager, A.
Miller, John
Winnerwessing, John,   Hazardville.

Shirt and Drawers Manufacturers.

Enfield Manufacturing Co.

Stoves and Tinware.

Law Brothers. Hazardville.

Surgeon.

Grant, H. A.

Tailors.

McIlroy, James
Robinson, David
Wilson, D. S.

Tinware.

Pease & Killam.

Tobacco Dealers.

Barber & Pease.

T. PEASE & SON,

DEALERS IN

Lumber, Lime & Cement.

Particular attention paid to furnishing

SPRUCE AND HEMLOCK TIMBER,

THOMPSONVILLE, CONN.

LONG MEADOW, MASS., a post town about 4 miles south of Springfield, and one mile east of the river. Buttons, Spectacles, Thimbles, Paper Collars, and Carriages are manufactured quite extensively here. Agriculture is the chief pursuit of the larger portion of the people.

The boundary line betwen the Massachusetts and Connecticut runs a short distance south of the village, which was first settled in 1644.

27

BUSINESS DIRECTORY.

Blacksmithing.

Dion, Joseph

Button Manufacturers.

Calvert & Bennett.

Carriage Manufacturer.

Taylor, Newton E.

Collar Manufacturers, Paper.

Reed & Cordis.

Groceries.

Noble, Lester

Spectacle Manufacturer.

COOMES, W. W.   See adv. index.

Thimbles, Gold and Silver.

COOMES, W. W.   See adv. index.

SPRINGFIELD, HAMPDEN COUNTY, MASSACHUSETTS, situated on the east bank of the Connecticut River, 76 miles from its mouth, 134 from New York, 100 from Boston, from Montreal Canada, 310 miles, Albany 100 miles, is the second of size of the cities in the Connnecticut Valley, and contains about 28,000 inhabitants, which is double its population as estimated by the census of 1860. This rapid increase of numbers propro- tionately enhanced the wealth and beauty of the city as is seen by the large number of public buildings, business blocks, and tenement houses erected during the last few years, still the de- mand for tenements exceeds the supply. Springfield is the old- est town in Massachusetts, on the Connecticut River, having been settled in 1636, by a company from Roxbury. It is also the shire town of Hampden county, and was incorporated February 20th, 1812.

Springfield is the great Railway centre of New England, and it being the junction of the Western, Hartford, New Haven & Springfield and Conn. River Railroads. This is the terminus of the Hartford and New Haven Road, which extends a distance of 62 miles. The Conn. River Road, 50 miles in length, extending up the river valley, terminating in South Vernon, at the state line between Vermont and Massachusettss, and connects with the Vermont and Massachusetts Railroad from Fitchburg, Boston and Northern Vermont. The Western Railroad connect- ing at Worcester with the Boston and Worcester Railroad, passes west through the city and terminates at Albany, N. Y., is about 160 miles in length. Here are located the repair shops of the Western and Conn. River railroads, giving employment to several hundred men. The extensive manufactory of the Norwalk Iron Works, making the Earl patent Steam Pump, is situated here. The United States Armory, established here in 1795, has propa- bly done more towards building the city than any other one cause. Previous to 1860, the hands employed in the Armory did not ex- ceed 500, but during the war the number increased to 2,992. At the present time about 1000 men are employed. The num- ber of muskets made in the month of April, 1864, was 26,000. Armory square which contains a portion of the workshops, and the residence of the commandant, paymaster, master armorer and other officers, is situated on the high grounds in the eastern portion of the city. A number of the armory buildings, known as the water shops, are situated one mile south of armory square where is done the heavy work of rolling the barrels, trip ham- mer and drop work, &c. The armory grounds are surrounded with an iron fence 8 feet high. The arsenal building, 3 stories high will hold 300,000 guns. The view from the tower is very fine and in a clear day, one can see twelve miles down the river.

Hampden Park, inaugurated September 29th, 1857, was purchased and improved by the Hampden County Agricultural Society, for an exhibition ground, at a cost of about $32,000, is beautifully situated on the river bank, in the northwestern portion of the city. These grounds, containing about 60 acres, are very level and are enclosed on the river side by a levee, and on the other by a substantial fence. The grounds comprise a mile and half mile race track, graded and kept in good condition, also buildings for sheltering stock during Agricultural and Horse fairs. Springfield contains many excellent Hotels.

SPRINGFIELD BUSINESS DIRECTORY.

Agricultural Implements and Seed.

Bliss, Benj. K. 231 Main St.

Artificial Limbs.

Douglas, D. D. F. 7½ Burt's Block, Main St.

Architects.

Chapin, A. L. Barnes Block, Main St.
WASHBURN, JASON, 17 Foot's Building, cor Main and State Sts.

Attorneys at Law.

Beach, E. D. Main St.
Brown, Timothy E. (Internal Revenue assistant assessor,) Pynchon House Block.
Davis, L. L. Foot's Block, Main St.
Dewey, T. A. Main St.
Donnelly, H·   "
GREEN & BOSWORTH, 4 Elm St.
Hildreth, R. B. 269 Main St.
Manchester, C. A. 263   "
Morris, H.   "
Morris, Edward, 263   "

McIntire, Jas. E. Chicopee National Bank, Main St.
Pierce, H. H. Main St.
Sanders, Sidney, Goodrich Block, Main St.
Shurtleff, Wm. S. 1 Elm St.
Soule, A. L. cor. Main and Court Sts.
Stearns & Knowlton, 4 Elm St.
Stebbins, J. M. Main St.

Album, Photograph Manufacturers.

BOWLES, SAMUEL & CO., Franklin Block, Main St.

Auction and Commission.

Eldredge, J. A. & Co., 243 Main St.

Babbitt Metal Dealers.

Brown, Charles & Co., Cypress cor. Fulton St.

Bakers.

Allen & Lobsitz, 301 Main St.
Childs, W. H. & Co., 254 "
Ross, Henry, East Worthington St.

Banks.

Agawam, National, cor. Main and Lyman Sts., capital $300,000,
    Marvin Chapin Prest., F. S. Bailey, Cash.
Chicopee National Bank, cor. Main and Elm, H. S. Lee, Pres.
    Thomas Warner, Jr., Cash., capital $400,000.
First National Bank, Main St., James Kirkham, Pres., Jas. D.
    Safford, Cash., capital $300.000.
John Hancock National Bank, 110 Main St.
Third National Bank, Main St.
Pynchon National Bank, 212 Main St., H. N. Case, Pres.,
    Chas. Marsh, Cashier, capital $150,000.
Second National Bank, 205 Main St., Henry Alexander, Jr.,
    Pres., Lewis Warriner, Cashier, capital $300,000.

Barbers.

Adams, J. B. 114 East State St.

Adams, Wm. cor. Main and East Court Sts.
Harley, T. H. 30 East State St.
Hobson, Wm. 25 East State St.
King, David, 85 Main St.
Montague, W. H. 75 North Main St.
QUEEN, GEO. Sanford St. See adv. index.
SAMPSON, J. D. Union House Block, Main St.
Wilson, James S. 317 Main St.
Wagnecury & Erb, Chicopee Bank Block, Main St.

Beer, (Root,) and Soda Manufacturer.
BROOKS, F. A. 52 North Main St. See adv. index.

Bell Hangers.
Moody, G. Z. Barnes* Block, Main St.

Billiards.
Hawkes, E. R. & Brothers, cor. Main and Hampden Sts.
Phelan Billiard Rooms, Sanford St.
Springfield Billiard Hall, Union Block.
WINKLER, BERTHOLD, 299 Main St.

Blacksmiths.
Avery, John
QUIMBY & HUDSON, East Court St. See adv. index.
Wardwell, Charles
Hood, John, Taylor St.
Sibley & Weeks, Liberty St.

Boarding and Eating House.
Morgan, Mary Mrs. 115 Main St.

Book Agents.
Fisk, D. E. & Co., 4 Vernon St.
Jones, E. & Co., 190 Main St. Up stairs.

Book Binders and Blank Book Manufacturers.
BOWLES, SAMUEL & CO., 207 Main St.
BRIDGMAN & WHITNEY, cor. Main and State Sts.

Books and Stationery.

BRIDGMAN & WHITNEY, cor. State and Main Sts.
Burt & Clark, 190 Main St.
Burt, A. & Co., 175 "
Jennings, A. F. 257 "
Ryan, J. 157 "
Rude, H. 189 "

Book Publishers.

Bill, G. & Co., 73 Main St.
BOWLES, SAMUEL & CO., Franklin Block, 207 Main St.
Merriam, G. & Co., West State St.

Boots and Shoes, Wholesale.

Cutler, McIntosh, Tibbetts & Co., 99 Main St.
Hixon, Birnie & Shaw, Main St.
Morse, O. D. & Co., Shaw's Block, Main St.

Boot and Shoe Makers.

Adams, W. J. 58 Main St.
Buchanan, John, cor. Market and Harrison Avs.
Marsh, E. Allis' Block, North Main St.
Stewart, A. State St.
Stewart, Austin, cor. State and Walnut Sts.
Swallow & Burke, Sanford St.

Boot and Shoe Dealers.

Bailey & Marsh, 9 East State St.
Bradley & Fay, 24 " "
Gibbs, J. W. & N. G. opposite Massasoit House.
Hart, Wm. H. 131 Main St. Wholesale and Retail.
Kendall, Joel, 241, 243 "
PAULK, G. W. 106–7 East State St.
Shaw, H. A. 5 " " Wholesale and Retail.
Warner & Smith, 265 Main St.

Bottling Establishment.

BROOKS, F. A. 52 North Main St. See adv. index.

UNION PRINTING CO., cor. Main and Taylor Sts.   See
adv. index.

Brass Finishing and Jobbing.

MORGAN, H. & J. Hampden St., near Water St.

Brass Finishers and Machinists.

Barnes & Curtis, Market St.
Morgan, H. & J. Hampden St.

Brass Founders.

Brown, Chas. & Co., Cypress, cor. Fulton St.
Emory, P. P. & Co., Hampden St.

Brewers.

Shaw & Co., 1 Water St.

Bridge Builders.

BRIGGS, A. D. & CO., Main St., Foot's Block. See adv. index.
HARRIS, D. L. & CO., 1 Charles St.   See adv. index.

Brick Yards.

Agawam Brick Co., 2 Allis' Block, North Main St.
Allis, W. H. 1 Allis' Block   "   "

Broker, (Money.)

Jordan, Josiah, 5 Elm. St.
Kimball, C. W. Water St.
Smith, Henry, 5 Elm St.
Rice & Clark,   (Real Estate.)
Winchell, V. 192 Main St.

Broom Manufacturer.

Morse, David, 319 Main St.

Building Materials.

Walker, T. M. & Co., 253 Main St.

Button Manufacturers.

Goldthwait, M, Ivory Button Manufacturer, Market St.
Hampden Button Co.
Newell Brothers, foot Howard St.
Swazey, G. W. cor. Stockbridge and Willow Sts.

Cabinet Manufacturers.

Belcher, D. E. Liberty St.
FISHER, BUCKHAUSE & KNAPP, 5 1-2 Burt's Block, Main
St. See adv. index.

Canal Companies.

Agawam Canal Co., Pynchon House Block, Main St.

Canceling Stamps and Seal Presses.

Hill, B. B. Liberty St., near Chase's Planing Mill.

Car Builders.

Wason Manufacturing Co., Lyman St.

Car Axles Manufactory.

Talcott, N. W. Liberty St.

Card Manufacturers.

Hampden Card Co., W. E. Montague, Agt., Sanford St.

Carriage and Saddlery, Hardware and Trimmings.

LEE & BAKER, 78 Main St. See adv. index.

Carpenters and Builders.   .

Rose Brothers, Taylor St.
Gough, H. A. 40 Water St.
Hubbard & Hendrick, 10 East Union St.
Kingsbury, G. O. Main St.

King, J. A. Liberty St.
Shaw, C. L. cor. Water and Elm Sts.
Scott & Merritt, Dwight St.
Shattuck, E. W. Taylor St.
Mouton, C. C. East Worthington St.

Carriage Trimmers.

SMITH, DAVID & CO., 2 Park St.   See adv. index.
QUIMBY & HUDSON, East Court St.   See adv. index.

Carriage Manufacturers.

Loomis, J. & W. Sanford St.
Rogers, John, 329 Main St.
SMITH, D. & CO., 2 Park St.   See adv. index.
Bailey, H. F. East Court St.
QUIMBY & HUDSON, East Court St,   See adv. index.

Carriage Repairer.

Bliss, H. A. Taylor St.

Casket, (Burial,) Manufacturers.

WASHBURN & CHASE, cor. Market and Sanford Sts.   See
adv. index.

Carver, (Wood.)

GARDNER, J. A. Taylor St.

Cigar and Tobacco Manufacturers and Dealers.

Doan, Whitcomb & Co., 88 Main St.
Margerum, H. J. 206 Main St.
Mort & Whitney, 66 North Main St.

Civil Engineers.

Briggs, A. D. & Co., Fort Block, Main St.

Clock Repairer.

Stearns, Wm. 9 Dwight St.

Clothing Dealers.

Brigham, D. H. & Co., 199, 201 Main St.
Baldwin, J. A. 138   "
Haynes, J. L. & Co., Main cor. Pynchon St.
Miller & Culver, 80 Main St.
Keyes, Henry & Co., 235 Main St.
Sweeny, Wm. 59 North   "
Page, S. E. cor. Main and State Sts.
Woodward & Merrill, Main cor. Court St.
VAUGHAN, GEORGE, 2 Fort Block, Main St.

Clothing, (Wholesale and Retail.)

Brigham, D. H. & Co., 199, 201 Main St.

Coal Dealers.

BANKS, J. H. & SONS, 238 Main and 38 West William Sts.
See adv. index.
Bemis, S. C. & Co., Taylor St.
Chapin, A. W. 13 West State St.
Gray, Henry & Sons, cor. Lyman and Spring Sts.
Wells, Isaac cor. Water and Court Sts.

Coal and Iron Dealers.

Bemis, S. C. & Co., Taylor St.

Coal and Wood Dealers.

BANKS, J. H. & SON, 38 West William St. See adv. index.
Chapin, A. W. 13 West State St.
Gray, Henry & Sons, Main St. under Massasoit House.
Abbey, N. B. East Worthington St.

Coffee and Spice Manufacturers and Dealers.

Barber, M. E. Market St.
Fowler, Geo. Commercial Row.

Coffin and Casket Manufacturers.

WASHBURN & CHASE, Sanford St.   See adv. index.

Coffin Dealers.

Pomroy & Fisk, 17 State St.
Ross, Sidney 267 Main St.
Skahan & Bourke, 113 "
WASHBURN & CHASE, cor. Sanford and Market Sts.   See adv. index.

Collar Manufactory.

Nonpariel Paper Collar Co., William St. near Main.

Commercial College.

Burnham's Business College, Main cor. State St.

Commission Merchants.

Dorman, A. E. 5 Union House Block, Main St.
Crosby, D. W. Lyman St.
King, Norton & Ladd, 83 Main St.
Lane, Adams & Co., 59   "
Palmer, Samuel & Co., 21 Hampden St.

Confectionery Manufacturers.

Cowles & Bliss, 281 Main St.
Kibbie Brothers & Co., 109 Main St.

Confectionery and Fruit.

Burr, Edwin C. 136 Main St.
Cowles & Bliss, 281   "
Gunn & Merrill, cor. Main and Lyman Sts.
Quimby, H. A. 267 Main St.
Shattuck, W. H. 115   "

Copper Work and Brass Castings.

EMORY, P. P. & CO., Hampden St. See adv. index.
Knight, A. & M. Pynchon St.

Cork Manufacturer.

Springfield Cork Manufacturing Co., Hillman St. near Main.

Cotton Batt Manufacturers.

Keith & Bunstead, Mill.

Cotton Waste Dealers.

Arms, William S. Commercial Row.
Olmsted & Taylor & Olmsted.

Cracker Bakers, (Wholesale.)

Carr, L. B. & Co., near cor. Harrison Avenue and Central Market St.

Crockery and Glass Ware.

Dearden, William, 112 Main St.
Eldredge, J. S. & Co. Main St. Fountain Row.
Hamilton & Co., 197 Main St., Wholesale and Retail

Croquet Manufacturers.

Bradley, Milton & Co., 241 Main St.

Curtain Hanging Dealers.

BRIDGMAN & WHITNEY, Main cor. State St.
FISHER, STOCKHOUSE & KNAPPE, Burt's Block, Main St.
See adv. index.

Dentists.

Ames, N. B. 253 Main St.
Collins, J. 6 Fallon's Block, Main St.
Hurlburt, J. S. Shaw's Block "
Hurlburt, C. 4 Vernon St.
Derby, P. H. opposite Court Sq.

Die Sinkers.

STACY, E. S. & CO., Shumway's Building, Harrison Avenue.

See adv. index.
Morgan, N. 190 Main St.
Perkins, C. 263   "
RENSLOW, M. B. 247 Main St.   See adv. index.
Searle, F. 279 Main St.

Drain and Sewer Tubing.

Wilcox, J. P. & Co., 16 State St.
Willis, Henry cor. State and Willow St.

Dress and Cloak Making.

Adams, E. Miss East State St.
Brown, S. C. Mrs. & Co., 92 Main St.
Chever, M. H. 7 Fallow's Block   "
Cheever, M. H.   "   "
Cadwell, Jennie Miss Commercial Block.
Demorest, Madame 241 Main St.
Henry, K. A. Commercial Block, Main St.
Hollis, Mrs. S. 6 Barnes Block,   "
Murdock, S. Mrs. 121 Main St.
Murless, B. Miss Townsleys' Block.
Warren, Mrs. 138 Main St.
Wheeler, Mrs. Barnes' Block.
Welton, J. W. Mrs. 7 Barnes' Block, Main St.
Wood, A. H. Mrs. Townsley's Block.

Druggists.

Alden & Brewster, opposite Massasoit House, Main St.
Bigelow, E. opposite Court Square.
Brewer, H. &. J. 263 Main St.
Dickinson, F. S. & Co., cor. Main and State St.
Doyle, John E. Allis Block, North Main St.
Hooker, John, 210 Main St.
Hutchins, H. & Son, cor. Main and Pynchon St.
Stebbins, E. C. 4 Union House Block, Main St.
Merritt & Sinclair, 112 East State St.
Moulton, E. B. 98 Main St.
Webber, J. T. & Co., 7 East State St.

Dry Goods.

Carter & Cooley, 106 Main St.
Chapin & Spencer, 191   "
Currier & Hodskins, cor. Main and Court Sts.
Hale, D. F. cor. Main and Pynchon Sts.
Hallock L. E. & Co., 4 Barnes' Block, Main St.
Holt, L. J. 108 East State St.
Labaree Brothers & Co., 1 Fallows' Block, Main St.
Lincoln, A. W. 1 Main St.
McKnight, Norton & Hawley, 1 Haynes' Block, Main St.
Strain, John 211 Main St., Wholesale and Retail.
Tinkham & Co., 184   "
Forbes & Smith, cor. Main and Vernon.

Dying and Cleaning.

Broadhurst & Walker, 2 West Worthington St.

Dye House.

Springfield Dye House, Adams, Patten & Co., 159 Main St.

Eave Trough Manufacturer.

BARTLETT, CHILD & CO., Taylor St.   See adv. index.

Eating Houses.

Dubois & Wright, 117 Main St.
Gilmore, D. cor. Pynchon and Main Sts.
Jennings, J. Court St.
Pierce, L. 18 East State St.
Thomas, Thomas 119 Main St.
Waverley House, Sanford St., H. S. Lane, Proprietor.
Quimby, H. A. 267 Main St.

Electrotypers.

BOWLES, SAMUEL & CO., Main St., Franklin Block.
LOCKWOOD & MANDEVILLE, Main St.   See adv. index.

Emigration Office.

Ryan, J. 157 Main St.

Engineers, Civil.

BRIGGS, A. D. & CO., Fort Block.   See adv. index.

Envelope Manufacturer.

Morgan, E. & Co., cor. Hillman and Dwight Sts.

Engravers.

Chubbuck, T. 265 Main St.
Bradley, Millton & Co., 247 Main St.
Martin, F. W. Main St.

Extension Table Manufacturer.

BELCHER, D. E. Liberty St.   See adv. index.

Express Offices and Agents.

MERCHANTS UNION EXPRESS CO., J. H. Osgood, Agent,
Franklin Block, Main St.   See adv. index.
American Express, 3 Court St.
Thompson & Co., 3 Court St.

Fancy Goods and Notions.

Coleman, M. & B. 108 Main St.
Fallon, J. 1 Opera Block, Main St.
Gardner & Young, Townsley Block.
KINMAN, W. D. 214 Main St.   See adv. index.
Jennison & Kendall, 2 Court St.
McFarland & Niebuhr, 216 Main St.
Lord, A. G..& Co., 182   "
Paquettee, Henry, 187   "
Pierce, William, 4 Shaw's Block.
Stern, Jacob, 3 East State St.
Malley, M. W. 180 Main St.

Fancy Goods and Millinery.

Baumgarten, J. L. 177 Main St.

Fancy Goods and Straw Bleachers.

Sayles & Stockbridge, 173 Main St.
WALLACH, SCHWAB & BINSSER, 233 Main St.

Fancy Goods and Stationery.

Jennings, A. F. 259 Main St.
Jennings, A. F. Post Office Building, Pynchon St.
Sterns, F. H. & E. H. 2 Fallon's Block, Main St.

Fishing Tackle.

GIFFORD, J. H. 3 State St., up stairs. See adv. index.

Fish and Oysters, (Wholesale and Retail.)

AMES, S. (Wholesale Oysters,) 121 Main St.
Gilmore, Bond & Co., 6 Market St., basement Massasoit House.
Jennings, C. L. 85 Main St.
Lillibridge & Batchelder, 323 Main St.
Webber, J. W. & Co., 1 Cypress St.

Fire Arms Manufacturers.

GIFFORD, J. H. 3 State St., up stairs. See adv. index.
Smith & Wesson, (Revolvers,) Stockbridge St.

Florist and Nursery.

Olm Brothers, 350 Main St.
Sheehan, J. Morris St.

Flour, Feed and Grain.

Bangs, John, 10 East State St. Wholesale and Retail.
Barker, S. & Co., 1 Union House Block, Main St.
Dorman & Strong, Union Block,   "
Sibley & Rathbun, 295, 297 Main St.
Worthy, J. L. & Co., 117   "

29

Flouring Mills.

Bangs, John, Mill St.
Worthy, J. L. (Agawam.)
Wright, C. G. South Main St.

Flour, Lime and Cement.

Bigelow, S. Commercial Block.

Foundries, Brass.

Stebbins, Erastus, Taylor St.
Hampden Iron Foundry, 42 Water St.
Springfield Brass Foundry.

Fruit, (Foreign and Domestic,) Dealers.

Bau, E. C. 156 Main St.
Collins, Wm. M. 283 Main St.
Gunn & Merrill, cor. Main and Lyman Sts.

Fresco Paintings and Window Shades.

WIESE, F. 13, 15 Pynchon St.   See adv. index.

Fruit and Confectionery, Wholesale and Retail.

AMSDEN & CO., 92 Main, 2 Hampden Sts.
Dill, Dexter, 139 Main St.
Goddard, H. T. 204   "
Judd, Wm. A. 26 East State St.
Lyon, C. T. Allis' Block, North Main St.
Shattuck, W. H. 115   "
Sleeper, M. D. 1 Railroad Row.

Fruit Dealers, (Wholesale.)

Gunn & Merrill, cor. Main and Lyman Sts.
Gilmore, Bond & Co., Railroad Row.

Furniture Manufacturers.

FISHER, BUCKHAUSE & KNAPPE, Burt's Block, Main St. See adv. index.

Furniture Dealers.

Dickinson, E. W. & Co., 2 Union Block, Main St.
FISHER, BUCKHAUSE & KNAPPE, 5 1-2 Burt's Block, Main St. See adv. index.
Eldredge, J. A. & Co., Fountain Row.
Maxfield & Kellogg, Hampden Hall.

Furriers.

(See also Hats, Caps, and Furs.)
Avery, S. W. 195 Main St.
Sanderson, Harvey, 271 Main St.

Gas Burner Manufacturers.

Berg, C. H. & Co., Market, near Market St.

Gas Fitters and Fixtures.

BRIGGS, H. J. & Co., Vernon St. See adv. index.
Elwell, E. M. Main St.
Hamilton & Co.
Roche Brothers, Liberty St.
Howard Steam Heating Co., 101 Main St.
Springfield Steam and Gas Pipe Co., 123 Main St.

Gasometer Manufacturers.

BULLEN & GRIMES, Liberty St. See adv. index.

Gas Light Company.

Springfield Gas Light Co., cor. Main and State Sts.
Marvin Chapin, Pres., Geo. Dwight, Supt., J. D. Brewer, Treas.

Gas Fixtures.

Elwell, E. M. Shaw's Block, Main St.

General Repairers.

ELDRIDGE & HASTINGS, 283 Main St., up stairs. See adv. index.

Gents. Furnishing Goods.

Avery, S. W. 195 Main St.
Baldwin, J. A. 138   "
Haynes, T. L. & Co., cor. Main and Pynchon Sts.
Miller & Culver, 80, 82 Main St.
RAY, SAMUEL C. Main St., opposite Court Square. See adv. index.
Keyes, Henry & Co., Main St.
VAUGHAN, GEO. 2 Fort Block, Main St.
Brigham, D. H. & Co., Main St.

Gold Chain Manufacturer.

SHUMWAY, R. G. Harrison Av. See adv. index.

Gold Pen Manufacturer.

C. N. PACKARD, 247 Main St. See adv. index.

Grocers, (Wholesale.)

Downing & Sturtevant, Main St.
Pynchon, Leo & Co., cor. Main and State Sts.
West, Stone & Co.

Grocers, (Retail.)

Bliss, Jas. H. cor. Main and William Sts.
Brown & Pinney, Water Shops.
Bly, E. 120 Main St.
Breerly & Eveans, Walnut St.
Camp, A. Day & Jobson's Block, North Main St.
Cate, N. cor. State & Walnut Sts.
Couch & Miller, 260 Main St.

D. L. HARRIS & CO.,

NO. 1 CHARLES STREET, SPRINGFIELD, MASS.

Builders of Machinists' Tools, Turn Tables, Bolts, Shafting, Foundry and Mill Work, Bolt Cutters and Tapping Machines. Also manufacturers of Howe's Patent Truss for Bridges and Roofs for Railroads and Highways. Also Builders of the Littlefield Steam and Power Pumps, for Fire Purposes, Supply or Boilers.

D. L. HARRIS.   R. F. HAWKINS.   W. H. BURRALL.

Coulding & Co., 3 Burt's Block, Main St.
Craig, A. 3 Union House Block,   "
Cutler, Luther, 303   "
Davison, H. J. 230   "
Downing & Sturtevant, cor. Main St. and Western R. R.
Dwight, E. Allis' Block, North Main St.
Elmer, M. & Co., 112 East State St.
Field, Chas. P. 9 Hampden St.
Gilmore, Bond & Co., cor. Main and Broad Sts., Westfield.
Haskell, E. B. & Son, 79 Main St.
Houghton & Eddy, North   "
Houston & Smith,   "   "
Hudson, Chas. T. 38 East State St.
Joy & Chandler, 293 Main St.
Kimberly, E & Co., 190 Central St.
Lyman, Harvey, 70 East Worthington St.
Macombee & Cornell, 305 Main St.
Marsh, J. S. & Co., 193   "
McCarty, J. 17 Hampden St.
Newell, Nox H. S. & C. S. Burt's Block.
Niles, A. F. & H. L. cor. Main and Cypress Sts.
Pember & Jenks, 3 Allis' Block, North Main St.
Pynchon, Lee & Co., cor. Main and State Sts. Wholesale and Retail.
Quimby & Aikens, 28 East State St.
Rice, Wight & Co., 141 Main St.
Shaw, Geo. D. & Co., 12 East State St.
Waite, E. H. 111   "   "
Weeks, John, 50 Main St.
West, Stone & Co., cor. Main and Court Sts. Wholesale and Retail.
Miller, W. S. 118 Main St.
Winter, L. S. & J. K. Main St.
Woolson, Chas. A. 12 Water St.

Gun Smiths.

Ashton, Wm.
GIFFORD, J. H. 3 East State St. See adv. index.

Hair Restorative.

QUEEN, GEORGE, Sandford St.   See adv. index.

Hand Drill Press.

Sessons, Asa, Jr., Mill St.

Harness Makers.

PAYNE, Wm. 3, 5, 7 Dwight St.   See adv. index.

Hardware and Cutlery.

Bemis, A. Main St.
Bemis & Call, Taylor St.
Brown & Graves, opposite Massasoit House.
Brewer, J. D. State cor. Main St.
Foot, Homer & Co., cor. State and Main Sts.

Harness and Saddlery.

Cummings, Josiah, 111, 113 Main St.
White & Coolidge, 200 Main St.
Wilkinson, W. H. 109   "
PAYNE, WILLIAM 3, 5, 7 Dwight St.   See adv. index.
Russell & Barber, cor. State and Walnut Sts.

Hardware and Tool Manufacturers.

Bemis & Call, Taylor St.

Hats, Caps and Furs.

Avery, S. W. 195 Main St.
Trafton, John W. cor. Main and Sanford Sts.
Roberts, Dwight 96 Main St.
Sanderson & Son, 271 Main St.
Williams, E. A. & Co., 279 "

Hoop Skirt Manufacturers and Dealers.

CHACE, GEO. W. 179 Main St.   See adv. index.
Wheeler, M. M. 108 Main St.

Horse Shoers.

Bailey & Burke, East Court St.

Hosiery and Gloves, (Wholesale and Retail.)

KINSMAN, W. D. 214 Main St. See adv. index.

Hotels.

Carlton House, 1 Hampden St.

Cooleys Hotel, 75 North Main St.

EXCHANGE HOTEL, E. Adams & Co., Pro., 206 Main St.

Greundler's Hotel, cor. Bridge and Water Sts.

HAMPDEN HOUSE, H. N. Fish, Pro., cor. Court and Main Sts. See adv. index.

HAYNES' HOTEL, Tilly Haynes, Pro., cor. Main and Pynchon Sts.

MASSASOIT HOUSE, M. & E. S. Chapin, Main St. opposite Depot. See adv. index.

Myrtly Street House, Myrtle St.

MEAGHER'S HOTEL, 91 Main St.

MOULTON'S HOTEL, 117 East State St.

Nayasset House, J. S. Robinson, Railroad Row.

Park Street House, Main cor. Lyman St.

PYNCHON HOUSE, W. F. Gunn, Pro., Main near Depot.

ROCKINGHAM HOUSE, A. Nason, Pro., State cor. Walnut Street.

SANFORD STREET HOUSE, W. B. Cook Pro., Sanford St.

SPRINGFIELD HOUSE, 17 West St.

UNITED STATES HOTEL, G. Burbach Pro., Maine cor. State St.

Union House, H. M. French Pro., Union House Block, Main Street.

Ice Cream Saloon.

Barney, Charles E. 102 Main St.

Ice Cream and Dining.

Quimby, H. A. 267 Main St.

India Rubber Goods.

Frary, O. Mill St.

India Rubber Web Manufacturing Co., South Main St.

Insurance Agents.

Bond, A. H. Gurdian Life Ins. Co., Taylor & Olmsted Block.

Burt, A. & Co., 175 Main St.
Graves, J. L. cor. State and Main Sts.
Johnson, Jas. L. 192   "
Jas. M. Porter & Co., 4 Music Hall, Main St.
Miller, Henry D. 5 Fallons Block,   "
Pynchon & Marsh, Post Office Building, Pynchon St.
Ladd Brothers, cor. Main and Pynchon Sts.
Waterman & Bower, 2 Fallon's Block, Main St.

Insurance and Claim Agents.

Holmes, J. W. 1 Union Block.
Tifft, S. A. 265½ Main St.

Insurance Companies.

Holyoke Mutual Fire Ins. Co., 3 Fallon's Block, Main St.
Rice & Benjamin, 48 Main St.
Springfield Mutual Fire Assurance Co., cor. Main and Elm Sts.
    E. Blake, Pres., L. Gorham, Sec.
MASSACHUSETTS MUTUAL LIFE INS. CO., 8 Foot's
Block.
Springfield Fire and Marine Ins. Co., Foot's Block, 110 Main
St., Cash capital, $500,000, Surplus, $210,000.   Edmund Free-
man, Pres., J. N. Dunham, Sec., Sandford J. Hall, Asst. Sec.
See adv. index.

Intelligence Offices.

Ryan, J. 157 Main St.
Smith, Z. 271   "

Iron Works.

NORWALK IRON WORKS, William St.   See adv. index.

Jewelry Manufacturers.

Arthur Rumsill & Co., cor. Central and Maple Sts.
SHUMWAY, R. G. See adv. index.

Jewelry and Watches.

Bailey & Graves, cor. Main and Elm Sts.

Buckland, E. H. & Co., 94 Main St.
Kirkham, Wm. 277   "
Shaw, C. R. 100 Main St.
Smith, Henry, 5 Elm St.
STOWE, L. S. Post Office Building, Main St., (Wholesale.)
Robinson, M. F. 181 Main St.
Whipple, E. A. 299   "
Williams, T. A.

Job Printers.

Bowles, Samuel & Co., Main St.
Miller, Joseph Goodrich's Block, Main St.
Tannath, J. F. & Co., 3 Elm St.

Junk Dealers.

McCULLOUGH & BURT, 117 Main St.   See adv. index.
Hammond, S. T. & Co., rear of Springfield Dye House.   See
adv. index.

Kerosene Oil Dealers.

Hamilton, John & Son, Commercial Row.

Knitting Machine Manufacturers.

LAMB KNITTING MACHINE CO., Pynchon Bank Block,
Main St.   See adv. back cover.

Laundries.

Hampden Laundry Co., 4 Pynchon St.
Springfield Laundry, Hillman St.

Lime and Cement.

Crosby, D. W. 3 Lyman St.

Liquor Dealers, (Wholesale.)

Gunn, Wm. & Co., 9 West State St.

Livery Stables.

ALVORD, EDWARD, Market, rear Merchants' Express.   See
adv. index.

Bates & Kingsley, cor. Walnut and State Sts.
Beckwith, F. R. 208 Main St.
Briggs, J. L. Lyman St.
Cadwell & Stickney, 18 East State St.
COLLINS, WM. S. Sanford St.
Henry & Marsh, cor. Court and Market Sts.
Wilder & Houston, Main St., near Union Hotel.
Patch, E. H. Sanford St.
RICHMOND, F. & J. M. Sanford St. See adv. index.
Robinson, E. C. rear Massasoit House, Railroad Row.
Sexton & Nason, cor. Walnut & State Sts.
Simonds, Wm. Liberty St.

Lithographers.

Bradley, Milton & Co., 247 Main St.

Lock Smiths.

Ashton, Wm. Main, cor. Bridge St.
ELDRIDGE & HASTINGS, 282 Main St. See adv. index.
GIFFORD, J. H. 3 State St., up stairs. See adv. index.

Lumber Dealers.

Robinson, Marsh & Co., Lyman St.
SMITH & MARTIN, Taylor St.
Wells River Lumber Co., 4 Elm St.

Machine Screw Manufacturers.

HARRIS, D. L. & Co., 1 Charles St. See adv. index.
STACY, E. S. & CO., Harrison Av. See adv. index.

Machine Shops.

Dickinson, E. L. & J. Mill St.
HARRIS, D. L. & Co., 1 Charles St. See adv. index.
Roche Brothers, rear Chase's Planing Mill, Liberty St.

Machinists' Tools Manufacturers.

HARRIS, D. L. & Co., 1 Charles St. See adv. index.
STACY, E. S. & CO., Harrison Av. See adv. index.

Machinists.

Barnes & Curtis, Sanford and Market Sts.
BULLEN & GRIMES, Liberty St. See adv. index.
Dickinson, E. L. & J. Mill St.
HARRIS, D. L. & Co. 1 Charles St. See adv. index.
Kimball, C. W. Water St.
STACY, E. S. & Co., Harrison Av. See adv. index.

Machinery Manufacturers.

BULLEN & GRIMES, Liberty St. See adv. index.
Harris, D. L. & Co., 1 Charles St.
STACY, E. S. & Co., Harrison Av. See adv. index.
Lamb Knitting Machine Co., Main St.

Marble Yards.

SPRINGFIELD MARBLE WORKS, Crabtree & Short, No. 2
Burt's Block, cor. Main and Bliss Sts. See adv. index.

Meat Markets.

Allen, Thos. H. & Brother, 60 North Main St.
Allen, T. H. 2 Walnut St.
Byrnes, Jas. A. 56 North Main St.
Clark, Wm. L. 291 Main St.
Chaffee & Nye, 232   "
Hawes & Smith, 4 West State St.
Colwell & Whitney, 5 Elm St.
Hunt & Greenleaf, Sanford St.
Maynard, M. A. 24 East State St.
Moseley, A. A. 101   "   "
Medbery, J. C. 78 East Worthington St.
Miller, W. S. 116 Main St.
Nutting, Wm. 64 North Main St.
Perkins, V. 14 East State St.
Richards & Dumbleton, 258 Main St.
Smith, A. C. & S. B. 319 Main St.
Ward, Geo. W. Indian Orchard.

Metals. •

HAMMOND, S. T. & Co., rear Springfield Dye House. See adv. index.

McCULLOCH, & BURT, 117 Main St. See adv. index.

Mechanics' Tools Manufacturers.

Bemis & Call Co., Taylor St.

STACY, E. S. & Co., Harrison Av. See adv. index.

Mechanical Brokers.

Gardner & Hyde, 2 Vernon St.

KIMBALL, C. W. cor. Water St. and Railroad Row, opposite Depot. See adv. index.

Melodeon Dealers.

Burt & Hoadley, 190 Main St.

Hutchings, M. J. D. Shaw's Block, Main St.

Merchant Tailors.

Avery, Henry, 245 Main St.

Barber, J. D. 113 East State St.

Geraghty & Sullivan, 161 Main St.

Haynes, T. L. cor. Main and Pynchon Sts.

Kimball & Blodgett, 106 Main St.

King, C. H. 5 Stockbridge St.

Murdock, Henry, 120 Main St.

Merrick & Huber, 218   "

Paine, Charles, 275   "

Richardson, G. D. 227   "

RAY, SAMUEL C. 241   "   See adv. index.

Schober, Charles, cor. Main and Elm Sts.

Mineral Water Manufacturer.

BROOKS, F. A. 52 North Main St. See adv. index.

Millinery.

Bartlett, D. J. 2 Fallon's Block, Main St.

Coleman, M. & B. 108   Main St.
Pierce, Wm. 4 Shaw's Block, "
Smith, Mrs. R. F. 102   "
WALLACH, SCHWAB & ZINSSER, 233 Main St.
Wilcox, O. W. & Co., 187   "
Winslow, G. T. 185   "

Mop Handle Manufacturer.

BELCHER, D. E. Liberty St.   See adv. index. '

Moulding Manufactory.

Springfield Moulding Manufactory, Viner, F. J. Dwight St.

Music and Musical Instruments.

Hutchins, M. J. D. Main St.
Mathews, J. W. 189 Main St.
Burt & Hoadley, 190   "

Musical Instrument Manufacturer.

Page, F. 17 1-2 State St.

Naturalist and Taxidermist.

Hosford, B. 115 Main St.

Newspapers. '

SPRINGFIELD DAILY REPUBLICAN, Franklin Block.
SPRINGFIELD DAILY UNION, Main St.   See adv. index.
SPRINGFIELD SEMI WEEKLY AND WEEKLY REPUB-
LICAN.
SPRINGFIELD WEEKLY UNION, Main St.   See adv. index.

Oil and Lamp Stores.

JOHNSON, G. D. 321 Main St.
Hamilton, Jason, Commercial Row.

Oil Tank Manufacturers.

BULLEN & GRIMES, Liberty St.   See adv. index.

Opticians.

Burbank, S. D. Stockbridge St.
Chapin, D. M. 184 Main St.

Ornamental Carver.

GARDNER, J. A. Taylor St.

Ornamental Hair Work.

Commeran, Miss, 14 Barnes' Block, Main St.
Montague, W. H. 77 North Main St.

Oyster Dealers.

AMES, S. 121 Main St. (Wholesale.)
Gilmore, Bond & Co., 6 Market St.
Webber, J. W. & Co., 1 Cypress St.

Paint and Chemical Manufacturers.

HAMPDEN PAINT AND CHEMICAL Co., cor. Armory St.
and Western Railroad.

Paints, Oils, Glass, &c.

Walker, T. M. & Co., 253 Main St. Wholesale and Retail.
Warner, D. 7, 8 Market St.

Paper Dealers, (Wholesale.)

Powers & Brown Paper Co., under Massasoit House, Main St.

Paper and Paper Stock Dealers, (Wholesale.)

HAMMOND, S. T. & Co., rear Springfield Dye House. See
adv. index.
Hollister & Co., 95 Main St.
McCULLOCH & BURT, 117 Main St. See adv. index.
Salsbury, Henry & Co., 137 Main St.
Smith & Dickinson, Commercial Row.
Taylor, Olmsted & Co., Main, cor. Taylor St.

Paper Hangings.

Prince, Wm. M. & Co., 86 Main St.
Bridgman & Whitney, cor. Main and State Sts.

Paper Box Manufacturers.

Elliott & Houghton, Shaw's Block, Main St.
Doane, G. Commercial Block, Main St.
Doane, G. W. cor. Main and Hampden Sts.
Taylor & Moseman, 5 1-2 Burt's Block, Main St.

Paper Collar Manufacturers.

Ray & Taylor, cor. Hillman & Dwight St.
Nonpariel Paper Collar Manufacturing Co., Hillman St.

Paper Box and Envelope Manufactory.

Taylor & Moseman, 5 1-2 Burt's Block, Main St.

Paper Manufacturers.

Greenleaf & Taylor Manufacturing Co., opposite Massasoit House, Main St.
Salsbury, H & Co., Main St.
Columbia Paper Company, cor. Main and Taylor Sts.
Union Paper Co., cor. Main and Taylor Sts.

Paper Stock.

Dickinson & Mays, 1 Commercial Row.
HAMMOND, S. T. & CO., rear Springfield Dye House.   See adv. index.
McCULLOCH & BURT, 117 Main St.   See adv. index.

Paper Warehouse.

Power & Brown, 90 Main St.

Patent Agents.

Buckland & Curtis, 1 Barnes' Block, Main St.
Sanders, Sidney, Goodrich Block,   "
Gardner & Hyde, 2 Vernon St.
KIMBALL, C. W. cor. Water and Railroad Row, opposite Depot. See adv. index.

Patent Eave Trough Manufacturers.

BARTLETT, CHILD & CO., Taylor St.   See adv. index.

Patent Medicines.

Leet, C. D. Hillman, near Main St.
Skinner, Orrin & Co., 6, 7 Taylor & Olmsted Block.

Pattern, Models and Machine Building.

Marshall, Morse & Sweetland, Market St.

Pattern and Model Maker.

BLISS, J. K. 18 Hampden St.   See adv. index.
Piper, E. J. Market St.

Patent Right Agents.

JOHNSON, L. C. 321 Main St.

Picture Frame Dealers.

Campbell, J. B. 19 State St.
Bradley, Milton & Co., Main St.
Powers, L. J. & Bro., 90 Main St.

Piano Forte Dealers.

Beebe, R. Foot's Block, Main St.
Burt & Hoadley, 190   "
Kingsbury, Geo. O.   "
Hutchins, M. J. D.   "

Photograph Album Manufacturers.

BOWLES, SAMUEL & CO., Main St.

Photographers.

Buckholz & Hendrick, 4 Pynchon Bank Block, Main St.
MOORE BROTHERS, Artists, opposite Court Square. Life size Photographs finished in all sizes, also, cabinet Photographs and Cartes de Visite on the most satisfactory terms.
Richardson, W. P. 34 Goodrich Block, Main St.
Spooner, J. C. cor. Main and State Sts.
Sweetser, A. T. cor. Main and Hillman.
TOWNSEND, A. C. & CO., Main St.   See adv. index.
Warren, R. 173½ Main St.

Physicians and Surgeons.

Allen, Paul W. 39 High St.
Allen, E. C. East Worthington St.
Anthony, Reily, Main St.
Calkins, M. East State St.
Buck, T. F. Main St.
Buck, W. G   "
Church, Jefferson 246 Main St.
Gardiner, W. W. 27 East State St.
Holmes, H. W. 90   "
Hooker, John 25   "
Kelley, J. Wesley, 28   "
Lambert, Alfred   "
Miller, Wm. B. Walnut St.
Peabody, Dr. 329 Main St.
Pomeroy, S. F. 7½ East State St.
Reed, A. G. 8 Barnes' Block.
Rice, A. B. East State St.
Smith, David P. "
Stebbins, Geo. S. 126 Main St.
Overand, Dr.   "
Reed, A. G. 8 Barnes' Block, Main St.
Stickney, H. G. 9 West Bridge St.
Vaille, H. R. 282 Main St.
Winans, Niles, cor Main and Fremont St.
Winans, S. 47 North Main St.
White, W. H. Rice Block.

Pistol Manufacturers.

Smith & Wesson, Stockbridge St.

Picture Frame Manufacturers.

Campbell, J. B. 19 State St.
Learned, E. E. opposite Court Square.
Talbot, Geo. W. 46 Main St.
Holcomb, E. M. 202 Main St.

Painters, (House and Sign.)

Bartlett, T. B. 3 Market St.

31

Clark, L. 62 Main St.
Rice, Nathan 3 Market St.
Powel & Tucker,   "

Peat Machine Manufacturer.
Leet, C. D. Hillman St.

Periodical and News Depots.
Jennings, A. H. Main St.
Powers, L. J. & Bro., under Massasoit House.

Plane Maker.
Crane, Harvey, Market St.

Planing Mill and Box Manufactory.
Chase, J. G. & Brother, Liberty St.
Miller, Francis, Taylor St.

Planing Mill and Lumber Yard.
Day, Jobson & Chase, Liberty and Chestnut Sts.

Plumbing and Gas Fitting.
Goodhue, C. L. 121 Main St.
Knight, Asa M. Pynchon St.

Briggs, H. J. & Co., 4 Vernon St.   See adv. index.

Plumbers and Gas Fitters.
Briggs, H. J. & Co., 4 Vernon St.
Knight, A. M. & Son 13 Pynchon St.

Polar Soda Fountain Manufacturer.
Bigelow, E. Market St.

Printers.
BOWLES, SAMUEL & CO., Franklin, Main St.

UNION PRINTING CO., cor. Main and Taylor Sts., Taylor & Olmsted Block. See adv. index.

Pump Manufacturers.

DWIGHT, GEORGE Jr. & CO., (Earle's Patent Steam.)   See adv. index.

Gardiner, J. B. Agent.

Harris D. L. & Co.

Knight, Asa W. (copper) Main St.

Roche Brothers, Liberty St.

Pump Manufacturers, (Steam and Power.)

HARRIS, D. L. & CO., (Littlefield's Patent,) 1 Charles St. See adv. index.

Publishers, (Book.)

G. & C. Merriam, 8 West State St.

Union Printing Co., Main St.

Holland, W. J. & Co., Taylor & Olmsted Block.

BOWLES, SAMUEL & CO., Main St.

Railroad Car Manufacturers.

Wason Manufacturing Co., Lyman St.

Railway Supplies.

Howard Brothers, 76 Main St.

Real Estate Agents.

Kingsbury, G. O. cor. Court and Main Sts.

Rice & Clark, Main St.

Reed Manufacturers.

TILLEY & CLARK, Commercial Row.   See adv. index.

Restaurants.

Adams, H. G. R. R. Depot.

Barney, Chas. E. 102 Main St.

Burr, Edwin C. 136 Main St.
Gilmore, D. O. Pynchon St.
Hefferan, C. 125 Main St.
Parsons, A. B.   "
Sleeper, M. D. Railroad Row.
Quimby, H. A. 267 Main St.
Thomas, Thomas 119 Main St.

Rubber, Boot and Shoe Dealers.

Bailey, Maish 9 State St.
Griswold & Bradley.
Shaw, H. A. 5 State St.

Saddle and Harness Makers.

Hewett, J. R. Patton's Block, Main St.

Saddlery and Hardware, (Wholesale.)

LEE & BAKER, 78 Main St.   See adv. index.

Saddlery Trimmings.

WESSON & MORRIS, Dwight St.
LEE & BAKER, 78 Main St.   See adv. index.

Sale Stables.

ALVORD, E. rear Merchants Union Express Co.   See adv. index.
Richmond, F. & J. M. Sandford St.

Sash, Doors and Blinds.

Currier, Richards cor. Liberty and Chestnut Sts.

Saving Banks.

Hampden Savings Bank, Main St.   Joseph C. Pynchon, Pres., Daniel J. Marsh, Treas.
Springfield Five Cents Savings Bank, 2 Court St.
Springfield Institution for Savings, Main cor. State St.

Saw Dealers.

Elwell, E. M. Shaw's Block, Main St.

Sewing Machine Agents.

CHACE, GEO. W. Agent (Singers,) 179 Main St. See adv. index.

Griswold, Ogden 12 Barnes' Block, Main St.

Lee, H. C. Elliptic Machine, Pynchon Bank, Main St.

Lee, C. M. 279 Main St.

Thomas, Mrs. Wm. 216 Main St., Wilcox & Gibbs.

Williams, H. S. 9 East State St., Agent Ætna Sewing Machine.

RAY, SAMUEL C. Main opposite Court St., Finkle & Lyons. See adv. index.

Shirt Manufacturer.

DEWEY, H. S. 24 Barnes' Block, Main St. See adv. index.

Sign Painters.

Drake, James C. 131 Main St.

Hancox, Albert, Hillman St.

Hooker, George, Willow St.

Silk Merchants.

Bartlett, H. H. & Co., Allis' Block, North Main St.

Slipper Manufacturers.

AMERICAN CARPET SLIPPER WORKS, Martin Wesson, Prop. cor. Stockbridge and Willow.

Soda and Syrup Apparatus Manufacturer.

Bigelow, E. 245 Main St.

Soap and Candle Manufacturers.

Arnold, Wm. & Co., Lyman St.

Cooley, R. N. 61 East State St.

Fisk, L. I. & Co.,Lyman St.

Spectacle Manufacturer.

Burbank, S. D. Stockbridge St.

Stair Builder.

Fitts, L. L. Taylor St.

Steam Table Manufacturers.

BULLEN & GRIMES, Liberty St.　See adv. index.

Steam Boiler Manufacturers.

SPRINGFIELD STEAM BOILER WORKS.
BULLEN & GRIMES, Liberty St.　See adv. index.

Steam Heating Apparatus.

Howard Steam Heating Co., 87, 89 Main St.

Steam Pump Manufacturers.

NORWALK IRON WORKS, Hillman St.　See adv. index.

Steam and Gas Pipe Dealers.

BRIGGS, H. J. & Co., Vernon St.　See adv. index.
Springfield Steam and Gas Pipe Works, J. H. Appleton & Co.,
Proprietors, 123 Main St.

Stencil Cutter.

GIFFORD, T. H. 3 State St.　See adv. index.

Stoves and Tinware.

Abbe, James, 114 Main St.
Alexander, John, Allis' Block, Main St.
Beach, T. D. 1 Elm St.
Clark, Leonard, 12 West State St.
Clark, Simpson, 31 East State St.
Lewis, L. S. 11　　　"　　"
Montague, D. B. 135 Main, and 2 & 4 Bridge St.
Spooner & Pease, 100 East State St.
Wilcox, W. L. & Co., 16 "　　"

Tea, Coffee and Spices.

Bourke Brothers, 113 Main St.
Japan Tea Co., 2 Elm St.

Telegraph Offices.

Franklin Telegraph Co., Franklin Block.
Western Union Telegraph, Haynes' Hotel Block, Main St.

Tin and Wooden Ware Dealers.

Dickinson & Mayo, 1 Commercial Row.

Tobacco and Cigars.

Frost, S. M. cor. Main and Bridge Sts.
Ryder, A. C. 255 Main St.
Warner, F. G. 133 "
Wright, W. H. 273 "

Tobacco Dealers.

Smith, H. & Co., 20 Hampden St.

Tool Manufacturers.

Bemis & Call Co.
STACY, E. S. & Co., Harrison Av. See adv. index.

Troughs, (Eave.)

BARTLETT, CHILD & Co., Taylor St. See adv. index.

Trimming Goods.

KINSMAN, W. D. 214 Main St. See adv. index.

Undertakers.

Pomeroy & Fisk, 17 East State St.
Ross, Sidney, 267 Main St.
Skahan & Bourke, 113 Main St.
WASHBURN & CHASE, cor. Market and Sanford Sts. See adv. index.

Upholstering and Repairing.

Ellis, A. cor. Willow and Stockbridge Sts.

Upholsters' Goods.

FISHER, BUCKHAUSE & KNAPPE, 5 1-2 Burt's Block. See adv. index.

Variety Stores.

Bartlett, Miss R. A. 22 East State St.
Cogswell, J. W. 20 " "

SANDERSON, W. Grimes' Block, East State St.
Tiffany, W. S. 76 East Worthington St.

Waste Dealers.

Howard & Brothers, Mill St.

Watches and Jewelry.

Williams T. A. 84 Main St.
Porter & Prince, 86 Main St.
Chandler A. C. 243   "
Kirkham, Wm. Jr., 277 "
⁕　Howard, J. C. 277   "
Whipple, E. A. 229   "

Wire Cloth and Sieve Manufacturer.

Bigelow, Cheney, 3 Sanford St.

Woolen Manufacturers.

Alden, Gaylord, Mill St.,
King, Lyman,   "
Smith, Fall & Bucklaird, Mill St., foot of Maple.

Wooden Eave Trough Manufacturers.

BARTLETT, CHILD & Co., Taylor St. See adv. index.

Wrapping Paper and Paper Stock.

McCULLOCH & BURT, 117 Main St. See adv. index.

Yankee Notions, (Wholesale.)

Patton, William, 100 Main St.

SINGER'S IMPROVED

SEWING MACHINES

Head-quarters at

Springfield, Mass., 179 Main Street.

GEO. W. CHACE, General Agent.

GEO. W. CHACE,

Hoop Skirt Manufacturer,

WHOLESALE AND RETAIL DEALER IN

Hoop Skirts, Corsets, and Skirt Materials.

179 Main St., Springfield, Mass.

Office of the Singer Mfg. Co's
IMPROVED SEWING MACHINES.

J. H. BANKS.   H. H. BANKS.

J. H. BANKS & SON,

WHOLESALE AND RETAIL

COAL DEALERS.

ANTHRACITE AND BITUMINOUS.

Lehigh and Schuylkill, Very Superior Quality.

City Office, 253 Main St., Opp. Court Square,

No. 38 West William St. Yard and Office, }   **Springfield, Mass.**

E. S. STACY & CO.,

Tool Makers and Machinists.

MACHINE SCREWS OF ALL KINDS MADE TO ORDER.

*Models of Wood or Metal, Die Sinking, Stamp
Cutting, &c., &c.*

HARRISON AVENUE, SPRINGFIELD, MASS.

32

W. D. KINSMAN,

(Successor to Howard & Kinsman,)

WHOLESALE AND RETAIL DEALER IN

HOSIERY AND GLOVES,

Trimmings, Zephyr Worsteds, Embroideries,

AND

THREAD STORE GOODS,

Pynchon Bank Block, 214 Main Street,

SPRINGFIELD, MASS.

SPRINGFIELD MARBLE WORKS.

CRABTREE & SHORT,

MANUFACTURERS OF

Marble Mantles, Monuments,

Gravestones, and

ORNAMENTAL MARBLE WORK.

No. 2 Burt's Block, Main Street, and No. 2 Bliss Street,

SPRINGFIELD, MASSACHUSETTS.

GERMANIA FURNITURE WAREROOMS.

FISHER, BUCKHAUSE & KNAPPE,

PRACTICAL UPHOLSTERERS, AND CABINET MAKERS,

Dealers in Parlor, Dining Room and Chamber Furniture,

Mattresses, Curtains, Curtain Trimmings, Shades, &c., &c.

ALSO COMMON FURNITURE OF ALL KINDS.

5 1-2 BURT'S BLOCK, SPRINGFIELD, MASS.

A. C. FISHER.   CHAS. BUCKHAUSE.   H. KNAPPE.

WASHBURN & CHASE,
WHOLESALE MANUFACTURERS,

And Dealers in

WALNUT, ROSEWOOD AND GRAINED
CASKETS AND COFFINS,
AND

GENERAL UNDERTAKERS,

Corner Market and Sanford Streets,
SPRINGFIELD, MASS.

WILLIAM PAYNE,
MANUFACTURER OF

Saddles, Harnesses and Collars,
Nos. 3, 5 and 7 Dwight Street,
SPRINGFIELD, MASS.

TILLEY & CLARK,
MANUFACTURERS OF EVERY DESCRIPTION OF

WEAVING REEDS AND HARNESSES,
Commercial Row, Near Western Depot,
SPRINGFIELD, MASS.
All orders by Mail, for Reeds or Harnesses, promptly attended to, and satisfaction guaranteed.

Paper and Paper Stock Warehouse.

McCULLOCH & BURT,
DEALERS IN

Writing and Wrapping Papers,
Envelopes, Paper-Bags, Twine,
PAPER STOCK, &c.

117 Main St., Opposite Fort Block, Springfield, Mass.

Cash paid for Rags and Old Junk.

J. W. McCULLOCH.   A. BURT, Jr.

E. ALVORD,
LIVERY, FEED, SALES
And Exchange Stables,
Rear Merchants' Union Express,
MARKET ST., SPRINGFIELD, MASS.

H. S. DEWEY,
MANUFACTURER OF
COTTON AND WOOLEN SHIRTS,
Collars, Bosoms, Drawers and Under Flannels, Custom Made,

24 BARNES' BLOCK, - - - - SPRINGFIELD, MASS.
Shirt Patterns Cut and all orders promptly attended to.

QUIMBY & HUDSON,
MANUFACTURERS OF
EXPRESS, PEDDLER AND GROCERY WAGONS, PHÆTONS,
TOP AND NO TOP BUGGIES,

ROCKAWAYS, CABROILETS, BEACH WAGONS, &c., &c.

We fully warrant our work to be equal to any in the country.

Orders promptly attended to.

SPRINGFIELD, MASS.
M. G. C. QUIMBY.   R. H. HUDSON.

S. T. HAMMOND & CO.,
(Successors to Coburn & Hammond,)
DEALERS IN
Old Iron, Metals & Paper Stock,
Rear of Springfield Dye House, SPRINGFIELD, MASS.
S. T. HAMMOND.   JOHN DAY.

F. A. BROOKS,
MANUFACTURER OF
MINERAL WATER, SODA & SPRUCE BEER.
Bottle Ale, Porter and Cider constantly on hand.

Orders promptly attended to.

52 North Main St., - - - - Springfield, Mass.

J. H. GIFFORD,
GUN, LOCKSMITH & STENCIL CUTTER,
No. 3 State Street, Up Stairs,
SPRINGFIELD, MASS.
ALSO DEALER IN
GUNS, RIFLES, PISTOLS, FISHING TACKLE & AMMUNITION.
ALL KINDS OF STENCIL WORK.
*Locks and Keys fitted, Sewing Machines, Cutlery, Umbrellas
and Parasols repaired, and all kinds of small work.*

Silver Door Plates and Numbers.
SAFE REPAIRING.

LEE & BAKER,

(*Successors to Howard & Brothers,*)

MANUFACTURERS AND DEALERS IN

CARRIAGE AND SADDLERY HARDWARE AND TRIMMINGS.

Also, Manufacturers of the

Patent Universal Harness,

Dealers in all kinds of Twines, Burlaps, &c.

Close Plating done to order.

MASSASOIT BLOCK, 78 MAIN STREET, SPRINGFIELD, MASS.

SAMUEL K. LEE. HENRY K. BAKER.

ELDRIDGE & HASTINGS,

GENERAL JOBBERS.

Locks, Keys, Umbrellas, Parasols, Jewelry, &c., &c.

All kinds Jobbing done at Short Notice.

283 Main Street, (up stairs,) Springfield, Mass.

H. J. BRIGGS & CO.,

Dealers in Wrought Iron

Steam and Gas Pipe

AND FITTINGS.

STEAM AND GAS FITTING

Done in the best and most Workmanlike manner.

Vernon Street, near Main, Springfield, Massachusetts.

M. A. WHIPPLE, FOREMAN.

A. D. BRIGGS & CO.,

CIVIL ENGINEERS AND BUILDERS

O F

Iron and Timber Bridges,

Of the most approved kind.

Also Drawbridges, Proprietors of Truesdell's Patent Iron Bridge.

Also of Howe's Patent.

Office, Fort Block, Springfield, Mass.

33

UNION PRINTING COMPANY,
STEAM
JOB PRINTERS,
And Publishers of the
DAILY AND WEEKLY UNION,
Office, corner Main and Taylor Streets.

THE PEOPLE'S PAPER.
THE SPRINGFIELD DAILY UNION.
PUBLISHED EVERY EVENING,
Containing all the Local News ,and Latest Telegrams from all parts of the world. Issued on a Double Sheet every Saturday.

Terms, $6.00 a Year.

SPRINGFIELD WEEKLY UNION,
PUBLISHED EVERY FRIDAY MORNING,
On a Large Double Sheet, containing more reading matter than any other journal in Western Massachusetts. Choice Miscellany, Poetry, and a carefully prepared RESUME of the news of the week.

Terms, $2.00 a Year.

MASSASOIT HOUSE,

Springfield, Mass.

M. & E. S. CHAPIN,

Proprietors.

WEST SPRINGFIELD, MASS., opposite the City of Springfield, on the west bank of the river, includes the villages of Ashleyville and Agawam. Carriages and Leather are manufactured quite extensively here, but it is largely an Agricultural Community.

BUSINESS DIRECTORY.

Blacksmith.

Bliss, H. N. Springfield.

Carriage Manufacturer.

CLARK, EDSON.   See adv. index.

Carriage, Coach and Sleigh Builder.

CLARK, EDSON.   See adv. index.

Leather Manufacturers.

ELY, C. (P. O. Ashleyville.)   See adv. index.
ELY, HOMER, (P. O. Ashleyville.)   See adv. index.

Tanners and Curriers.

ELY, C.   See adv. index.   (P. O. Ashleyville.)
ELY, HOMER.   See adv. index.   (P. O. Ashleyville.)

HOMER ELY,

TANNER AND CURRIER,

MANUFACTURER OF

Oak Harness, Russet Skirting and Bridle, Buff Leather
for Emery Wheels, Picker, Calf Lace, Suspender
Leather, &c., &c.

Post Office Address, - - - *Ashleyville, Mass.*

C. ELY,

MANUFACTURER OF

LEATHER

Of all Descriptions,

West Springfield, Mass.

Post Office Address, - - Ashleyville, Mass.

CHICOPEE, Hampden County, Mass., is situated on the east
bank of the Connecticut Rivers, at the confluence of the Chicopee
and Connecticut River, 3½ miles north of Springfield. Chicopee
comprises the villages of Chicopee Falls, nearly 2 miles east,
where there is a large manufacturing business of Cottons and
Agricultural Implements. The Lamb Knitting Machine Manufactory is located here.

At Chicopee are the large cotton mills, 7 in number, of the
Dwight Manufacturing Company, with a capital of nearly two
million dollars.

BUSINESS DIRECTORY.

Agricultural Implements Manufacturers .

BELCHER & TAYLOR, Agricultural Tool Co. Geo. S. Taylor, Agent, (C. Falls.) See adv. index.

WHITMORE, BELCHER & CO., (C. Falls.) See adv. index.

Apothecaries.

Johnson, Wm. W. 9 Merchants Row.
Kent, C. F. Exchange St.
Page, E. H. Front St., (O. Falls.)
Smith, Warren, Exchange St.

Attorneys at Law.

Knapp, Geo. H. Merchants Row.
Robinson, Geo. D.   "
Stearns, Geo.   "
Wells, John, Front St., (O. Falls.)

Belt Manufacturer.

PLIMPTON, J. D. opposite Depot. See adv. index.

Billiards.

Bartlett, A. Front St., (O. Falls.)

Boots and Shoes.

Beers, W. P. Exchange St.
Donovan, Daniel, (O. Falls.)
Fogg & Bickford, Exchange St.
Hitchcock, J. W. & Co.,   "
Robbins, J. S.   "

Cigar Dealer.

Bond, Amos, 8 Merchants Row.

Clergymen.

Ballamy, R. K. (Bap.)   (C. Falls.)
Clark, (Cong.)
Cone, L. H. (Cong.)
Foster, (Cong.)   (C. Falls.)
Johnson, Chas. F. (Meth.)   (C. Falls.)
Hathaway, (Epis.)
Stevens, (Univ.)

Clothing Dealers.

Barnes, M. H. Front St., (C. Falls.)

Bliss, Wm. G. 10 Exchange St.

HALL, TYLER & CO., opposite Chapin House.

Hill & Moody, Exchange St.

HITCHCOCK & HOSLEY, Exchange St.   See adv. index.

Coal Dealers.

Johnson & Stoddard, Springfield.

Coffin Trimmings.

Wetherell, Wm. F. Exchange St.

Coffins and Caskets.

Hostey, D. P. & Co., Market Square.

Confectionery and Notions.

Downing, H. 3 Merchants Row.

Jacobs, Simeon, Exchange St.

Watson, T. P. Front St., (C. Falls.)

Corn Shellers, Feed Cutters, Store Trucks, Manf's.

BELCHER & TAYLOR, Agricultural Tool Co., (C. Falls,)
Geo. S. Taylor, Agent.   See adv. index.

WHITTEMORE, BELCHER & CO., (C. Falls,).   See adv.
index.

Cotton Goods Manufacturers.

Chicopee Manufacturing Co., (Sheetings and Shirtings,) C.
Falls.)

Dwight Manufacturing Co., (Sheetings and Shirtings.)

Cotton Waste and Paper Stock.

Matoon & Hubbard.

Curtain Fixture Manufacturer.

BELCHER, B. B. (C. Falls,) (Perfected Pendulum Fixtures.)
See adv. index.

Dentist.

Porter, J. Exchange St.

Dress Makers.

GASNER, SUSAN J. Mrs., (C. Falls.)
Thompson, E. M. Miss

Druggists.

Johnson, Wm. W. 9 Merchants Row.
Kent, C. F. Exchange St.
Page, E. H. Front St., (C. Falls.)
Smith, Warren, Exchange St.

Dry Goods.

Merrick, C. H. 8 Exchange St.
Munn, Eugene, Main St., (C. Falls.)
Oakes, Bragg & Co.,
Rockwood, J. T. cor. Exchange and Springfield Sts.
SPITTLE BROS. & THOMPSON, Front St., (C. Falls.)
Taylor & Gilbert, Center St., (C. Falls.)
Wood, J. B. 2 Exchange St.

Foundries.

Ames Manufacturing Co.
Belcher & Taylor, (C. Falls.)
LAMB KNITTING MACHINE CO.   See adv. back cover.
Whittemore, Belcher, & Co., (C. Falls.)

Furniture Dealers.

Hostery, D. P. & Co., Market Square.

Gent's Furnishing Goods.

Barnes, M. H. Front St., (C. Falls.)
Hall, Tyler & Co., (C. Falls.)
HITCHCOCK & HOSLEY, Exchange St.   See adv. index.
Parshley, S. W. cor. Exchange and Cabot Sts.

Grocers.

Boyd & Holcomb, Front St., (C. Falls.)
Bullens, Isaac & Son, Exchange St.
Carter, J. A. & Co., Market Square.
Devin, Thomas, Exchange St.
Dixon, John   "
Kimball, E. P. 3 Merchants Row.
McKing, J. Exchange St.
Lankton & Pond,   "
Munn, Eugene, (C. Falls.)
SPITTLE BROS. & THOMPSON, Front St., (C. Falls.)
Taylor & Gilbert, Center St., (C. Falls.)

Hair Dressers.

Adams, Jas. B. Front St., (C. Falls.)
Blackman, C. H. 6 Merchants Row.

Harness Makers.

Johnson, Thos. M. 10 Merchants Row.
Riley, Geo. L. Front St. (C. Falls.)

Hotels.

CABOT HOUSE, Front St., W. H. Dickinson, Pro.
Chapin House, (C. Falls,) C. L. Round, Pro.
CHICOPEE HOUSE, opposite R. R. Depot, E. P. Belding,
Pro.

Iron Founders.

Ames Manufacturing Co.
Belcher & Taylor, (C. Falls.)
Gaylord Manufacturing Co.
Whittemore, Belcher & Co., (C. Falls.)

Knitting Machine Manufacturers.

LAMB KNITTING MACHINE CO., (C. Falls.)   See adv.
back cover.

Lathe Manufactureres.

Ames Manufacturing Co.

34

Lawyers.

Knapp, Geo. H. Merchants Row.
Robinson, Geo. D.   "   .
Stearns, Geo.   "
Wells, John, Front St., (C. Falls.)

Lock Manufacturers.

GAYLORD MANUFACTURING CO.

Machinery Manufacturers.

Ames Manufacturing Co.

Machinists'.

Ames Manufacturing Co.
BELCHER & TAYLOR, (C. Falls.)   See adv. index.
LAMB KNITTING MACHINE CO., (C. Falls.)   See adv. back cover.
WHITTEMORE, BELCHER & CO., (C. Falls.)   See adv. index.

Manufacturing Companies.

Ames Manufacturing Co., (Machinery.)
BELCHER & TAYLOR, Agricultural Tool Co., Geo. S. Taylor, Agent. See adv. index.
Chicopee Manufacturing Co., (Cottons.)
Dwight Manufacturing Co., (Cottons.)
GAYLORD MANUFACTURING CO., (Locks.)
LAMB KNITTING MACHINE CO., (C. Falls.)   See adv. back cover.
WHITTEMORE, BELCHER & CO. See adv. index.

Meat Markets.

Brown, J. S. Exchange St.
Fanner, J. K. Center St., (C. Falls.)
Stoddard & Stedman, Springfield.
Taylor, A. C. & Co., Center St., (C. Falls.)

Millinery and Fancy Goods.

Dixon, John Mrs. Exchange St.

Fuller, A. J. Miss Exchange St.
'Reilly, S. M.   "
Rice & Ferry,   "
Wait, A. Miss   "

Newspapers and Periodicals.

McFarland, Albert, Front St., (C. Falls.)

Painters and Glaziers.

Hamersley, J. C.
Watson, T. P. Market St., (C. Falls.)

Pistol Manufacturers.

STEVENS, J. & CO., (C. Falls.) See adv. index.

Physicians.

Alford, Church St., (C. Falls.)
Barton, Jarvis, Merchants Row.
JENNESS, W. W. Cabot Hall Building.
Sawin, Wm. J. cor. Front and Church St., (C. Falls.)
Shepard, Ransom, Exchange St.,
Wilbur, John R. Center St., (C. Falls.)

Pruning Shear Manufacturers.

STEVENS, J. & CO., (C. Falls.) See .adv. index.

Printer, (Job.)

Wheelock, Geo. V. Cabot Hall Building.

Postmasters.

Havens, J. C.
McFarland, A. (C. Falls.)

Stove and Tinware Dealers.

Bliss, Wm. G. 10 Exchange St.
Hill & Moody,   "
Wallace, Geo. Front St., (C. Falls.)

Steel Dividers Manufacturers.

STEVENS, J. & CO., (C. Falls.)   See adv. index.

Tailors.

Buckingham Bros., 6 Exchange St.
Moffat, B. Exchange St.

Trunks and Valises.

Johnson, Thos. M. 10 Merchants Row.
Riley, Geo. L. Front St., (C. Falls.)

Undertakers.

Hostey, D. P. & Co., Market Square.

Variety Store.

Blackman, Wm. L. 4 Merchants Row.
McFarland, A. (C. Falls.)

Watches and Jewelry.

Parsons, C. G. Exchange St.
Stackpole, J. & Son,   "

WHITTEMORE, BELCHER & CO.,

Manufacturers and Dealers in all kinds of

AGRICULTURAL IMPLEMENTS.

Our Doe-Eagle, and Premium Stubble and Stony Land Plows,

Know no rivals at our Agricultural Fairs, in taking first Premiums.

SHARE'S PATENT HARROW CANNOT BE EXCELLED.

ALSO GEDDE'S AND IMPROVED HINGE HARROWS,

CULTIVATORS, HORSE HOES,

Whittemore's Patent Vegetable Cutter,

Magic and Improved Eagle Feed Cutters,

The most simple and durable machines in the market, and cut faster and easier than any other. HIDE ROLL CUTTERS and GRANT PATENT LEVER FEED CUTTER, with Curved Knife, (very cheap and good.) CORN SHELLERS, both right and left hand, with and without Separators and Wrought Shafts.

Whittemore's New Horse Rake,

(That cannot be excelled for ease of operation.)

Haying Tools and Seeds we make a prominent part of our business.

Wareroom and Seed Store at

84 MERCHANTS' ROW, BOSTON.

Manufactory, - - - - - Chicopee Falls, Mass.

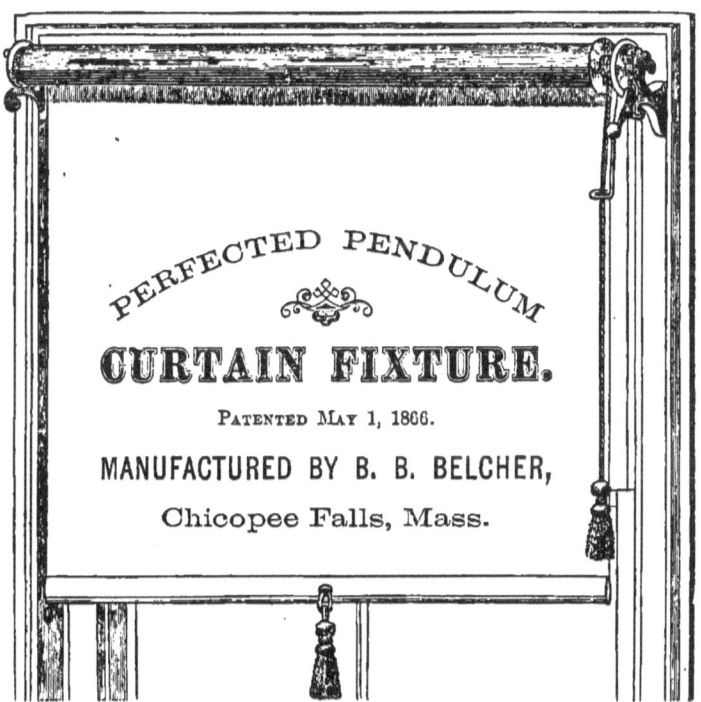

PERFECTED PENDULUM

CURTAIN FIXTURE.

PATENTED MAY 1, 1866.

MANUFACTURED BY B. B. BELCHER,

Chicopee Falls, Mass.

THE Subscriber begs to call the attention of his former patrons, and the million others who use and are to use Curtain Fixtures, to his recently PERFECTED AND PATENTED PENDULUM FIXTURE. The original White's Pendulum Fixture, that I extensively manufactured and sold some years since, is a good Fixture, but the one I now offer is the NE PLUS ULTRA. The two objections to that Fixture were, that it was noisy and sometimes failed to hold the Curtain from running down. The PERFECTED is operated with but little noise, and is sure to hold the Curtain permanently in place at any desired height. It is neat and tasty in design, is manufactured of the best of material and in a thorough and workmanlike manner. It is durable and easily put up for use. A moment's inspection will make its superiority apparent to every observer.

J. STEVENS & CO.,

MANUFACTURERS OF

Stevens' Patent Breach Loading

POCKET AND TARGET PISTOLS.

ALSO, SUPERIOR SPRING CALLIPERS AND DIVIDERS,

Pruning Shears, Iron, Steel, and Brass Screws, Flyer Pins,

And Steps for Spinning Frames.

Small Lathes, Models and Machines made to order,

CHICOPEE FALLS, MASS.

HOLYOKE, MASS., located on the west bank of the Connecticut river, 8 miles north of Springfield, and distant from New York 144 miles. Here in October, 1849, a dam was constructed across the river, 1017 feet in length, and 30 feet high, making the largest water power in New England. There are three canals along which are located the factories, and so situated that the water is used three times over. This water power is owned by the Holyoke Water Power Company, with a capital of $350,000. Here are a large number of Manufacturing Companies and corporations, representing some 15 millions of dollars, employed in manufacturing Cottons, Woolens, Writing Paper, Paper Collar Paper, Manilla Paper, Envelopes, Balmoral Skirts, Cotton Warps, Cotton Thread, Machinery, &c.

Holyoke is pleasantly situated, and at present contains about 7,000 inhabitants.

BUSINESS DIRECTORY.

Apothecaries.

Bassett, A. G. High St., Exchange Block.
Browning Bros.   "
Goodell & Fitch, Holyoke House Block.
Morrill, J. E. High St.

Banks.

Hadley Falls National Bank, capital $200,000, C. W. Ranlet, Prest., H. P. Terry, Cash.

Barber Shops.

Gilmore, John R. Exchange Block.
Wetherston, L. N. Holyoke House Block.

Blacksmiths.

Newton & Brothers, Main St.

Boot and Shoe Dealers.

Clark, C. opposite Holyoke House.
Craigin, H. H. Holyoke House Block.
Butler & Stratton, High St.
Corser, Chas. A. 5 Exchange Block, High St.
Wolcott, Geo. M. High St.

Boot and Shoe Maker.

Sullivan, B. M. Maple St.

Coal and Wood.

Martin, W. L. High St.

Confectionery.

Brierley, Margaret A. High St.

Cotton Goods Manufacturers.

Hampden Cotton Mills, J. E. Chase, Agent.
Lyman Mills.

Dentist.

Wheeler, H.

Druggists.

Bassitt, A. G. Exchange Block, High St.
Browning Bros. High St.
Goodell & Fitch, Holyoke House Block.
Morrill, J. E. High St.

Dry Goods.

Bowler, John Maple St.
Gilbert, Potvin, High St.
Higginbottom, A.   "
King, S.   "
Manning, Mrs. H.   "
Rockwood, J. T.   "
Shumway, A. S.   "
Tuttle, O. S.   "
Webber & Seaver, 1 Holyoke House.

Dress and Cloak Makers.

Prickett, Mrs. Exchange Block, High St.
Wellington, C. H. Mrs.

35

Dyers.

Sculler, John, Maple St.

Express Companies and Agents.

Gilmore, S. M. Agent Merchants Union Express Co.
Prescott, C. B. Agent Thompson & Co. Express.

Furniture.

Crafts, R. P. 4 Exchange Block.

Gent's Furnishing Goods.

Burnham, P. H. High St.
Kingman, L. S. & Co., Exchange Block, High St.
Miller & Co., 6   "   "   "
Mitchell Brothers, High St.

Hardware Dealers.

Farrington & Burditt, Holyoke House Block, Dwight St.
SNOW, GUSTAVUS, High St.

Grocers.

Baker, J. R. Dwight St.
Crafts, R. P. High St.
Connor, W. J. Maple St.
Coran, F. L. Canal St.
Downs, J. Maple St.
O'Donnell, John "
Ely, J. E. & Son, Holyoke House Block.
Flynn & Doyle, High St.
Gay, John, Maple St.
HIGGINS, DENNIS, High St.
Lynch, Michael.
Richards & Thayer, Main St.
Munsell & Sears, opposite Holyoke House.
Stephenson, E. C. North St.
Tuttle & Moore, High St.
Welch, M. & Co. Canal St.

Harness Maker.

Martin, W. L. High St.

Hotels.

HOLYOKE HOUSE, H. Brown, Pro. See adv. index.
SAMOSETT HOUSE, Maple St., Myron E. Green, Pro. See adv. index.

Insurance Agents.

Johnson, R. B. High St.
Underwood, Porter "

Iron Founders.

HOLYOKE MACHINE CO. See adv. index.

Lawyers.

Chapin, E. W. Exchange Block.
Pierson, High St.
Underwood, Porter, High St.

Lumber Dealers.

Chase, E. & Sons.

Livery Stables.

Bernier, Joseph.
Mosher, R. Main St.
Wellington, T. H. Maple St.

Machinists' Tool Manufacturers.

HOLYOKE MACHINE CO., T. B. Flanders, Agent. See adv. index.

Machinists.

HOLYOKE MACHINE CO., T. B. Flanders, Agent. See adv. index.

Meat Markets.

Allyn, A. & S. B. High St.

Allyn, J. F. & Co., High St.
PERKINS, L. & W. Hampden St.

Manufacturing Companies.

Barker, J. (Cloth.)
Germania Mills, (Woolen.)
HADLEY COMPANY, (Thread,) J. L. Davis, Agent. See adv. index.
Hampden Cotton Mills, (Cottons,) J. E. Chase, Agent.
Hampden Paper Co., Newton, J. C. Agent.
Holyoke Thread Co., (Thread,) T. Merrick, Agent.
Lyman Mills, (Cottons.)
New York Woolen Co.
Parsons Paper Co.
Whiting Paper Co., (Paper,) Wm. Whiting, Agent.

Millinery and Fancy Goods.

Chapin & Nichols, Main St.
Booden, Mrs. J. W. High St.
Gilbert, J. F.   "
Hardy, Mrs. Emma, Exchange Block.
Worswick, A. & A. High St.

Newspapers.

Holyoke Transcript, Lyman, C. H. Editor.

Painters. (House and Sign.)

Grisworld & Wishheart.

Paper Manufacturers.

Hampden Paper Co., J. C. Newton, Agent.
Parsons Paper Co.
Whiting Paper Co., Whiting, Wm. Agent.

Paper Machinery Manufacturers.

HOLYOKE MACHINE CO. See adv. index.

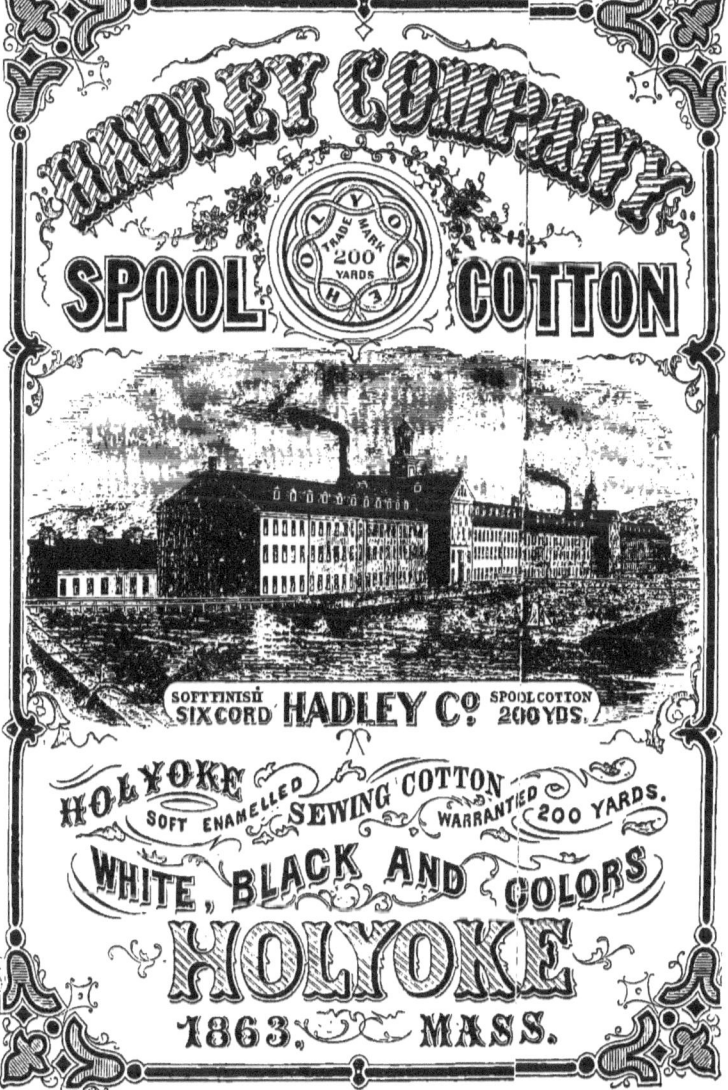

Photographers.

Prew Brothers, Hutchins' Block, High St.
Haskins, F. W.   "

Physicians.

Booth, S. Exchange Block.
Blodgett, Chas. "   "
O'Connor, Jas. J. High St.
Huntington, L. F.   "
Newport, E. opposite Holyoke House.
Taylor, F. L. Exchange Block.

Postmaster.

Prescott, C. B.

Reed, (Weaving,) Manufacturers.

WHITAKER, EDMUND. See adv. index.

Restaurants.

Blanchard, J. M. Maple St.
Burk, James,   "
Graham, James,   "
Sawtelle, O. H.   "
Shehan, William,   "

Savings Banks.

Holyoke Savings Bank, Incorporated Feb. 23, 1855.
  Joel Russell, Pres., R. B. Johnson, Treas.

Shafting and Pulleys.

HOLYOKE MACHINE CO. See adv. index.

Spool Cotton Manufacturers, (White and Colored.)

HADLEY COMPANY, J. S. Davis, Agt. See adv. index.

Stove Dealers.

Buckley, P. M. High St.
TOWN BROTHERS, opposite Holyoke House.

Telegraph Office.

Western Union, Holyoke House Block.

Thread Manufacturers, (White and Colored.)

HADLEY COMPANY, J. S. Davis, Agt. See adv. index.
Holyoke Thread Co., T. Merrick, Agt.

Variety Stores.

Draper, E. L. High St.
Gilmore, C. R. Mrs. High St.
Loomis, E. W.   "
McCabe, Filley, Maple St.
Onell, E. A. Mrs. High St.
Palmer, J. H. Hampden St.

Water Wheel Manufacturers.

HOLYOKE MACHINE CO. See adv. index.

Watches and Jewelry.

Cain, A. Dwight St.
Taber, L. A. High St.

Wire Manufacturer.

PRENTISS, GEO. W. See adv. index.

Woolen Goods Manufacturers.

Germania Mills.
New York Woolen Co.
Barber, J.

HOLYOKE MACHINE COMPANY,
PRACTICAL MACHINISTS & FOUNDERS,
MANUFACTURERS OF

Water Wheels, Gearing, Shafting,
AND MILL WORK OF ALL KINDS.

*Paper Engines, Callenders, Hydraulic Presses,
Ruling Machines, Elevators, &c.,*

MACHINISTS' TOOLS, HYDRANTS AND HYDRANT VALVES,
Bolts, Nuts, Washers, Set Screws, &c.

CASTINGS of all descriptions, including CAST IRON PIPES of all sizes, made to order.

PATTERNS on hand or made to order.

Address, Holyoke Machine Co., Holyoke, Mass.

GEORGE W. PRENTISS,
MANUFACTURER OF

REFINED IRON WIRE
of every description,

Tin Plated, Plain and Annealed ; Piano Pin and
Covering Wire, Spring, Machinery, Reed,
PIN AND HOOK AND EYE WIRE.

PATENT BROOM WIRE of the BEST QUALITY.
HOLYOKE, MASS.

Orders for exact or sample sizes will receive special attention. As we use nothing but the best of Norway and Swedes Iron, satisfaction is guaranteed.

Holyoke House, Holyoke, Mass.

H. BROWN, Proprietor.

HOLYOKE REED FACTORY.

EVERY DESCRIPTION OF

WEAVING REEDS,
MADE AND WARRANTED BY
EDMUND WHITAKER, Holyoke, Mass.
ORDERS PROMPTLY ATTENDED TO.

HADLEY, Hampshire County, Massachusetts, is situated on the east bank of the Connecticut River, about 15 miles north of Springfield, Mass., and comprises the villages of South Hadley, North Hadley and Hockanum. Agriculture is the chief business of the town. The "Hadley Meadows" comprise several thousand acres, and much of it the finest in the whole river valley. Broom Corn and Tobacco are raised very extensively. A large business is done in manufacturing brooms and brushes.

Hadley is one of the oldest towns on the river, it having been settled as early as 1650. West street is one of the finest streets any where to be found, it being nearly one mile long and 17 rods wide. At South Hadley Falls, are large manufactories of Ginghams and Paper.

BUSINESS DIRECTORY.

Blacksmiths.

Cook, S.   (S. Hadley.)
Dickinson, C. D.   (N. Hadley.)
Whittemore, W.   (S. Hadley.)

Boot and Shoe Dealers.

Gaylord, John,   (S. Hadley Falls.)
Grimes, J. N.   "   "

Broom Manufacturers.

Cook, Chester,   (N. Hadley.)
Cook, James,   (Hadley.)
Cook, Chas. 2d   -   "
Cook, Horace,   "
Edson, F.   "
Jones, Lyman,   (N. Hadley.)
Marsh, C. S.   "
Smith, S. S.   :   "
Smith, H. E.   "
Smith, Thaddeus,   "
Smith, Francis,   "
Lawrence, Hubbard,   "
Reynolds, P.   (Hadley.)

Carriage Manufacturers.

Adams, J. & Son,   (N. Hadley.)
Chapin, A. T.   (S. Hadley.)
Esterbrook, Geo.   "
Chapin & Pond,   "   Falls.

Cigar Manufacturer.

Cook, William,   (S. Hadley.)

Clergymen.

Ayres, Rowland, Cong.
Beaman, W. H.   "
Dwight, E. S.   "
Knight, Richard,   "   (S. Hadley Falls.)
Mead, Hiram,   "   "
Merwin, S. J.   "   (S. Hadley Falls.)

Cotton Goods Manufacturers.

Glasgow Co.,   (Ginghams,)   (S. Hadley.)

Hotels.

Hadley Falls Hotel, C. C. Barrett, Pro.
Prospect House, Mt Holyoke, French, Pro.

Lumber Dealers.

Adams, J. & Sons, (N. Hadley.)
Granger, L. N.   (Hadley.)
Nutting, J. H.   "

Machinist.

Harris, Wm. F.   (S. Hadley.)

Merchants.

Barrett & Dunkler,   (S. Hadley.)   Dry Goods, Groceries, &c.
Cooley, S. F.   (N. Hadley.)   "   "   "
Chamberlain, Geo.   (S. Hadley.)   "   "   "
Guy, Alice Miss, Dry Goods.
Montague, E.   (S. Hadley.)   "   "   "

36

Porter, W. P.   (Hadley.)   Dry Goods, Groceries, &c.
Shipman, W. S.   "   "   "   "
Smith, T. & Co.,   (N. Hadley.)   "   "   "
Smith, Hiram Jr.,   (S. Hadley.) "   "   "
Vinton, Geo.   "   "   "   "
Wright, Ira B.   "   "   "   "

Painter, (House and Sign.)

Preston, J. H. (S. Hadley Falls.)

Paper Manufacturers.

Carew Manufacturing Co., (Letter Paper.) (S. Hadley.)
Hampshire Paper Co.,   "   "   "
Salisbury & Bolton, (Wrapping.)   "
Taylor & Cook, (Manilla.)   "

Physicians.

Bonner, F. (Hadley.)
Pierson, Wm. (S. Hadley Falls.)

Postmasters.

Cooley, S. F. (N. Hadley.)
Shipman, W. S. (Hadley.)
Smith, G. Morgan, (S. Hadley.)
Smith, Hiram Jr. S. Hadley Falls.)

Sash, Door and Blind Manufacturers.

Howard, Gaylord & Co. (S. Hadley.)

Saw Mills.

Adams, J. & Son.   (N. Hadley.)
Congdon & Son.   (S. Hadley.)

Selectmen.

F. Edson,
Geo. C. Smith,
Horace Cooke.

Stove and Tinware Dealer.

Harris, Wm.   (S. Hadley.)

Town Clerk and Treasurer.

Wm. S. Shipman.

Tub Manufacturer.

Kellogg, J. E.   (S. Hadley.)

Wire Manufacturer.

Prouty, Geo.   (N. Hadley.)

Woolen Manufacturers.

Agawam Company, (Flannels and Cassimeres.)
Arnold, L. H. (Tweeds and Cassimeres.)   (S. Hadley.)

EASTHAMPTON, MASS., is a pleasant and thriving town, with a population of about 3000, beautifully situated in the valley, just north of and at the foot of Mt. Tom, four and one-half miles south-west of Northampton, and is reached by cars on the New Haven and Northamption Railway, which passes through this town.

Easthampton is noted for its large manufactories of Buttons, Vulcanized Rubber, Elastic Suspenders, Rubber Thread and Cotton Yarns, &c., &c.

The prosperity of Easthampton, to a large extent, is due to the enterprise and energy of Hon. Samuel Williston, who is largely interested in several large manufactories.

Williston Seminary, which is located here, was founded by the munificence of Hon. Samuel Williston. It was first opened for the reception of pupils in Dec., 1841, and has since enjoyed uninterrupted prosperity. Additions have been made from time to time by the founder, to its buildings, apparatus and funds, until the whole amount of donations, including $50,000 for the new Dormitory recently completed, has reached the sum of $225,000.

BUSINESS DIRECTORY.

Apothecaries.
Fay, C. R. & Co., Main St.

Attorney at Law.
Bassett, W. G. Union St.

Banks.
First National Bank of Easthampton,
Samuel Williston, Pres., C. E. Williams, Cashier.

Barber.
Maynard, W. C. School St.

Blacksmiths.
O'Connell, James, School St.
Holcomb, N. A.

Bobbin Manufacturer.
BASSETT, JOEL L. See adv. index.

Books and Stationery.
Bardwell, J. Main St.

Boot and Shoe Dealers, (Retail.)
Hutchinson, B. W. Main St.
Waite, Joseph, Union St.

Boot and Shoe Makers.
Colgan, T. Union St.
Hutchinson, B. W. Main St.
Waite, Joseph, Union St.

Burial Caskets.
Searle, W. R. Main St.

Business Wagon Manufacturers.

CLARK, OLIVER N. School St.
Smith, Ralph

Button, (Covered,) Manufacturers.

National Button Co.
Samuel Williston, Pres., H. G. Knight, Treas.

Carpenter and Builder.

Bosworth, E. R. Union St.

Carriage, Coach and Sleigh Builders.

CLARK, OLIVER N. School St.
Smith, Ralph

China, Earthern and Glassware Dealers.

Putnam, F. H. & Co., Main St.
Wells, John H. Union St.

Clergymen.

Colton, Aaron M. (Cong.)
Furber, Franklin, (Meth.)
Seelye, Samuel T. (Cong.)

Cloak and Dress Maker.

Kent, Emma, Union St.

Cotton Yarn Manufacturers.

Williston Mills.
Samuel Williston, Pres., M. H. Leonard, Treas.
Samuel Williston, J. Sutherland, General Agents.

Dentist.

Strong, R. E. Main St.

Dry Goods, (Retail.)

Lambie, R. M. & J. E. Main St.
Langdon, C. W. Union St.

Rust & Pulsifer, Union St.
Wells, John, Union St.

Engine, (Steam,) Manufacturers.
Easthampton Pump and Steam Engine Co.
Samuel Williston, Pres., Jas. Sutherland, Treas.

Express Agents and Companies.
Campbell, J. L. American Express Co.
Putnam, F. H. Merchants' Union Express Co.

Gas Company.
Easthampton Gas Co.
Samuel Williston, Pres., H. S. Clark, Treas.

Gas Fitter.
Manchester, Geo. H.

Gents. Furnishing Goods.
Preston, Lucius, Main St.
Strong Brothers,   "

Grain Dealer.
Jepson, D. S. Union St.

Grist Mills.
Jepson, D. S. Union St.
Strong, Sheldon

Grocers, (Retail,)
CHAPMAN & PARSONS, Pleasant St.
Johnson, Hannum & Co., Main St.
Putnam, F. H. & Co.,   "
Rust & Pulsifer, Union St.
Thayer, J. T. Pleasant St.
Wells, John, Union St.

Hair Dresser.
Maynard, W. C. School St.

Hides and Leather.

Shoals, H. B. Mill Lane.

Hotel.

UNION HOUSE, Main St., G. M. Fillebrown, Proprietor. See adv. index.

Internal Revenue Collector.

Clapp, Lafayette

Lawyer.

Bassett, W. G. Union St.

Leather Dealer.

Shoals, H. B. Mill Lane.

Livery Stables.

Alvord, Whitney
Avery, M. W.·
JEPSON, D. S. Union St.
STRONG, H. C. rear Union House.

Lumber Dealers.

BASSETT, JOEL L. See adv. index.
Bosworth, E. R. Union St.

Manufacturing Companies.

Easthampton Gas Company.
Easthampton Pump and Steam Engine Co.
Easthampton Rubber Thread Co.
National Button Co.
Nashawannuck Manufacturing Co., (Suspenders.)
Williston Mills, (Yarns.)

Milliners.

Kent, Emma Miss, Union St.
Thrall, Misses, Main St.

Physicians.

Winslow & Ward, Main St.

Plumbers.

Manchester, Geo. H.
Mayher, John, Union St.

Postmaster.

Bardwell, J.

Pump, (Steam,) Manufacturers.

Easthampton Pump and Steam Engine Co.

Railroad Agent.

H. H. Strong, New Haven and Northampton R. R.

Rubber, (Vulcanized,) Suspender Manafacturers.

NASHAWANNUCK MANUFACTURING CO.
E. H. Sawyer, Treasurer. See adv. index.

Rubber Thread Manufacturers.

EASTHAMPTON RUBBER THREAD CO.

Saw Mill.

BASSETT, JOEL L. See adv. index.

Sewing Machine Agent.

Webb, O. G. Pleasant St.

Selectmen.

Soloman Alvord.
Quartus P. Lyman.
L. W. Harmon.

Sheet Iron Workers.

Mayher, John, Union St.

Spool (Thread) Manufacturer.

BASSETT, JOEL L. See adv. index.

Livery Stables.

Alvord, Whitney.
Averey, M. W.
JEPSON, D. S. Union St.
STRONG, H. C. rear Union House.

Stove Dealer.

Mayher, John, Union St.

Tailors.

Preston, Lucius, Main St.
Strong Bros.   "

Tanner and Currier.

Shoals, H. B. Mill Lane.

Teachers, (Williston Seminary.)

Marshall Henshaw, LL. D. Principal.
Russell M. Wright, M. A. (Chemistry and Natural History.)
Francis A. Walker, M. A. (Latin and Greek.)
Henry H. Goodell, M. A. (Modern Languages & Gymnastics.)
Joseph H. Sawyer, B. A. (Mathematics & Mental Philosophy.
Chas. H. Chandler, B. A. (Latin and Greek.)
Thos. S. Smith, B. A. (Arithmetic and English Grammar.)
Prof. Wm. S. Clark. P. H. D. (Chemistry.)
A. L. Strong, Esq., (Penmanship.)
Henry J. Rudd, Esq., (Vocal Music.)

Thread (Rubber) Manufacturers.

Easthampton Rubber Thread Co.

Tin Ware Manufacturer.

Mayher, John, Union St.

37

Undertaker.

Searle, W. R. Main St.

Watchmakers and Jewellers.

Yarn (Cotton) Manufacturers.

Williston Mills.

Miscellaneous,—Churches.

First Congregational Society, Main St., Rev. Aaron M. Colton, Pastor.

Payson Congregational Society, Main St., Rev. Sam'l T. Seelye, Pastor, C. B. Johnson, Clerk.

Methodist Episcopal Society, Rev. Franklin Furber, Pastor.

Societies, Good Templars.

Silver Star Lodge, Good Templars, No. 150. Number of members, 125, meet Wednesday evenings, Lambie's Hall, officers elected quarterly.

UNION HOUSE,
EAST HAMPTON, MASS.

The Proprietor would announce to the public, that he has the UNION HOUSE refurnished, and additions made, thus rendering the accommodations suitable for transient customers, or summer boarders. The place is a delightful summer retreat, for persons wishing to get away from the city.

Rooms single or in suites.

Trains daily from New York, Northampton and Springfield. A good livery connected with the Hotel.

G. M. FILLEBROWN, Prop.

NORTHAMPTON, MASS., The shire town of Hampshire County, on the west bank of the Connecticut River, 18 miles above Springfield, and 76 miles north of New Haven. It is located on the rising ground ½ mile west of the river, giving a complete view of Mts. Holyoke and Tom and Hadley Meadows. It is irregularly laid out; the winding avenues and crooked streets lined with Elms and Maples, giving it an inviting and picturesque appearance, and making it one of the pleasantest towns in the river valley.

The first settlers numbering 21 persons, came from Springfield and Windsor, and located here in 1654. Town officers were chosen in 1655, though there is no record of any act of incorporation. The town is supposed to have been named after Northampton in England, though that is somewhat doubtful.

The first church was erected in 1655, it was 26 feet long by 18 wide, built of sawed timber, and cost 14 pounds sterling. At present there are six Protestant societies and one Roman Catholic. Northampton has long been noted for the excellence of its Public Schools, and at the present time contains several large and commodious school buildings, well supplied with competent teachers in all departments.

Its stores are large and numerous and well filled with large stocks of seasonable goods, and its business men are alive to the wants of the public, many of them having had long years of experience in this place. There are three good Hotels here, well kept by *live* Landlords, who study to provide for the comfort and convenience of their guests. The travelling public and all those who wish to find a pleasant summer resort are recommended to try the Round Hill Hotel and Water Cure, or the Warner House, Main Street.

The Florence Sewing Machines which are so extensively used the world over, are manufactured in the beautiful village of Florence in this township. Here are employed several hundred hands in making what is acknowledged to be the best Sewing Machine now in use. The machine makes four distinct stitches, Lock, Knot, Double Lock, and Double Knot, either of which are much stronger, more durable and elastic than that made by many other machines. It has become so popular that it has been nearly impossible to fill the large orders for it.

BUSINESS DIRECTORY.

Agricultural Implement Dealer.

Todd, W. H. 3, 4 Warner Block.

Apothecaries.

EDWARDS, OSCAR, 32 Merchants Row.
Kingsley, C. B.   "
PARSONS, S. C. 28   " See adv. index.

Architects.

GARDNER & PERKINS, (Florence.)   See adv. index.
PRATT, WM. F. 2 Union Block.   See adv. index.

Artist.

HOTCHKISS, W. cor. Main and King Sts.

Baker.

CARR, SMITH, State St. See adv. index.

Banks.

First National Bank, Main St.
HAMPSHIRE COUNTY NATIONAL BANK, Main St.
Northampton National Bank, Main St.

Banker.

Clarke, John, Clarke Block, Main St.

Basket Manufacturers.

WILLIAMS MF'G CO.

Beer and Soda Manufacturers.

Lovell, J. H. & Co., South St.

Billiard Saloon.

DANIELS, CHAS. H. & GEO. H. Main St.

Bitt Stock Manufacturers.

Goodell Patent Brace Co.
Rose Bitt Brace Co.

Blacksmiths.

DAVIS, R. B. & CO., South St.   See adv. index.
Francis, V. Court St.
Kingsley, E. L. Main St.
PHELPS, GEO. S. Masonic St.   See adv. index.

Blank Book Manufacturers.

BRIDGMAN & CHILDS, 19, 20 Merchants Row.   See adv. index.

Book Binders.

BRIDGMAN & CHILDS, 19, 20 Merchants Row.   See adv. index.
CORNWELL, E. J. 34 Merchants Row.

Book and Job Printers.

Metcalf & Co., Court St.

Book Sellers and Stationers.

BRIDGMAN & CHILDS, 19, 20 Merchants Row. See adv. index.

Marsh, Joseph, 3 Merchants Row.

S. SCHOOL BOOK DEPOSITORY, Bridgman & Childs, 19, 20 Merchants Row. See adv. index.

Book Seller, (Subscription.)

- CORNWELL, E. J. 34 Merchants Row.

Boot and Shoe Dealers.

CLARK, C. & CO., 2 Clarke Block, Main St.
BRIDGMAN & GRAVES, 31 Merchants Row.
Slate & Baker, 18 Merchants Row.
WILSON & CO., 1 Warner Block.

Boot and Shoe Makers.

Anderson, J. 2 Pleasant St.
Maurer, John T. Warner Block.

Broker, (Bond and Note.)

Dawson, L. A. 6 Merchants Row.

Broom Corn Dealers.

THAYER, SERGEANT & CO. See adv. index.

Brush Manufacturers.

Florence Mf'g Co., (Florence.)

Burial Caskets.

Smith, S. M. & Co., 8 Court St.

Business Wagon Manufacturers.

DAVIS, R. B. & CO., South St. See adv. index.
PHELPS, GEO. S. Masonic St. See adv. index.
Hartwell, N. S. (Florence.)

Button Manufacturer.

Critchlow, P. (Leeds.)

Carpenters and Builders.

Breck, Moses, South St.
Brewster, Edward, Gothic St.
Bosworth, G. S. & Co., cor. Main and State Sts.
Curriers & Smith, Gothic St.
Drury, Geo. B. (Loudville.)
Eldredge & Smith, (Florence.)
Parents, A. D. Central St.
Smith, L. W. King St.

Carriage, Coach and Sleigh Builders.

DAVIS, R. B. & CO., South St. See adv. index.
Hartwell, W. S. (Florence.)
PHELPS, GEO. S. Masonic St. See adv. index.

China, Earthen and Glass Ware.

Arnold, W. F. & Co., Main St.
SKILTON, O. A. 8 Pleasant St. See adv. index.

Cigar Manufacturer.

GABB, CHAS. N. Main St. See adv. index.

Clergymen.

Hall, Gordon, (Cong.)
Hunt, Geo. L. (Bap.)
Jenkins, Wm. L. (Unit.)
Leavitt, Wm. S. (Cong.)
Mansfield, Joseph A. (M. E.)
Moyce, Patrick B. (Cath.)
Tomkins, E. D. (Epis.)

Cloak and Dress Makers.

Hamilton & Bliss, Main St.
Tamplin, Kate Miss, "

Clothing Dealers, (See Tailors.)

Clark, Merritt, Main St.
Cohn, S. & M. 4 Pleasant St.
French, M. M. 26 Merchants Row.
Kingsley, Daniel, 29 "
OCKINGTON, B. F. cor. Main and Pleasant St. See adv. index.
Smith and Prindle, 5 Granite Row.

Coal.

Williams, J. C. Lyman Block, Main St.

Cracker Manufacturer.

CARR, Smith, State St. See adv. index.

Crockery, China, Glass and Earthen Ware.

Arnold, W. F. & Co., Main St.
SKILTON, O. A. 8 Pleasant St. See adv. index.

Cutlery Manufacturers.

Bay State Hardware Co., (Table.)

Deatists.

Davenport, J. N. Main St.
Jones, W. H. Main St.
Meekins, T. W. "
Rust, L. 19 Merchants Row.

Doors, Sash and Blinds.

SMITH & JONES, 3 Court St. See adv. index.
Renney F. L. 3 "

Druggists.

EDWARDS, OSCAR, 32 Merchants' Row.
Kingsley, C. B. 35
PARSONS, S. C. 28   See adv. index.

Dry Goods, (Retail.)

Cutler, H. F. (Florence.)
Delaney, J. W. (Loudville.)
Field, L. H. 25 Merchants' Row.
FLORENCE MERCANTILE CO., (Florence.) H. K. Parsons, Agent.
Hemenway, S. S. (Florence.)
Maynard, T. G.
Parsons, L. J. & Co. (Florence.)
PHILLIPS & SAMPSON, 7 and 8 Merchants' Row
Stoddard & Kellogg,   "   "
WAKEFIELD & SOUTHWICK, opposite Court House.

Dyers.

Carroll, Wm. King St.
Kaiser, W. F. Main St.

Eating Houses.

Dickinson, L. R. Conn. River R. R. Depot.
Edwards, L. B. Main St.
Morton, Levi, Lyman's Block.
PARKER, J. C., N. H. & N. R. R. Depot.

Edge Tool Manufacturers.

Bay State Hardware Co.

Engravers.

Phelps, E. 19 Merchants' Row.

Express Agents and Companies.

Benton, H. C. American Ex. Co., Main St.
BRIDGMAN, EDWARD, Merchants' Union Ex. Co., Main St.

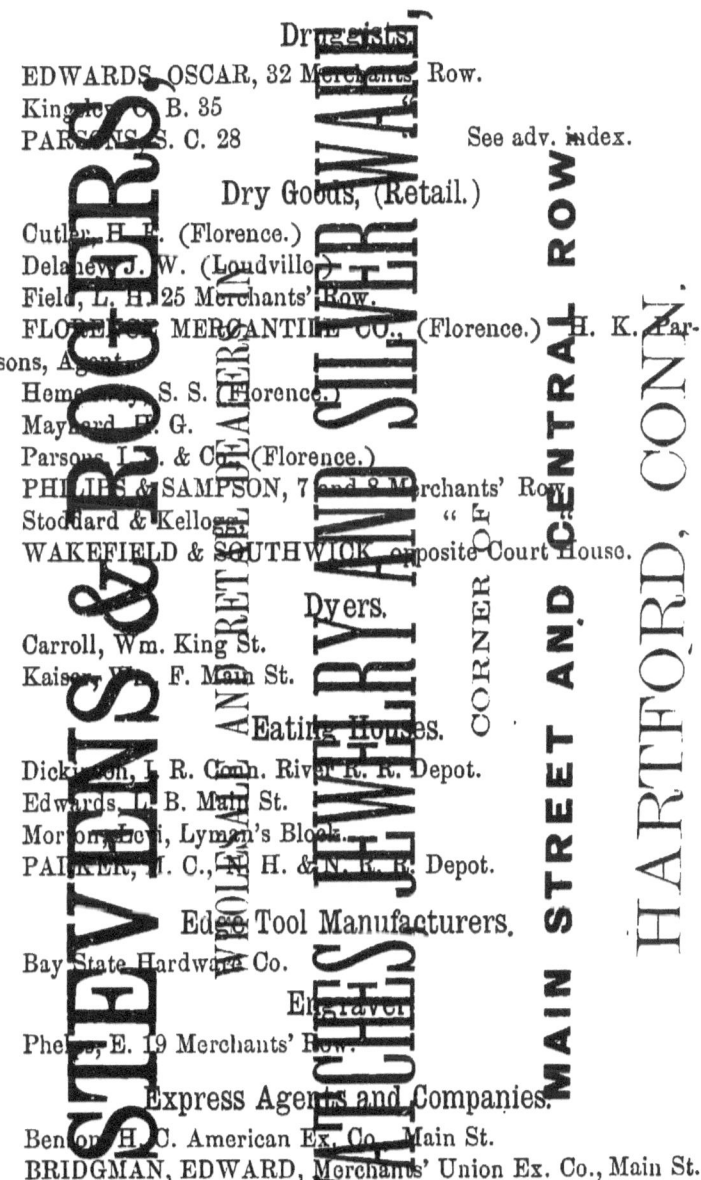

KELLOGG & BULKELEY, 245 Main St., Hartford, Lithographers. Checks, Drafts, Certificates of Stock, &c., Checks Stamped and Numbered, Lithographic work of every variety executed in the best style.

38

Fish Dealers.

JEPSON, F. Lyman's Block.
Rowe & Congdon, 2 Hunt's Building.
Thayer & Moody, 5 Union Block.

Flour and Grain, &c.

McIntyre, L.
THAYER, SERGEANT & CO. See adv. index.
Williams, J. C. Main St.

Flouring Mills.

Clark, S. D. Lower Mills.
THAYER, SERGEANT & CO., Main St. See adv. index.

Fruit and Confectionery.

PROUTY, B. 2 Pleasant St.
Dickinson, I. R., R. R. Depot.
PARKER, M. C., N. H. & N. R. R. Depot.
Strong, Geo. H. 2 Hunt's Building.

Furnaces and Ranges.

EAMES, SPRAGUE & CO., Main St.
Lee & Hussey, Main St.

Furniture Dealers.

Calder, H. M. (Florence.)
Smith, S. M. & Co., 8 Court St.

Gas Companies.

Northampton Gas Light Co.

Gent's Furnishing Goods.

Clark, Merritt, Main St.
Cohn, S. & M. 4 Pleasant St.
French, M. M. 26 Merchants' Row.
Kingsley, Daniel, 29   "   "

OCKINGTON, B. F. cor. Main and Pleasant Sts. See adv. index.

Smith & Prindle, 5 Granite Row.

Glassware Dealers.

Arnold, W. F. Main St.

SKILTON, O. A. 8 Pleasant St. See adv. index.

Grain Dealers.

Clark, S. D. Lower Mills.

Williams, J. C. Main St.

THAYER, SERGEANT & CO., Main St. See adv. index.

Grocers, (Retail.)

Clark, W. M. & Co.

Cutler, H. F. (Florence.)

Day & Loomis, Pleasant St.

Delaney, J. W. (Loudville.)

Dellehunt & King, Main St.

Dickinson, W. P. 4 Court St.

EDWARDS, OSCAR, 32 Merchants' Row.

Hemenway, S. S. (Florence.)

JEPSON, F. Lyman's Block.

Kingsley, C. B. 35 Merchants' Row.

KNOWLTON & NEWTON, 6 and 7 Granite Row.

Maynard, H. G.

Morton & Hayden, 6 Pleasant St.

PARSONS, S. C. 28 Merchants' Row. See adv. index.

Parsons, J. S. & Co., (Florence.)

Rust, T. & Son, Main St.

Stockwell & Spaulding, Union Block.

WRIGHT, A. & CO., Main St.

Hair Dressers.

MAUGER, C. E. Warner House Block.

Prouty, E. F. 3 Pleasant St.

Hardware and Cutlery.

SKILTON, O. A. 8 Pleasant St. See adv. index.

Todd, Wm. H. 3 and 4 Warner Block.

Hardware and Cutlery Manufacturers.

Bay State Manufacturing Co., (Table Cutlery.)
Clement & Hawkes Manufacturing Co., (Hoes.)

Harness Makers.

Eustis, A. Court St.
Hancock, E. B. Old Town Hall.
Hubbard, W. A. Court St.
Smith, H. P. Main St.

Hats, Caps and Furs.

Shepard, Geo. Warner Block.
Deming, R. 1 Union Block.
Draper, J. L. 30 Merchants' Row.

Hoe Manufacturers.

Clement, Hawkes & Maynard.

Hoop Skirt Manufacturers.

Arms & Bardwell Manufacturing Co.
Tinker, Myron A. 6 Merchants' Row.

Home for Invalids, (Springdale.)

E. E. Denniston, M. D., Proprietor.

Hotels.

FLORENCE HOUSE, (Florence,) Joel Abercrombie, Pro.
MANSION HOUSE, Main St., Wm. Hill, Proprietor.
ROUND HILL HOTEL, H. Halsted, M. D.,   "   See adv. index.
WARNER HOUSE, Main St., Roswell Hunt, Proprietor. See adv. index.

Insurance Agents.

JEWETT, J. H. & CO., Main St.   See adv. index.
KIRKLAND, HARVEY, (Court House.)   See adv. index.
Pray, J. Parker, Main St.
Peck, A. P. Main St.

Insurance Company.

HAMPSHIRE MUTUAL FIRE INS. CO.

Jewelry Dealers.

Cook, B. E. & Son, 24 Merchants' Row.
Davidson, D. F. 3   "   "
Fowle, J. H. 15 Main St.
Hannum, John, Main St.

Ladies furnishing Goods.

Dickinson, R. B. 27 Merchants' Row.
Gardner, D. D. Jr., Main St.
Kingsley, Mrs. F. A. 5 Merchants' Row.
PHILIPS & SAMPSON, 7 & 8 Merchants' Row.

Lawyers.

ALLEN, WM. Jr., 23 Merchants' Row.   See adv. index.
Bond, D. W. (Florence.)
Bond, Henry H. (Florence.)
Chilson, H. H. cor. Main and King Sts.
Delano & Turner. "   "   "
Peck, A. P. Main St.
Spaulding, S. F. "
Whitney, J. D. "

Lime, Plaster and Cement.

THAYER, SERGEANT & CO., cor. Main and Market Sts.
See adv. index.
McIntyre, L.

Livery Stables.

CLARK, C. S. & CO., opposite R. R. Depot.   See adv. index.
GRAVES BROTHERS, (Florence.)
HOLLEY, J. Main St.
Strong, Ebenezer, rear Warner House.

Lumber Dealers.

Barrister, Edwin, Gothic St.
Clapp, Wm. R. Pleasant St.

Smith, L. W. King St.
Shaw, S. A., D. Gibbs, Agent, King St.

Machinery Manufacturers.

GRANT & SON, GEO. M.   See adv. index.
HERRICK, W. (Circular Saw Mills,) Pleasant St.   See adv. index.

Machinists.

Boland, T. & Co., Pleasant St.
Clapp, Wm. R.   "
GRANT & SON, GEO. M.   See adv. index.
HERRICK, W. Pleasant St.   See adv. index.

Manufacturing Companies.

WITH KINDS OF GOODS MANUFACTURED.

Arms & Bardwell, Manufacturing Co., (Pocket Books and Hoop Skirts).
Bay State Hardware Co., (Cutlery.)
Clement & Hawkes Manufacturing Co., (Hoes.)
Florence Manufacturing Co., (Florence,) (Brushes,) S. S. Parsons, Sec.
FLORENCE SEWING MACHINE CO., (Florence,) Sewing Machines.
    J. M. Waidwell, Gen. Agent.   See adv. index.
International Screw Nail Co., (Wood Screws.)
Manhan Paper Mills, (Loudville,) (Paper.)
Indellible Pencil Co., (Pencils.)
Monotuck Silk Co., (Florence.)
Rose Bitt Brace Co., (Bitt Stocks.)
    (Silk Sewings and Twist, S. L. Hill Treas.
Williams Manufacturing Co., (Baskets.)
Williston & Arms Manufacturing Co., (Tapes, Bindings and Webbings.)

Marble Workers.

BLACK & FORD, Main St.   See adv. index.
Kinney Bros., Court St.

Meat Markets.

KNOWLTON & NEWTON, N. Granite Row.
THAYER & MOODY, 5 Union Block.
WARREN & GRAVES, Maple St., (Florence.)

Melodeons & Cabinet Organs.

CLARKE, KIDDER & CO., 4 Union Block. See adv. index.
Wright, W. K. Main St.

Milliners and Millinery Goods.

Dickinson, R. B. 27 Merchants Row.
Gardner, Jr. D. D. Main St.
King, F. A. Mrs. 5 Merchants Row.
PHILIPS & SAMPSON, 7, 8   "

Musical Instruments.

CLARKE, KIDDER & CO., 4 Union Block. See adv. index.
Cook, L. C. & Son, 24 Main St.
Fowle, J. H. 15 Main St.
Hannum, John,   "
Wright, W. K.   "

Music & Musical Merchandise.

CLARKE, KIDDER & CO., 4 Union Block. See adv. index.

Newspapers.

Gazette & Courier, (Trumbull & Gere, Editors.)
New England Homestead, (Henry M. Burt & Co., Editors.)
NORTHAMPTON FREE PRESS, (Albert R. Parsons, Editor.)
See adv. index.

Notaries Public.

Delano, Chas. cor. Main and King Sts.
Peck, A. P. Main St.
Spaulding, S. F. "
Turner, Wm. E. cor. Main and King Sts.

Oil Dealers.

SMITH & JONES, Court St. See adv. index.

Oyster Dealers.

JEPSON, F. Lyman Block.
Rowe & Congdon, 2 Hunt's Building.
THAYER & MOODY, 5 Union Block.

Painters. (House, Sign and Carriage.)

GOODELL, RALPH, Main St.
Hamilton, L. W.   "
PRENTISS, WM. C. Court St.
Renney, F. L. 3   "
SMITH & JONES,   "   See adv. index.
Whitcomb, David B.   "

Paints and Oils.

SMITH & JONES, 3 Court St.   See adv. index.

Paper Manufacturers.

Clark, Wm. & Co., (Writing.)
Delaney, Wm. (Wrapping,) (Loudville.)
Manhan Paper Mill,   "   "
Loud, Caleb,   "   "
Watson, John,   "   "

Paper Stock Dealers.

CORNWELL, E. J. 34 Merchants Row.

Patent Medicines.

EDWARDS, OSCAR, 32 Merchants Row.
Kingsley, C. B. 35   "   "
PARSONS, S. C. 28   "   "   See adv. index.

Patent Spring Pocket-Book Manufacturers.

Arms & Bardwell Manufacturing Co.

Photographers.

Biddle, James, 3 Pleasant St.
Houghton & Knowlton, 2 Union Block.
Ingraham Bros., P. O. Building.
ONEIL, JAMES, cor. Main and King Sts.

Physicians.

Dunlap, James, 29 Merchants Row.
FISK & DeWOLF, 20 "   "
Harding, E. B. Union Block.
HALSTED, H. (Round Hill.)
Peck, G. D. 29 Merchants Row.
Roberts, O. O. Main St.
Sornborger, Lyman Block.
Thompson, A. W. 34 Merchants Row.
Thompson, Daniel, 34 "   "

Piano Forte Dealers.

CLARKE, KIDDER & CO., 4 Union Block.   See adv. index.

Planing Mills.

Clapp, Wm. R. Pleasant St.
SMITH, L. W. King St.

Plumbers and Gas Fitters.

EAMES, SPRAGUE & CO., Main St.
Lee & Hussey, Main St.

Pocket Book Manufacturers.

Arms & Bardwell Manufacturing Co.

Porcelain Pictures.

(SEE PHOTOGRAPHERS.)

Postmasters.

Joy, L. W.
Parsons, I. S. (Florence.)

Printers.

FREE PRESS PRINTING CO.   See adv. index.
Metcalf & Co., Court St.
Trumbull & Gere, "

39

Publishers.

BRIDGMAN & CHILDS, 19, 20 Merchants Row. See adv. index.

Ranges and Furnaces.

EAMES, SPRAGUE & CO., Main St.
Lee & Hussey, Main St.

Railroad Agents.

DWIGHT, Henry O., N. & W. Street Railway Co.
JOHNSON, E. A. Conn. River R. R.
PARKER, M. C., N. H. & N. R. R.

Real Estate Agents.

KIRKLAND, HARVEY, Court House. See adv. index.

Restaurants.

SEE LIST EATING HOUSES.

Roofers.

EAMES, SPRAGUE & CO., Main St.
Lee & Hussey, Main St.

Root Beer Manufacturers.

Lovell, J. H. & Co., South St.

Saddle and Harness Manufacturers.

(SEE HARNESS MAKERS.)

Sawing and Planing Mills.

Clapp, Wm. R. Pleasant St.
SMITH, L. W. King St.

Savings Bank,

Northampton Institute for Savings.

Sewing Silk Manufacturers.

Nonotuck Silk Co., (Florence.)
WARNER, JOSEPH

Screw Manufacturers.

International Screw Nail Co.

Sewing Machine Manufacturers.

FLORENCE SEWING MACHINE CO., (Florence,)
John M. Wardwell, Gen. Agent.   See adv. index.

Shafting and Pulleys.

HERRICK, W. Pleasant St.   See adv. index.
GRANT & SON, GEO. M.   See adv. index.

Sheet Iron Workers.

EAMES, SPRAGUE & CO., Main St
Lee & Hussey,   "

Sleigh Manufacturers.

(SEE LIST CARRIAGE AND SLEIGH MANUFACTURERS.)

Soap Manufacturer.

Sawyer, Amos

Soda Water Manufacturer.

Lovell, J. H. & Co., South St.

Stables.

CLARK, C. S. & Co., opp. R. R. Depot.   See adv. index.
GRAVES BROTHERS, (Florence.)
HOLLEY, J. Main St.
STRONG, E. rear Warner House.   See adv. index.

Stationers.

Bridgman & Childs, 19, 20 Merchants Row.   See adv. index.

Stove Dealers and Tinsmiths.

EAMES, SPRAGUE & CO., Main St.
Lee & Hussey, Main St.

Tape Manufacturers.

Williston & Arms Manufacturing Co.

Tobacco (Leaf) Dealers.

Fuller, Geo. M. Agent, Main St.
Graves, Henry B.   "
GABB, CHAS. N.   "   See adv. index.

Wallet Manufacturers.

Arms & Bardwell Manufacturing Co.

Wagon Makers.

DAVIS, R. B. & CO., South St.   See adv. index.
Hartwell, W. S. (Florence.)
PHELPS, GEO. S. Masonic St.   See adv. index.

Water Cures.

ROUND HILL, H. Halsted, M. D.   See adv. index.
SPRINGDALE, E. E. Denniston.

Watchmakers and Jewellers.

Cook, B. E. & Son, 24 Merchants Row.
Davidson, D. F. 3   "   "
Fowle, J. H. 15 Main St.
Hannum, John,   "

Wire Manufacturer.

LAMB, HORACE.   See adv. index.

Miscellaneous.

BUSINESS INSTITUTIONS.

Hampshire Mutual Fire Insurance Co.
Samuel F. Lyman, Pres., Harvey Kirkland, Sec. and Treas.

HAMPSHIRE COUNTY NATIONAL BANK, Capital $250,000.
Luther Bordman, Pres., Lewis Warner, Cashier.

First National Bank, Capital $400,000.
Joel Hayden, Pres., Henry Roberts, Cashier.
Wm. B. Hale, Vice Pres., New York Correspondent National Park Bank.

Northampton National Bank, Capital $400,000.
E. Williams, Pres., Jas. L. Warriner, Cashier.
New York Correspondent, National Mercantile Bank.

Northampton Institution for Savings, Main St.
Dr. Benj. Barrett, Pres., L. Maltby, Treas.

Northampton Gas Light Company, Main St.
M. M. French, Pres., Wm. B. Hale, Treas., D. W. Crafts, Supt.

Northampton Bridge Company, Capital $40,000.
E. Williams, Pres., John Clarke, Treas.

Northampton Dyke Company.
Ansel Wright, Jr., Pres., Henry S. Gere, Clerk, Ansel Wright, Treas.

NORTHAMPTON & WILLIAMSBURGH STREET RAILWAY COMPANY. Cars run every 20 minutes.
J. Wyman Jones, Pres., Emery B. Wells, Supt., Henry O. Dwight, Sec. and Treas.

SOCIETIES.

Northampton Society for the detection of Thieves and Robbers, Organized, 1782.
B. E. Cook, Pres., Oscar Edwards, Clerk, C. Clarke, Treas.

Northampton Young Mens' Institute.
Lafayette Maltby, Pres., Dr.' Wm. H. Jones, Cor. Sec.,
J. R. Trumbull, Rec. Sec.,'C. Clarke, Treas.

Northampton Public Library.
L. Maltby, Pres., J. R. Trumbull, Sec., C. Clarke, Treas.,
Miss Caroline S. Laidley, Librariau.

Hampshire-Medical Society.
Dr. A. W. Thompson, Pres., Dr. D. W. Miuer, Vice Pres.,
(Ware,) Dr. E. M. Johnson, Sec., (Williamsburgh,) Dr.
James Dunlap, Treas.

Insane Hospital.
Dr. Pliny Earle, Supt., Dr. C. K. Bartlett, Asst. Supt.

Hampshire, Franklin and Hampden Agricultural Society.
Milo J. Smith, Pres., A. P. Peck, Sec., H. K. Starkweather,
Treas.   Annual Fair at Northampton first Thursday and
Friday in October.

Northampton Horticultural Club.
A. P. Peck, Pres., L. C. Ferry, Sec. and Treas.

Workingmens' Association.
Rowland Lewis, Pres., H. M. Converse, Sec.   Meet every
Wednesday night, over Skilton's Store.

Northampton Choral Union.
Dr. Thomas W. Meekins, Director, C. Clarke, Treas.

MASONIC.

Jerusalem Lodge, F. and A. M., Instituted in 1797.
Joseph C. Williams, W. M., Sidney E. Bridgman, S. W.,
Wm. C. Pomeroy, J. W., Albion P. Peck, Treas., Chas.
B. Carlisle, Sec., John A. Prentiss, Marshall, James O.
Mantor, S. D., Henry W. Morgan, J. D., Edward F. Ham-
lin, S. S., Isaac P. Davis, J. S., C. Clarke, Chorister, T.
W. Meekins, Organist, Henry Childs, Trustee, D. B.
Whitcomb, Jr., Tyler.

Northampton Royal Arch Chapter, Instituted in 1825.
J. H. S. Prindle, H. P., J. A. Prentiss, K., A. C. Barton, S.,
Edward F. Hamlin, C. H., Geo. S. Phelps, } M.
J. C. Williams, P. S., Alvin Rust, } of
O. O. Roberts, R. A. C., O. A. Parent, } V.
Ansel Wright, Jr., Treas., A. P. Peck, Sec., D. B. Witcomb,
Jr., Tyler.

GOOD TEMPLARS.

"Spirit of Forty" Lodge of Good Templars, No. 149.
Number of Members, 150.
H. K. Noble, W. C. T., L. F. Hunt, W. S. Meet every Monday Night, Agricultural Hall.

The Trustees of the Smith Charities.
Osmyn Baker, Northampton.
Chas. Arms, Deerfield.
Ezra Ingram, Amherst.

RELIGIOUS SOCIETIES.

First Congregational, Main St.
Rev. Wm. S. Leavitt, Pastor, S. C. Parsons, Clerk.

Edwards Congregational, Main St.
Rev. Gordon Hall, D. D., Pastor.

Baptist, Main St.
Rev. Geo. L. Hunt, Pastor.

Methodist Episcopal, Center St.
Rev. Joseph A. Mansfield, Pastor.

St. John's, (Episcopal,) Bridge St.
Rev. E. D. Tomkins, Rector, Wm. H. Raynor, Clerk.

Unitarian, Main St.
Rev. Wm. L. Jenkins, Pastor, Ansel Wright, Jr., Clerk.

Roman Catholic, King St.
Rev. Patrick B. Moyce, Priest.

Young Mens' Christian Association, Rooms First National Bank Building. Organized October, 1864.
S. C. Parsons, Pres., Wm. P. Strickland, Cor. Sec.

Hampshire County Mass., incorporated May 7th, 1662, shire town, Northampton.

COUNTY OFFICERS.

Judge of Probate and Insolvency, Samuel F. Lyman.
Register of   "   "   "   Luke Lyman.
Clerk of Courts, Wm. P. Strickland.
Register of Deeds, Harvey Kirkland.
County Treasurer, Henry S. Gere.
Overseers of House of Correction, Wm. P. Strickland, Luke Lyman, Daniel Kingsley.
Sheriff, H. A. Longley.

TOWN OFFICERS, 1867.

Selectmen, Assessors and Overseers of the Poor, H. K. Starkweather, Milo J. Smith, Ebenezer Strong, Chas. Strong, Nath'l Day.

W. F. Arnold, Town Clerk.
M. H. Spaulding, Town Treas.
W. F. Arnold, Town Liquor Agent.

School Committee, Wm. D. Clapp, H. S. Gere, Sidney Bridgman, Rev. Wm. Jenkins, Rev. L. C. Cobb.

Post Master, L. W. Joy.

ROUND HILL HOTEL
AND
MOTORPATHIC WATER CURE.

The Round Hill Hotel and Water Cure, a Scientific Institution, free from the Ultraism of the day at

NORTHAMPTON, MASS.

The tables are spread with the luxuries of the season. The buildings are on a high hill, in a grove of 50 acres, overlooking one of the finest Landscapes in the world. Both are open the year around.

THE PARTIALLY INSANE,
OPIUM-EATERS AND STIMULUS-TAKERS,

The unhappy sufferers dependent upon such means of keeping up their spirits and strength, or for warding off mental or physical pain or oppression, who desire to break up habits so ruinous to health and mental well-being, will do so with comparative ease under the vitalizing and health-sustaining effects of Motorpathy, mountain air, and cold and hot baths.

TO INVALID GENTLEMEN.

The Motorpathic Treatment, a system of saturninating vitalization, aided in particular cases by a few celebrated vegetable alteratives and a discriminating use of medicated hot and cold baths, speedily removes most diseases. This treatment is of especial merit in breaking up those insidious and dangerous diseases dependent upon impurities of the blood, and of scrofula in the system. In the cure of nervousness, sleeplessness, debilitating dreams, loss of memory, dyspepsia, bronchitis, liver complaint, rheumatism and gout, its success is unparalleled.

TO PHYSICIANS AND LADIES.

Dr. Halsted, in the course of thirty years practice, has been able to discover the adaptation of certain chemical agents, which act in harmony with the natual functions of special organs, remedying their diseased condition, and, motorpathically used, vitalizing them into healthy and vigorous action; thereby removing sterility, curing *prolapsus uteri* and other functional derangements, with ease and certainity, and without using any of the appliances of the day. This Motorpathic treatment restores the whole system to pristine health and vigor. These facts are indisputable. Ladies and physicians without number can be referred to who will vouch for their correctness. The Profession can have all the evidence they desire.

B. F. OCKINGTON,
MERCHANT TAILOR,
FINE READY-MADE CLOTHING & GENTS' FURNISHING GOODS,
Corner Main and Pleasant Streets.
NORTHAMPTON, - - MASS.

40

FLORENCE SEWING MACHINE CO.,

FLORENCE, MASS.,

MANUFACTURERS OF THE CELEBRATED

REVERSIBLE FEED

SEWING MACHINES.

The following are some of the advantages possessed by the FLORENCE over other Machines :

The feed may be reversed at any point desired without stopping the Machine.

It sews light and heavy fabrics with equal facility.

The work will run either to the right or left. It runs quietly and sews rapidly. It has no springs to get out of order. It has the most practical hemmer in use. It turns wide and narrow hems, and will *fell beautifully*.

There is no danger of oiling dresses, the entire machinery being on the top of the table.

The needle is more readily adjusted than in any other machine. There is no difficulty experienced in sewing across thick seams. It is adapted to a larger range of work than any other.

It has a self adjusting shuttle tension. The amount of tension always being in exact proportion to the size of the bobbin.

The taking up of the slack thread is not performed by the irregular contraction of a wire coil, or uncertain operation of wire levers. The precision and accuracy with which the Florence draws the thread into the cloth, is unapproached in any Sewing Machine hitherto offered in the market.

Read what is said of it by some who have thoroughly tested its qualities.

Derry, N. H., May 30th, '67.

Florence Sewing Machine Co.

Two years ago I purchased a Florence Sewing Machine for the use of my family. It has never been out of order since, and works to our perfect satisfaction. I have examined many others, and think this preferable to any I have ever seen. I should not be willing to exchange it for any other Machine that I have ever examined.

Yours, &c.,

G. C. BARTLETT.

Oswego, New York, June 7th, '67.

Florence Sewing Machine Co.

We have for some months past been using one of your Machines with entire satisfaction, having previously used two different kinds. We have thoroughly tested it on various kinds of Cotton, Silk and other fabrics, and we believe that for ease and accuracy of motion, simplicity of construction, for variety, strength and excellence of the stitch, it has no superior, and probably combines more desirable qualities than any other Machine.

E. W. WARNER.

Lancaster, Ohio, June 1st, '67.

Agent Florence Sewing Machine Co.

I have been using a Florence Machine in my family for more than four years, and am better pleased with it every day. It gives no trouble, never gets out of order, is simple in construction and easily managed.

DR. G. MIESSE.

Office & Salesroom No. 505 Broadway, N. Y.

Principal New England Offices,

No. 141 Washington St., Boston,

No 83 Asylum Street, - - - Hartford, Conn.

CHAS. N. GABB,
CIGAR MANUFACTURER,
WHOLESALE AND RETAIL DEALER IN

Tobacco, Cigars, Snuff and Pipes,
Masonic Hall Building, - Northampton, Mass.

SMITH CARR,
Manufacturer and Wholesale Dealer in

All kinds of Crackers and Biscuit,
NORTHAMPTON, MASS.

GEO. M. GRANT & SON,
MANUFACTURERS OF

Machinists' Tools, Shafting, Hangers, Pulleys,
AND MILL WORK OF ALL DESCRIPTIONS.
LOWER MILLS,
NORTHAMPTON, MASS.

NORTHAMPTON MONUMENTAL WORKS.
BLACK & FORD, Proprietors.
MANUFACTURERS OF

MONUMENTS, HEAD STONES,
AND ALL DESCRIPTION OF CEMETERY WORK.
ORDERS SOLICITED AND SATISFACTION GUARANTEED.
Main Street, Northampton, Mass.
ISAAC H. BLACK. JOHN FORD.

GEO. S. PHELPS,
MANUFACTURER AND DEALER IN

Carriages, Business Wagons, Sleighs, &c.
REPAIRING NEATLY AND PROMPTLY DONE.
MASONIC STREET, - - NORTHAMPTON, MASS.

W. F. PRATT,
ARCHITECT,
Northampton, Mass.
NO. 2 UNION BLOCK.

HATFIELD, MASS., on the west bank of the Connecticut, 4 miles north of Northampton, and 14 miles south of Greenfield. The principal business of the town is agricultural. But very little manufacturing is done except of Brooms. Population about 1800.

BUSINESS DIRECTORY.

Broom Manufacturers.

Bragg, Theodore
Bardwell, Elijah
Colby, Samuel & Son.
Curtis, L. G.
Jones, A. S.
Marsh, Elihu
Sanderson, Alvin

Drugs and Medicines.

Bliss, L. S.

Merchants.

Billings, W. D.	Dry Goods, Groceries, &c.
Dickinson, J. G.	" " "
Fitch Bros. & Doane,	" " "
Marsh, Orsemus	" " "
Mosher, Solomon	" " "
Wells & Bardwell,	" " "

Painters, (House and Sign.)

Jones, J. R. & C. H.

WHATELY, MASS., a small post village, 8 miles north of Northampton, on the right bank of the river.

Agriculture constitutes the chief business of the town.

Considerable is done manufacturing Woolen Goods, Pocket Books, Hosiery, Brooms and Leather. The town contains about 1600 inhabitants.

BUSINESS DIRECTORY.

Broom Manufacturer.

Woods, Eliphalet H.

Grist Mill.

Wells, Charles & Co.

Hosiery Manufacturer.

Stockbridge, Charles D.

Merchants.

Lesure, Samuel, Dry Goods, Groceries, &c.
Stone, Daniel   "   "   "

41

Thayer, Caleb L. Dry Goods, Groceries, &c.
White, Samuel B.   "   "   "

Pocket Book Manufacturer.

Belden, Stephen

Tanner and Currier.

Sanderson, J. C.

Woolen Goods Manufacturers.

Bardwell, Seth
James, H. L.
Nash, Thomas

SUNDERLAND, MASS., a pleasant village on the east bank
of the Connecticut River, and nearly opposite South Deerfield.
Agriculture is the chief business of the people. Sunderland is
connected with South Deerfield by a covered toll-bridge across
the Connecticut.

BUSINESS DIRECTORY.

Blacksmith.

Read, Geo. B.

Carpenters and Builders.

Armstrong, J. M.
Batchman, G. L.
Darling, B. C.

Carriage Manufacturer.

Abbey, Geo. F.

Grocers. .

Dunlap, Samuel
Lyman, I. T.

Hotel.

Sunderland Hotel, Norman P. Clark, Proprietor.

Lumber Dealers and Manufacturers.

Delano, A. C. & Son.
Whitmore, D. D.

Merchant.

Lyman, Horace, Dry Goods, Groceries, &c.

Postmaster.

Lyman, Horace

Selectmen.

W. W. Russell.
J. K. Smith.
G. S. Cooley.

Town Clerk and Treasurer.

John M. Smith.

DEERFIELD, MASS., 3 miles south of Greenfield, and comprises the villages of South and Old Deerfield. In South Deerfield several firms are engaged in manufacturing Wallets, Pocket Books, Carriages, &c.

No finer farming country can be found in the Connecticut Valley, than Deerfield Meadows, and large crops of Tobacco, Broom Corn, &c., are raised.

BUSINESS DIRECTORY.

Boots and Shoes.

Arms, O. S.

Carriage Manufacturers.

Billings, Ira
Billings, J. E. & Co.
Ockington, John

Druggist.

Ware, W.

Express Agent.

Arms, O. S.

Flouring Mills.

Goddard, D.
Porter, R. M.

Hotel.

Bloody Brook House, C. B. Fell, Proprietor.

Harness Maker.

Fisher, T.

Livery Stable.

Mosher, C.

Millinery.

Arms, O. S.

Merchants.

Graves, R.
Smith, D. T.
Sammis, D. L.
Tilton, C. B.
Pratt, ——

Nursery.

Davis, W. T.

Physicians.

Eaton, J. S.
Eaton, J. M.

Postmaster.

Arms, O. S.

Pocket Book Manufacturers.

Arms, Charles
Eaton, L. L.
Hamilton & Co.
Palmer, G. K. & Co.
Pease & Ruddock.

Saw Mills.

Tilton, Alvin
Phelps, Smith

MONTAGUE, MASS., is situated on the East bank of the Connecticut, nearly opposite Greenfield, and Distant from Springfield 36 miles north. Piano Forte Cases, Rakes and Lumber are manufactured to some extent.

The Turner's Falls Water Powers Co. are to have one of the most extensive water powers in New England, by constructing a dam across the Connecticut River at Turner's Falls in this town.

BUSINESS DIRECTORY.

Clergyman.

Edward Norton.

Croquet Manufacturers.
Richardson, Geo. F. & Co.

Dentist.
Barrett, Wm. C.

Flouring Mill.
Bangs, S. W. & Co.

Furniture Dealers.
Dike, A. & Co. & Brothers.
Richardson, Geo. B.

Furniture Manufacturers.
Dike, A. & Brothers.

Lumber Manufacturers.
Lawrence, C. & H. C.

Merchants.
Ball, F. M. Dry Goods, Groceries, &c.
Bangs, J. C.   "   "   "
Bangs, Dwight C. "   "   "
Clapp, Geo. A. "   "   "
Goss, R. L. & D. W. (M. City,) Dry Goods, Groceries, &c.
Larned, J. H. & C. H.   "   "   "
Larned, James,   "   "   "

Piano Forte Case Manufacturers.
Goss, R. L. & D. W.

Physicians.
Bradford, David
Deane, A. E.
Cobb, A.

Rake Manufacturer.
Rugg, Amos

Saw Mills.

Lawrence, C. & H. C.
Goss, R. L. & D. W. (M. City.)

Selectmen.

Oakman, R. N.
Root, J. H.
Taylor, Z.

Stove and Tinware Dealer.

Clapp, Geo. A.

Tanner and Currier.

Pond, Benj. F.

Town Clerk and Treasurer.

Root, J. H.

Watches and Jewelry.

Newton, Albert

Water Power.

Turner's Falls Water Power Co.

GREENFIELD, MASS., is one of the many thriving towns in the river valley, situated 36 miles north of Springfield, about one mile west of the Connecticut, and is located on high ground which commands fine views of the surrounding country.

Greenfield is the shire town of Franklin County, and is the centre of a large agricultural community, and contains about 3800 inhabitants.

· The Green River, which flows through the lower part of the town, furnishes power for considerable manufacturing of cutlery and machinery of different kinds. Here is the junction of the Conn. River, Vermont and Mass., and the to be Hoosac Tunnel Railroads.

BUSINESS DIRECTORY.

Agricultural Implement Manufacturers.

FELT & Co., Green River Machine Shop and Furnace. (Plows.)
See adv. index.
Simonds, S. (Rakes,) (Nash's Mills.)

Agricultural Warehouses.

Allens Sons S. cor. Main and Bank Row.
Arms, Geo. A. & Co., cor. Main and Court Square.

Apothecaries.

Hovey, Daniel, Hovey's Block.
Hovey, Geo. H. Court Square.
Howland, R. 5 Bank Row.

Attornies at Law.

Aiken, David, Main St.
Bartlett, Geo. W. 4 Sanborn Block, Main St.
Brainard, A.   "
Conant, C. C. Court House.
DAVIS & DEWOLF, Main St. See adv. index.
 (Wendell T. Davis, Austin Dewolf.)
Griswold, W. Main St.
Hopkins, W. S. B. Pond's Block.
Lamb, S. O. cor. Main and Federal Sts.
MATTOON, CHAS. Main St.
Reed, S. H. Sanborn's Block, Main St.

Auctioneer.

Guinan, Wm. Federal St.

Bakers.

Jones & Guillon, Chapman St.

Ball Bat Manufacturer.

PARKER, BOWDOIN S.

Banks.

FIRST NATIONAL BANK, Bank Row.
Franklin County National Bank.

Basket Manufacturers.

WILLIAMS, T. A. & Co., (Oak and Rattan, hand made.) See
adv. index.

Bit Brace Manufacturers.

Gunn & Amidon.

Blacksmiths.

EWERS, JAS. B. Depot.
MOORE & PERSONS, Davis St.

Book Binders.

Rice, L. W. & Co., Main St.

Book Sellers and Stationers.

Merriam, L. 3 Bank Row.
Rice, L. W. & Co., Main St.

Boot and Shoe Dealers.

Childs, J. R. 8 Main St.
Fellows, M. S.   "
Ford, H. S. 8 Bank Row.
Kean, Edward, Main St.
McFarland, J. 11   "

Business Wagon Manufacturers.

MOORE & PERSONS, Davis St.
Warner, H. W. School St.

Carpenters and Builders.

Embury, H. C. Ames St.
Pierce, Edwin
Stratton & Chapin, School St.
Traver, Philip

42

Carriage, (Children,) Hardware Manufacturers.

MUNSON, J. M. & CO.   See adv. index.

Castings, Manufacturers.

FELT & CO.   See adv. index.

Childrens' Carriages.

Field, Chas. R. Union St.
Noyes, B. B.

Cigar Manufacturer.

Strecker, E. & Co.. Main St.

Clergymen.

Finch, Peter V.   (Epis.)
Lee, S. H.   (Cong.)
Moors, John F.   (Cong.)
Moyce, P. V.   (R. Catholic.)
Potter, E. S.   (Cong.)
Schwartz, P. A.   (Germ. Luth.)
Tupper, Sam'l.   (M. E.)

Cloak and Dress Makers.

Frost, E. Mrs. Main St.
Martin & Sweeney, Misses. Main St.
Wilson, J. A. Mrs. Main St.

Clothing Dealers.

BAILEY, L. N. 10 Bank Row.   See adv. index.
Cohn, M. Main St.
Keuran, H. F. Federal St.
Pond, George, 15 Main St.
Seward, Willard & Co., Main St.
Schuler, Wm.   "

Commission Merchants, (Flour and Grain.)

Potter, W. N. opposite Depot.

SHATTUCK, S. L. Depot Store. See adv. index.

Crockery, China, Glass and Earthen Ware.

Pierce, Jr. Geo. Main St,

Cutlery Manufacturers:

J. Russell Manufacturing Co., Green River Works. (Table.)

Croquet Manufacturer.

PARKER, BOWDOIN S.

Dentists.

Beals, J. Main St.
Leonard, S. Bank Row.
Morgan, R. "
Phelps, C. B. Federal St.

Doors, Sashes and Blinds.

WILSON, J. & CO., Main St. See adv. index.

Druggists.

Hovey, Daniel, Hovey's Block.
Hovey, Geo. H. Court Square.
Howland, R. 5 Bank Row.

Dry Goods.

Brown, F. Main St.
Browning & Co., Hovey's Block.
Eddy & Mann, 2 Pond's Block.
Root, T. D. 5 Sanborn's Block.

Dyers.

BURG, PHILIP, Main St. See adv. index.

Eating Houses.

Lamb, J. H. adjoining Reeds Hotel.
Tyler, M. H. Court Square.

Edge Tool Manufacturers.

Greenfield Tool Co., (Planes.)
Mitchell, R. B. & Co., (Molding and Plane Irons.)

Express Agents and Companies.

Ford, H. S. (Adams Ex. Co.)
STEBBINS, F. L. Mansion House Block, (M. U. Ex. Co.)

Fish and Oyster Dealers.

Damon, D. N. Main St.

Flour and Grain.

Potter, W. N.
SHATTUCK, S. L. Depot Store.   See adv. index.

Foundry, (Iron.)

FELT & CO.   See adv. index.

Fruit and Confectionery.

Coller, D. L. Main St.
Gascoigne, J. T. Federal St.
Lamb, J. H.
Tyler, M. H. Court Square.

Furnaces and Ranges.

CHASE, G. A. 1 Wiley's Block, Main St.   See adv. index.
Lester, Edward, Main St.
Wiley, Oren, Federal St.

Furniture Dealers.

Chamberlin, S. W. Am. House Block.
Miles & Lyons, Main St.

Gas Company.

Greenfield Gas Light Co.
  Rufus Howland, Pres., S. O. Lamb, Sec.

Gents Furnishing Goods.

BAILEY, L. N. 10 Bank Row.   See adv. index.
Cohn, M. Town Hall Building.
Keuran, H. F. Federal St.
POND, GEORGE, 15 Main St.
Schuler, William,   "
Seward, Willard & Co.   "

Gold and Silver Platers.

Phelps & Remington, Federal St.

Grain Dealers.

(See Flour and Grain.)

Grocers.

Hall, Jackson & Co., Main St.
Kellogg, B. & Son,   "
Luey, Henry N.   "
Persons, E. S. & Bro.,   "   Lime Cement.
Potter & Bryant, 4 Pond's Block.
Shattuck, S. L. Depot Store, Com. Merchant, Flour.
Wise, Wm. M. 2 Phoenix Block, Federal St.
Wait, T. & Co., Main St., 1 Washington Hall.

Gun and Locksmith.

Grant, W. A. Main St.

Hair Dressing Saloons.

Arcey, Salmon, D. Mansion House Block.
MILLER, FREDERICK, American House Block.
Adams, Geo. H. Main St.

Hardware Dealers.

Allen's S. Sons, cor. Main & Bank Row.
Arms, Geo. A. & Co., cor. Main and Court Square.

Harness Manufacturer.

PAYNE, H. W. 12 Main St.   See adv. index.

Hotels.

AMERICAN HOUSE, Main St., Simons, Pro.
MANSION HOUSE,   " H. B. Stevens & Sons, Props.
REED'S HOTEL, C. N. Reed, Pro.
Union House, John Cogan, Pro.

Insurance Agents.

Buddington & Childs, 8 Bank Row.
Elliott, William, 13 Main St.
LYONS, SAMUEL J. Sanborn's Block, Main St.
Phelps, A. Main St.

Insurance Companies.

FRANKLIN MUTUAL FIRE INS. CO.
   Sam'l H. Reed, Pres., Chas. Matoon, Sec.

Internal Revenue Collector.

Alvord, D. W. 8 Bank Row.

Job Printers.

Franklin Job Printing Office, Main St.

Livery Stables.

Burr, E. W. Federal St.
Joslyn & Kimball, Main St.
Miller, Valentine, School St.
Wood, Henry S. Main St.
Stetson, Amos,   "

Lumber Dealers.

Nourse, A. G. Main St.
Goss, R. L. & D. W.
Newton, James & Son.

Machinists.

GREEN RIVER MACHINE SHOP AND FURNACE. (Felt
& Co.) See adv. index.
MUNSON, J. M. & CO. See adv. index.

Marble Workers.

Bolter & Woods.

Meat Markets.

Clark, J. A. & Co., Federal St.
Coombs, Jesse A. Federal St.
Persons, E. S. & Brothers, Main St.

Merchant Tailors.

BAILEY, L. N. 10 Bank Row. See adv. index.
Keuran, H. F. Federal St.
Pond, Geo. 15 Main St.
Schuler, Wm.   "
Seward, Willard & Co., Main St.

Millinery and Fancy Goods.

Bigelow, M. P. Miss, 1 Pond's Block, Main St.
Taylor, R. R. 7 Main St.
Wunsch, Wm. 4 Mansion House Block.

Molding and Plane Irons.

Mitchell, R. B. & Co.

Newspapers.

Gazette and Courier, S. S. Eastman & Co., Proprietors.

Notaries Public.

Wm. H. Allen,
Charles K. Grennell,
Lewis Merriam.

Organs and Melodeons.

FORBES & FOSTER, 1 Mansion House Block. See adv. index.

Painters, (House and Sign.)

Lyon, David, School St.
Mark, G. W. Main St.
Rice, E. J. Federal St.
WILSON, J. & Co., Main St. See adv. index.

Paper Hangings.

Merriam, L. 3 Bank Row.

Paper Stock Dealers.

CHASE, G. A. 1 Wiley's Block, Main St. See adv. index.

Photographers.

Bradford, P. cor. Main and Federal Sts.
Taylor & Knoulton, 3 Pond's Block.

Physicians.

Broons, Frederick, Main St.
Dean, A. C.
Fisk, C. L. Main St.
FISK, Jr., Chas. L. Sanborn's Block, Main St.
Harding, W. F. Pond's Block.
Osgood, J. W. D. Main St.
Stone, Mrs.
Severance, Wm. S. Main St.
Ulrich, F.
Walker, A. C. Union Block.
Wunsch, Mrs. Wm.

Postmaster.

Merriam, Lewis

Rake Manufacturer.

Simonds, Sylvester, (Wash's Mills.)

Railroad Agent.

HOWARD, H. E. Conn River, & Vt. and Mass. Railroads.

Saddle, Harness and Trunks.

PAYNE, H. W. 12 Main St. See adv. index.

Sash, Doors and Blinds.

WILSON, J. & CO., Main St. See adv. index.

Saw Mills.

Goss, R. L. & D. W.
Newton, James & Son.

Sheriff.

Samuel H. Reed.

Sheriffs, (Deputy.)

Jos. P. Felton.
L. D. Joslyn.

Stove and Tinware Dealers.

CHASE, G. A. 1 Wiley's Block, Main St. See adv. index.
Lester, Edward, Main St.
Wiley, Oren, Federal St.

Tanner and Currier.

Barton, Lyman G.

Truckmen.

WOOD, E. W. Main St.
Wood, N. J.   "

Trunk Dealer.

PAYNE, H. W. 12 Main St. See adv. index.

Trial Justice.

Wendell T. Davis.
43

Trip Hammer Manufacturers.

FELT & CO.   See adv. index.

Town Clerk.

Noah S. Wells.

Watches and Jewelry.

FORBES & FOSTER, 1 Mansion House Block, Main St.   See adv. index.

Hollister, J. H. 14 Main St.

Water Wheel, (Whitney & Rose,) Manufacturers.

FELT & CO.   See adv. index.

Wheel Wrights.

MOORE & PERSONS.   Davis St.

Wood Working Machinery Manufacturers.

FELT & CO.   See adv. index.

Woolen Manufacturers.

Greenfield Manufacturing Co., Theo. Leonard, Agt.

Miscellaneous.

Franklin County, Mass., Incorporated June 24, 1811.   Shire Town, Greenfield.

County Officers.

Judge of Probate and Insolvency, Chas. Mattoon.
Register of Probate and Insolvency, Chester C. Conant.
Clerk of Courts, Edward E. Lyman.
Register of Deeds, Humphrey Stevens.
County Treasurer, Bela Kellogg.
Overseers of House of Correction, Lewis Merriam, Rufus Howland.

Town Officers.

Selectmen, Humphrey Stevens, Anson K. Warner, Fred G. Smith.

Assessors, M. H. Tyler, Lyman G. Barton, Wm. Keith.

Town Clerk, Noah S. Wells.

Banks.

The First National Bank, Incorporated 1822, Capital, $300,000.
Wm. B. Washburn, Pres., E. W. Russell, Cashier.
Franklin County National Bank, Capital, $200,000.
Ira Abercrombie, Pres., R. A. Packard, Cashier.
Franklin Savings Institution.
H. W. Clapp, Pres., Theo. Leonard, Sec., Wm. H. Allen,
Treasurer.

Societies.

Greenfield Library Association, 2300 Volumes.
Theo. Leonard, Pres., Chester C. Conant, Sec., Miss Frances
E. Moody, Librarian.
Franklin Co. Agricultural Society.
Thos. J. Field, Pres., Northfield, E. D. Lyman, Sec. and
· Treas.
Franklin District Medical Society.
C. Stratton, Northfield, Pres., Wm. Dwight, Bernardston,
Sec.

Good Templars.

Green River Lodge Good Templars, No. 154, number of members 125. Meet every Tuesday evening. Officers elected quarterly.

Churches.

First Cong. Society, (Nashs' Mills,) Rev. E. S. Potter.
Second Cong. Society. Rev. S. H. Lee, Pastor, Daniel H.
Newton, Clerk.
Third Cong. Society, Unitarian, Main St., Rev. John F Moors,
Pastor, M. H. Taylor, Clerk.
First Baptist Society, W. L. Fisk, Clerk.
Methodist Episcopal Church, Church St., Rev. Samuel Tup-
per, Pastor, Recording Steward, Samuel E. Brown.
St. James' (Episcopal) Church, Federal St., Peter V. Finch,
Rector, Chas. K. Grinell, Clerk,

German Lutheran Church, Rev. P. A. Schwartz, Pastor, Geo. Zeiner, Clerk.

Roman Catholic Church, P. V. Moyce, Priest.

Masonic.

Connecticut Valley Encampment, (under dispensation,) Wendell T. Davis, G. C. Titus Strong, Council. E. P. Graves, T. I. G. M. Geo. H. Hovey, Rec. Franklin, R. N. Chapter. Wm. S. Severance, M. E. H. P. Geo. H. Hovey, Sec. Republican Lodge, Bowdoin S. Parker, W. M. E. P. Sec'y.

Religious Society.

Greenfield Young Mens' Christian Association, C. C. Conant, Pres., Bowdoin S. Parker, Sec'y.

T. A. WILLIAMS & CO.,
MANUFACTURERS OF
SPLINT AND RATTAN BASKETS,
HAND MADE.
Corn, Clothes, Laundry, Market, Rice, Cotton and Fruit Baskets,
GREENFIELD, MASS.

L. N. BAILEY,
DEALER IN
READY-MADE CLOTHING, GENTS' FURNISHING GOODS.
Custom Clothing made to order in the most approved style.
AGENT FOR WEED'S SEWING MACHINES.
No. 10 Bank Row,   GREENFIELD, MASS.

J. WILSON & CO.,
DEALER IN
Windows, Doors, Blinds, Window Glass, Paints,
OILS, VARNISHES, PAPER HANGINGS AND BORDER,
Window Shades and Fixtures,
Paint, Varnish and Whitewash Brushes.
A few doors west of the }
American House,   }   GREENFIELD, MASS.
A. G. MINER.   J. WILSON.

GEORGE A. CHASE,
DEALER IN
STOVES, RANGES, HOT-AIR FURNACES,
Iron Sinks, Tin, Glass, Britannia and Wooden Ware.
Guttering, Tin Roofing, and every description of Tin, Copper and Sheet Iron work done to order.
Dealer in Improved Coal and Wood Burning Cook Stoves,
Eldorado, Aetna, Model, Magnet, Tropic, Senator, Loyal, Placer and other Cooking Stoves.
Agent for Boynton's Patent Calorifie Furnace, Boynton Empire Gas Burner, Church's Gas Burner,
Gas Burning Parlor Stoves, with and without Ovens, Parlor Magnet,
COPPER AND IRON PUMPS, LEAD PIPE, &C.
No. 1 WILEY'S BLOCK, }
Main Street,   }   GREENFIELD, Mass.
☞Particular attention given to Custom Work.   Cash paid for Rags, Paper Stock,
Old Junk, &c.

WHOLESALE DEPOTS OF DENTISTS' MATERIALS,
PORCELAIN TEETH, GOLD FOIL, etc., etc.
528 Arch St., Philadelphia, Pa.   769 Broadway, N. Y.   16 Tremont Row, Boston, Mass.   100 and 102 Randolph St.,
Chicago, Illinois.
SAMUEL S. WHITE.

NORTHFIELD, Franklin County, Mass., is situated on the east bank of the Connecticut, about 45 miles north of Springfield. A small business is done in manufacturing Brooms, Pails, Medicines, &c.

Northfield is a fine agricultural town, and contains about 1400 inhabitants.

BUSINESS DIRECTORY.

Broom Manufacturer.

Hibbard, Cornelius

Merchants.

Lyman, Jonathan, Dry Goods, Groceries, &c.
Osgood, Charles,   "   "   "
Smith, Dwight & Son, "   "   "
Walker, S. T.   "   "   "

Sash, Doors and Blinds.

Parker, H. B.

Millinery.

Atkins, Mary T.
Smith, M. & A. Misses

Ointment and Salve Manufacturers.

Elmer, A. D. & Co.

Pail and Bucket Manufacturer.

Johnson, Henry

Stoves and Tinware.

Rose, Amos W.
Gale, James O.

BERNARDSTON, MASS., situated near the southern border of Vermont, 7 miles north of Greenfield, 43 miles from Springfield, and 17 miles south of Brattleboro, has a station on the Conn. River Railroad. Population about 1000. There is some Manufacturing done here of Hoes, Lumber, &c., but the principal business is Agriculture.

BUSINESS DIRECTORY.

Blacksmiths.

Dewey, I. N.
Day, Josiah

Boarding House.

Cushman Hall, Ira O. Lucy, Steward. .

Boot and Shoe Makers.

Alexander A.
Sanders, A. P.

Cigar Manufacturer.

Lane, Geo. W.

Clergymen.

Canfield, C. T. Rev.
Butler, H. B.   "
Crowl, J. F.   "
Merrill, T.   "
Wrinkle, T.   "

Distiller.

Connable, S.

Dress Making.

Chapin, Miss H.
Crafts, Mrs. F.

Dry Goods and Groceries.

Cook, L. W.
Stratton & Slate.

Temple, G. W.
Wright, L. B.

Express Offices.

American Express Co., O. Dickinson, Agent.
Merchants' Union Express Co., Wm. Dwight, Agent.

Fancy Goods.

Pierce, L. S.

Halls, (Public.)

Sanderson Hall.
Town Hall.

Harness Maker.

Hoyt, R.

Hoe Manufacturer.

Hurlbut, E. S.

Hotels.

New England House, H. Denham, Proprietor.
Union House, L. Weatherhead, Proprietor.

Library, (Free.)

Cushman Library, Wm. Dwight, Librarian. (2500 volumes.)

Lumber Dealers.

Carter & Cameron.
Bagg, R. & Co.
Hale, S.
Park, H.
Newton, Jas. & Son.

Millinery.

Bascom, Mrs. L. P.
Cowles, Miss R.

44

Physicians and Surgeons.

Bowker, C.
Dwight, Wm.

Postmaster.

Wm. Dwight.

Sash, Doors and Blinds.

Haynes, Jas. & Son.

Telegraph Office.

O. Dickinson, Operator.

Wool Carding.

Bagg, R. & C.

HINSDALE, Cheshire County, New Hampshire, nearly opposite and a little north of South Vernon, and 8 miles south-east
of Brattleboro, was originally called "Fort Dummer." The town
was incorporated Sept. 3, 1753. Population at the present time
about 1500.

Considerable business is done in the manufacture of Woolen
Goods, Carriages, Machinery, Leather, &c.

BUSINESS DIRECTORY.

Blacksmith.

Merrill, Pliny

Box Manufacturer.

Snow, James

Clergyman.

Balchelder, J. S. (Cong.)

Carriage Manufacturer.

Butler, John W.

Harness Maker.

Parker, Samuel

Iron Founders.

Howe & Sabin.

Knobs and Bobbins.

Priest, Joseph

Machinists.

Newhall & Stebbins.
Tolman, J. R.

Merchants.

Cook, L. W. Dry Goods, Groceries, &c.
Fisher Brothers, "   "   "
Holland, George "   "   "
Holland & Williams, Dry Goods, Groceries, &c.
Martin, Edward H.   "   "   "
Martin, Oscar J.   "   "   "

Painters, (House and Sign.)

Pratt, N. E.
Wyman, T. E.

Palm Leaf Hat Manufacturer.

Gilbert, Richmond

Physicians.

Boyden, Frederick
Leonard, Wm. S.

Postmaster.

Chas. J. Amidon.

Publishers.

Hunter & Co.

Shoe Maker.

Thayer, John M.

Stoves and Tinware.

Mitchell, J. B.

Tanner and Currier.

King, J. L.

Woolen Manufacturers.

Boydon & Amidon.
Hailo & Frost.

GUILFORD, Windham County, Vermont, located 17 miles north of Greenfield, Mass., contains about 1300 population.

Guilford includes the villages of Guilford Center and Green River. Considerable manufacturing is carried on here in Paper, Axle Springs, Slate, Childrens' Carriages, &c.

BUSINESS DIRECTORY.

Broom Handles Manufacturers.

Franklin, Philip (Hinesbury.)
Franklin, George   "
Keith, Vinal   "

Blacksmith.

Tubbs, S. N.

Brick Manufacturers.

Houghton, G. & J.

Cider Brandy Manufacturers.

Jacobs, Herbert
Tan, Truman

Carriage Manufacturers.

Ashcraft, Francis
Edwards & Smith.

Clergymen.

Bennett, Jonas G. (Bap.)
Allen, Ethan (Epis.)

Childrens' Carriage Manufacturers.

Boylston, F. & S. (Green River.)
Edwards & Hubbard, (East Guilford.)
Smith, Sanford "

Flour, Meal and Feed.

Squires & Eddy.

Grist Mill.

Eddy & Halliday.

Insurance Agent.

Field, R. B.

Lumber Dealers.

Franklin, Geo.
Maxwell, John

Axle Spring Manufacturer.

Bangs, N.

Machinist.

Bangs, N. J.

Merchants.

Field, Rodney B. (East Guilford,) Dry Goods, Groceries.
Stowe, Henry, (Green River,) " "
Thayer, John, (Center,) " "

Paper Manufacturers.

Robinson & Stoddard, (Green River.)

Physician.

Webster, Norman

Postmasters.

Barney, C. L. (Center.)
Field, R. B. (Guilford.)
Putnam, A. W. (Green River.)

Saw Mills.

Boyden, Samuel B.
Taylor, G.

Slate Quarries.

Waite & Johnson.
Brattleboro & Guilford Slate Co., Tyler L. Johnson, Supt.
Pierce, Willard.

VERNON. Windham County. Vermont, 50 miles north of Springfield. Mass., and ten miles south of Brattleboro, contains about 900 inhabitants. Principal business is farming and lumbering. At the south village is the junction of the Conn River and Vermont and Mass. Railroads.

BUSINESS DIRECTORY.

Blacksmiths.

Lee, Geo. M.
Miller, S. S.

Brick Manufacturers.

Brown, J. A.
Green & Dickinson.

Clergymen.

Hodgdon, N. C.

Hotels.

Burrows, J. F.
Merrill & Clark.
WHITHED, ADDISON

Lumber Manufacturers.

Cone, Hunt & Co.
Merrill & Clark.
Trask, J. T. & Co.
Wright, S. S.

Merchant.

WHITHED, ADDISON, Dry Goods, Groceries, Drugs, Hardware.

Physicians.

Goodwillie, Thomas, (Allo.)

Postmasters.

ADDISON WHITHED.

Match Manufacturers.

Trask, J. T. & Co.

Restaurant.

Weller, Geo. B.

BRATTLEBORO, Windham County, Vermont, is situated on the right bank of the Connecticut river, and distant from New York 194 miles; Hartford, Conn., 84; Springfield, Mass., 60; Montreal, 250 miles. For business it is one of the principal towns in the river valley, there being a large amount of manufacturing carried on, principally Organs, Melodeons, Furniture, Woolen and Silk. Whetstone Brook which flows through the south part of the town furnishes the water power. Situated on an uneven surface with hills and mountains in all directions, the scenery is grand and beautiful. Population about 4500.

Across the Connecticut to the east are Wantastiquet and Mine Mountains, the former rising from the river to the height of nearly 1100 feet.

The Vermont Asylum for the Insane is located here, and is one of the best conducted Institutions of the kind in the country. Many distinguished people make Brattleboro their summer resort, and truly there is no pleasanter place or more charming drives, or finer fishing grounds, or grand and picturesque scenery to be found anywhere. The town is well supplied with good Hotels, Water Cures and summer boarding houses.

The Record and Farmer, the principal paper of Windham County, published in Brattleboro, and edited by Ed. P. Ackerman, is a large eight page sheet, full of original matter, and one of the most lively and enterprising newspapers in New England. The attention of the reader is called to the advertisment on inside Back Cover.

The Cottage Organ Manufactory of Mess. J. Estey & Company, located on South Main and Bridge Streets, and also on Flat street, comprising many buildings, is one of the most perfect and extensive of the kind in the world.

The most improved and perfected machinery known to modern times has been introduced, presenting one of the grandest displays of American genius anywhere to be found. The Cottage Organ contains the following great and important improvements which are patented and consequently found in no other instruments. The Patent Harmonic Attachment, which doubles the power of the instrument without increasing its size or number of reeds. Also, the Patent Manual sub-bass, which brings into use an independent set of large and powerful sub-bass reeds, which are played with the ordinary keys and controlled by a stop. Also the Patent Box Humana Tremolo.

BUSINESS DIRECTORY.

Ale and Beer Manufacturers.

Houghton & Warren, (West Brattleboro.)

Architects.

Wilkins, W. E. Fisher's Block.
Hines, Geo. A. Canal St.

Attorneys at Law.

Clarke & Haskins, Town Hall Building.
Field & Tyler, Main St.
   Chas. K. Field, Jas. M. Tyler.
Hall, Nathan, Williston Block.
Howe, Geo. Main St.
Kellogg, Daniel, Town Hall.
Keyes, Asa,   "   " Building.
Mead, L. G. Main St., N. P.
PHELPS, J. W. "
Tyler, Royall, Town Hall Building, County Clerk.

Auctioneers.

Campbell, E. B. Williston's Block.
Chapin, Charles, High St.
Herrick, S. N. Union Block, Main St.

Bakers.

Smith & Robbins, Main St., Cutler's Block.

Banks.

THE FIRST NATIONAL BANK OF BRATTLEBORO, Capital, $300,000. N. B. Williston, Pres., S. M. Waite, Cash., N. C. Sawyer, Ass't Cash.
Vermont National Bank of Brattleboro, Capital $150,000, Samuel Root, Pres., Frank Wells, Cash.

Billiard Rooms.

Howe, Moses B. Main St.
Sargent, I. & L. "
Revere House, "

Blacksmiths.

Bailey, C. W. (West Brattleboro.)
Horton & Streeter, Elliott St.

Blank Book Manufacturer.

Edwards, F. C. Main St.

Book Binder.

Edwards, F. C. Main St.

Booksellers and Stationers.

Carpenter, E. J. Main St.
Felton & Cheney, "
Steen, J. "

Boot and Shoe Dealers.

Boynton & Demarais, Main St.
Frost, Willard "
Frost, C. C. "
Judge, Thomas "
Simonds, E. G. "
Simonds, P. "

Brass Founders.

BURNHAM, H. & E. Main St.   See adv. index.

Carriage Manufacturers.

Allen, So. Main, (Children.)
Stebbins, J. H. Canal St.
Williston, N. B & Co., Elliott.

Cloak and Dress Makers.

Brown, L. A. Miss, Main St.
Dickerman, J. L. Mrs. "
Farnsworth, R. Mrs. Blake Block, Main St.
Miller, J. B. Mrs. (West Brattleboro.)
Sargent, O. Miss Main St.
Weatherhead, D. Mrs. Hudson St.
Wells, M. J. Mrs. Main St.

Clothes Cleaning and Repairing.

KAYE, THOMAS, High St.   See adv. index.

Cottage Organ Manufacturers.

ESTEY, J. & CO.   See adv. index.

Clothing Dealers.

Cune & Brackett, 4, 5, Granite Row.
Pratt, Wright & Co., 2, 3   "

Crockery, China and Glass Ware.

Barrows & Dillingham, Main St.
Doorn, M. T. Van   "

Dentists.

Pettie, A. L. Cutler's Block.
Putnam, A. D. Main St.
Post, O. R. Green St.

Dyer.

KAYE, THOMAS, High St.   See adv. index.

Druggists.

Thorn, I. N. & Co., Main St.
CLARK & WILLARD, "
THOMPSON, C. F.   "   See adv. index.
Clark, Joseph   "

Dry Goods.

McKnight, J. D. 1 Union Block.
Pratt, O. J. 1 Granite Row.
Houghton, Spencer & Co., 7 Granite Row.
Barrows & Dillingham, Fisk's Block.
Slate & Wilkins, Main St.
Newton, Wm. S.   "
Perry, P. F. (West Brattleboro.)

Eating Houses.

Brooks, E. S. Main St.
Eayrs, A. E.   "
Pratt, G. H. Main St.
Sargent, I. L.   "

Express Companies and Agents.

Am. Express, U. S. & Canada Express, Bemis, Willis Agent.
Merchants Union Express Co., Franks, F. H. Agent.

Fish Dealer.

Boyd, J. Main St.

Flour Dealers.

Buddington Bros., Main St.
Crosby, E. & Co., Union Block, Main St.
Frost & Goodhue,   "

Flouring Mills.

Buddington Bros. Bridge St.
Goodnough, J. P. (West Brattleboro.)
Stoddard, Elroy   "

Furniture.

Brown, C. L. Main St.
Dwinell, A. E.   "
Retting, John   "

Gents' Furnishing Goods.

Chamberlin & Franks, Main St.
Cune & Brockett, 4, 5 Granite Row, Main St.
Goodrich, H. A. Main St.
Pratt, Wright & Co., 2, 3 Granite Row, Main St.

Grocers.

Allen, J. M. So. Main St.
Davenport & Mansur, "
Frost & Goodhue, "
FAIRFIELD & PERRY, 2 Union Block.
Glover, Henry, Main St.
Newton, Wm. S. "
Perry, P. F. (West Brattleboro.)
Piper & Simonds, Main St., Exchange Block.

Gunsmith and Jobber.

Barrett, L. H. Main St.

Hair Dressing Saloons.

Clark, Orin, Elliott St.
Edwards, J. M. Main St.
GREEN, FRANCIS, "
Powers, O. M. Mrs. (Lady Hair Dressing,) Elliott St.
Remington, O. P. Main St.

Harness and Trunk Makers.

Heustis & Burnap, Main St.
Miller, N. Elliott St.
PROUTY, F. A. Main St.

Hardware.

Clark, Joseph, Main St.
THOMPSON, C. F. Williston Block, Main St. See adv. index.
Thompson & Ranger, Main St.
Perry, P. F. (West Brattleboro.)

Hats, Caps and Furnishing Goods.

Chamberlin & Franks, Main St.
Goodrich, H. A. Main St.

Hoop Skirt and Corset Maunfacturer.

Gross, A. E. Mrs. High St.

Hotels.

American House, Main St., G. A. Boyden, Pro.
Brattleboro House, " C. G. Lawrence.
Glen House, (West Brattleboro,) L. D. Thayer.
LAWRENCE HOTEL, Elliott St., (open summers.) Emil
Apfelbaum & Co.
Revere House, Knowlton Bros., Elliott St.
Vermont House, (West Brattleboro,) N. Holland.
Wesselhoet House and Water Cure Establishment, P. B.
Francis & John Knowlton, Prop's.

Insurance Agents.

Campbell, E. B. Williston Block, Main St.
CHAPIN, CHAS. High St.
Hull, Nathan, Williston Block, Main St.
Higby, L. E. Union Block, "
Jenne, B. R. Williston Block, "
Mead, Chas. L. Main St.
Putnam, A. D. "

Inventor.

Baldwin, Frederick, Main St.

Iron Founders.

Newman & Tyler, Main St.

Lathes and Upright Drills.

CRANE, L. H. Canal St.

Leather Dealers.

Kimball, S. W. (West Brattleboro.)

Simonds, J. H. Main St.
THOMPSON, C. F. (Patent and Enamelled Leather.) Williston Block, Main St. See adv. index.

Liquor Agent, (Town.)

Austin, Jno. Town Hall.

Machinists.

Baldwin, Frederick, Main St.
CRANE, L. H. Canal St.
Vinton & Hines, "
Newman & Tyler, Main St.
Weld, C. J. Asylum St.
Worcester, Leonard, (Centerville.)

Marble Workers.

Kathan, J. H. Bridge St.

Mathematical Instrument Manufacturers.

CRANE, L. H. Canal St.

Meat Markets.

Alexander, Chas. E. 2 Elliott St.
Hadley, H. Main St.
Richardson, W. F. Main St.

Manufacturers.

Alexander, Chas. E. (Whites' Patent Mop Wringers,) Elliott Street.
Allen, Geo. So. Main St., (Perambulator.)
Brattleboro Melodeon Co., Flat St., (Organs and Melodeons.)
Brattleboro Woolen Co., (Jordan, Marsh & Co., Boston,) Balmoral Skirts.
BURNHAM, H. & E. Main St., (Pumps.)
Cobb, J. B. (West Brattleboro,) (Axhelves.)
Dunklee, Bridge St., (Sewing Silk.)
ESTEY, J. & CO., office, Flat St., (Cottage Organs and Melodeons.) See adv. index.
Clark, Jacobs & Co., (West Brattleboro,) (Rice and Coffee Hullers.)

Milliken & Bissell, (Portable Photograph Apparatus.)
Sawyer, Cyrus W. (Centerville,) (Glue.)
Smith & Coffin, So. Main, (Sash, Doors and Blinds.)
Snow, Daniel & Co., (West Brattleboro,) (Vesper Organs and Melodeons.)
Spencer, S. M. & Co., (Centerville,) (Stencil Tools.)
Stanley Rule & Level Co., Canal St., (Rules and Levels,) C. L. Mead, Agent.
Stebbins, J. H. Canal St., (Carriages.)
Tyler & Newman, (Paper Machinery.)
Wardsworth, R. & Son, (Sidney,) (Presses.)
Woodcock & Vinton, Canal St., (Paper, Print.)
Wheeler, Geo. B. (Centerville,) (Skates.)
Williston, N. B. & Co., Elliott St., (Carriages.)

Melodeon Manufacturers.

Brattleboro Melodeon Co.
ESTEY, J. & CO. See adv. index.
Snow, Daniel & Co., (West Brattleboro.)

Millinery and Fancy Goods.

Avery, T. & Co., Mrs. Main St.
Gill, H. J. Miss 6 Granite Row.
Marsh & Ballard, Misses, Main St.
Pratt, O. J. 1 Granite Row.

Mop Wringers, (White's Patent.)

Alexander, Chas. E. 2 Elliott St.

Newspapers.

Vermont Phoenix, Brown & Prouty, Editors and Publishers.
VERMONT RECORD & FARMER, Main St.
  Ed. P. Ackerman, Editor and Proprietor. See adv. inside back cover.

Optician.

Tripp, Chas. A. & Co., Main St.

Organ Manufacturers.

ESTEY, J. & Co.   See adv. index.
Snow, Daniel & Co., (West B.)

Paint and Oil Dealers.

THOMPSON, C. F. Williston Block, Main St.   See adv. index.

Paper Machinery Manufacturers.

Newman & Tyler, Main St.

Paper, (Printing,) Manufacturers.

Woodcock & Vinton.

Photographers.

Henry, D. A. Cutter's Block.
Howe, C. L. Union Block.
Gilmore, J. M. Main St.

Physicians.

Bowles, S. W. North Main St.
Dearborn, D. P.   "
Frost, C. P. Green St.
Horton, Chas. W. Main St.
Higgimon, F. J. High St.
Ketchum, B. F. Main St.
Arms, E. B. Insane Asylum.
Steadman, J. H. (West B.)
Rockwell, Wm. H. Insane Asylum.
Rockwell, Wm. H. Jr., "   "
Warren, J. P. Green St.

Plumbers and Gas Fitters.

BURNHAM, H. & E. Main St.   See adv. index.
Gould, Wm. Clark St.
Putnam.   "

Postmasters.

Kellogg, Daniel Jr., Town Hall.
Perry, P. F. (West B.
46

Printers, (Job.)

COBLEIGH, F. D. Phœnix Office. See adv. index.
RECORD & FARMER, Main St., P. Ackerman, Editor. See
adv. index.
Selleck, Geo. E. Fisher's Block, Main St.
Stedman, D. B. 9 Granite Row, "

Pump Manufacturers.

BURNHAM, H. & E. Main St. See adv. index.

Railroad Agent.

Brooks, E. F. Vt. & Mass., and Burlington and Vt. Valley
Railroad.

Rule and Level Manufacturers.

Stanley Rule and Level Co., Chas. L. Mead, Agt.

Sash, Doors and Blinds.

Smith & Coffin, Main St.

Savings Banks.

Windham Provident Institution for Savings.
Lafayette Clark, Pres., L. G. Mead, Sec. and Treas.

Sewing Silk Manufacturer.

Dunkler, H. Bridge St.

Stables.

Liscomb, John, (West B.)
Morse, Sidney A. cor. Main and Elliott Sts.
Putnam, Lewis, Prospect St.
Ray, J. L. Main St.
Smith, Wilder, High St.

Stoves and Tinware.

Wood & Kathan, Main St.
Dickenson, L. P. Elliott St.

Tailors.

Cune & Brackett, 4 and 5 Granite Row.
Pratt, Wright & Co., 2 and 3   "

Tanners and Curriers.

Kimball, S. W. (West B.)
Warren, Geo. & Co., (Centerville.)

Watches and Jewelry.

Tripp, Chas. A. & Co., Main St.   Watchmaker.
Thompson & Ranger,   "   "

Woolen Goods Manufacturers, (Balmoral Skirts.)

Brattleboro' Woolen Co., cor. Elliott and Bridge Sts.

Masonic.

Fort Dummer Royal Arch Chapter, No. 12.
H. C. Pelter, Sec. Regular Convocations second Thursday
in every month.
Columbia Lodge, No. 36.
W. H. Vinton, W. M., J. W. Burnap, Sec. Regular meet-
ings Tuesday of or preceding full moon.

Odd Fellows.

Wautastiquet Lodge No. 5. Officers elected semi annually.
Regular meetings Monday evening of each week.

Good Templars.

Minnehaha Temple, No. 1, (Chartered 1867.) Regular meet-
ings first Thursday in each month.
Minnehaha Lodge of Good Templars, No. 31. Meet every
Wednesday night. Number of members, 300. O. B. Douglas,
Lodge Deputy. Officers elected quarterly.

Educational Institutions.

Brattleboro Academy for Boys, (West B.) Open Winters.
Hiram Orcutt, Principal.

Elm Hall Seminary, cor. Asylum and Common Sts.
Mrs. L. M. Chase, Principal.
Burnside School for Boys, (Newfane Road.)
C. A. Miles, Principal.
Glenwood Ladies' Seminary, (West B.)
R. E. Hosford, Fin. Agent.
Home School for Boys, North Main St.
Miss A. S. Tyler, Principal.
Laneside School for Girls, North St.
Miss Louise Barber, Principal.
Howland, L. A. Mrs. School for Young Ladies, Asylum St.

Miscellaneous.

Brattleboro Book Club.
Miss Annie Higginson, Sec.

Brattleboro Temperance Society, Annual meeting first Monday in May.

Brattleboro Freedman's Aid Society.
Miss A. Higginson, Sec.

Brattleboro Water Company.
K. Haskins, Sec. and Treas.

Brattleboro Gas Company.
S. M. Waite, Prop.

Brattleboro Library Association.
C. F. Thompson, Treas.

Brattleboro Drum Corps, 20 Pieces.
H. H. Hadley, Leader.

Brattleboro, (West,) Cemetery Association.
S. Clark, Samuel Earle, Committee.

Centerville Aqueduct Association.
Jno. Cutler, Pres.

Hinsdale Bridge Company.
Charles Chapin, Treas. and Agent.

Northern Aqueduct Association.
Nelson Crosby, Agent.

New Book Club.
A. C. Davenport, Sec.

Prospect Hill Aqueduct Company.
L. K. Fuller, Sec. and Treas.

Prospect Hill Cemetery Association.
Geo. Newman, Sec.

Southern Aqueduct Association.
Joseph Clark, Treas.

Western Aqueduct Association.
C. L. Mead, Sec. and Treas.

Windham County Agricultural Society.
W. A. Stedman, Sec.   Annual Fair at Newfane, Wednesday
and Thursday of first week in October.

Vermont Asylum for the Insane, Asylum St.
Wm. H. Rockwell, M. D., Supt.

Windham County Park Association.
Geo. A. Hunt, Sec. and Treas.

F. D. COBLEIGH,
Book and Job Printer,
PHOENIX OFFICE, Third Floor,
Brattleboro, Vermont.

Printing in Colors and every description of Job Printing neatly and promptly executed,
at the most reasonable rates.

DUMMERSTON, Windham County, Vermont, about 5 miles north of Brattleboro, and 20 miles south of Bellows Falls, located on the west bank of the river, and includes the village of West Dummerston.

It has a station on the Vermont Valley Railroad, and the prin cipal business is farming. Population, about 1200.

BUSINESS DIRECTORY.

Bedstead Manufacturers.

Townsend & Estey, (West D.)

Blacksmith.

Batchelder, (West D.)
Ormsbee, Ira, (D.)

Carriages, Sleighs and Lumber

Walker & Dix.

Clergymen.

Carpenter, Mark, (Bap.)

Good Templars.

West River Lodge, No. 24, I. O. G. T. (West D.)

Grist Mills.

Crosby, Franklin
Knight, Wilder

Lumber Dealers.

Crosby, George (D.)
Crosby, Franklin (D.)

Stickney, Peter (West D.)
Townsend & Estey, (West D.)
Stickney, Benjamin   "

Merchants.

Birchard, Roger (D.)   Dry Goods, Groceries.
Knapp, J. (West D.)   "   . "

Postmasters.

Greenwood, John (West D.)
Miller, Wm. O. (D.)

Wheelwrights.

Dutton, Winslow
Dutton, Charles

PUTNEY, Windham County, Vermont, a quiet town on the west bank of the Connecticut River, and a station on the Vermont Central Railroad, about 10 miles north of Brattleboro. Contains a population of about 1400. There are here several manufactories of Woolen and Paper. Putney includes the village of East Putney.

BUSINESS DIRECTORY.

Attorney at Law.

Kimball, John

Blacksmiths.

Hinman, Frank
Willard, W. & W.

Boot and Shoe Makers.

Veasy, J. A.
Wilbur, L.

Carriage Manufacturer.

Roberts, J. C.

Grist Mills.

Holmes, L.
Houghton, James

Harness Maker.

Houghton, W. L.

Hotels.

SALSBURY'S HOTEL, H. Salsbury, Pro.
Vermont House, A. Hosford, Pro.

Insurance Agent.

Darling, La Forest C.

Merchants.

Baker & Hewett, Dry Goods, Groceries, &c.
Pierce, G. L.   "   "   "
Walker, J. W.   "   "   "

Millinery.

Walker, E. M.

Paper Manufacturers.

Robertson, John
Robertson, William

Physicians.

Allen, D.
Halton, H. D.

Postmasters.

Chamberlain, H. K. (East P.)
Hewett, A. B. (P.)

Sawing and Planing.

Knight, J. H.

47

Wood Turning.

Underwood & Stowell.

Woolen Manufacturers.

Putney Woolen Co., (Fancy Cassimeres.)

WESTMINISTER, Windham County, Vermont, is situated on the west bank of the Connecticut, 20 miles north of Brattleboro, and has a station on the Vermont Valley Railroad.

The township contains the villages of East and West Westminister, and the population numbers about 1400. Baskets, Carriages and Lumber are manufactured to some extent.

BUSINESS DIRECTORY.

Basket Manufacturer.

Stearns, Olin

Blacksmith.

Metcalf, George

Carpenter and Builder.

Willard, H. A.

Carriage Manufacturer.

Cobb, George

Clergymen.

Fairbanks, (Cong.) (W.)
Stevens, Alfred (Cong.) (West W.)

Grist Mills.

Gage, W. P.
Mayo, Peter

Merchants.

Chase, C. C.   Dry Goods, Groceries, &c.
Safford, R. S. & Co.   "   "   "
Wilcox, E. (West W.)   "   "   "

Physicians.

Chandler, Joseph H.
Safford, Pliny

Postmasters.

Chase, C. (W.)
Ranney, Russell (West W.)

Silver Plated Goods Manufacturers.

Watkins, A. S. & Co.

WALPOLE, Cheshire County, New Hampshire, (formerly call-ed Great Falls, or Bellows Town,) incorporated February 13th, 1752, contains a population of some 2000 people. Walpole township includes the village of Drewsville, and is chiefly a farm-ing community. It is located some 20 miles north of Brattle-boro, and 4 miles south of Bellows Falls. A bridge crosses the Connecticut at this place. Walpole is one of the neatest and prettiest villages in the Connecticut Valley. Its streets are wide and the dwellings are large and elegant, and many fine residences may be seen in the town, which has become of late years quite a place of resort during the summer.

The Cheshire Railroad passes through this town, and about one mile distant is Walpole Station, on the Vermont Valley Railroad.

Attorneys at Law.

Bellows, J. G.
Vose, F.

Blacksmiths.

Hooper, Ira H.
Smith, Joseph

Books and Stationery.

Martin & Davis. ·

Boots and Shoes.

Ball, R. L.
Maynard, A. K.

Dentist.

Ball, W.

Drugs and Medicines.

Lovejoy, J. W.
Martin & Davis.

House and Sign Painters.

Benson, James
Brown, H. W.
Ward, Wm.

Hotels.

Todd's Hotel, Thos. Todd, Proprietor.
Wentworth House, H. A. Perry, Proprietor.

Gristmill.

Fisher, Charles, (Drewsville.)

Harness Maker.

Allen, Henry

Insurance Agent.
Seabry, Edwin

Watches and Jewelry.
Kendall, Chas. W.

Meat Markets.
Brown, O.
Farnham, Wm.

Merchants.
Buffum & Co., Dry Goods, Groceries, &c.
Britton, M. J.   "   "   "
Aldrich, B. F. & Co.
Lathrop, H. (Drewsville,) Dry Goods, Groceries, &c.
Putnam, E. T.   "   "   "   "

Millinery.
Hodskins, H. Mrs.
Miller, Ellen R.

Photographer.
Ball, H.

Railroad Agent.
C. B. Lucke.

Physicians and Surgeons.
Kittredge, J. N.
Martin, S. D.
Richardson, A. P.
Watkyns, Hiram

Postmaster.
Sherman, Wm.

Shirt Manufacturers.
BATES & ALDRICH.

Stables.

Maynard, W. A.

Stoves and Tinware.

Clark, J. B.

Summer Boarding House.

Makepeace, G. R.

Tailor.

Bradford, S. W.

Tanner and Currier.

Maynard, G. (Drewsville.)

Veterinary Surgeon.

Weir, F. A.

ROCKINGHAM, Windham County, Vermont, contains the villages of Bellows Falls, Saxton's River, Cambridgeport and Bartonsville, and has a population of about 3000. Bellows Falls, in this township, on the Connecticut River, is 114 miles from Boston, and 220 miles from New York, on the direct route to Saratoga Springs, the White Mountains, Montreal, &c.

BUSINESS DIRECTORY.

Attorneys at Law.

Bridgman, J. D. Square.
Eddy, C. B.
Meyers, W. S.
Stoughton, H. E.
Arnold, C. E.
Campbell, A. S.

Banks.

National Bank of Bellows Falls, Rockingham.
N. Fullerton, Pres., J. H. Williams, Cashier.

Basket Manufacturer.

Gage, Wm. P. Westminister.

Blacksmith.

Ames, Otis B. Square.

Books and Stationery.

Johnson & Babbitt. Square.

Boots and Shoes.

Hapgood, E. Square.
Streeter, H. "

Circular Saw Mill Manufacturers.

CLARK & CHAPMAN. See adv. index.

Clergymen.

Pierce, N. (Bap.)
Stevens, M. A. Cong.)
Wight, W. H. (Meth.)
Wainwright, F. C. (Epis.)

Dentist.

Blake, S. M. Square.

Druggists.

Johnson & Babbitt. Square.
Woods, O. F. "

Furniture

Conant, William, Square.

Gristmill

Wilson & Co.

Grocers.

Arms & Wilson, Square.
Cragan, S.   "
Thompson, A. L. Canal.
Hyde, Russell, Westminister.
Viall, H. B. Square.

Hair Dressing Saloon.

Whitney, M. M. Square.

Hardware.

Arms & Wilson, Square.

Harness Manufacturers.

Goodwin, J. C. & Co., Square.

Hotels.

Bellows Falls Hotel, O. F. Woods, Proprietor.
Island House, Chas. Turns, Proprietor.

Insurance and Express Agents.

Johnson & Babbitt, Square.

Insurance Agent.

Eddy, C. B. Square.

Insurance Company.

Conn. River Mutual Fire Insurance Company.
   Asa Wentworth, Pres., A. S. Campbell, Sec.

Iron Founders.

CLARK & CHAPMAN.   See adv. index.

Lodging and Eating House.

GEORGE, F. A. at Railroad Depot.   See adv. index.

Marble Workers.

Evans, R. A. Square.
ANDREWS, GEO. Westminister.   See adv. index.

Meat Market.

Young, H. M. Square.

Merchants.

Chase & Hooper, Westminster, Dry Goods, Groceries, &c.
Guild & Fau, Square, Dry Goods and Paper Hangings.
Gray, O. D. 　" 　Dry Goods, Groceries, &c.

Mill Gearing and Shafting Manufacturers.

CLARK & CHAPMAN. 　See adv. index.

Millinery.

Guild, S. S. & Co., Rockingham.
Wood, A. S. Mrs. near P. O.

Newspaper.

Bellows Falls Times, A. N. Swain, Editor and Publisher.

Pension Agent.

Campbell, Alex. S. Square.

Photographers.

Blanchard, J. W. F. Square.
Taft, P. W. 　　　"

Physicians.

Nichols, S. Rockingham,
Whitman, F. Square.

Postmasters.

Divoll, J. B. (Rockinghan.)
Fletcher, —— (Bartonsville.)
Osgood, E. R. (Saxton's River.)
Swan, A. N. (B. Falls.)
Perry, Solon, (Cambridgeport.)

Printer, (Job.)

Swain, A. N. Square.

Railroad Agent.

A. A. Jacobs, Vermont Central.

Railroads.

Vermont Central, G. Merrill, Supt., J. W. Hobart, Transportation Agent.

Cheshire Railroad.

Restaurants.

Brown, Geo. (Rockingham.)

GEORGE, F. A., R. R. Depot.   See adv. index.

Wightman, J. G. (Rockingham.)

Sanders, S. Square.

Sash, Doors and Blinds.

Underwood & Richardson.

Scythe Snath Manufacturers.

Frost, Derby & Co.

Stoves and Tinware.

Hadley, F. B. Westminster St.

Tailors.

GUILD, S. H. Square.

Saker, J. F. Square.

Watches and Jewelry.

Amadon, L. Square.

Water Wheel Manufacturers.

CLARK & CHAPMAN, (Chapman's Improved Turbine.) See adv. index.

CHARLESTOWN, Sullivan County, New Hampshire, originally called number Four, includes part of Langdon. Incorporated July 2d, 1753, is situated on the east bank of the Connecticut

River, 8 miles above Bellows Falls, and 34 miles north of Brattle-
boro. The township includes the villages of North and South
Charlestown. There is but very little manufacturing done here.
Along the valley adjoining the river, lies a fine farming country.

BUSINESS DIRECTORY.

Attorneys at Law.

Cushing, E. L.
Hubbard, Henry

Banks.

Connecticut River National Bank.
  Geo. Olcott, Cash., H. Lathrop, Prs.

Boot and Shoe Manufacturers, (Wholesale.)

HARRISON & WEST, near R. R. Depot.

Boots and Shoes, (Retail.)

Holbrook, Charles E.

Blacksmiths.

Smith, Hiram
Kendall, B.

Children's Carriage Manufacturers

De Haven, Harlow & Co.

Druggists.

Tyrrill, S. M.

Dry Goods and Groceries.

White, Josiah
Josselyn, J. O.
Smith, O. & Co.

Groceries.

Cooley, S. O. & Son.
Bowman, Jas. M.
Slade, John W.

Harness Shop.

Sparrow, W.

Hotels.

Robertsons' Hotel, G. H. Hoyt, Pro.
Cheshire Bridge House.

Insurance Agent.

Olcott, Geo.

Livery Stables.

Josselyn, J. O.
Robertson & Porter.

Meat Markets.

Taylor, John

Physicians and Surgeons.

Webber, Samuel
Whittaker, J. M.

Postmaster.

Kendall, C. C.

Saw Mill.

Crosby & Fish.

Stoves and Tinware

Bond, George S.

Town Clerk.

Kendall, C. C.

R. R. Agent.

Sloughton, D. G.

SPRINGFIELD, Windsor County, Vermont, 10 miles north-west of Bellow Falls, and about 5 miles west of the Connecticut River. Contains about 3500 population.

Black River, which flows through this town, furnishes a valuable water power for manufacturing, which is carried on very extensively. Woolens, Cottons, Woolen Machinery, Children's Cabs, Horse Rakes, Agricultural Implements, Stoves, &c.

BUSINESS DIRECTORY.

Attorneys at Law.
Closson, H.
PIERCE, J. W. Main St.
Porter, E. W.

Banks.
First National Bank of Springfield, capital, $200,000.
Henry Barnard, Pres., Chas. E. Richardson, Cash.

Barrel Vent Manufacturers.
Smith, Mason & Co., (Patent,) Main St.

Blacksmith.
Kimball, Geo. Jr., Main St.

Bobbin Manufacturers.
Barker & Washburn, (Block River Village.)

Boots and Shoes.
Cook, Selden, Main St.
Merritt, George,   "

Carriage Manufacturers.
ELLIS, BRITTON & EATON, (Childrens' Carriages.)
Graham, G. W.   .

Chair Manufacturers.
Leland, G. (North S.)
Martin, D.   "

Churn Manufacturers.
Diamond Churn Co., Amos Brown, Agent.

Clergymen.
Bass, E. C. (Epis.)   .

Cobb, L. M. (Cong.)
Chedel, (Chris.) (North S.)
Cook, S. (Chris.) "
Lewis, G. E. (Ind. Meth.)
Pickwell, W. S. (Bap.) (North S.)

Clothes Pin Manufacturers.

Smith, Mason & Co., Main St., (Smith Block.)

Cotton Goods Manufacturers.

HOLMES, JOHN & CO., (Sheetings and Battings.)

Dentist.

Bowers, G. W. Main St.

Druggists.

Chase, C. S. Main St.
Porter, F. W. & Co. Main St.

Flouring Mills.

Parker & Washburn, (Black River Village.)
GILBERT, JAMES, Main St.

Fruit and Confectionery.

Kimball, Thomas, Main St.
Long, Francis "

Furniture.

Sanders, Charles

Hair Dressing Saloons.

Hastings, J. W. Main St.
Stiles, John "

Harness Makers.

Ball & Harlow, Main St.

Hooks and Eye Manufacturers.

Smith, Mason & Co., (Eagle Talon,) Main St.

Horse Rake Manufacturer.

KIMBALL, GEO. Main St. (Kimball's Patent Wheel Rake.)
See adv. index.

Hotels.

SPRINGFIELD HOUSE, E. R. Backus, Pro.

Iron Fence Manufacturers.

MITCHELL, JAMES & CO.   See adv. index.

Iron Founders.

MITCHELL, JAMES & CO.   See adv. index.

Machinists.

Gilman & Townsend, Main St.
PARKS & WOOLSON.
Smith, Mason & Co., Main St.

Machine Castings.

MITCHELL, JAMES & CO.   See adv. index.

Manufacturers.

Ball & Thompson, (Scythe Snaths.)
Ball & Harlow, (Harnesses.)
Barrett, M. S. (Lumber.)
DIAMOND CHURN CO., (Churns.)
ELLIS, BRITTEN & EATON, (Children's Carriages & Toys.)
Graham, G. W. (Carriages.)
Gilman & Townsend, (Machinists.)
HOLMES, JOHN & CO., (Sheetings, Satinet, Warp Batting.)
Holmes, Whitmore & Co., (Cassimeres & Doeskins.)
KIMBALL, GEO., (Wheel Horse Rakes.)   See adv. index.
MITCHELL, JAS. & CO., (Iron Founders, Plows, Stoves,
Water Wheels. See adv. index.
PARKS & WOOLSON, (Woolen Machinery.)
Smith, Mason & Co., (Hooks and Eyes, Paper Holders, Machinists.)

Marble Worker.

Barney, Franklin

Meat Market.

Way & Hammond, Main St.

Merchants.

Burke & Tenney, Main St., Dry Goods, Groceries, &c.
Chipman, John,   "   Hats, Caps, &c.
Closson, G. L. Main St., Clothing, Boots and Shoes, Gents' Furnishing Goods.
FLOYD, H. W. Main St., Cloths, Clothing, &c.
Frost, M. P.   "   Groceries, Crockery, Boots & Shoes.
Howe, S. R.   "   Dry Goods, Clothing, &c.
Harlow & Kirk,   "   Hardware, Stoves Tinware, &c.
Keyes, C. M.   "   Millinery, Cloaks, &c.
LABARRE, C. K.   "   Dry Goods, Groceries, Boots and Shoes, &c.
Porter, F. W. & Co., Main St., Drugs, Books, Stationery, Fancy Goods, Jewelry, &c.
Porter, G. W. & Co., Main St., Dry Goods, Groceries, &c.
ROBINSON, A. L. & H. L., Main St., Crockery, Groceries, Agricultural Implements.
SPILLANE & COBB, Main St., Cloths, Clothing, &c.

Millinery and Fancy Goods.

Harvey & Grover, Main St.
Keyes, C. M.   "
Knight, G. P. Miss   "

Mop Manufacturers.

Smith, Mason & Co., Main St.

Newspaper.

RECORD & FARMER, D. L. Milliken, Editor. See adv. inside back cover.

49

Ox Bow Manufacturer.

Smart, A. Main St.

Packing Box Manufacturer.

BARRETT, M. S.

Pail and Tub Manufacturer.

Ellis, L. (North S.)

Painters, (House, Sign and Carriage.)

Ellis, Oliver
Howe, H. F.

Paper Holder, (Smith's Patent.)

Smith, Mason & Co., Main St.

Photographer.

Powers, J. D. Main St.

Physicians.

Chase, L.
Crane, H. F.
Knight, E. A.
Martin, M.
Sawyer, L.
Tuttle, M.

Plow Manufacturers.

MITCHELL, JAMES & CO.   See adv. index.

Postmaster.

Porter, F. W. Main St.

Sash, Doors and Blinds.

BARRETT, M. S. Pearl St.   See adv. index.

Satinet Warp Manufacturers.

HOLMES, JOHN & CO.

Savings Bank.

Springfield Savings Bank, Main St.
Henry Closson, Prest., Geo. W. Porter, Sec'y and Treas.

Saw Mills.

Batchelder, A. Main St.
Parker & Washburn.
BARRETT, M. S. Pearl St.   See adv. index.

Sawing and Planing Mill.

BARRETT, M. S. Pearl St.   See adv. index.

Sawed Shingle Manufacturer.

BARRETT, M. S. Pearl St.   See adv. index.

Scythe Snath Manufacturer.

Ball & Thompson.   ˙

Stable.

Wood, B. F. Main St.

Stencil Tool Manufacturer.

Fullam, A. J. Main St.

Stove Manufacturers.

MITCHELL, JAMES & CO.   See adv. index.

Tailors.

FLOYD, H. W. Main St.
SPILLANE & COBB, "

Toy Manufacturers.

ELLIS, BRITTON & EATON.

Watches and Jewelry.

Porter, F. W. & Co., Main St.
Smith D. M.   "

Water Wheel Manufacturers.

MITCHELL, JAMES & CO.   See adv. index.

Woolen Machinery Manufacturers.

PARKS & WOOLSON, (Shearing and Finishing Machines.)

Woolen Manufacturers.

Black River Woolen Mills, Holmes, Whitmore & Co., (Fancy Cassimeres and Doeskins.)

Miscellaneous.

Masonic.

St. John's Lodge, No. 41.
   H. W. Floyd, W. M., Sam'l Chipman, Sec'y, meet first on or preceding full moon.

Good Templars.

Social Lodge Good Templars, No. 41.
   Meet Wednesday evenings.   Officers elected quarterly.

Springfield Thief Detecting Society.

Daniel A. Gill, Pres., Benj. F. Dana, Clerk, Fred W. Porter, Sec'y.

Springfield Agricultural Society.

Horace Hubbard, Pres., D. O. Gill, Sec'y.

Springfield Central Library, 1,100 volumes.
   J. W. Pierce, Librarian.

Springfield Agricultural Library.
   Daniel Rice, Librarian.

Springfield Farmers Club.
   C. K. Hubbard, Pres., Henry M. Arms, Sec'y.

JAS. MITCHELL & CO.

Manufacturers, Wholesale and Retail Dealers in

Gen. Dix, No 3, 2¾ feet.   Gen. Dix, No. 4, 3 feet.   Hot Air Furnace, 3½ and 4½ feet.

Ploughs, Cultivators, Bucklin's Patent Harrow and Cultivator, Ox Shovels, Hot Air Furnaces, Box, Parlor and Cook Stoves, Farmer's Portable Boiler, Caldron Kettles, Sinks, Sap Pans, Sap Pan Mouths and Grates, Hollow ware, Arch, Oven and Boiler Mouths, Arch Tops and Circles, Scroll and Pipe Registers, Stove Flues and Safes, Stove Backs, Fire-Dogs, Coal Shovels, Sad Irons and Stands, Clothes Reels, Window Weights, Grind-stone Hangings, Door Hangings, for Wood and Iron Trucks, Door Trucks, Door Scrapers, Boot Jacks, Brackets, Bedstead castings, Pegging Jacks, Stitch-ing Clamps, Boot Crimpers, Copying Presses, Wagon and Cart Boxes, Wagon Jacks, Sleigh, Sled and Wagon Shoes, Portable Forges, Boxes and Tweers, Tire Formers, Mandevill's Saws, Water Wheels, Water Cisterns, Woolen Mill Steam Boxes, Head-block Castings, Pump-log Couplings, Cemetery Fences, Ionic Capitals, Taylor's improved Press Irons, Carver, C. C. Blodget's Pat. Har-poon Horse Pitch-forks and Grapler,

Improved Cottage.

Snatch Blocks, Corn Crackers, and a large assortment of Mill and Machinery Castings.

SPRINGFIELD, VERMONT.

KIMBALL'S
IMPROVED HORSE RAKE,
PATENTED DECEMBER 20, 1864.

Here is an article that justly claims the attention of every man who has hay to make. The Rake being in front of the Wheel, is within sight of the driver, and he can manage it at pleasure to suit the uneven surface of the ground. No other Rake can have any such contrivance.

The driver on this Rake has the advantage of working it with his feet or hands, as he may choose. It is so simple and so securely made that it is not liable to get out of order; and the low price at which it is sold will enable every farmer to buy it. Try one, by all means.

REFERENCE TO EVERY PERSON WHO HAS USED THIS RAKE.
MADE AND SOLD BY
GEORGE KIMBALL, - - - Springfield, Vt.

CLAREMONT, Sullivan County, New Hampshire, 14 miles north of Bellows Falls, and 12 south of Windsor, was incorporated Oct. 26, 1764, and now contains a population of about 4,500.

Sugar River, which flows through the town, furnishes water power for the many manufactories of Cotton, Woolen, Paper, Lumber, Flour, &c.

BUSINESS DIRECTORY.

Agricultural Implements.

STOWELL, GEO. H. Tremont Square.

Attorneys at Law.

Baker, Edward D. Farwell's Block.
Chase, Arthur, Brown's Block.
Colby, Ira Jr., Farwell's Block.
Freeman, P. C.
Parker, H. W. Sullivan St.
Prentiss, J. J.   "
Woodell, Edward, W.
Vaughn, E. Farwell's Block.

Banks.

The Claremont National Bank, Capital 150,000.
Geo. N. Farwell, Pres., Jno. L. Farwell, Cashier.

Billiards.

Fitch, Henry, 2 Tremont St.
Moulton, Charles,   "

Blacksmiths.

Abbee & Smith, Tremont St.
Henry, W. B. Main St.
Watriss, H. B. & L. W. Main St.
Woodbury, Jacob, Spring St.

Book Binders.

CLAREMONT MF'G CO., E. L. Goddard, Treasurer.   See adv. index.

Bookseller and Stationer.

Merrifield, G. W. Brown's Block.

Boots and Shoes.

Bigley, W. H. Tremont St.
Bliss, A. J. Sullivan St.
Corey & Nevers, 2 Tremont Row.
Dickinson, H. A. & Co., Sullivan St.
Noyes, Henry C. 3 Brown's Block.

Cabinet Ware Manufacturers.

Briggs, Wm. Spring St.
Briggs, Fred. A. Broad St.
Briggs, J. G. Lower Village.

Carriage Manufacturers.

HARRIMAN, L. Lower Village.
ROYS, HENRY F. North St.

Cigars and Tobacco, (Wholesale.)

BARRETT, HENRY E. cor. Broad and Tremont Sts.   See adv. index.

Clergymen.

Babcock, D. C. (Meth.)
Clark, Edward W. (Cong.)
Moore, Asher, (Uni.)
Peck, John M. (Epis.)
Smith, Henry,   "
Towle, Francis W. (Bap.)

Clothing.

Haubrich, 4 Perry's Block.
Parkhurst & Tutherley, Brown's Block.

Confectionery Manufacturer.
BARRETT, HENRY E. Broad St. See adv. index.

Cotton Manufacturers.
Home Mills, (4-4 Cottons,) Arnold Briggs, Agt.
Monodnock Mills, (Sheetings, Drill.,) D. W. Johnson, Agt.

Cracker Manufacturer.
BARRETT, HENRY E. cor. Broad and Tremont Sts. See adv. index.

Cutlery Glassers Manufacturers.
BRIGGS, WM. H. Main St. See adv. index.

Dentists.
Bock, J. Tremont St.
Kidder, Frederick A.
Sabine, Silas A.
Smith, Wm. M.

Deputy U. S. Assessor.
Clark, Wm. 7 Perry's Block.

Druggists.
Ainsworth, Edwin, 5 Perry's Block.
Brooks, L. Main St.
Ladd, Wm. M. 2 Brown's Block.

Dry Goods.
Baker & Hurd, Farwell's Block.
Brigham, C. M.   "
Heywood & Co., Tremont Square.
Emerson & Haskell,   "
Putnam & Pierce, Main St.
True, Henry O. Brown's Block.
Patten, Henry, Main St.

Express Company and Agent.
Fisk & Co., Ex. O. J. Brown, Agent.
50

Fancy Goods.

Heywood & Co., Tremont Square.
Spencer, Reuben   "

File Manufacturers.

CLAREMONT FILE WORKS, Main St.
Henry E Austin, Agent. See adv. index.

Firkin Manufacturer.

Shepardson, R.

Fish Dealer.

Johnson, Ed. Broad St.

Flour Manufacturers.

SUGAR RIVER MILLS, Stowell, A. & Co.

Flouring Mills.

STOWELL, A. & Co., Main St.

Fruit and Confectionery.

Gowdey, T. R. Tremont St.
White & Eels, 3   "

Grain Dealers.

STOWELL, A. & Co., Main St.

Grocers.

CHASE BROTHERS, Tremont St.
Jewett, M. L. 1 Perry's Block, Tremont St.
Johnson & Fisher, Fisher's Block.
Putnam & Pierce, Main St.
Stowell & Bradford, 1 Tremont Row.
Redfield, A. (West Claremont.)
White, J. & Co., 9 Pleasant St.

Hair Dressing Saloons.

Jacques, E. H. Tremont House.
TENNEY, H. A. Tremont St.

Handle Manufacturer.

Howard, J. B. Broad St., (Rake, Fork and Hoe.)

Hats, Caps and Gents' Furnishing Goods.

Emerson & Haskell, Tremont Square.
Hanbrich, F. 4 Perry's Block.
Parkhurst & Tutherly, Brown's Block.

Hardware.

Putnam & Pierce, Main St.
Stowell, Geo. H. Tremont Square.

Harness and Trunk Makers.

Bowen, E. J. 11 Pleasant St.
Dart, T. Main St.

Hoop Skirt Manufacturer.

White, E. H. Miss, Tremont St.

Hotels.

SULLIVAN HOUSE, James Leet, Pro., Broad St.   See adv. index.
TREMONT HOUSE, Tremont Square, James S. Pickard, Pro.

Insurance Agent.

HARRIS, THOS. J. 1 Brown's Block, up stairs.

Listing Yarn Manufacturer.

Moore, A. B. Lower Village.

Lumber Dealers.

Richardson & Co.

Machinists.

UPHAM, J. P. & CO., Main St.

Marble Workers.

Blood & Woodcock, Broad St.

Meat Markets.

Dole, Lemuel, 8 Perry's Block.
Dole, C. H. Tremont St.
Dole, G. W.   "

Meat and Vegetable Chopper, (Patent.)

Smith, Collins & Co., Main St.

Men's Half Hose Manufacturer.

Silsbee, R. W. 7 Perry's Block.

Milliners.

Andrews, M. S. Main St.
Babcock, M. H. Broad St.
Niles, M. S. Miss Pleasant St.

Millinery and Fancy Goods.

Noyes, H. N. Tremont St.
Thompson, A. Sullivan St.
Rogers, M. M.   "

Newspapers.

The National Eagle, Simeon Ide, Editor and Pro.
The Northern Advocate, Joseph Weber, Editor.

Newspapers and Periodicals.

GOWDY, T. R. Tremont St.

Painters, (House and Sign.)

Abbott, Geo. H.
Taylor, John W.
Walker, S. W.
Rowell, Granville, North St.

Paper Manufacturers.

CLAREMONT MANUFACTURING CO., E. L. Goddard, Agent and Treas., (Print.) See adv. index.
Farrington, John, (West Claremont,) (Wrapping.)

Photographers.

Coffin, Wm., 2 Perry's Block.
Johnson, J. H. Pleasant St.

Physicians.

Baker, Cyrus E.
Cooper, Sherman
Cummings, A. R.
Gleason, Robert S.
Jarvis, Samuel G.
Squire, William C.
Tolles, Nathaniel
Volk, Carl A.

Plow Manufacturers.

LUFKIN PLOW CO., J. P. Upham, Agent.

Postmaster.

Chas. O. Eastman, Brown's Block.
Henry A. Redfield, (West C.)

Printers, (Book and Job.)

CLAREMONT MANUFACTURING CO., E. L. Goddard,
Treas. See adv. index.

Savings Bank.

Sullivan Savings Institution, John I. Farwell, Treas.

Saw Mill.

Richardson & Co.

Sewing Machine Agent.

Woodbury, W. O. C. Sullivan St., (Singer's.)

Stables.

Brown, A. Spring St.
Heywood, J. Broad St.
Hubbard, Henry L. Pleasant St.

LEET, JAMES, rear Sullivan House.
Leonard, Chas. Broad St.

Stoves and Tinware.

GOULD & CO., Main St.
Rand, S. S. 13 Pleasant St.

Tailors.

Backus, Geo. H. 6 Farwell's Block.
CHAMBERLAIN, John B. over Emerson & Haskell.
Perry, Chas. L. 3 Perry's Block.
REDFIELD, S. F. 1 Tremont St.

Tanner and Currier.

Eastman, C. H. North St.

Tinware Manufacturers.

GOULD & CO. Main St.

Town Clerk.

GOWDEY, T. R. Tremont St.

Toys and Variety Store.

Bardwell, Chas. Sullivan St.

Turning, Planing and Sawing.

BRIGGS, WM. H. Main St.   See adv. index.

Undertaker.

Briggs, Fred. A. Broad St.

Watches and Jewelry.

Heywood & Co., Tremont Square.
Spencer, Reuben,   "
Silsby, Solon, 4 Brown's Block.
WAIT, G. W. Sullivan St.

Water Wheel Manufacturers.
UPHAM, J. P. & Co., Main St.

Wool Carder.
Shepardson, R.

Woolen Flannels Manufacturers.
Monodnock Mills, D. W. Johnson, Agt.

Miscellaneous.

MASONIC.
Hiram Lodge, No. 9, meet first Wednesday each month.
Hosea Parker, W. M.

Webb Chapter, No. 6, meet third Monday each month.
John J. Prentiss, H. P.

Columbian Council, No. 2, meet third Wednesday each month.
Lewis Woodman, T. I. G. M.

Sullivan Commandery.
L. J. Graves, E. C.

TEMPERANCE.
Claremont Division Sons of Temperance, No. 21, Instituted
February 6th, 1861, meet Friday evenings.

THE CLAREMONT MANUFACTURING COMPANY,
CLAREMONT, N. H.
*Manufacturers of Paper and Books, and Wholesale and Re-
tail Dealers in the same,*
Will furnish proposals, on application, for any kind
of work in their line of business.

AND HAVE FACILITIES
For the manufacture of Books on contract, equal to any
concern in New England.
PLEASE TAKE NOTICE,
That they MAKE PAPER, PRINT and BIND, all under one roof.

WEATHERSFIELD, Windsor County, Vermont, situated on the west bank of the Connecticut River, 15 miles north of Bellows Falls, includes the villages of Perkinsville, Upper Falls, Ascutneyville and Weathersfield Center. It is mostly an agricultural town, although to some extent articles of Soap Stone, Bobbins, &c., are manufactured. Partly in Weathersfield stands Ascutney Mountain, 3,320 feet high.

BUSINESS DIRECTORY.

Clergymen.

Cudworth, N. (Bap.) (P.)
Kimball, Moses, (Cong.) (A.)
Smith, J. L. (Meth.) (Upper Falls.)
Spaulding, A. (W. Center.)

Cotton Manufacturer.

Proctor, M. S.

Merchants.

Brock, R. (A.) Dry Goods, Groceries, &c.
Henry, H. (P.)   "   "   "
Proctor, M. S. (P.) "   "   "

Physicians,

Atwood, Robert, (A.)
Cram, R. B. (P.)
Kendrick, Ariel, (North Springfield P. O.)

Postmasters.

Breck, R. (Ascutneyville.)
Danforth, L. C. (W.)
Goldsmith, (W. Center.)
Henry, V. R. (Perkinsville.)
Warner, J. L. (Upper Falls.)

Soap Stone Stoves Manufacturers.

Darling, L. B. (Perkinsville.)
Henry, H.   "

WINDSOR, Windsor County, Vermont, distant from New York 246 miles, and from Hartford, Conn., 136 miles, is a quiet town on the west bank of the Connecticut, containing about 2000

51

· population. A large business is done manufacturing Fire Arms
and Machinery, by the Windsor Manufacturing Company.

BUSINESS DIRECTORY.

Attorneys at Law.
Coolidge, C.
Edminster, J. N. Main St.
Farnsworth, J. B. State St.

Bank.
Ascutney National Bank, Capital $100,000.
  Hiram Howe, Pres., Henry Wardner, Cashier.

Billiards.
Amsden, A. G. & E. G. Main St.

Blacksmiths.
Carr & Benton.
Watriss, L. W.

Bookseller and Stationer.
MERRIFIELD, PRESTON, Main St.

Boots and Shoes.
Damon, U. E. Main St.
Lawrence, L. W. "
Miller, Harvey,   "

Clergymen.
Dyington, E. H. (Cong.)
Dexter, S. K. (Bap.)
Douglass, M. (Epis.)
Butler, Frank, (State's Prison Chaplain.)

Coffins and Caskets.
Fenney, Mather & Co., Main St.

Dentists.
Hale & Mather, Main St.

Druggist.

Paine, M. K. Main St.

Eating House.

Fadden, J. M. Main St.

Express Companies and Agents.

Cheney & Co's Express, L. W. Lawrence, Agent.
Fisk & Co.,   "   "   "

Fancy Goods, Notions, &c.

McIndoe, L. J. Main St.

Fire Arms Manufacturers.

Windsor Manufacturing Co., E. G. Samson & Co.

Flour and Grain.

Steele & Wheeler, Main St.

Furniture.

Edminster, F. S. State St.
Fenney, Mather & Co., Main St.

Gas Company.

Windsor Gas Light Co.
H. Harlon, Pres., Wm. Fullerton, Treas.

Groceries.

Lawrence, S. L. Main St.
Whittaker, C. W. State St.

Hair Dressing Saloons.

Tarby, C. H. Main St.

Hardware.

Cross, C. C. Main St.
POLLARD, J. A. Main St.

Harness Makers.

Harris, Wm. Main St.

Hotels.

ARMORY HOUSE, Main St., James Gifford, Proprietor.
WINDSOR HOUSE, Geo. R. Cushing, Proprietor.

Iron Founders.

Draper, Francis, Main St.

Machinists.

Windsor Manufacturing Co., E. G. Lamson & Co.

Meat Market.

Patrick & Moore, State St.

Merchants.

Hubbard, M. C. & Co., Main St., Dry Good, Groceries, &c.
Story, C.   "   "   "   "
Tuxbury & Stone,   "   "   "   "
Sabin, E. D.   "   "   "   "

Millinery.

Colby, Miss Main St.
Porter, Sarah Miss Main St.

Newspapers.

VERMONT CHRONICLE, Rev. Franklin Butler, Editor.   See
adv. index.
VERMONT JOURNAL, L. J. McIndoe, Editor and Proprietor.   See adv. index.

Physicians.

Clark, Ripley
Phelps, E. E.
Stiles, J. N.
Everett, W.

Postmaster.

Albert G. Hatch, Main St.

Railroad Agent.

Thomas Keefe, Vt. Central R. R.

Savings Bank.

Windsor Savings Bank, Main St.
J. T. Freeman, Pres., L. C. White, Sec'y and Treas.

Scythe Snaths Manufacturers.

LAMSON & GOODNOW MF'G CO., Hiram Harlow, Agent.

Stables.

Thurston & Stevens, Main St.
Young & Billings,   "

Stoves and Tinware.

Butman, Wm. Main St.
Stone, J. & Son, State St.

Tailors.

Howard, Ralph, Main St.
Stuart, Jr. W. State St.

Watches and Jewelry.

Bullard, L. O. Main St.

Masonic.

Vermont Lodge, No. 18, F. & A. M. A. L. 5867.
J. N. Stiles, W. M., E. D. Sabine, Sec'y.
Regular communications Thursday, of or preceding full moon.
Windsor, R. A. Chapter, No. 6, A. L. 2397. Meet first Friday every alternate month, commencing with December.
Windsor Council, No. 8, convocations held in connection with R. A. Chapter, No. 6.
Vermont Commandery, No. 4, regular convocations 4th Wednesday of January, March, May, July, September and November.

HARTLAND, Windsor County, Vermont, 4 miles north of Windsor, on the west bank of the Connecticut, and contains about 1800 population. Hartland comprises the villages of Hartland Four Corners, and North Hartland.

BUSINESS DIRECTORY.

Clergymen.

Bryant, (Meth.)
Clark, C. W. (Cong.)

Door, Sash and Blinds.

Martin, A. C. (H.)

Inventor and Machinist.

English, A. F. (H Four Corners.)

Iron Founders.

Darling & Gilbert, (H. Four Corners.)

Leather Manufacturers.

Warren, C. W. & Son, (H.)

Lumber.

Sumner, D. H. (H.)

Marble Worker.

Harding, John, (H. Four Corners.)

Merchants.

Elmer, H. J. (North H.) Dry Goods, Groceries.
Leonard & Marcy, (H. Four Corners,) Dry Goods, Groceries.
Pierce, F. M. (H.)   "   "
Woodward, Geo. (H.)   "   "

Physicians.

Emmons, Lewis, (H. Four Corners.)
Richmond, L. A. (H.)

Postmasters.

Elmer, H. J. (North H.)
Patch, G. M. (H.)
Leonard, T. F. (H. Four Corners.)

Tinware.

Bagley, E. H. (H.)

Woolen Manufacturers.

Paine & Horton, (H.)

HARTFORD, Windsor County, Vermont, 66 miles north of Brattleboro, contains the villages of White River Junction, West Hartford and Quechee. At White River Junction, Railroad trains meet from north, south, east and west, it being the Junction of Vermont Central, Conn. & Passumpsic Rivers, and Concord Railroads. Population of the town about 2500.

BUSINESS DIRECTORY.

Attorneys at Law.

Pingree, S. E & S. M.
Tenney, George

Clergymen.

Kingsbury, (Quechee.)
Ray, B. F. (H.)
Wellington, H. (West H.)

Carriage Manufacturer.

Dutton, B. (H.)

Chair Manufacturers.

Morris, E. W. & E. (H.)

Furniture Manufacturer.

Thurston, C. H. (H.)

Hay Forks and Potato Diggers.

Van Oenum, Brailey & Co., (H.)

Wooden Ware Manufacturers.

Clark, Henry & Downing, (H.)

Hotel.

Junction House, (White River J.,) A. T. Barrow & Co.

Merchants.

Brooks, J. C. (H.
Cone, G. E.   "
Bragg, W. L. (Quechee.)
Dimick, J.   "
French, M. (H.)
Gates, T.   "
Hazen, J. W. & Co.
Holt, F. & Co., (West H.)

Goff, W. H.   (W. R. Junction.)
Grover & Blodgett,   "
Tinkham, A. B. & Co.   "
Tinkham, Chas. (Quechee.)
Thurston, C. H. (H.)

Leather Manufacturer.

Allen, J. (West H.)

Physicians.

Allen, S. J. (W. R. Junction.)
Rand, J. B.   (H.)
Tenney, C. H.   "
Ross, (Quechee.)
Tucker, Laban, (West H.)

Postmasters.

Brooks, J. C. (H.)
Hazen, J. W. (West H.)
Lyman, Geo. (W. R. Junction.)
Russ, S. (Quechee.)

Tin Ware Manufacturer.

Tarbell, G. L. (H.)

Woolen Manufacturers.

Dewey, A. G. & Co., (Quechee.)
Parker, J. C. & Co.   "

LEBANON, Grafton County, New Hampshire, is situated on
the east bank of the Connecticut, and nearly opposite White
River Junction, Vermont. The township was incorporated July
4th, 1761, and includes the villages of East and West Lebanon;
population about 2,500. Tilden Female Seminary is located

52

here. Rakes, Scythes and Carriages are manufactured here to some extent.

BUSINESS DIRECTORY.

Attorneys at Law.

Cragan, Aaron H.
Morris, Lewis R.

Bank.

Lebanon National Bank, Capital $100,000.
Jas. H. Kendrick, Cashier.

Blacksmiths.

March, H. & J.

Boots and Shoes.

Burnham, John
Chase, P. M.
Cragin, R. W.
Cutting, A.

Carriage Manufacturers.

Garland, Elliott
Greenough, Lyman
Richardson, A. W.

Clergymen.

Bryant, George N. (Meth.)
Donns, Charles A. (Cong.)
Edwards, John H.   "
Fisher, Judson (Univ.)
McKinley, John (Bap.)

Drugs and Medicines.

Town, C. O.

Fish Dealer.

Carter, Elijah W.

Flour and Grain.

Butman, J. H.
Moose & Wright.

Furniture.

Durant, Edwin J.

Gristmill.

Morse, John J.

Hardware.

Hildreth, C. M., Agent.

Harness Makers.

Ticknor, J. G. & E.

Hotel.

Benton's Hotel, H. B. Benton, Proprietor.

Merchants.

Blood & Burton, Dry Goods, Groceries, &c.
Cummings, Farris   "   "   "
Coolidge, M.   "   "   "
Houghton, Geo. W. "   "   "
House, Lester   "   "   "
Kendrick, Geo. S.   "   "   "
Kimball, Robert B.   "   "   "
Laighton, E. T.   "   "   "
Morey, R.   "   "   "
Richardson, W. A.   "   "   "
Whipple, G. C.   "   "   "
Worthen, Geo. W.   "   "   "

Millinery.

Colburn, C. E. Mrs.
Morey & Philips, Misses
Sampson, M. N. Mrs.
Smith, Lizzie
Thompson, E. H.

Newspaper.

Granite State Free Press, (Weekly.)
Elias H. Cheney, Editor and Publisher.

Painter, (House and Sign.)

Crosby, G. R.

Peddler.

Carter, Henry W.

Photographer.

Hough, Billings

Physicians.

Bean, Luther C.
Clough, John
Fuller, Geo. H.
Smalley, Adoniram
Town, Charles O.

Planing Machines.

Cushman, F. A. Agent.

Postmasters.

Cushing, C. A. (West L.)
Hosley, Jewett D. (L.)
Liscomb, Elisha P. (East L.)

Rake and Scythe Manufacturers.

Sterns, Leonard & Co.

Sash, Doors and Blinds.

Sturtevant, J. C.

Seminary.

Tilden Female Seminary.

Stoves and Tinware.

Gustin, John
Spear, N. D.

Tailors.
Gore & Fitch.

NORWICH, Windsor County, Vermont, 5 miles north of White River Junction, contains about 1800 population, and includes the village of Pompanoosuc. Norwich University is located here, about one mile and a half from Dartmouth College.

BUSINESS DIRECTORY.

Attorneys at Law.
Burton, Harvey
Loveland, Aaron

Carriage Manufacturer.
Knapp, A. W.

Clergymen.
Bourns, Edward, (Epis.)
Cheese, M. R. (Meth.)
Fuller, C. D. (Bap.)
Pettingill, E. (Meth.)
Sewall, Wm. (Cong.)

Fork and Hoe Manufacturer.
Miner, Daniel

Flour and Meal.
Dodge, J. S.

Leather Manufacturers.
Wadsworth & Felch.

Lumber.
Kibling, G. W.

Literary Institution.

Wheelock Seminary, L. H. Wheelock, Principal.

Merchants.

Edgerton, J. K. Dry Goods, Groceries, &c.
Gill, E.   "   "   "
Lewis, E. M.   "   "   "
Olds, F. L. & E. W. "   "   "
Russ, Harrison,   "   "   "

Postmaster.

Olds, F. L.

Physicians.

Converse, Shubael
Currier, S. H.

HANOVER, Grafton County, New Hampshire, is situated on the east bank of the Connecticut, 5 miles north of White River Junction. The town was incorporated July 4, 1761, and numbers about 2500 inhabitants. Here is located Dartmouth College, founded in the year 1769, and one of the oldest and most useful Colleges in New England. A large number of the prominent men of our country have graduated here.

The principal business is agriculture. The town has one bank of issue, and one Savings Bank. The township includes the village of Hanover Center.

BUSINESS DIRECTORY.

Attorneys at Law.

Blaisdell, Daniel
Duncan, Wm. H.

Bank.

Dartmouth National Bank, Capital, $50,000.
N. S. Huntington, Cashier.

Baker and Confectioner.
Smith, E. K.

Books and Stationery.
Hall, Benjamin W.
Howe, B. D.

Boots and Shoes.
Chase, J. W.
Rock, A.

Carriage Manufacturers.
Haynes, Frank A.
Pardee, Wm.

Clergymen.
Brown, Samuel G., D. D.
Fairbanks, Henry
Merriam, F. (Bap.)
Noyes, Daniel J., D. D.
Lord, Nathan, D. D.
Leeds, Samuel P.
Smith, Bezaleel
Parker, Henry E.
Packard, Wm. A.
Rood, Heman
Richardson, Daniel F. (Bap.)
Sanborn, Edwin D.
Smith, Asa D., D. D.

Clothing and Gent's Furnishing Goods.
Gibbs, Wm. H.

Confectionery.
Smith, Everett K.

Dentist.
Norton, James

Drugs and Medicines.

Smith, James A.

Furniture.

Rand, G. W. & Co.

Grocers.

Carter, E. W.
Cobb, Samuel W.

Hotels.

American House, S. S. Davis, Proprietor.
Dartmouth Hotel, Horace Frary, Proprietor.

Insurance Agents.

Fields, C. A.
Ingalls, O. S.

Merchants.

Clough & Sterns, Dry Goods, Groceries, &c.
Cobb, S. W.   "   "   "
Dodge, J. W.   "   "   "
Sawyer, J. K.   "   "   "

Millinery.

Dennison, Mary S. Mrs.

Physicians.

Crosby, A. B.
Crosby, Dixi
Crosby, Thomas R.
Smith, James A.

Painter, House and Sign.

Maxham, A. E.

Postmasters.

Camp, David, (Center.)
Fields, Cornelius A. (H.)

Savings Bank.

Dartmouth Savings Bank.
Daniel Blaisdell, Pres., N. S. Huntington, Treas.

Stable.

Allen, Ira B.
McCabe, E.
Thompson & Nash.

Tailors.

Carpenter, E. D.
Gibbs, N. H.

Tin and Hardware.

Wainwright, Albert

Railroad Agent.   .

Mack, W. F.

THETFORD, Orange County, Vermont, opposite Lime, New Hampshire, contains about 1800 inhabitants, and is distant from White River Junction, 15 miles north, and comprises the villages of East Thetford, Thetford Center, North Thetford, Post Mills and Union Village.

BUSINESS DIRECTORY.

Attorneys at Law.

Gleason, S. M. (Thetford C.)
Howard, A. (T.)

Clergymen.

Hosford, Isaac, (Cong.) (North T.)
Johnson, Geo. (Meth.) (T. Center.)
Pettingill, E.   "   (Union Village.)
Scott, George, (Cong.) (Post Mills.)

53

Merchants.

Barnes, W. N. (North T.) Dry Goods, Groceries, &c.
Howe, T. F.   "   "   "   "
Marsh, J. B. (T.)   "   "   "
Pratt, John, (Post Mills.)   "   "   "
Taylor, Truman, "   "   "   "
Walker, M. J. (Union Village.) "   "   "

Physicians.

Goodwin, Martin, (T. Center.)
Niles, H. H. (Post Mills.)
Worcester, E. C. (T.)

Postmasters.

Barnes, W. W. (North T.)
Clough, J. B. (T. Center.)
Gleason, R. M. (Union Village.)
May, Cyrus (Post Mills.)
Marsh, J. B. (T.)
Slack, F. S. (East T.)

Paper Manufacturers.

Rogers, S. G. & Son, (Board and Wrap.) (T. Center.)

Scythe and Axe Manufacturer.

Briggs, A. S. (T. Center.)

Schools.

Thetford Academy, A. S. Howe, Princ.

Woolen Manufacturers.

Cambridge, A. C. (Union Village.)

LYME, Grafton County, New Hampshire, is situated on the east bank of the Connecticut, 15 miles north of White River Junction, and directly opposite Thetford, Vermont. Very little manufacturing is done here. The town was incorporated July 8, 1761, and numbers about 1600 inhabitants.

BUSINESS DIRECTORY.

Clergymen.

Smith, Edmund H. (Bap.)
Tenney, Erdix, (Cong.)

Harness Maker.

Gilbert, Elam

Hotel.

Perkins Hotel, Thos. Perkins.

Merchants.

Churchill, David C. Jr. Dry Goods, Groceries, &c.
Clark, H. M. & Co.   "   "   "
Conant, F. D.   "   "   "
Thurston, Asa   "   "   "
Webster, Moses K. Agent, "   "   "

Physicians.

Dickey, Abraham O.
Kingsbury, Chas. F.

Postmasters.

Clark, Holmes M.

Shoe Manufacturer.

Balch & Churchill.

Stoves and Tinware.

Clark, C. M.
Smith, O. F.

Tanner and Currier.

Balch, Samuel W.

FAIRLEE, Orange County, Vermont, a small station on the Connecticut and Passumpsic Rivers Railroad, of about 600 population.

BUSINESS DIRECTORY.

Clergymen.

Hosford, Isaac (Cong.)
Haynes, Z. S. (Meth.)

Hotels.

Bailey's Hotel, Jerome Bailey, Pro.

Lumber.

Everett, J.
Pierce, J. D.

Axe Handles and Spokes.

Kelley, E. L.

Lumber, Flour and Grain.

Abbott, W. E. & D. C.

Merchants.

Bailey & Driggs, Dry Goods, Groceries, &c.

Postmaster.

Bailey, J. B.

ORFORD, Grafton County, New Hampshire, situated on the east bank of the Connecticut, nearly opposite the town of Fairlee, Vermont. Orford is mostly an agricultural town, but chair manufacturing is carried on to some extent. The town was incorporated September 25th, 1761. Population at present time, about 1400. The township includes the village of Orfordville.

BUSINESS DIRECTORY.

Blacksmith.

Demick, Thomas L.

Books and Stationery.

Palmer, A. B.

Chair Manufacturers.

Beale, D. & R.

Clergymen.

Cross, J. D. (F. W. Bap.)
Lawrence, Edward A. (Cong.)
Pratt, Horace,   "

Dentist.

Hale, Samuel W.

Grist Mills.

Dayton, James

Harness and Saddlery.

Conant, H. H.

Hotels.

Clark's Hotel, B. M. Clark.
Gould's Hotel, L. F. Gould.

Merchants.

Cutting, H. G.	Dry Goods, Groceries, &c.		
Gage, Adam H.	"	"	"
Howard, Wm. Jr., & Co.,	"	"	"
Morse, W. S.	"	"	"
Soule, Amasa	"	"	"
Tillottson & Richardson,	"	"	"
Wheeler, Daniel	"	"	"
Willard, David E.	"	"	"

Millinery.

Locke, M. L. Miss

Painter, (House and Sign.)

Sargent, N. B.

Peddler.

Dow, E. B.

Physicians.

Hosford, Willard
Marston, Daniel G.
Russell, Timothy

Postmasters.

Strong, Alexander, (Orfordville.)
Tillottson, Daniel F. (O.)

Tailor.

Fifield, Thos. J.

Watches and Jewelry.

Hale, S. W.

Wheelwright.

Jeffers, Gilbert

BRADFORD, Orange County, Vermont, in the Connecticut Valley, west of the river, is one of the most important towns north of Brattleboro. There is considerable manufacturing done here. Waits River, which runs through the town, furnishing the water power. Patent Medicines, Paper and Fish Kitts are manufactured here; population about 1500. The Trotter House is one of the best kept Houses in the river valley.

BUSINESS DIRECTORY.

Agricultural Implements.

SHEPHERDSON & DAVIS, Main St.
PRICHARD, GEO. Agt.   "   See adv. index.

Attorneys at Law.

Batchelder, J. W. Main St.
Dickey, A. M.   "
Farnham, R.   "
Ormsbee, R. M. K.   "
Worthen, H. A.   "

Auctioneer.

Bliss, Ellis, Main St.

Book Store.

Parr, H. Main St.

Boots and Shoes.

Davis, S. E. Main St.
KELLEY, S. W. Main St.
Martin & Andrus,   "

Carriage Manufacturers.

Brown Brothers, cor. Armory and Pleasant Sts.

Caskets and Coffins.

BUTLER, L. G. Main St.   See adv. index.

Dentist.

Mowe, A. M. Main St.

Drugs and Medicines.

LEONARD & DAY, Main St.
PRICHARD, GEO. Agt. "   See adv. index.

Express Company and Agent.

Cheney & Co's Express, A. M. Stevens, Agt., Main St.

Fish Kitt Manufacturers.

Aldrich & Barrett.

Flour (Bradford Mills,) Manufacturers.

PRICHARD & PECKETT, Main St.

Flour and Grain Dealers.

Osborn, A. Main St.
PRICHARD & PECKETT, Main St.

Furniture.

BUTLER, G. L. Main St.   See adv. index.

Gristmills.

Howe, J. H.
PRICHARD & PECKETT.

Hardware.

Osborn, A. Main St.
PRICHARD, GEO. Agt., Main St.   See adv. index.
SHEPHERDSON & DAVIS, "

Hotels.

Vermont House, Main St., D. H. Cheney, Proprietor.
TROTTER HOUSE, John Finnigan, Proprietor.

Insurance Agents.

Palmer & Stearns, Main St.

Machinist.

Strickland, H. Main St.

Mandrake Bitters Manufacturers.

DOTY, C. C. & CO.   See adv. index.

Marble Worker.

Jenkins, Geo. Main St.

Merchants.

BASCOM & CLARK, Main St., Dry Goods, Groceries, &c.
Hallett, R. C. Main St., Dry and Fancy Goods.
STEVENS, W. B. & C. S. Main St., Dry Goods, Groceries, &c.
   PRICHARD, GEO. Agt., Dry Goods, Groceries, Crockery and
Hardware.   See adv. index.

Millinery.

Andrus, Geo. R. Mrs. Main St.
Gage, W. E. Mrs.   "
Shaw, M. S. Mrs.   "

Newspaper.

THE NATIONAL OPINION, (Weekly.)
D. W. COBB, Editor and Proprietor.

Painters, (House and Sign.)

CLARKE, A. T. Main St.
WHITCOMB, R. E.   "

Paints, Oils and Glass.

CLARKE, A. T. Main St.

Paper Hangers.

CLARKE, A. T. Main St.
WHITCOMB, R. E.   "

Paper Manufacturers.

Granite Mills, A. Low, Agt. (Wrap., Printing and Book.)

Patent Medicine Manufacturers.

DOTY, C. C. & Co.   See adv. index.

Piano Fortes and Organs.

BUTLER, GEO. L. Main St.   See adv. index.

Photographers.

Allen, E. H. Main St.

Physicians.

Carter, W. H. Main St.
Doty, A. A.   "
Poole, J.   "
Scott, M. L.   "

Postmaster.

FLANDERS, THOS. J. Main St.
54

Restaurants.
Clough, E. Main St.
Johnson, D. Main St.

Schools.
Bradford Union High School.
Francis Farrell, Principal.

Scythe Stone Manufacturers.
PRICHARD & PECKETT.

Stable.
Carlton, Oscar, rear Trotter House.

Stoves and Tinware.
Pillsbury, D. T. Main St.

Tailors.
Hatch, G. Main St.
Wilt, H. B. "

Watches and Jewelry.
Hardy, Wm. G. Main St.
Warden, J. M. "

Variety Store.
FLANDERS, T. J. Main St.

Vegetable Cough Balsam Manufacturers.
DOTY, C. C. & CO. See adv. index.

Masonic.
Charity Lodge, No. 43.
  A. T. Clark, W. M., D. Hurlburt, S. W., A. P. Shaw, Jr.,
  J. W.
Mount Lebanon, R. A. Chapter No. 13.
  H. Strickland, H. P., Rev. J. Britton, Sec., Mills O. Barber, Treas.

C. C. DOTY & CO.,

BRADFORD, VERMONT,

PROPRIETORS OF

DOTY'S CELEBRATED MANDRAKE BITTERS,

The Great Family Medicine.

These Bitters cure all complaints arising from a DISEASED LIVER. Try a bottle if suffering from Dyspepsia, Jaundice, Costiveness, Piles, Sick Headache, Foul Stomach, Loss of Appetite, &c., and you will be pleased with the result. These Bitters have been used with great success for more than fifteen years. The sales, although large, are very fast on the increase.

M. S. BURR & CO., GENERAL AGENTS,

BOSTON, MASS.

GEO. PRICHARD, Agt.,

DEALER IN

DRY GOODS, GROCERIES, CROCKERY AND GLASS WARE,

Hardware, Drugs and Medicines, Iron and Steel,

SALT, FLOUR & COUNTRY PRODUCE.

Also Manufacturers of Fish Kitts,

BRADFORD, VERMONT.

GEO. L. BUTLER,

DEALER IN

PARLOR, CHAMBER & COMMON

FURNITURE,

Coffins, Caskets, Grave Clothes, Trimmings, &c.

ALSO AGENT FOR THE SALE OF

CABINET AND AMERICAN ORGANS AND PIANOS.

First door south of Trotter House, - - - BRADFORD, VT.

PIERMONT, Grafton County, New Hampshire, is situated on the east bank of the Connecticut River, nearly opposite Bradford, Vermont. The town was incorporated November 6th, 1764, and now numbers about 1200 inhabitants. Farming and stock raising is the principal business of the town, though something is done in manufacturing Carriages and Scythe Stones.

BUSINESS DIRECTORY.

Carriage Manufacturer.

Goodwin, Asahel

Clergymen.

Cilley, Moses T. (Meth.)
Marder, Augustus L. (Cong.)

Hotel.

Bean's Hotel, Stephen M. Bean.

Merchants.

Cutting & Dodge, Dry Goods, Groceries.

Peddler.

Hodgen, Cyrus K.

Physician.

Knight, Jonathan

Postmaster.

Cutting, Hezekiah

Saw Mill.

Cutting, D. C. & H.

Scythe Stone Manufacturer.

Dodge, Cordon

Shoe Maker.

Mead, Moses

Stoves and Tinware.

Evans, Joseph C.

HAVERHILL, (formerly called Lower Cohoes,) Grafton County, New Hampshire, is a half shire town, situated on the east side of the Connecticut River, about 28 miles north of White River Junction.

The township includes the villages of East and North Haverhill, Woodsville, and Haverhill Center.

The county records are kept here. The town was incorporated May 18th, 1763, and contains about 2400 inhabitants. Paper, Scythe Stones and Carriages are manufactured to some extent. Haverhill in former days was the head-quarters of the numerous stage lines extending through northern New Hampshire.

BUSINESS DIRECTORY.

Attorneys at Law.

Dale, C. A.
Chapman, George S.
Bryant, J. S.
Marsh, L. W.
Page, David
Putnam, G. F.
Felton, N. B.
Westgate, N. W.

Auctioneer.

Batchelder, Daniel

Railroad Agent.

Wilson, George

Blacksmiths.

Poole, Caleb
Harriman, James

Carpenters and Builders.

Burbeck, Wm. H.
Page, James

Clergymen.

Beane, J. M. (Meth.)
Emerson, J. D. (Cong.)

Cattle Dealers.

Putnam, A. W.
Webster, J. P.

Carriage Manufacturers.

Batchelder & Carleton.
Colburne, Josiah
Carlton, M. Jr.
Carlton, Charles

Carriage Painters.

Durgin & Hovey.
Carlton, M.
Carlton, Horace

Drugs and Medicines.

Woodward, C. B. M.
Hooks, S. F.
Merrill, Henry

Harness Makers.

Leonard, Thomas
Page, James A.
Sinclair, H. B.
Sinclair, John
Woods, A. A.

Hotel.

Smith's Hotel, C. G. Smith.

Lime Manufacturers.

Haverhill Lime Co., M. Mason, Agent.

Machinist.

Butterfield, Solomon

Marble Workers.

Chandler, Harvey
Thompson, J. P.
Jenkins, Robert

Meat Market.

Pike, Samuel

Merchants.

Bailey, Allen,	Dry Goods, Groceries, &c.
Bailey, Milo	"	"	"
Ober, E. T.	"	"	"
Page, Wm. H.	"	"	"
Poor, Joseph	"	"	"
Cook, J. L.	"	"	"

Millinery.

Currier, Misses.
Gove, George Mrs.

Paper Manufacturers.

Haverhill Paper Co., J. V. Webster, Agent.

Photographers.

Merriam, Chas.
Williams, J. M.

Physicians.

Corbor, S. P.
Spaulding, P.

Printers, (Job.)

Reding, H. W.
Reding, S.

Route Agent.

Whitney, A.

Scythe Stone Manufacturer.

Pike, A. F.

Shoe Manufacturer.

Currier, Bagley C.

Shoe Makers.

Smith, J. B.
Tabor, Norman

Stoves and Tinware.

Ham, L. B.

Tanners and Curriers.

Currier F. P.
Currier, John
Currier, O. A.

Tailors.

Leath, George
Whipple, George

Ticket Agent.

Tabor, E. N.

NEWBURY, Orange County, Vermont, is situated in the Connecticut valley, 295 miles from New York, and 35 miles north of White River Junction.

Newbury includes the villages of West Newbury, South Newbury and Wells River, where is the Junction of the Conn. & Passumpsic Rivers, Boston & Montreal, and White Mountain Railoads.

BUSINESS DIRECTORY.

Attorneys at Law.

Leslie & Rogers, (Wells River.)
Underwood, Abel   "

Clergymen.

Connell, David (Cong.) (West N.)
Burton, H. N.   "   (N.)
Palmer, W. S.   "   (Wells River.)
Spencer, H. A. (Meth.) (N.)

Literary Institution.

Newbury Seminary, S. E. Quimby, Prin.

Merchants.

Buchanan, J. & W. S. & Co., (Wells River,) Dry Goods, Groceries.

Deming, H. H (N.)   Dry Goods, Groceries, &c.
Deming, Frank & Co., (W. River,)   "   "   "
Farewell, A. S.   '   "   "   "   "
Keyes, F. & H. T. & Co. (N.)   "   "   "
Wilson & Carlton, (West N.)   "   "   "

Paper Manufacturers.

Durant & Adams, (Wells River.)

Physicians.

Brown, ———(Wells River.)
Crosby, A.   "
McNab, John   "
Watkins, E. V. (N.)
Watson, H. L.   "

Postmasters.

Morse, H. B. (N.)
Brock, W. W. (South N.)
Deming, Frank (Wells River.)

Stoves and Tinware.

Ladd, P. W. (West N.)

Watches and Jewelry.

Holton, Harry (Wells River.)
Wallace, W. R. (N.)

55

BARNET, Caledonia County, Vermont, a small town situated in the Connecticut River Valley, near where the Passumpsic River enters the Connecticut.

The township of Barnet includes the small villages of West Barnet, Passumpsic and McIndoes Falls. At each of the two last named places there are good water privileges and considerable manufacturing is carried on. At Barnet, are the Mills of the Caledonia Manufacturing Co., making heavy fancy Woolen Goods.

BUSINESS DIRECTORY.

Boots and Shoes.

Johnson, J. A.

Clergymen.

Bradford, M. (Cong.) (McIndoes.)
Goodwillie, T. (Pres.) (Barnet.)
Reed, W. H. (West B.)
Underwood, J. (Cong.) (Barnet.)

Leather Manufacturers.

Abbott & Clement.

Literary.

McIndoes Falls Academy.
Union School, Barnet.

Merchants.

Abbott & Clement,	Dry Goods, Groceries, &c.		
Dutton, A. (McIndoes,)	"	"	"
Goss, F. (Passumpsic,)	"	"	"
Bochops, A. (West B.)	"	"	"
Nelson, W. H. (McIndoes,)	"	"	"
Hazen, L. D. & L. H.	"	"	"
Parks, L. (Passumpsic,)	"	"	"

Physicians.

Eaton, B. F.

Hazleton, H. J..
Downs, (McIndoes.)
Tuttle, Socrates.
Thompson, A. B.

Postmasters.

Hoyt, J. Q. (Barnet.)
Parks, L. P. (Passumpsic.)
Dartwell, R. (McIndoes.)
Warden, O. H. (West B.)

Woolen Manufacturers.

Caledonian Manufacturing Co.
Gould & Hildreth, (Passumpsic.)

ST. JOHNSBURY, Caledonia County, Vermont, 311 miles
from New York, Montreal, 148, Hartford, Conn., 203 miles, is
the most important station on the Conn. and Passumpsic Road.
This is the shire town of the county, and is the centre of a large
country trade. Population about 4500. The township includes
St. Johnsbury Village, St Johnsbury Center, and East St. Johnsbury. Most of the business is done in the village.

The principal manufacturing is the Fairbanks Scale, employing from 400 to 500 hands. A large business is done in the
manufacture of Machinery, Water Wheels, Ploughs, Horse
Power Machinery, Mowing Machines and Boots and Shoes, &c.

The Passumpsic River which flows through the town, furnishes
a valuable water power for manufacturing purposes.

BUSINESS DIRECTORY.

Attorneys at Law.

BURKE, O. S. Railroad.
Stoddard, J. D. Union Block.
Pierce, W. A. Railroad.
Ross, Jno. Main St.
Willard, A. J. "

Axles and Spindles, (Wholesale.)

FLETCHER, J. Depot Store, Eastern Ave.   See adv. index.

Bakers.

Cross & Brigham, Main St.

Banks.

First National Bank, St. Johnsbury, capital, $250,000.
L. P. Poland, Pres., Geo. May, Cash.

Blacksmiths.

Lawrence, S. R.
HARROUN, J. C. Eastern Avenue.

Board, Starch, Grist and Saw Mill Manufacturer.

BUZZELL, LUKE, Railroad.   See adv. index.

Boots and Shoes, (Wholesale.)

Mooney, H. A. Railroad.   See adv. index.

Boots and Shoes.

Bishop, W. I. Eastern Avenue.
Lonigan, P. P. Railroad.
MOONEY, H. A.   "   See adv. index.
Howe, R. C. M. Main St.

Boot and Shoe Manufacturer.

MOONEY, H. A. Railroad.   See adv. index.

Cabinet Ware Manufacturer.

HEYER, JAMES H.   See adv. index.

Carriage Trimmings, (Wholesale.)

FLETCHER, J. Depot Store.   See adv. index.

Carriage Manufacturers.

Brown, A. (St. J. Center.)
Miller, J. D. near R. R. Depot.

Casket and Coffin Manufacturer.
HEYER, JAMES H.   See adv. index.

Caskets and Coffins.
BABCOCK, F. J. Railroad.

Circular and Drag Saw Manufacturer.
ROLLINS, B. F. (Horse-power Machines.)   See adv. index.

Circular Saw Mill Manufacturer.
BUZZELL, LUKE, Railroad.   See adv. index.

Clergymen.
Braston, Lewis O. (Cong.)
Cummings, E. C.   "
Daniston,——— (Cath.)
Titus, E. A. (Meth.)

Cutlery Manufacturer.
Belknap, A. K. & J.

Dentists.
FALES, F. H. Union Block.
Perkins, J. L. cor. Main and Eastern Avenue.

Doors, Sash and Blinds.
Colby, Gay & Co., Railroad.
Morris, L. C.
Carpenter, Horace, near Depot.

Druggist.
Bingham, J. C. Main St.

Dry Goods.
Jewett, S. Main St.
Johnson, N. M. Railroad.

Edge Tools Manufacturer.
Belknap, A. K. & J.

Express Companies and Agents.

Cheney & Co., Express.
Cook, A. M. & Co., Agents.

File Cutters.

NUTT, JAMES, near Depot. See adv. index.

File Manufacturer.

NUTT, JAMES, near Depot. See adv. index.

Flour and Grain, (Wholesale.)

FLETCHER, J. Depot Store, Eastern Ave. See adv. index.
Learned, W. N. R. R. Depot.

Flouring Mill.

Goss, H. & L. Railroad.

Flour and Grain.

Aldrich & Hancock, Eastern Avenue.

Furniture.

Armington, I. (St. J. Center.)
Cassino, J. T. Eastern Avenue.
BABCOCK, F. J. Railroad.

Groceries and West India Goods, (Wholesale.)

FAIRBANKS, E. & T. & Co., (Fairbanks Village.)
FLETCHER, J. Depot Store, Eastern Avc. See adv. index.

Grocers.

Barney, Geo. O. Main St.
DANIELS, BARTLETT & CO., Railroad.
Fuller, Wm. Main St.
Howe, R. C. M. "

Hair Dressing Saloon.

Blackstone, R. B. Union Block.

Harness Makers.
Flynt, R. B. Railroad St.
KENISON, A. H. "
Baker, Wm. A. Eastern Ave.

Hats, Caps and Furnishing Goods.
MOORE, G. P. Railroad St.

Hotels.
Passumpsic House, Railroad St., Samuel R. Remick, Prop.
St. JOHNSBURY HOUSE, Main St., Hiram Hill, Prop.   See
adv. index.

Hoe and Fork Manufacturers.
Ely, Balch & Co.

Insurance Agents.
SHAW, GEO. S. Main St. (General Agt.)
Steel, J. H. Caledonian Building.

Iron and Steel, (Wholesale.)
FLETCHER, J. Depot Store, Eastern Ave.   See adv. index.

Iron Founders.
BUZZELL, LUKE, Railroad St.   See adv. index.
FAIRBANKS, E. & T. & Co.

Leather Belting, Laces, Leather & Belt Hooks, (Wholesale.)
FLETCHER, J. Depot Store, Eastern Ave.   See adv. index,

Leather Manufacturers.
Bacon, Jr., J. & Co. (St. J. Center.)

Leather Dealer.
MOONEY, H. A. Railroad St.   See adv. index.

Lime, Cement, Plaster and Grindstones, (Wholesale.)
FLETCHER, J. Depot Store, Eastern Ave.   See adv. index.

Lumber Dealers.
Colby, Gay & Co., Railroad St.

Machine Castings.
BUZZELL LUKE, Railroad St.   See adv. index.

Machinists.
BUZZELL, LUKE, Railroad St.   See adv. index.
Belknap, K. & J.
FAIRBANKS, E. & T. & Co.
Spaulding, C. F.
Paddock Iron Works.
WARNER, J. M. & SON, near Depot.   See adv. index.

Marble Workers.
Bryant & Taplin, Railroad St.
Hill, W. H.   "

Meat Market.
DANIELS, BARTLETT & Co., Railroad St.

Merchants.
Bacon & Ide, (St. J. Center,) Dry Goods, Groceries, &c.
Brown, E. F. Main St., Groceries, Crockery and Hardware.
Cook, A. M. & Co., Eastern Av., Groceries, Crockery, &c.
Clark, B. B. Union Block, Clothing, Hats, Caps and Furnishing Goods.
Chapman, D. & Sons, (East St. J.) Dry Goods, Groceries, &c.
FAIRBANKS, E. & T. & Co., Groceries and Crockery.
Gorham, I. B. Main St., Hats, Caps, Furnishing Goods, Boots and Shoes.
Goodall, G. E. (East St. J.,) Dry Goods, Groceries, &c.
Hall, Emerson, Main St.,   "   "   "
Higgins & Cutting, "   Dry and Fancy Goods, &c.
Hoyt & Drew, cor. Railroad and Eastern Av., Dry Goods, Groceries, &c.
Hazleton, L. A. & Co., Union Block, Dry Goods, Millinery, &c.
Remick, J. K. & C. E. Railroad St., Dry Goods and Clothing.
Silsby, David, Railroad St., Clothing and Furnishing Goods.
Weeks, H. (St. J. Center,) Dry Goods, Groceries, &c.

Millinery.

Crossman, Miss, Main St.
Senter, Geo. W.   "

Mowing and Reaping Machine Manufacturers.

WARNER, J. M. & SON, near Depot.   See adv. index.

Music Teacher.

Stoddard, J. Miss, Union Block.

Newspaper.

The Caledonian, (Weekly,) C. M. Stone & Co., Proprietors.

Paper Manufacturers.

Bacon & Ide, (St. J. Center.)
Pierce, A. A.   "

Photographers.

Haynes, T. C. Eastern Ave.
Gage, F. B. Main St.

Physicians.

Browne, H. S.
Bullard, G. B.
Brooks, S. T.
Ferrin, —— Dr.
Houghton, M.
Hunter, H. P.
Hoyt, H. P.
Newell, S.
Sanborn, B.
Varney, E. A. Miss

Plow Manufacturer.

BUZZELL, LUKE, Railroad St.   See adv. index.

Postmasters.

Bacon, John, (St. J. Center.)
FLEETWOOD, H. W. Main St.
Chapman, David, (East St. J.)

56

Railroad Agent.

Learned, W. N. Conn. and Passumpsic Rivers R. R.

Restaurant.

Poor, J. W. Main St.

Scale Manufacturers.

FAIRBANKS, E. & T. & Co.

Shoe Peg Manufacturers.

Flynt & Magoon.

Savings Bank.

Passumpsic Savings Bank.
  A. G. Chadwick, Pres., Jno. Rose, Sec. and Treas.

Stoves and Tinware.

Boynton, David, Union Block.

Tailor.

Corser, D. G. Main St.

Threshing Machine Manufacturer.

ROLLINS, B. F. (Paddock's Village.)   See adv. index.

Watches and Jewelry.

Childs, C. C. Main St.
Brown, L. R.   "
DOW, O. C.   "
Howard, T. M.   "

Water Wheel Manufacturer.

BUZZELL, LUKE, Railroad St.   See adv. index.

Miscellaneous.

MASONIC.

Passumpsic Lodge No. 27.
  Silas Martin, W. M., H. C. Hastings, Sec.   Meet every
  Thursday eve.

Harwell Chapter No. 11.
Silas Martin, H. P., E. L. Adams, Sec. Regular meetings Friday eve., on or preceding full moon.
Palestine Commandery No. 5.
J. L. Perkins, E. C., F. J. Dalton, Rec. Regular meetings Tuesday eve., on or preceding full moon.

GOOD TEMPLARS.

Harmony Lodge No. 17, meet every Tuesday eve.

J. FLETCHER,

Wholesale Dealer in

Teas, Tobacco, West India Goods,

GROCERIES, FLOUR, GRAIN, SALT FISH,

Pork, Lard, Nails, Lead Pipe, Lime, Cement,

PLASTER, GRIND STONES,

IRON & STEEL, AXLES AND SPRINGS, MALLEABLE IRON,

BOLTS,

And a General assortment of CARRIAGE TRIMMINGS.

Sporting and Blasting Powder, Fuse, Lace Leather,

BELTING AND BELT HOOKS,

Depot Store, Eastern End of Eastern Avenue,

ST. JOHNSBURY,   *VERMONT.*

St. Johnsbury House,

MAIN STREET,

ST. JOHNSBURY, VERMONT.

HIRAM HILL, Proprietor.

LYNDON, Caledonia County, Vermont, a town on the Conn. and Passumpsic Rivers Railroad, about 8 miles north of St. Johnsbury, includes the villages of Lyndon Corners and Lyndon Center. At the Center the Railroad Company have located their Repair Shops, and have erected large and commodious brick buildings for manufacturing and repairing their engines and cars.

BUSINESS DIRECTORY.

Attorneys at Law.
BARTLETT, T. Main St.
BELDEN, H. C.   "
Cahoon, G. C. & G. W. Main St.

Bank.
Lyndon National Bank, capital, $200,000.
E. B. Chase, Pres., L. B. Mattocks, Cash.

Boots and Shoes.
Bradshaw, J. W. Main St.

Business Wagons and Sleigh Manufacturer.
DARLING, JOHN A. Main St. See adv. index.

Carriage Manufacturers.

DARLING, JOHN A. Main St. See adv. index.
Hoyt, E. H. & C. D.

Dentist.

Mills, G. W. Main St.

Druggist and Fancy Goods.

JOHONNOT, L. R. Main St.

Flouring Mills.

Cole, L. P.
Lincoln, B. F. & Co.

Flour and Lumber Manufacturer.

Hall, Fairbanks & Co.

Grocers.

Welch, J. C. & J. Main St.

Hardware, (Saddlery.)

Bartlett & Tenney, Main St.

Harness Makers.

Powers, W. C. & Co.
Currier, D. C. (Center.)

Hotels.

Lyndon House, J. M. Hubbard, Pro.
Lyndon Center Hotel, Wm. F. Ruggles, Pro.
Walker's Hotel, (Center,) Geo. B. Walker, Pro.

Leather Manufacturers.

Ingalls, C. (Center.)
Weeks, G. H. & J. M. Main St.

Masonic.

Crescent Lodge, F. & A. M. No. 66.
  L. K. Quimby, W. M., B. F. Lincoln, Sec'y.

Merchants.

Hall, J. H. & H. E. (Center.)
McGaffey, Wm. H. Main St., Dry Goods, Groceries, &c.
Weeks, G. H. & J. M. "   "   "   "

Newspaper.

Vermont Union, (Weekly,) C. M. Chase, Editor.

Physicians.

Cahoon, C. S.
Scott, C. W.

Postmaster.

McGaffey, Main St.

Railroad Agent.

L. P. Brown, Agent, Conn. & Passumpsic Rivers R. R.

Silver Platers.

Bartlett & Tenney, Main St.

Starch Manufacturer.

Whipple, D. (Center.)

Stencil Manufacturer.

Mathewson, G. L. (Center.)

Stove and Tinware Dealers.

QUIMBY, L. K. & CO., Main St.

Tailors.

Underwood, E. Main St.

Tin Ware Manufacturer.

QUIMBY, L. K. & CO., Main St.

Watches and Jewelry.

Applebee, Cephas, Main St.

JOHN A. DARLING,
(Successor to Trull and Miller.)
Carriage Manufacturer,
AND DEALER IN
IRON, RIMS, MALLEABLE IRON,
Bolts, Spokes, Springs, Bands, Paints. Varnishes, &c.

Manufacturing and Repairing of all kinds, done to order, with fidelity and promptness.

LYNDON, VT.

BURKE, Caledonia County, Vermont, a small town in the Passumpsic Valley, with a station on the Conn. and Passumpsic Railroad, 16 miles north of St. Johnsbury.

Burke includes the villages of East and West Burke, and contains about 1200 inhabitants.

BUSINESS DIRECTORY.

Attorney at Law.
Chadwick, David

Clergymen.
Hitchcock, A. (Meth.)
Joslyn, W. R. (Cong.)

Merchants.
Beckwith, Silas & Co., (West B.) Dry Goods and Groceries.
Newell, C. C. (East B.)   "   "   "
Smith, G. P. & F. H. (East B.)   "   "   "
Humphrey & Smith,   "   "   "   "
Rowell, Tyler   "   "   "   "
Nichols, S. L. (West B.)   "   "   "

Physicians.

Brown, Abel (B.)
Carpenter, Warner (West B.)
Spaulding M. C. (B.)
Dutton, T. T. (East B.)

Postmasters.

Beckwith, Silas (West B.)
Newell, C. C. (East B.)
Nichols, S. L. (B.)

Starch Manufacturer.

McNeal, J.

BARTON, Orleans County, Vermont, is a station on the Conn. and Passumpsic Rivers Railroad, 25 miles south of Newport, and 29 miles north of St. Johnsbury. It includes the villages of South Barton and Barton Landing. There is considerable manufacturing done in this town. The Walter Haywood Chair Co. manufacture large quantities of Chairs, which are exported to different foreign countries.

BUSINESS DIRECTORY.

Blacksmith.

Buchanan, Wm. Main St.

Boots and Shoes.

Hunt, D. R. Main St.
Floyd, I. G.   "
Woodman, J. L. Main St.

Carriage Manufacturer.

Bickford, H. S.

57

Clergymen.

Robinson, Wm. A. (Cong.)
Tabor, C. (Meth.)

Dentist.

Perry, F. M. Main St.

Druggists.

Joslyn, Wm. & Sons, Main St.
Willson, L. D. (B. Landing.)

Express Company and Agent.

CHENEY & CO'S EXPRESS, A. C. Robinson, Agt.

Flour and Grain, (Wholesale.)

ROBINSON, A. C. Main St.

Furniture Manufacturers.

Dromnell, C. H. Main St.
Walter Haywood Chair Company, Main St.
MOSSMAN, BENJAMIN,   "

Harness Makers.

Rogers, D. Main St.
Lucius, A.   "
Young, L.   "

Hotel.

CRYSTAL LAKE HOTEL, R. H. Little, Proprietor.   See adv. index.

Iron, Steel, Groceries, &c., (Wholesale.)

ROBINSON, A. C. Main St.

Marble Worker.

Bowler, J. T. Main St.

Merchants.

Hall & Joslyn, Main St., Dry Goods, Groceries, &c.
Kimball & Pierce, " " " "
Robinson, W. F. " " " "
Twombly, A. & J. L. " " " "
Parker, W. O. (B. Landing,) " " "
Webster, L. D. " " " "
SKINNER & DREW, Main St. " " "

Millinery.

Cutler, A. J. Miss, Main St.
Woodman, Mary P. Miss, Main St.

Newspaper.

Orleans Independent Standard, A. A. Earl, Proprietor.

Photographer.

Webster, Joseph, Main St.

Physicians.

Ruggles, —— Dr.
Skinner, R. G.
Skinner, J. F.

Postmaster.

RAWSON, E. E. Main St.

Stoves and Tinware.

Chamberlain, Henry, Main St.
Whitcher, H. O. "

Town Clerk.

Wm. Graves.

Watches and Jewelry.

Graves, Wm. Main St.
RAWSON, E. E. "

MASONIC.

Keystone Chapter No. —.
M. M. Scott, Sec. Regular Communication Monday eve., on or preceding full moon.

Orleans No. 55, F. & A. M.
J. P. Baldwin, W. M., C. H. Dwinnell, Sec. Regular Com munications Friday eve., on or before full moon.

GOOD TEMPLARS.

Phœnix Lodge Good Templars, No. 12. Meet Tuesday eve. Officers elected quarterly.

CRYSTAL LAKE HOTEL,
R. H. LITTLE, Proprietor,
BARTON, VERMONT.

Located 5 rods from Crystal Lake, which is 3 miles long and 1 mile wide. 6 miles to Willoughby Lake, (one of the most remarkable lakes in the world,) 6 to Willoughby Mountains, where a fine view may be obtained. Good fishing ponds within one mile of Hotel.
A good Livery connected with the House.

NEWPORT, Orleans County, Vermont, on the Shore of Lake Memphremagog, about 2 miles from the Canada Line, 54 miles north of St. Johnsbury, numbers about 2000 people, and is rapidly growing in wealth and population.

Large numbers of Tourists visit Newport every season. The Memphremagog House, by Messrs. Buck & Pender, is equal to any of our city Hotels, and will accommodate about 300 guests. Tables are supplied with all the delicacies of the season, including Lake Trout, fresh from the Lake. There is not much manufacturing done here.

BUSINESS DIRECTORY.

Attorneys at Law.

Allen, J. T. Main St.
Bisbee, L. H.   "
Crane, W. D.   "

Bakers.

SNELL, W. L. & CO., Main St.   .

Blacksmiths.

Preston, J. F. First St.
FIELD, L. D.   "
Wood, Moses, Main St.

Bark Extract Manufacturers, (Hemlock.)

American Bark Extract Co., N. C. Page, Agent.

Carriage Manufacturers.

DEWEY, A. S. Main St.
RAND, W. H.   "

Clergyman.

S. T. Frost, (Bap.)

Dentist.

Huntington, E. Main St.

Druggists and Booksellers.

GREEN, J. Y. Main St.
Hall, James R.   "

Dry Goods and Hoop Skirts.

GILMAN, W. C. & SON, Main St. See adv. index.

Engraver.

Shaw, B. E. Main St.

Flour, Grain and Hardware, (Wholesale.)

BAKER, BROWN & CO., Main St.

Fancy Goods and Notions. '

GILMAN, W. C. & SON, Main St. See adv. index.

Hotels.

LAKE HOUSE, Railroad St., Horace Bean, Pro.
MEMPHREMAGOG HOUSE, Main St., Buck & Pender, Pro's.

Marble Worker.

Fuller, Warren, Main St.

Meat Market.

BUCK & PENDER, Main St.

Millinery.

Cushing, J. H. Mrs. Main St.
Goodwin, A. A. Mrs. "
Green, A. F. "
Scott, P. "

Merchants.

Babcock & Co. Main St., Groceries, Hardware, &c.
CUSHING, J. H. " Dry Goods, Millinery, Groceries, &c.
Goodrich & Pratt, Main St., Dry Goods, Groceries, Furniture.
GILMAN, W. & C. & SON, Main St., Dry, Fancy, Notions, Cloths, Hoop Skirts. See adv. index.
Huntley & Barrow, Main St., Dry Goods, Groceries, &c.
McCLARY, O. R. Main St., Cloths, Clothing, Fancy Goods, &c.
Prouty, R. & Co., Trues Block, Main St., Dry and Fancy Goods, Notions.
TRUE, E. B. & CO., Main St., Dry Goods, Groceries, Hardware, &c.
Warren, W. W. Main St., Groceries, Boots, Shoes, &c.

Newspaper.

The Newport Express, Main St., Camp & Cummings, Pro's.

Photographer.

Blanchard, H. T. Main St.

Physicians.

Carpenter, H. H. Main St.
Currier, J. M. "
Patch, L. "
Rutherford, J. C. "

Postmaster.

Cushing, J. H. Main St.

Printers, (Job,)

Camp & Cummings, Main St.

Railroad Agent. •

SHERMAN, F. M. Agent Conn. & Passumpsic Rivers R. R.

Restaurants.

English, D. G. Main St.
SNELL, W. L. & CO., Main St.

Sash, Doors and Blind Manufacturers.

Haiding, J. D. Main St.
Stimpson & Co., "

Sawing and Planing.

Harding, J. D. Main St.
Stimpson & Co. "

Stables.

Bean, Horace, Railroad St.
SNELL, W. L. & CO. Main St.

Stoves and Tinware.

Barnes, J. G. Main St.
REYNOLDS, C. D. "

Tailors.

LIVINGSTON, L. D. Main St.
McCLARY, O. R.   "

Town Clerk and Treasurer.

Royal, Cummings, Main St.

Watches and Jewelry.

Shaw, B. E. Main St.

Masonic.

Memphremagog Lodge, F. & A. M. No. 65.
E. B. Fairchild, W. M., H. S. Root, Sec'y.

MEMPHREMAGOG HOUSE,

NEWPORT, VERMONT.

BUCK & PENDAR, Proprietors.

W. C. GILMAN & SON,

Dealers in

𝕯𝖗𝖞 𝕲𝖔𝖔𝖉𝖘, 𝕵𝖆𝖓𝖈𝖞 𝕲𝖔𝖔𝖉𝖘, 𝕹𝖔𝖙𝖎𝖔𝖓𝖘,

HOOP SKIRTS AND CORSETS, CLOTHS,

Gents' Furnishing Goods, Groceries, &c.

Main Street,   -   -   NEWPORT, VT.

58

Merriam Manufacturing Company,

Japanned and Stamped Tin Ware, Toilet Ware,

HOUSE FURNISHING GOODS, TIN TOYS, &C.,

DURHAM, CONN.

E. C. MALTBY,

MANUFACTURER OF

COCOA DIPPERS,

And Preserved Cocoanut Meat,

NORTHFORD, CONN.

TERMS:—Rimmed, per doz., $3.75 ; Plain, per doz., $3.25 ; Net Cash, at New Haven Depot.

J. WHITLOCK,

MANUFACTURER OF

Whitlock's Patent Self-Oiling Boxes,

GUARANTEED TO RUN SIX MONTHS WITHOUT RE-OILING,

Also, Shafting, Hangers and Pulleys, Water Wheel Regulators, Twisters for
Woolen Yarn, Reels for Woolen or Cotton Yarn, Braiding Machines,
Button Machinery, Lathes, and General Machinery.

ATLANTIC HOTEL,

OPPOSITE NEW YORK AND NEW HAVEN DEPOT,

BRIDGEPORT, CONN.

A. R. HALE, PROPRIETOR.

Turbine Water Wheel Manufacturing Company.

J. D. CHASE & SONS, Agents. ⎫
L. KILBURN, Treasurer.   ⎬
L. E. HOLMES, Secretary. ⎭

⎧ L. KILBURN & CO.
⎪ D. POMROY.
⎨ J. R. DERBY.
⎩ S. POLAND.

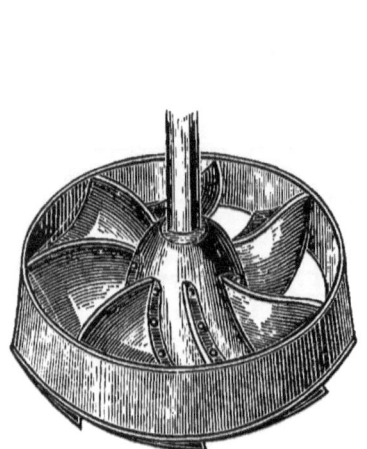 

CHASE'S
IMPROVED EXCELSIOR JONVAL TURBINE

WATER WHEEL.

J. D. CHASE & SONS and D. POMROY'S Patent, July 31, 1866.

Manufactured by TURBINE WATER WHEEL MANUFACTURING CO., and warranted to give a superior per cent. of power, *low price*, and unequalled in convenience and durability.

Also, Circular Saw Mills, with most simple and durable Lever Setts in use, convenient and durable ; Grist, Woolen and Paper Mills constructed, Shafting, Gearing, Pulleys, &c., furnished, and surveys for Mill sites made.

Circulars representing, furnished on application. Address,

J. D. CHASE & SONS, Agents, Orange, Mass.

L. KILBURN & CO.,

MANUFACTURERS OF

CANE SEAT CHAIRS,
Pine and Chestnut Chamber Sets,
STANDS AND TABLES.

L. KILBURN, ⎫
R. FRENCH,   ⎬
G. E. POLAND. ⎭

Orange, Mass.

J. S. DEWING is connected with the firm of L. K. & Co. in the manufacture of Furniture.

HARTFORD AND NEW YORK
STEAMBOAT CO.

REGULAR DAILY LINE.

THE NEW AND SPLENDID STEAMERS

"STATE of NEW YORK,"

AND

"CITY OF HARTFORD,"

Leave NEW YORK from PECK SLIP, East River, alternately at 4
P. M., connecting at HARTFORD with early trains
running North and East.

Leave HARTFORD at 4 P. M., arriving in NEW YORK at 5 A. M.

THE FAST STEAMER

"SILVER STAR,"

Leaves HARTFORD for Saybrook daily at 4½ P. M., stopping at all
landings on the river, and connects with the regular New York
boats, thus allowing passengers one hour longer in
Hartford than the regular boats.

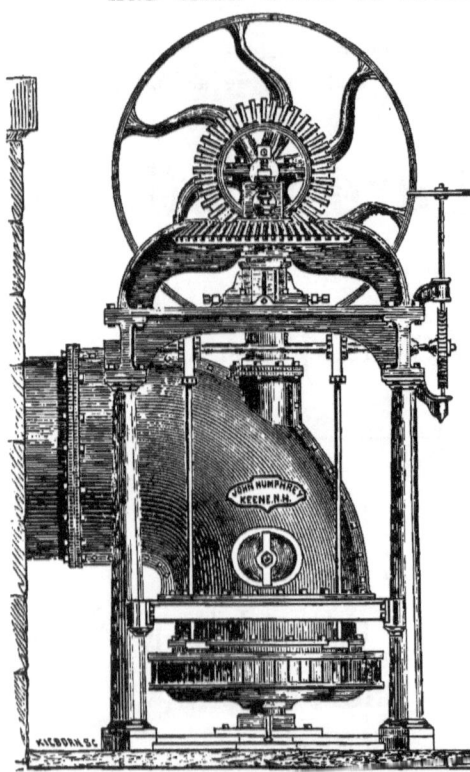

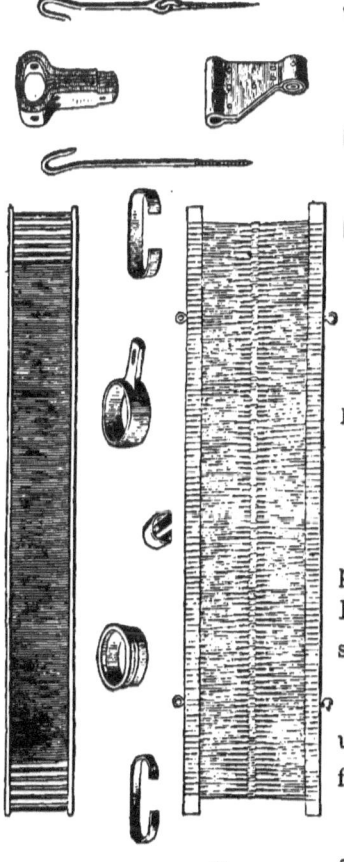

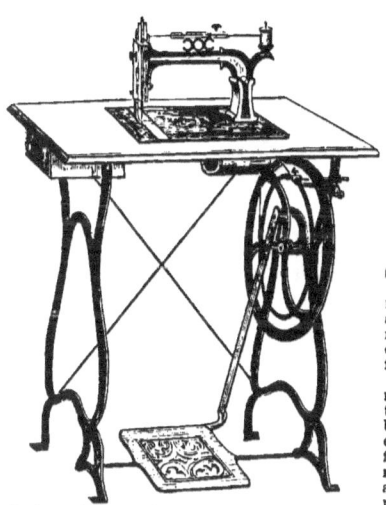

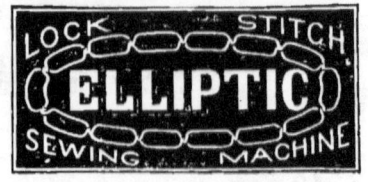

Volute Tension,
Crystal
Presser,

Adjustable Drop
Feed,
Elliptic Hook.

THE improved *Elliptic* Sewing Machine, (formerly known as the Sloat Elliptic,) is now owned by one of the strongest companies in the United States, with a capital of ONE MILLION dollars, which, employing the finest machinery in the world in its manufacture, and owning the latest patented improvements, *confidently presents the* ELLIPTIC as INCOMPARABLY *the most perfect family sewing machine ever made.*

Believing that a thorough investigation (which we particularly desire) can not fail to satisfy every one of the *entire truthfulness of our assertions, and of the preëminent superiority of our machine,* we cordially invite all who may wish to see a *Perfect Family Sewing Machine,* (whether desiring to purchase or not,) to call at our establishment in this city, or at any of our agencies throughout the country, and examine it for themselves.

The Elliptic Machine, (which is the strongest and most durable in use,) while eminently adapted to the wants of the *dress-maker, seamstress, tailor, or manufacturer of shirts, collars, mantillas, cloaks, corsets, clothing, ladies' gaiters, linen and silk goods, etc.,* etc., (for all of which purposes it is unequaled, performing with ease and perfection the work of a dozen hand-sewers, or almost any other two machines,) is *incomparably superior* to all others for the *use of the family,* and now stands "*par excellence,*" and by the *common consent of all* who have seen it, as the great *Family Sewing Machine of the age,* having established itself, wherever adopted, as the *great and exclusive favorite,* especially with the ladies, to whose *invariable recommendations* the great success of the machine, as a family machine, is in a great measure due.

PERFECTION OF MECHANISM.

The following is a condensed synopsis of the chief desiderata which, *combined only in this machine,* render it incomparably superior to all others:

1. **Pre-eminent Beauty and Elasticity of Stitch,** alike on both sides of the fabric sewed.
2. **Unequaled Strength and Durability of Seam,** that will not rip nor ravel.
3. **Great Economy of Thread,** costing less than one half as much as most other machines.
4. **Unexampled Rapidity of Movement,** making from 1000 to 2000 stitches per minute.
5. **Remarkable Ease of Operation and Management;** a child ten years old can use it without difficulty
6. **Noiselessness of Movement;** it can be used where quiet is necessary.
7. **Its many Improvements and Attachments,** and consequent unequaled range of work.
8. **Its wonderful Simplicity of Construction and Mechanical Perfection,** rendering derangement almost impossible.
9. **Compactness and Elegance of Model and Finish,** rendering it a real ornament for the parlor.
10. **An adjustable Feed-Bar,** readily adapting it to material of any class or thickness.
11. **The Elliptic Hook,** a most ingenious device for making the lock-stitch with unequaled precision.
12. **It will Seam, Hem, Fell, Tuck, Gather, Braid, Bind, Cord, Quilt and Embroider** with unequaled perfection.

In the above, and all other requisites of a *Perfect Sewing Machine,* it stands *unrivaled and unapproachable.*

The Elliptic is now in use by A. T. Stewart & Co., I. E. Walraven, O'Sullivan & Grey, James Cox, and other of the best houses in New York.

Report of Committee on Sewing Machines, at N. Y. State Fair, 1866.—"We, the Committee on Sewing Machines, after a careful and thorough investigation into the respective merits of the various machines submitted for examination, find the Elliptic Lock-Stitch Sewing Machine to be superior to all others."

From the Reports of the Maryland Institute Fair, 1866.—"We find the Elliptic Lock Stitch Sewing Machine to excel all others."

PRICES:

No. 1 Machine.	Plain,	- - - - -	$55	No. 3 Machine.	In Half-Case, Waxed,	$82
No. 2	"	Ornamental Bronze, -	65	No. 2	" " " Polished,	75
No. 3	"	Silver Plated, - - -	75	No. 3	" " " "	85
No. 2	"	In Half-Case Waxed, -	72	Full Cases from $100, upwards.		

Machines (which are warranted for two years) forwarded to any part of the world, with printed instructions (which will enable any one to operate them without the slightest difficulty) for use, on receipt of the price in current funds or by draft. Agents wanted in territory unoccupied. Address,

ELLIPTIC SEWING MACHINE CO.,
543 Broadway, N. Y.

D. S. COVERT, Gen. Agt.